Fantastic
Companions

Realms of Wonder

Fantastic
Companions

Edited

by

Julie E. Czerneda

Fitzhenry & Whiteside

Published in Canada by Fitzhenry & Whiteside, 195 Allstate Parkway, Markham, Ontario L3R 4T8

Published in the United States by Fitzhenry & Whiteside, 121 Harvard Avenue, Suite 2, Allston, Massachusetts 02134

First Printing of the following:

A Special Introduction © 2005 Kristen Britain, House of Cats © 2005 Catherine Dybiec Holm, Mountain Challenge © 2005 John Mierau, Just Hanah © 2005 Doranna Durgin, The Day Michael Visited Happy Lake © 2005 Matt Walker (Derryl Murphy), Eggs for Dinner © 2005 Jay Lake, Dances with Coyotes © 2005 John C. Bunnell, Riverkin © 2005 K.D. Wentworth, Wings to Fly © 2005 Fran LaPlaca, Last of Her Kind © 2005 Janny Wurts, Blood Ties © 2005 Sarah Jane Elliott, Dragon Time © 2005 Ruth Nestvold, Robes and Wands © 2005 Janet Elizabeth Chase, Uncle Ernie Was a Goat © 2005 Kent Pollard, A Sirius Situation © 2005 Daniel Archambault, Once Upon a Toad © 2005 Wen Spencer, The Power of Eight © 2005 Jane Carol Petrovich, Darkbeast © 2005 Mindy L. Klasky, Kitemaster © 2005 Jim C. Hines, Singing Down the Sun © 2005 Devon Monk.

www.fitzhenry.ca   godwit@fitzhenry.ca

10 9 8 7 6 5 4 3 2 1

Library and Archives Canada Cataloguing in Publication

Fantastic companions / edited by Julie E. Czerneda.
(Realms of wonder)
ISBN 1-55041-863-7
    1. Fantasy fiction, American. 2. Short stories, American. 3. Fantasy fiction, Canadian (English) 4. Short stories, Canadian (English)
5. American fiction—21st century. 6. Canadian fiction (English)—21st century. I. Czerneda, Julie, 1955- II. Series.

PN6071.F25F33 2005   813'.087660806   C2005-900046-5

United States Publisher Cataloguing-in-Publication Data
Fantastic companions / edited by Julie E. Czerneda
[448] p. : ill. ; cm.
Summary: An anthology of short stories, illustrating the use of anthropomorphism in fantasy. Stories range from more traditional techniques, such as talking animals, to more unusual, such as the personification of constellations, ancient gods, and story itself.
ISBN 1-55041-863-7 (pbk.)
1. Fantasy. I. Czerneda, Julie E. II. Title.
813.54 22 PS509.F3 2005

Fitzhenry & Whiteside acknowledges with thanks the Canada Council for the Arts, the Government of Canada through the Book Publishing Industry Development Program (BPIDP), and the Ontario Arts Council for their support of our publishing activities.

Cover Art and Interior Illustrations by Heather Bruton
The illustrations on pages 1, 247, and 321 are copyright 2002 by Alderac Entertainment Group and are reprinted by permission.
Series Cover Design by Kenn Brown and Chris Wren, Mondolithic Studios
Text Design by Karen Petherick, Intuitive Design International Ltd.

Printed in Canada

Contents

✌•✌

A Special Introduction

by Kristen Britain

≈•≈

I admit it. If my dog ever decided to strike up a conversation with me about, say, the fine bouquet of *l'eau de commode*, his whiskers dripping, I'd keel over in a dead faint. (Then I'd be appalled.) Yet, I truly enjoy stories that contain such improbabilities, and there is much to choose from – just search the fantasy section of any bookstore or library and you'll find numerous books featuring sentient wolves, mind-speaking dragons, empathic raptors, and ultra-intelligent horses, to name a few. What is it that readers (and writers) crave from such tales?

To begin with, the stories of fantastic companions have been entwined with the human story since the beginning of history, when ancient peoples painted animals on cave walls and spoke of them over campfires. Animals, gods, and monsters were woven into the belief systems of countless cultures in myriad ways to explain the world: the Chinese used bat motifs in artistic designs to bring good luck; the Egyptians worshipped the cat goddess, Bast; the world of the Iroquois was carried on the back of a great turtle; and Noah built an ark so humans could continue on after the Biblical flood in the company of all the Earth's species.

In more recent history, various creatures inhabited fables and fairy tales – the big bad wolf, Cinderella's mice, the cow that jumped over the moon – to teach moralistic, and sometimes frightening, lessons that are still read and interpreted today. While many classic children's books took a gentler tack, such as Peter Rabbit and Winnie the Pooh, modern storytellers are as likely to deliver their message using opinionated sponges or hamsters that fight evil.

The fantasy genre continues the tradition of endowing creatures (and even inorganic objects) with human attributes. The fantastic companion becomes a more personal ally and guardian, not necessarily to explain the meaning of life or the origins of the world, but to explain ourselves. We yearn for that "other" who, whether good, evil, or otherwise, knows our deepest fears and innermost selves, and who accepts us for who we are, banishing isolation and loneliness. They touch us on a profound level, allowing us to look in a skewed mirror at ourselves. Who do we see in the looking glass? The fairest one of all, or the beast? What lies below the surface?

I think it's a normal human trait to desire complete empathy from another being, and such a rapport between fantastic companion and protagonist is often featured in today's fantasy. In a sense, it could be classified as simple wish fulfillment, but it's more than that. The fantastic companion reflects the story's protagonist, transforms him so he grows and learns, and becomes an engine of change. Confidence blossoms and the protagonist is empowered to make things happen, and the story moves forward. We read on, transformed as well.

Scientists and naturalists may frown at the concept of endowing creatures and objects with human traits, but it's the stuff of fantasy, and the inspirations for fantastic companions abound and are seemingly mundane – teapots, pets that provide unconditional love, wildlife, you name it. Fantasy allows one to bend reality so that the teapot sings and one can hear the thoughts of the wolf. It's the sense of wonder factor, the cool stuff that makes it so fun to read. The book you hold in your hands is full of wondrous stories – a neighborhood watch group of cats? Most excellent. A kite with attitude? Wicked! A sage old salmon that dispenses advice? Definite coolness.

Consider this book your gateway to magical realms, and each fantastic companion your extraordinary guide.

Kristen Britain

Companions
Familiar

House of Cats

by

Catherine Dybiec Holm

A low hiss slid from Milo's throat, and his sixth sense surged into full alert. "The magic's off," he muttered. He lifted a paw, touching the air gingerly. "Here." He drew back his whiskers.

Milo waited a few seconds, raised his paw again, and brushed against something hard and flinty. His orange tail jerked involuntarily and he narrowed his amber eyes.

"Feel it?" he whispered to Kali Ma. She crouched next to him, the gold around her eyes accentuated by the blue/white of the street lamp that towered above them in the alley behind Tamarack Street. Kali didn't answer.

There'd been a time when Kali could monitor the magic around Ironton as well as Milo did. Until hatred and bitterness hardened her heart and shut off the sixth sense that cats were renowned for.

"There's a gap in the Ironton magic dome. A hole," said Milo.

Kali snarled and pulled her whiskers back against her cheeks. Her face amused and worried Milo. Such a tough little female, with the wide face and attitude of a tom. So sensitive and bitter inside.

"How can that be?" she growled.

How indeed? Since the beginning of time, cats had maintained and monitored the magic domes that protected the places they lived. They learned the songs and the rituals as kittens; they incorporated magic into their daily lives. Cats' extraordinary sixth sense made this possible.

"Sing the song," whispered Kali.

"Sing with me," he challenged, but she shook her head. If only she would try to channel. Maybe something would come to her that would break down the walls around her heart. He closed his eyes and went into trance, uttering the yowls and purrs and tones that the Universal Great Cat sent him. When the song no longer flowed, he opened his eyes and tested the air with a paw again.

"It's still not right." Again he brushed against something like fine metal shavings. His paw felt full of slivers. Burning rubber lingered in the air.

He walked quickly down the alley, Kali next to him and staring at him with wide, worried eyes.

"Fine here." His sixth sense let him sense the magic and he breathed the normal smell of cinnamon/cardamom, felt the soft plush of something like a giant cotton ball, tasted a just-right feeling of fizz and softness all at once. Some cats could see the dome of white light, but Milo did not have that gift. Nor did any human.

He backtracked to where they'd discovered the discrepancy, then walked several paces in the other direction and tested. Normal. They returned to the place under the street lamp and Milo again smelled burning rubber and felt the metallic slivers.

The bite of the coming winter hung in the dry, cold air. Between the houses, Milo glimpsed the hills that surrounded the town, the overburden from open pit mining. Black silhouettes against the clear, moonless sky. A shiver ran along his backbone and he sat down for a moment, licking his tail furiously.

"It's near this house," he said. The nondescript two-story older home looked like many of the others in this neighborhood. Housing for the miners, when iron ore was king in this town.

Low arrhythmic growls came from Kali, starting and stopping of their own volition. They echoed Milo's mood. He didn't like feeling as if he wasn't in control. If the magic was off how could cats use telepathy, open portals, do any of the things that cats learned from birth? What kinds of forces could affect Ironton if there was a tear in the protective magic that covered the town?

"Check the house out," he muttered to himself. They both crept closer, slithering between a picket fence gate that hung ajar. Weeds grew up around the bottom of the gate; white paint curled off the fence, ready to drop to the ground. Now the metal shavings felt as if they covered Milo's entire body. The smell smothered him, making it hard to breathe. Kali walked next to him, throwing worried looks his way. They came around the front.

"Try to open a portal," Kali suggested.

Milo moved close to the picket fence that surrounded the house. A narrow sidewalk led to the front door; crabgrass pushed through cracks in the pavement.

The orange cat narrowed his eyes and recited the words in his mind. He pictured the portal that should come; a circular opening with an orange rim; big enough for a cat to hop through.

Nothing.

"Try opening one the next fence over," he said to Kali.

She narrowed her eyes, then went over to the next house with its chain-link fence. He wondered if she'd pull it off. After waiting a few moments, he joined her but she refused to meet his eyes. Again, he murmured the words in his mind and focused his intentions on the fence. A small portal opened, shimmering in the night. He closed it, then looked back at the other house.

"I wonder how long it's been since a cat prowl was done here," he said. How long had this rip in the magic been in place?

"This neighborhood is pretty far from town," Kali pointed out. "It's possible that no one's been out here in awhile."

That was probably true. But cats were responsible for making sure that Ironton was protected. Milo's tail twitched nervously as they headed back into the town center.

—•—

In the early morning, Milo left Kali to join his queen Karma. Kali Ma turned down her alley and crawled under the old steps she called home, the outdoor access to a now-abandoned, second-story apartment.

Kali had hunted successfully and her stomach no longer growled, but her paws were sore and the phantom pain from her missing leg throbbed with annoying repetition. It happened every year when the air turned drier. Snow would come soon. Trotting around town on three legs tired her, even though Milo had slowed his pace.

Kali licked her underside where the leg had been amputated several months ago, her tongue running across the raised tissue of the incision scar. Brady had put a rubber band on her leg and left it there. She had loved Brady, the ten-year-old boy from the family of humans she'd lived with.

She growled, hoping to banish the memory.

Brady and his mother had taken her to the vet for the operation. Maybe they were motivated by guilt; she supposed they had considered putting her down. It would have been cheaper than amputation. Humans always worried about money.

They needed to worry. The mines in town kept shutting down and laying off people. Brady's dad had "gotten the ax," as he put it, a few months before her leg had been taken.

Kali licked the scar furiously.

She'd waited until the incision was healed and she'd regained her strength. She'd slipped out of the house and never looked back. From that point on, humans would have no place in her life, or any of her remaining lives, if she had any say about it.

—•—

The next night Milo led a team of five cats back to the house. They had at least one more night of complete dark before the moon began to wax. By the time they crept into the neighborhood, near midnight, the lights in all the houses were out.

Milo had asked Kali to join them. She'd thrown him a nasty look, but what could she say? Milo was head of the Ironton Cat Contingent and she had agreed to re-apprentice with him after she'd lost the basic magic skills of any cat, after her surgery when her bitterness began to build.

Kali had been skilled with telepathy. Milo remembered instances when she'd performed at a level that was surprising for a cat in her first life. But Kali refused to talk about her life before the amputation.

Still, Milo held onto hope. Kali hadn't given up on regaining her gifts; otherwise she would not have asked for his help.

"Great Cat," Kali blurted.

The smell hit them, about three houses away from the stucco house. Something above and beyond the burnt rubber smell of torn magic.

Milo's ears flattened and he narrowed his eyes. Several of the group held their mouths open slightly, smelling with the special organ on the roofs of their mouths.

Cat urine. The smell of fear, sickness, rage.

They crept closer to the house, bellies low to the ground, unnerved by the scent that pervaded the air and burned their eyes. Everything Milo smelled screamed at him to turn tail and run away; he could sense the others struggling to keep on. It was warmer than it had been the previous night and as they got close to the house, Milo noticed an upper window slightly ajar; wide enough for a mouse to get through, but nothing bigger.

"Listen," whispered Kali, her eyes wide.

The other cats fell silent.

Untold numbers of cats howled and suffered inside that house. Milo heard hisses of desperation, cries of pain. Around them the air sizzled with the metallic hardness of magic gone wrong.

Milo and the others went straight to the house and tried to open a portal. Even Kali made an effort. Milo could barely concentrate. The overpowering smell made it difficult to breathe. The wailing of the cats inside the house formed a continuous, rending din.

"Great Cat," stuttered Kali, "I don't know how much longer I can keep this up."

No one could open a portal.

The cats crept around the house, unsuccessfully looking for ways in. Hyperventilating and shaking, they tried to at least look inside, but the window shades were down. Milo's group opened their mouths and yowled toward the window, singing songs of hope and courage and rescue.

"Don't give up," Milo sang, trying not to think about what the house might actually contain. "We'll get you out." He could only hope that the ones inside were well enough to understand the message.

—•—

On Milo's orders, the cats in the group began to watch the house at all hours, rotating shifts. The tenor of the sound from the house had changed.

If Milo listened carefully, he could discern the beginning of a death song; the chilling, sad noise that cats sung when they sensed death approaching too soon.

Several, maybe many, were beginning to die in that house.

Dry leaves rustled behind him. Kali squeezed in next to him under cover of a juniper bush. The blue juniper berries looked silver in the waning darkness. He turned to greet her and they both froze, hearing the car.

Headlights spilled over the dark street and a sedan pulled up in front of the house. A woman got out, her silhouette illuminated by the first quarter moon. She moved with a strange, slow gait; almost a limp. One leg dragged on the ground more than the other.

Kali hissed.

"Shhh." Milo smacked her with a paw.

The woman looked behind her, then pounded the trunk door a few times before it sprung open. She hauled out a large bag of cat food and slung it over her shoulder. With that strange childlike gait, she walked to the front door, glancing left and right.

The smell hit Milo in the face when the woman opened the door. He and Kali narrowed their eyes and covered their faces with their paws. The woman stumbled over the threshold and shut the door.

Kali glared past Milo, and the gold outline around her eyes stood out. A long, low growl built in her throat, and her tail thrashed back and forth, hitting the juniper branches and making the berries tremble.

"Cursed Cat," she swore. "I know that woman. It's Brady's aunt."

—•—

Kali hid under her steps, unable to do what she had to do.

"Didn't you know where the kid's aunt lived?" Milo had asked her after the woman had gone inside and Kali had settled down.

She would have to see Brady again. She didn't know if she could bear it.

She'd explained to Milo that she'd had no idea where Brady's aunt lived. Brady and his parents hardly saw the woman, only referred to her as The Crazy Aunt.

As if the rest of that family wasn't crazy. Just thinking about them drove Kali crazy. Why, oh why, did she have to dwell on this again?

The Crazy Aunt had come to Brady's home once a year at Christmas. She always bought Brady a special Christmas gift. The Crazy Aunt seemed to care about Brady, like they were two of a kind.

Sure. They both liked to torture cats.

Kali's incision throbbed.

Milo and Kali had watched the house, hoping that the woman would make a mistake. Perhaps she'd crack a window too far open and some cats would escape. Maybe she'd turn on a light and open a shade and a passing car would illuminate the house in just the right way, and the driver would glimpse the horrible scene in the house.

It didn't happen. The Crazy Aunt was obviously not far gone enough to ignore the details.

Kali shook with the numbing remembrance of the death songs. She couldn't wait any longer. With a mixture of revulsion and anger and fear, she forced herself out of hiding and toward Brady's house.

—•—

She'd guessed correctly. On an early Saturday morning, Brady would still be at home.

Why, she asked herself. *Why does it have to be me?*

Kali knew the answer. Telepathy worked best when there was or had been a clearly established relationship between the cat and the other party.

You couldn't get a much more 'clearly established' relationship than the one she'd had with the boy.

She bit her tail, tasting the blood.

She had trusted him and loved him. He'd said he loved her. Even as he'd put the rubber band around the upper part of her rear leg, twisting it and tightening it several times, he told her he loved her. Even as she howled in pain, as she tried to bite it off. It had imbedded into her skin quickly and she couldn't get a tooth under it. Soon she shook with pain.

It could have happened yesterday. She stared at the boy's ground-level basement window. The damp soil chilled her hind end and she'd trampled a clump of dead hosta stems to get to the window. One window over, Kali smelled the wet linty exhaust of a clothes dryer.

By the time Brady's mother discovered what Brady had done, the muscle in Kali's leg was dead and she couldn't have stood on it if she tried.

Cats are dying in that crazy woman's house, she reminded herself. *They are singing their death songs, thinking that no free cat will know of their pain.*

Could she face the boy? What if he decided to torture her while she tried to make contact? What if she couldn't reach him? What if she did reach him and he didn't listen?

What if you don't try, and hundreds of cats die because of your inaction? What kind of joke will your name become? What kind of warrior are you?

Snarling, she smacked the window with a front paw, wishing she never had to see Brady again.

—•—

"Callie!" The wide-eyed face of Brady looked up at her through the window.

"Kali Ma," she growled, but of course, Brady didn't understand her. Humans didn't know that cats chose their real names at birth.

The same intelligent-looking boy with intense eyes and blonde hair, Brady had grown taller. He opened the window and she jumped down and scurried out of his range.

Forgive him completely, Milo had said. It's the only way to guarantee clear telepathy.

What if she forgave him and there wasn't clear telepathy? What if whatever-the-hell was happening around that house had spread to the entire town? Beyond?

What if. What if.

Brady tried to come closer and she hissed at him, pulling her ears back and squeezing under an old couch.

"I just want to pet you," he said. "I'm sorry about what happened."

Sure you are.

"Really." He stuck his hand under the couch and she could almost taste the blood. She had to do everything in her power to resist chomping into the meaty part of his hand. She felt a sharp pain in her skull behind her forehead and her incision kept throbbing.

"The guy I hafta go talk to says that I do this because I'm mad at my dad. It's why I hurt you."

Maybe you can teach the kid, Milo had said.

Maybe. It had been so long since she'd felt the stroke of a human hand.

"Come on, Callie. Come on, come on," he crooned.

Part of her wanted to, and part of her mistrusted him completely. She hissed again and flattened her ears, even as she inched forward toward his hand. At least he couldn't see her moving.

What kind of warrior are you? How deep does courage lie in your heart? Milo's words nagged her memory, with the persistent drone of a bee after a catnip blossom. *Do you have the courage to find forgiveness?*

Would it be her life, or the lives of many others? How could she carry the name Kali Ma if she didn't try to give those cats the only chance they might have?

Achingly slow, she inched forward. The tip of the boy's finger touched her head.

Kali hissed and pounced on the finger, instincts and anger taking over. She bit and drew blood. Her claws dug into skin.

"Ow!" Brady pulled his hand out from under the couch.

Frayed black material from the couch underside brushed her fur. Dustballs made her want to sneeze.

Great Cat. She couldn't mess this up. Other cats' lives depended on it. She couldn't let her bitterness drive her down. Slowly, impossibly, she forced the angry thoughts out of her mind. *If you can't feel love yet, start from a neutral place,* she told herself.

"Callie?" Brady's voice cracked. "I'm sorry. I really am. I just want things to be the way they were again. Please forgive me."

She made her mind a blank sheet, as nondescript as the concrete she walked on around town, as flat as the top of the mining overburden that surrounded Ironton.

Brady's hand snaked under the couch, cautiously, slowly.

I hurt him, she thought. Humans had no tolerance for pain. *Did his finger throb as her leg had throbbed? Worse?* She made her mind blank again and prepared herself.

His finger touched the top of her head. She could feel the trembling that traveled through his hand.

Breathe, she told herself. *Forgive. Purr.*

She gave into the sensation and let her purr take over and wash the anger away. When she was able, Kali aimed her thoughts at him.

—•—

Kali and the boy hurried to the Crazy Aunt's house, after Brady called the pound. Kali Ma wasn't sure what she thought of that. She'd told Brady to hurry; she wanted to get there before the pound arrived and chaos erupted.

What's meant to be will be, she heard, and knew that Milo was communicating with her. Once again she could talk cat to cat, mind to mind.

Milo met them both at the house. Kali's tail twitched and she cast a nervous glance over her shoulder. Could they save any cats? Were there any cats to save?

Brady opened the door to the house and Kali and Milo slipped in. They reeled and gagged from the smell.

"Ohhhh!" gasped Brady.

She'd never seen anything like it. She hoped she never did again. Piles of excrement. Urine. Sick cats. Starving cats. Dead cats. Cats who'd gone mad, who wandered in circles and muttered gibberish. Their death songs made her want to die.

"Cursed Cat," Kali spat, numbed and unable to move. The pain in the house was too much to bear. The jumbled telepathic confusion, the keens from the dying cats, and the scared sickness that hung in the air made her feel as if she was drowning in an ocean.

"Move." Milo nudged her. "Now! I'll take the upstairs. You work down here. Brady! Open all the windows and doors."

Kali stumbled into action. "Out, out of here!" Light poured into the living room from the open door. Brady stared at the horrific sight in the room — dead cats, excrement, vomit — before he turned toward the windows. Poor kid was as shaken by the whole thing as she was. Brady would grow up today.

Kali and Milo urged every cat that was well enough to move out the doors or windows. Ironton cats surrounded the house, hiding in gutters, bushes, and under cars. These cats would help the sick ones and take them to warmth and food. The death songs rose in a fierce crescendo and Kali thought she'd never heard anything so heart-rendingly horrible. A cat that had started its death song would not reverse the process. These cats would stay. It was another Truth that cats learned at birth, but it didn't make it any easier to witness.

—•—

Milo and Kali hid in the shrubbery of a house across the street. The pound and the local Humane Society had arrived shortly after Milo and Kali had urged every living cat toward escape.

Milo had seen a lot in his lives, but never anything like this. It would take days to get the dying and dead cats out of the house. What made the situation sadder was that the woman had simply been lonely.

"I just wanted to take care of the cats," she'd told Brady. Milo had seen the beginning of maturity flash in the boy's eyes. "I wanted something to love, something for company." She'd told Brady how she'd tried her best, how she'd spent the little money she had to feed her cats. The cats had multiplied and she couldn't keep up with the food or cleaning up after them.

"I'm not crazy, am I?" she'd asked. Milo had felt a numb juxtaposition of sorrow and anger just listening to her. The police would press charges.

"They said there were cats in the walls," muttered Kali.

Milo no longer sensed the aura of anger around Kali; if he had to put a name to her aura now, he'd describe it as shocked pain.

Two firemen emerged from the house with breathing masks, wearing heavy clothing. They held pet carriers full of cats, and Milo smelled that these animals were dead. It would take time to recover all the bodies.

"Over two hundred cats, they think," Kali said.

"Yes." He studied the house, eyes narrowed, tail perfectly still. "They'll have to burn it down. They're calling it a health hazard." Milo wondered if the magic in the area of the house would ever be right again, even after the house was torched.

"I hope that those who died still have some lives to come back to," said Kali.

Milo was heartened by the empathy in her voice, even though it was heavy with sadness. Kali Ma would feel again, she would work magic, the birthright of cats.

"Will you go back to live with Brady?" he asked.

She shook her head and Milo understood. Freedom, even with the harsh weather and the constant pressure to hunt for food, was hard for a warrior to give up. "I'll visit him," she said.

A fireman came out the front door and pulled down his facemask, gagging. Before he could shut the door, a small white kitten, skinny and bedraggled, ran from the house, blinking and stumbling in the light. It took off across the yard, smelling Milo and Kali as it got closer, heading toward the shrub where they hid.

"Hey!" yelled the fireman, making a halfhearted attempt to go after the kitten. He gave up, impeded by his heavy clothing. The kitten pushed in under the shrubbery; speechless, confused, scared. Milo smelled that she was female. They cuddled around her and she gradually relaxed as Kali groomed her with long, soothing strokes.

"Welcome to the Ironton Cat Contingent," said Milo.

Mountain Challenge

by

John Mierau

An old wolf stands motionless and silent at the foot of a tall, snow-capped mountain. The chill water of a mountain stream soothes the ache in his bones, before he reluctantly presses across to the far bank. Long ago scents and sights of his brothers and sisters frolicking on the slopes of this very mountain play in his mind as his paws sink into pebbles on the shore. He walks along the shore, not wanting to leave the sounds of the stream, but the slowly healing wounds between his shoulders and on his left haunch remind him of how far he has left to travel. Growling at the pain he trots once more toward the mountain, sharp eyes scanning the slopes for the easiest ascent. A puff of smoke rises high above, and the gray-muzzled predator returns to his former stillness.

—·—

A herd of elk stampeded down the mountain, smashing against each other in their haste. Aleyku licked his lips, but had fed well the night before and watched the fevered run of the animals with the clarity of a full belly. Aleyku could almost smell the elk's panic, and

scanned higher on the mountain for the strange smoke that had caught
his eye. Nothing. He watched the long-legged animals barrel towards
him and wondered what predator had spooked them from their high
mountain plains.

Aleyku bared his fangs at a flare of pain in his withers, and
whipped his head around to chew at long fresh scar across his back. His
chest felt cold and hollow as the pain reminded him that he was now
packless, defenseless. He crept to a thick patch of grass and crouched
low as the elk approached, surprised by the number of strong young
males running scared. Aleyku stayed hidden long after the herd
splashed loudly through the stream and rumbled over the low, rolling
hill beyond, and his eyes did not leave the mountain pass. He listened
and breathed deep for scent but caught nothing. It shook him that a
predator powerful enough to warn off a whole herd could evade his
senses. A dozen heartbeats, then a dozen more passed and still there
was no sign of what had stalked the elk. Finally, Aleyku trotted warily
from the grasses and continued slowly up to the path, sniffing deep
with each step. Growing bolder, he began to run while the temporary
relief of the waters still lent him the strength, stretching his legs out full
and slapping the ground with just the clawed tips of his feet. He sensed
no eyes on him, but he would feel safer when the wide path closed
again to narrow turns and twists higher up the mountain.

—•—

Aleyku did not slow his gallop until he was deep into the last thick
stand of trees on the mountain. Creeping into the shadow of a low
bough he fought to still his panting enough to catch any chasing scent,
any stealthy footfall on his trail. Recovering from the run took too long,
and his hackles rose in nervousness until quiet returned and he could
listen with hard ears. He had seen many seasons, led his pack through
lean times and plenty, and now felt each step he had taken, each bite
he'd not been quick enough to evade.

He turned in a circle, nostrils flaring, but again there was no scent.
No animal scent at all. No rabbits, no elk, not even birds. Are *all the
animals gone?* Aleyku found the silence eerie, wondering what had

become of the seemingly endless number of rabbits he and his brothers and sisters had chased at play in his first years. He remembered a scary moment as a cub, chasing behind an elk three times his height to impress his littermates, to see how close he could get before it turned and stabbed at him with its antlers, in annoyance. A smile came to Aleyku's face, remembering how he'd always gotten closer than all the others. Forcing his mind back to the present, he tasted the empty air again: the hunter no longer prowled nearby, or so his nose said. Nothing did. He continued up the trail, but his hackles still pointed skywards, and he took care to step lightly.

—•—

Fire.

Mother Instinct backed Aleyku up against a jutting rock when the horrible scent filled his nostrils. When he met the rock he stopped, and thought of following the elk back down the trail. *No.* He waited, ears twitching in vain for sound, but refused to slink back off the mountain. *All that matters is reaching the top.* When he was satisfied that nothing moved around him save swaying branches, he continued on. In part he was frightened how easy it had become to override life-preserving reflexes, but another part was eager to face whatever came. *Stupid, looking for challenge like this.*

Both relief and sadness tugged at him as he completely abandoned the cry of his Instincts for the first time in his life. Aleyku was saddened by the thought he might be running his last race, but also eager to see what lay at the end. He stooped to chew long, cool grass to settle his nervous stomach and stoke his courage. He caught it again, the strange fire scent. Sure enough it was close now, wafting down the only pass leading upwards. Baring his teeth, Aleyku cantered ahead.

Stupid, but exciting!

—•—

The air was crisp, the ground chill beneath the pads of Aleyku's paws as he clawed his way up a steep incline, and he hoped the snow of the mountaintop was near. He could feel his energy fade, his will along with it.

I will decide when it's time to lay down!

Growling, drawing every ounce of pride to spur him on, Aleyku bounded over the crest onto a wide field and a view of the Moon, rising pale in the face of the sun. The scent of snow grew strong in his nostrils. So close now. He felt the Moon was calling him forward, his last ally, cheering him on from its beautiful perch in the sky. Looking at the eternal Moon Aleyku felt his resolve grow, and opened his mouth to bay in thanks. As he drew in that breath, the choking scent returned, and he jerked his head down to the path just in time to see the rabbits leap past. A plague of rabbits, bounding around and off of him in terror-inspired haste.

One of the poor creatures' tail was on fire, yet it was in too much of a hurry moving its legs to roll in the loose dirt. One of the last of the rabbits bounced off Aleyku's chest, chittering in panic. It found its legs and took flight again, ignoring the shocked wolf in its single-minded flight.

Aleyku's nose filled with rabbit dander from the collision and he sneezed, shaking his head to clear it even as the thumping of crazed feet disappeared behind him. He was left alone on the edge of a field, to stare through teary eyes at a monstrous thing at the far side: a giant of red and gold, scaled skin shining like pebbles in the clear streams that ran through the mountains. It had a head the size of a bear, rear legs the size of buffalo, and front legs longer than Aleyku from nose to tail. As it laughed, the air grew thick with bitter smoke.

Tremble, wolf! The thoughts grew in Aleyku's head, as if they had been his own. **For if you survive this day you will remember it always as the day you learned true fear!** It laughed again, smoke curling from black nostrils at the end of a mouthful of the largest, sharpest teeth Aleyku had ever seen.

What is it? Mother Instinct spurred the wolf into a fighting stance even as his thoughts fell on each other like watery-legged newborn pups. All other scent was gone, replaced by the reek of fire such as he'd only once encountered before — in the glowing embers of a forest laid to ash. Only a hunter's knowledge gave him the courage to stand his ground: if he ran, this monster would surely follow.

A chuckling filled his brain. **The animal tries to think!** In a flurry of motion, red and gold blurred like running water in a stream, and the giant stopped halfway to Aleyku. It fell to all fours, thick, fish-like scales along its spine rising at the back of its neck. Aleyku scrabbled back a step but did not turn, meeting his adversary's — *enormous!* — eyes as his thoughts began to flow again. The way it now stood, the way its scales rose along its back — almost like a wolf might, come to meet a challenge.

It was making sport of him, Aleyku realized, anger pushing back fear and Instinct. He let out a low growl. For all his shock, and despite the long day's journey, Aleyku felt his body respond to the challenge before him. *Let him test me, he'll remember this old wolf!*

Now the monster blinked, huge cat eyes reflecting light as they opened again, head cocked quizzically. *It Does Think!* came the pleased musing of Aleyku's challenger. Again, the emotions and thoughts appeared inside his skull, and Aleyku shook his head to clear it.

Of course I think, mountain spirit! Aleyku felt a strange thrill that he would know the thoughts of this opponent, even clearer than he had read each nip and whine of his pack. *Come closer, learn what else I can do!*

A cold wind blew across the field between them, carrying snow-scent that replaced the smoke in Aleyku's nostrils. He looked further up the mountain, into the grating wind, and saw the line of snow he'd come so far to lay down on, a white so bright it hurt his eyes. The ache in his bones settled deeper at the sight. Then alien laughter brayed between his ears and the monster standing in his way made the whiteness, so close now, seem almost unreachable.

Are you here to die, wolf? Never fear — for your trespass I will see to it myself!

Aleyku's answering growl vibrated to the pads of his feet. He sniffed deeper for the scent of his opponent, finding the smoke and strange odor of the thing again and breathing deep, focusing. *It would not be a bad end to die with my fangs in its throat.*

It laughed again, this time rearing into the air, startling Aleyku into springing up on his own haunches — but the strange creature did not leap. It flung itself onto its back, shuddering, waves of emotion pressing in on Aleyku, who snarled and paced nervously back and forth at the mouth of the pass. His warning growl was tinged with a questioning whine. *What was the thing?* It was nearer the size of the mountain than of any beast Aleyku had seen in his years of hunting and avoiding.

What … what am I? It repeated in equal surprise, turning its head upside down on the ground towards Aleyku —and digging a trough in the ground as it did. **I am dragon, furry morsel.** It pulled itself back to its feet; then, to Aleyku's terror, it climbed even higher, surging into the air with each snapping beat of unfurling leathery wings. **The ground quakes in fear at our presence, the air shrieks a warning to all who would fly our spaces! We are immortal, invincible. We are Dragon!**

Dragon. Aleyku's legs continued to trot across the mouth of the pass, never ceasing movement, head turned skyward, forgetting his fear. He wondered what those alien thoughts would feel like once he'd sunk his fangs in their maker's side. A part of him noted that no voice in his head answered his assessing thought. *I'm no rabbit or elk to scare away,* Aleyku thought 'at' the thing, gathering strength to reach the pure snow laying thick and white and cool just a few footfalls past his adversary. *My life comes with a cost. You hear, 'dragon?' Be off! Find another for your own, and mother Dragon won't have to lick your wounds tonight!*

It shrieked. Aleyku flattened his ears to his head as the cry of a thousand birds mixed with the roar of a mountain lion, shaking the mountain and the inside of his head. The dragon beat its wings again and Aleyku's vision filled with red and gold as angry eyes swooped closer, eyes large enough for him to see all of his body reflecting back.

Varas fears nothing, retreats from no one! Let alone a skinny bag of fur sneaking onto his mountain home!

Aleyku felt the world slow down, his senses becoming more acute as they always did during challenge or attack. He watched Varas the dragon throb backwards in the air, carried by the crack of his wings. The fanged cavern of its mouth widened in time with that first stroke, moving forward with the next to snap at Aleyku and a wide strip of ground beneath him —

— but the jaw snapped closed with only dirt between its teeth when Aleyku leapt between Varas's tree trunk-sized rear legs before it could complete its assault. Golden-yellow eyes wide with the thrill of the chase, he tore across the field towards the snow, feeling the ground shake as his opponent plowed into the earth where four wolf paws had stood a heartbeat before.

You should fear your own clumsiness, Varas! Even as the first rush of battle began to wash from his muscles and he struggled with the deepening snow, Aleyku's mind planned. He turned to run beside an outcropping of rock to prevent the dragon from flying over him. A part of his mind reeled: a flying creature that size! Pressing close to his shield of rock to race along the snow made the best use of his fleeing strength, let him choose the site of their next encounter.

A shadow blotted out the light above him, and Aleyku barked again in surprise as he dodged a spray of rocks loosed by the dragon's violent landing on a ledge just above his head. **I'll tear your tongue out for that!** Varas called, the thought shrill, reminding Aleyku of a wolf cub's breaking voice trying its first cry.

Some actions betrayed much about an opponent, no matter the skin they wore: Aleyku knew now that Varas was a youngling, unskilled in the use of his body as a weapon. He reveled in the knowledge. Perhaps this old wolf's strength will fade, he thought, but not his cunning!

Aleyku barked over his shoulder. *Have to catch me first!*

Varas leaped, farther and faster than Aleyku thought anything ever could. Claws dug into the snow inches from Aleyku, very nearly hitting their mark but with a last, painful burst of speed, he avoided death again. *Almost, little dragon!* Aleyku thought, wincing at the pain the evasive leap had cost him. *Keep coming, and you'll learn something about a fight!*

The young dragon radiated anger and exhaustion: from the strained thoughts chasing after him, Aleyku judged it had never been made to fight for its victories before.

We are dragon! ... Immortal! ... In ...vincible!

Aleyku's toes spread wider for balance in the snow as he scanned the height of the few scrawny trees growing this high up the mountain. Pick your stand, Aleyku, or the dragon will do it for you. There! A small stand of trees dipped to barely half the height of the last stand he had passed, while ahead the trees stood taller again. He leapt from the protection of the rocks, galloping flat-out for the deeply buried trees. The air filled with flapping, and he knew his hunter followed.

What's the matter, mighty dragon? Aleyku's thoughts taunted his pursuer in time with his own gasping breaths. When the snow was deep enough, he spun again to race uphill, far out from his protective outcropping of rock. *Do you tire of the chase?* The only answer was a louder clap of wings, closer, ever closer. When his foot caught against rock under the snow, Aleyku spun and pushed himself down onto the flat shelf hidden just beneath the whiteness.

The dragon landed badly, tumbling in even deeper snow than Aleyku had hoped for, and shrieked its surprise. Aleyku read murder in Varas' eyes, the same look he had faced from other threats to his den … and other challengers to his rule. A cloud dropped over his thoughts, and he forced his mind from that last challenge, the only battle he'd ever met and lost. Now was not the time.

The dragon's wings heaved, its rancid and sulphurous breath fouling Aleyku's nostrils. There were no cocky or angry thoughts invading his head now, just a struggle for breath like his own. The dragon laid there, all four limbs sunk to half their length in the snow too close to Aleyku for comfort, both those tremendous catlike eyes locked on him.

Aleyku knew he couldn't let his opponent rest. *Are you stuck, Varas? Tired? Perhaps you are too fat to fly!* he jeered, his tongue panting playfully in and out of his mouth.

Enjoy the chase while it … lasts! Be thankful you did not choose a different … mountain to die on. The voice grew stronger in the passage of moments. **I am youngest, true, and you would not have lasted a second breath trespassing the lands of my brethren.**

The thoughts grew sure again as they rattled in Aleyku's skull. The wolf could not say the same as he watched, awestruck, as all sign of the effort the massive dragon had expelled in his chase disappeared. *You're welcome for the lesson, then, child,* Aleyku panted, pushing his opponent to keeping him off-balance. *Ask me tomorrow on my way back down, and perhaps I'll give you another.*

Varas reared up again, and Aleyku watched it sink even deeper in the snow when it struggled to free its front legs. **You should have scampered after the other furry things as they left my mountain. When the Moon reaches its crest tomorrow, all this will be mine alone!**

You're sure you wouldn't like a little more time to prepare? You haven't used up all that pretty fire of yours chasing off those deadly rabbits, have you? Aleyku wished for a moment that he had scampered away with them, but locked his limbs to the ground, forcing his arguing body not to move in the face of the dragon's gathering anger.

The thoughts grew painfully loud in his head. **How dare you!** Thick, black smoke billowed from the dragon's scaled nostrils. **I should roast your bones where you lay, animal!**

Aleyku struggled to stay put, his body and Mother Instinct fighting against the effort of his mind. How deep is it? he wondered, just managing not to turn the snow under him yellow as the dragon's jaws snapped at him — just out of range! He summoned the courage to offer a last taunt. *Roast my bones, whelp? If you can melt the snow between us I'll die of shock!*

Do not doubt my flame, cur! Varas's head shook from the strength of the breath he drew in and, with a roar that almost shook Aleyku's eyes from his head, blew out again. A wall of fire grew between him and the dragon, and heat and steam blistered Aleyku's snout before roiling into the sky. When the air cleared, he saw the dragon standing tall on his hind legs in a deep crater of crackling ice, collecting a second breath.

A pity this has to end, wolf, but tradition demands I hold this mountain empty in the palm of … my …

Thunder clapped the ground. The ice beneath the dragon shattered, large chunks falling into the deep dark space below. Aleyku jumped back as the dragon flung itself at the rocks under Aleyku's feet, now blasted free of snow. The dragon missed, and tumbled into the chasm etched in the mountainside by the ice of other ages. **Woooolff!**

Tail wagging, Aleyku stood and lapped at a pool of fresh water on the flame-blasted rocks. He panted happily as the wordless fury lashing at him from far below faded. Then, before starting back up the mountainside he lifted his hind leg above the chasm, very glad that he hadn't turned the snow yellow before.

—•—

The light was dying before Aleyku came close to the summit. His paws were numb from vaulting drifts of snow, the pain in his haunches a constant companion now, and sleep was almost a solid thing pulling him toward the ground. He shook himself awake and raised his head to the Moon, majestic and full: just one last tower of rock obscured its surface. The Moon was his ally, calling to him not to quit, to climb that last height, sing to Her one last time. *Then I can lay down to sleep.*

Aleyku savored his victory over the dragon, Varas. Through his exhaustion, a strong pride lingered. Aleyku relished his victory, won by the strength in his old but not yet frail limbs and sealed in a split-second of cunning.

If only there was someone to share it with. Aleyku froze when something tickled the scruff of his neck -from the inside. Then a distant rumble echoed up the mountain, followed closely by the dragon's own victory cry as it gained its freedom.

I come for you, Aleyku.

Aleyku whined, confused, despairing. The dragon was too powerful to outrace again, especially on legs exhausted from their last gambit. And, though it was young, he knew his opponent would not be fooled again. *The Moon.* Aleyku spurred himself faster towards the peaks in the hopes that the night and snow would slow Varas' search just long enough.

He growled as the pain in his back leg grew worse, and hid from it in happy memories of family. *Lovely Ursa, lifemate. Chetan, his firstborn, fiercest and wisest of all the children of the pack.* He knew it was only right he'd been challenged, that a younger, stronger wolf now protected all those Aleyku loved. All that Aleyku had lost. He knew it, but couldn't accept it.

Why must it be this way?

Barely half the way up that final peak, Aleyku heard the clap of dragon wings, and knew his race was lost. He snarled, cursing that last shelf of rock that seemed to stab at the heart of the eternal Moon, and then cursed the harsh codes that had exiled him from all he loved in order that they might thrive. Finally, with the claps of giant wings coming closer and louder, he cursed the cruel world that pitted an old wolf — not ready for death, nor for the loneliness that was left of his life — against a solitary dragon that would destroy anything that dared share its world.

Eyes wet from more than the chill, Aleyku sat in the snow and waited.

The ground shook when Varas landed close behind, but Aleyku kept his gaze on the imperfect Moon. A heavy footstep fell, then came the leathery crackle of wings furling and unfurling. The heat of the dragon's massive body warmed Aleyku's snow-crusted fur, but nothing touched his mind, and no final blow fell. Was the dragon nervous? *Don't be afraid of an old wolf, Varas,* he called. *I've no tricks left.*

Varas laughed, but it was a shadow of his earlier glee. **There could be no other outcome, foolish animal. Why would you seek this death?** Varas' mental touch was thoughtful now, almost reverent. Aleyku decided he'd been right, that the dragon had never known any thoughts but another dragon's, let alone one he'd been bested by.

Aleyku had always hated waiting. *Why else would the proud beast put off the kill I robbed him of before?*

Varas wouldn't be deterred. **You are strong enough and fast enough to catch stupid rabbits, or even fish in the stream if it came to that. With cunning enough to thrive for seasons more. Why fight so hard for death?**

Aleyku lifted one paw, licking at an age-cracked pad. *Without a pack to share the catch, or to warm my side on cold nights? That's no life, to me.*

Another heavy foot smashed down in frustration close behind. Snow and pulverized stone sprayed Aleyku. **If passing your days alone is such pain, why not simply show me your throat in our first meeting!**

Aleyku's eyes pored over each ripple of shadow and light on the brightening Moon, and wondered distantly at Varas' confusion. *I love every scent left to my fading nose, every changing leaf yet to fall before my dulling eyes, but succumbing in challenge is a better end than dying alone.*

The dragon roared in anger, but like the laughter before it, this sound too was curiously empty. **I don't desire your end. I only wanted you to run from my domain!**

Aleyku cocked its head at the Moon, in search of some angle, some view he had not yet feasted on in his lifetime. Such a lonely domain. *Why live on this rock alone? To me, without another to share your prize it seems a prison, at best a beautiful place to die.*

Dragons do not share, animal. The ground shook again as Varas sat beside Aleyku, quizzically following the wolf's raised snout to the Moon above. **Every dragon must fight to carve out their domain, must fight to keep it. I will shield these lands with my blood each day of my life. It is an honor to claim such a majestic peak for my home.**

Aleyku watched his breath rise across the Moon. *But who will know this honor?*

You know, wolf, and I will remember the lesson you have taught me, and honor you for it. The thoughts dimmed, colored with regret as they settled in Aleyku's mind. **But I am dragon, and you must pay for your trespass.**

Aleyku almost laughed, wondering what lesson the youngling would remember. *You will miss me, Varas? From what you have said, that's not very like a dragon.*

I shall not forget the night I was bested by a wolf, it promised. **Yet, the world is what it is.**

Aleyku blinked away the water in his eyes, choked away the desire to beg the dragon for a little more time as it leapt to its feet and paced away. His head never left the precious jewel in the sky as the dragon's breath came quicker and his wings once again beat in preparation. **The world is the world, and we are each born what we must be,** Varas's thoughts entered Aleyku's mind reverently, as if at prayer.

Aleyku shook his head, teasing the thought apart. *You are wrong,* he decided, *the world is not unchanging: ice thaws, rivers change their course ... perhaps even the rabbits down the mountain will one day see a dragon learn new ways.* Only the Moon remains unchanged, Aleyka thought inwardly.

It could not be, Varas rumbled, drawing himself up to its full height, breathing deep. **It would be seen as weakness, another of my brethren would issue challenge and the rabbits would just have to run again.**

Aleyku cocked his head, surrendering in his last moments to the curiosity of a younger wolf, and feeling a shadow of his once-joyful smile twist his lips. *But wouldn't that be something to see? A dragon defending a land not stripped bare, but full of rabbits and elk. Perhaps even wolf. I would like to see the look on your challenger's face, Varas, with all of that standing in league with a dragon.*

Enough, the dragon said. **It cannot be.** Steel found its way into the thoughts washing over Aleyku. **It is past time.**

Anticipation gripped Aleyku and he stood, eyes locked on the Moon. He felt a hope stir that perhaps even in death there would be yet more to discover, new fields to run, perhaps not alone. *Perhaps in death,* he mused, *even the Moon knows change.*

The dragon reared itself back. Its claws splayed wide, its jaws open in fearful readiness, as Aleyku began to howl.

Aleyku's call to the Moon was steeped in the joys and victories of his life. It told of a pup named Aleyku pouncing at a butterfly, then racing back to his mother's side, proud of the pounce, though its quarry had floated safely away. It spoke of the first time he caught scent of Chetan, his first-born. It spoke of the scars collected as leader of his pack, defending all he knew and loved. It spoke of a life well lived, of a wolf now waiting — calmly, if not accepting — for his end.

The cold world listened to Aleyku's howl, and was changed again.

Aleyku felt the ground shiver beneath him, even before he had breathed the last of his call. Mildly curious as he waited for a death blow, his eyes left the Moon and trailed down the intruding peak just as its white face seemed to melt. Masses of ice and snow shifted from their millenia-long perch on the mountaintop and fell, crashing into more ice and snow and setting it, too, loose.

Aleyku watched the growing wall of white surge down towards him, struck by the enormity and absurdity of the onslaught.

The dragon's voice was gone. In its place, awe and terror rolled through Aleyku's mind. As the bombarding ice raced to meet the two, surely the fastest thing he had ever seen, Aleyku cocked his head back over his shoulder, tongue lolling. *Think you can outrun that? I can't.*

No! Your life is mine to take!

The dragon's claws reached for him, racing against the cataclysm brought to life by his howl as it swallowed them both.

—•—

Aleyku dreamed of painful things. He howled through the green boughs of his pack's forest home, cursing the Moon with his song. At his feet lay Ursa, strong mother of all his pups. Unmoving. Not yet gray in the muzzle, as Aleyku had become, she had been taken from him too young. He pawed fearfully at her cold neck, could not bear the way she lay there. She would not growl, would not move. In despair, he howled at the Moon and even Chetan, bravest of his children, dare not come close enough to mourn his mother.

Then the dream changed. Gray now streaked not only his muzzle, but all through his coat. He crouched and growled in warning to a new challenger seeking to lead the pack, ignoring the blood dripping from scratches on his face and pulsing from the tear on his left haunch. He'd sat too long in the woods, as food had dwindled and drought worsened, unable to leave where Ursa had fallen the season before. She'd nourished her pack, bones and all, and returned to the ground. Soon enough, he was sure, the ground would turn rich again, and Aleyku would not lead the pack away until he'd seen something good come from her death. Chetan snarled, and Aleyku watched his own blood dripped from those teeth. Chetan wanted to lead the pack to the wet plains, and he had challenged Aleyku to decide the matter. Aleyku stumbled, feeling his leg weaken, but could not back down. It was too late for that, and even if it weren't …he didn't want to leave her. Not yet.

The dream changed again. Aleyku was limping from the forest now, as the howls of the pack rose and fell in celebration of their new leader. He stood at the edge of the forest, shocked from loss of blood but more shocked from the loss of his pack. Mother Instinct had betrayed him, sent him scurrying from what could have been a proud death beneath his son's jaws. To fall where Ursa had fell. It was a mistake he could not bring himself to turn around and correct. Aleyku jumped about on three legs, terrified to leave the shelter of the trees and unsure of even where he was going ... until he saw the mountain-tops glowing white in the distance.

—•—

The cold woke him, a slow rousing accompanied by crushing weight pushing in from all sides. Then a lack of feeling, a numbness that seemed to have cloaked the fur, flesh, and sinew along one side of his body. Slowly at first, but then with greater urgency, Mother Instinct again rescued Aleyku, forcing tremors through his body, setting his legs kicking and heart pounding. He snapped back to himself, alert, instantly terrified to find himself blind and immobile, buried in ice.

Body spasming out of his control, kicking as if the snow were a thing of flesh he *could* kick away, his uppermost front leg caught painfully on something warm, very hard, and scaly.

The dragon.

Aleyku kicked again, but the snow packed all around him was unyielding. He could only claw back toward the warmth of the rough skin. Both front paws found a perch around a massive limb and he climbed. Wriggling along the blazingly warm dragon-flesh, stabs of pain blossomed as Aleyku's frostbitten skin warmed despite the crush of snow all around him. Hardpacked ice fell back into empty space behind him as he burrowed higher up the immobile frame of his adversary. Aleyku whimpered as pain lanced along his back, but with each whisker-length he dragged himself, the motion came easier. Night-scent reached his nose: the snow was giving way!

Aleyku thrashed and kicked and crawled, and an old wolf rebirthed itself into the Moon-bright world. Crawling a long dragon's-arm's length away, he fell, nose to tail, panting and freezing and Alive!

Time passed, and the Moon fell behind the last high cliff high above him. In all that time, Aleyku's eyes never left the red and gold flesh of the dragon, unsure of even an avalanche's ability to slay that magical

beast. All the time, as he waited for morning, for the strength to stand
and to run, Aleyku watched it carefully. Boulders pinned one of its front
legs, snow and more stone hid the rest. So much mountain had come
down, Aleyku wondered his fur still held him together. He thought of
the powerful dragon's body so very nearly buried, and how he'd woken
caught between heat-snatching cold and the dragon's warmth. Aleyku
cocked his head, snow-glazed whiskers twitching in confusion.

He relived Varas's final angry leap in the moments before the ice
caught them, his defiant refusal to let the snow rob him of his victory.
No, Aleyku thought, that's not right. *The dragon had never sought his
victory!* The chill of night retreated from Aleyku, remembering how
Varas's claws had hurried to close around him before the mountain
slammed over them. Yet its powerful grip had not victoriously crushed
him, they had protected him from the onslaught of snow and ice.

Aleyku owed Varas his life.

The ground shuddered, and the dragon's head lifted ever so slightly
from the snow. Aleyku snarled weakly, dragging himself painfully to
his feet and crept further back. Aleyku could see one giant eye was
swollen shut, the cheek below it covered with frozen blood as Varas
turned awkwardly to stare across the field at the retreating wolf.

Did I not...say your life was mine to take? Pain was laced
through the words, and Aleyku shook his head to clear a dizziness that
was not his own. The ground shifted again, and again, but the dragon
moved no further. The dragon really was trapped now, even his head
unable to turn any further. A wordless bellow of dragon rage sizzled up
and down Aleyku's spine … but below the rage, he could taste its fear.

Aleyku's stepped closer, sniffing cautiously. Even the dragon's
smoky scent had disappeared. How long could the dragon live trapped
in the ice? he wondered.

Longer than you or your children will walk the world. Aleyku
was struck by the brave acceptance of its fate. **The hunger will be
worst. Perhaps you'd like to place your head between my teeth?**

Aleyku barked his laughter. *Humor too, majestic Varas?* A young
Aleyku had once been trapped in a rotten tree trunk for a day and a
night before his mother heard his wailing and freed him from his
prison at the foot of this very mountain. The courage of the dragon

struck Aleyku. *I'm sorry I'll not be able to teach you any more lessons, youngling.* The wolf sniffed again, head low to the ground to remember the scent of this last foe, pleased this battle hadn't ended with the death of one or the other.

You're welcome for your life, furry thing, Varas called to the back of the wolf limping up the hill again. Sadness tinged the next thought: **Even though you mean to throw it away.**

Aleyku's paws and tail froze, a low growl tearing his throat as he swung his head around to glare at the head of the dragon. *Be quiet, or I might stay a while and still all your thoughts.* By tearing out your throat, the wolf snarled to himself.

For what purpose? No, you've bested me and I'm no threat to you. You have no need of my strength to climb one peak, lay down and die. Coward.

Rage added fuel to Aleyku's next growl, and he padded back towards the dragon. *Coward?! There's no shame in accepting an end, child!* He skirted around it, keeping carefully out of range of its mouth. *To live alone on a barren hill, chasing off all those who might speak truth to you, that reeks of cowardice!*

Varas pounded his head against the ground again and again, wordless anger reaching out to Aleyku, whose mane stiffened at the promise of violence. **A life alone is the way of the dragon! We are immortal, invincible!**

Immortal, invincible masters of dirt and grass, Aleyku lashed pitilessly at his captive audience. *Tremble, all, before the lord of rock and daisies, lest he huff and puff and chase you from his kingdom of loneliness!*

Not so, wolf, I'll have your bones to keep me company, and you'll be in the loneliest kingdom long before I!

Aleyku's eyes locked onto Varas' one. A light dusting of snow, late to the avalanche, fell across his foe. Slowly, Aleyku's anger dimmed, until he sat on the cold snow again, eyes turning round and sad. *It may be so, but there is nothing left for me. No companions to chase at play, or protect, no friends to ponder the sun and Moon with ... all the things you've turned your back on, Varas, have been stripped from me!*

The dragon's nostrils flared, and mildly steaming breath set snow spinning in a mockery of their former destructive flame. **A dragon**

takes no solace in the company of others, but bridles at their defiant presence and slaughters all who would stand on his ground.

Another fine speech to give to yourself. If it is truly so, why waste the words on me?

I ... do not consider our talks a waste, mangy one, Varas told him. **I am pleased I saved your life from the snow.**

Aleyku leapt back to his feet and slipped beneath the dragon's mouth, crouching in the snow just out of reach of its fangs. *I thought dragons didn't care about others, Varas!* How unfair, Aleyku thought, that this powerful beast should live and dedicate his life to shunning all that *is* life to me! And now this concern? He reared up and clawed at that powerful neck. *Perhaps I should send you to that kingdom first, to assure you do not stray from the solitude you crave!*

I would enjoy a spell arguing and fighting with you, my wiley quarry, but no blows you could land before freezing to death yourself would end me, Varas said softly. **Do not injure yourself, good Aleyku.**

Aleyku howled again, all four feet trampling the snow. The dragon made him want to chase his tail and chew it clean away. *Perhaps I won't make the climb up today, Varas! Perhaps I'll return to the stream for one of those fish that 'even an old wolf can catch', sleep a night on the warm grass and return tomorrow to chew on your scaly neck. And the day after that! This snow will not melt for a season, perhaps longer, and my old legs can make many trips before then!*

The ground shook with buried dragon's laughter under Aleyku's feet. **You risked your life to pass me, and now you'd spend your victory nipping at me instead of enjoying your last rest?**

The wolf stopped in mid-spin, forgetting his tail and snarling at the dragon's head and panting. *What is it to you, frightener of rabbits? Perhaps I should keep you here alive and find new ways to nip at you! Yes, I could spend the last of my days chasing every rabbit and elk and rodent back up here to keep you company in your prison.*

Even as the thoughts tumbled angrily out of him, they struck a chord deep within. The wolf wondered how long such a thing could last before Varas freed himself and ran the animals from their homes again — then his belly lit with fire at the thought of surrendering even the wisp of a dream to the bullying dragon and its ilk. The mountain had been his home, too, before he'd left his childhood den to command another pack. Spend my last days defending the helpless animals of this mountain? Aleyku decided he would sleep well after that challenge!

Varas writhed in the snow, but to no avail. Aleyku cocked his head as the dragon slumped again. **Were you to succeed in taking my life, my brethren would sense my end time and fall upon you as one, bent upon revenge and control of this mount.** Something very like wolfly concern wafted over Aleyku. **All those you fought for would die, as would you!**

What would a dragon-child know of concern for a lowly wolf, or the rest of them?

The cat-eye narrowed upon Aleyku. **Your life is mine to take!** the dragon rumbled.

Aleyku reared again and swatted at a smokeless nostril. *A fine trick! How will you slay me from your cold bed, hm? No, I will leave you in the ice and bring life back to your precious domain. Never fear, mighty icicle, I'll come tell you how the seasons treat your mountain!* An inner fire he thought he'd lost, limping at the edge of a forest, roared back to life as he considered it. Could he raise a new pack, a pack of all the animals of his childhood mountain home? *Should it bother you too much, I needn't leave you alive to suffer the changes I'll make, Varas.*

Don't take my life, Aleyku! Your life is mine, but I could not fight all of dragon to keep it! The concern beating against Aleyku in waves confused him, teetering in a defensive crouch and cocking an ear as he puzzled meaning from his foe's words.

What did Varas mean? Had his trickery impressed the dragon, or did it believe it could kill him with little effort, at any time he chose? *My life is my own, dragon!* He believed it, for some reason, and shuddered as his mind conjured up a sky full of dragons. *But … I only fight the battles forced on me. Perhaps we can strike a bargain, you and I.*

The eye narrowed down at Aleyku. **Bargain, wolf? Dragons have no need of those!** It wriggled weakly again, barely sifting the surface snow, but Aleyku didn't think it was really trying. **Then again, I could use the amusement. Say on.**

My life is yours to take — so say you. Have you sworn this as an oath? Aleyku watched the scaled head hesitate, then nod once, and felt a suspicion grow. *Yet what if I take your life? You say more dragons will come to avenge you —*

Not to avenge. Dragons care no more for their own kind than for others. To take revenge for my passing, yes, but then to fight each other for this land.

Aleyku snorted his contempt for the cold ways of dragons. *To seek revenge, then. The result is the same: you will have broken your oath. And if I should die protecting all the animals of this mountain while you sit and rot, so too rots your oath. Tell me Varas: what is a dragon's oath worth?*

Scaled lips pulled further back from sharp fangs, as if at a bad smell. **This is no subtle trap you bait me with, Aleyku. You would have me betray that which has given me life, an honorable code, in order to keep safe my word!**

Aleyku's white-haired muzzle mimicked the dragon's expression. *I see no dragon but you, Varas, and I see no betrayal.* His lips raised further, the tone of his thoughts turned lighter. *I see a challenge greater than any a dragon's ever attempted. All this, and the chance to see another season on this earth — not to mention the shared warmth of a pack.*

Oh, what great warmth there must be in that scrawny bag of fur! Varas began a shrill cry which his wolf companion took for laughter, but the dragon quickly shut its beak with a nervous glance at the snowy peak above him. **To live with your stink and nipping thoughts, I wonder if it is worth that price to see another season.**

Varas sighed, almost gusting Aleyku off his feet. **Answer a question, wolf.** These thoughts ran deep, and Aleyku could feel the first stirrings in the dragon of a desire to understand. **Answer, and I may consider your folly. Why? Why would you see the mountain slopes flush with chittering rodents, smelly elk, and so very many rabbits?**

Aleyku licked his lips as he might on a full stomach, enjoying this new game of wits. The dragon's supremacy and 'invincibility' had come tumbling down with the snow, and with its un-dragon-like concern for Aleyku himself. That raised interesting possibilities. He knew the dragon would not turn from a challenge once accepted, just as he couldn't. He savored the way his heart churned in a way he had thought lost to him, and he had hope now that the same desire could stir the heart of the dragon.

The image of a wolf cub not yet born came into Aleyku's mind. He saw it crawling along the ground behind Varas, inching ever closer, other wolf cubs watching nervously from a distance. Then the dragon turned, unleashing harmless smoke and a mock roar on the youngster, sending it yipping away in gleeful fright … too thrilled with its close shave to notice the smile on the fierce dragon's face. Aleyku pawed at the ground, eager to see what would take root in it. *I can promise you surprise, if you'll wait and see, Varas.*

Varas cocked his head to the side, a gesture Aleyku recognized as his own. Its next words were simple, to the point, and spoke of a curiosity growing beyond control. **I will wait,** it thought, **and see.** A huge sacrifice, Aleyku judged, from a powerful creature so recently bent on remaking its world.

The wolf swelled with hope, imagining the mountain flush again with life. And with a dragon at his side? He would not stray too close to those red and gold jaws just yet, but believed a silent bargain had been struck. *Then there will be time enough to answer 'why' another day, friend. Rest now.* Aleyku turned and picked his way carefully through loose snow and back down the hill, tail and soul wagging with an energy the rest of him would feel after sleep and a fish from a mountain stream.

I'll start small, Aleyku thought, not quite ready to corner bull elk and herd them home. *Perhaps tomorrow I'll bring a rabbit to make your acquaintance. If I can carry the thing without sneezing it into a grave.* Silent dragon's laughter warmed Aleyku more than the breaking dawn. A good start, he decided, breaking into a gentle run downhill. A good start to the pack a wolf and a dragon would build.

Just Hanah

by
Doranna Durgin

I linger near the slash of exposed rock, surrounded by stunted trees,
the cinder gravel rough beneath my pads. The power trickles up
through my paws ... it drifts on the air to set my hackles upright. It
tickles my nose.

This is why I'm here ...why I am. To find the power. To warn about
the hidden spots, the lurking spots ... the spots in becoming.

My HanahPup, do you hear?

— • —

Hanah slipped on volcanic cinders scattered over granite, caught
herself with a wild flail of arms, and felt irritation rise. She didn't see
the intensity of the sky, deepest clearest blue in this high ground. She
didn't see the intensity deepen between scrubby green leaves and the
rich, rusty trunks of the pines. Earlier in the day she'd seen those
things, and even appreciated them. She'd taken long, deep breaths of
the pine-scented air; she'd listened to the cocky songjays. She'd been
prepared for this to be the day when Sharlie found her voice.

When Sharlie finally found her voice.

But Sharlie had remained mute, and Hanah's pleasure in the
day faded.

Sharlie looked down at her now from high rock, her body language a confusion of signals. Her raised hackles ran in a faint ridge just behind her wide, solid head, down her black-on-tan merle back and all the way to the base of her normally graceful tail. That same fringed tail wagged low and quick and nervous and her ears — large and erect and beautiful, edged with black — flicked forward and back, signaling her anxious uncertainty. Beautiful, graceful, powerful ... that was Sharlie.

For Sharlie was of the best breeding. Sharlie, like her sire and dam and all the generations before them, had the instincts and temperament to protect Hanah's people — and to connect to her trainer in the rare symphony of unspoken communication that made the FlashGuard brace teams.

If only she found her voice.

Hanah put her fists on still-boyish hips and stared back at Sharlie with frustration making her throat a tight and painful squeeze. "You *know* they said I was too young for training," she told the caydog. Almost a dog and not quite, bred into specialization and symbiotic dependence; most people just called them brace dogs. "You're just going to prove them right."

Sharlie heard the blame in those words. She wagged her tail even faster, ducked her head slightly, and reached out with one beseeching paw, her spurclaw spread in submission.

"No!" Hanah's tight throat made the word harsh. "You're just not *trying.*"

Hanah knew the masters at Stark Academy doubted her — and thought that at fifteen, she was too young, no matter her aptitude with terrain and Flash theory. She'd quickly learned — if only in abstract — how to find the unpredictable openings to that strange plane of existence, how to survive the encounter, how to recognize the dangerous stray Flash creatures which sometimes blundered into her own world. The masters thought, too, that it would be a waste of a good caydog to assign her a puppy. That Hanah's tragic personal loss ten years earlier had left her too embittered to join the brace teams.

But Hanah herself knew that her bitter memories — those of her mother, father, and little sisters disappearing into the brightness of the Flash, of her sisters' terrified shrieks and her father's deep shout of despair echoing forever in her mind ... those things made her stronger. More determined. More prepared for what lay ahead.

For the Flash always lay ahead. The enigmatic and deadly Flash had been a part of this world for as long as written history could record. Appearing from nowhere, waxing and waning in activity and intensity ... teaching her people to survive its energies and its creatures.

Although Hanah couldn't help another layer of memories — Sharlie when she'd just been a young and squirmy armful, brindling still murky in her soft puppy fuzz, teeth too sharp to bear and tongue fast and neat against Hanah's cheek. Sharlie the youngster had held such promise — so responsive, so eager to please, so attached to Hanah. But now they had almost a year of brace exercises behind them, and still Sharlie hadn't found her voice. In fierce response to those suddenly painful thoughts, Hanah turned back on Sharlie's uncertainty. "They'll take you away from me!" she repeated. "I'll never join the FlashGuard, and you'll be stuck at some breeding kennel or used for basic handling classes!"

Sharlie lowered to her belly, paw still reaching.

Hanah closed her eyes. She and Sharlie had been sent out for extended freeform work in the woods and cinder hills north of the city, in the rolling prairie and earth-crack country south of it. Varied terrain and all of it rugged; all of it challenging. *Think positive and let the moments happen,* she'd been told.

For how long? How long would they wait, with Flash casualties rising and unpredictable disasters peppering the territory and the city of Sprenten? Not to mention the Flash leakage, too subtle for the average person to detect.

"They *need* us," Hanah told Sharlie. "And they don't have time to waste on failures." She sighed heavily. *Let the moments happen.* Another deep breath. Time to start moving. To find more *moments*, and to jar Sharlie out of her uncertainty and into boldness. And once she found her voice, they could move ahead into full brace training. They'd face the Flash...and they'd conquer it.

—•—

Uncertain, so uncertain! I need to be what she wants, to please my HanahPup.

She wants to leave this place. We should not, not without marking it. But I will.

For HanahPup.

— • —

Water skin empty, lunch sack depleted, leftover bits of roasted heart and liver still stinking up the small leather bag Hanah used for Sharlie's treats, Hanah headed for her cousin Guarie's house at the rim of the Sprenten city wheel she called home. In the center hub stood the stolid, practical administration buildings; one entire north-eastern spoke held the FlashGuard academy and barracks. The southern spokes of rolling grasslands and unimpeded views held the watch towers and the homes of the elite: the most successful merchants, the retired heroes and their land grants. The road from the south wound along those low hills to circle around the city to the west gate, giving the watch towers plenty of opportunity to assess new arrivals. And the west gate entered the merchant's section of town, leaving modest homes scattered north and east and the nastiest sections crammed into the central sections just beyond the merchants.

With Sharlie at her side, Hanah didn't fear to take those back streets, or the paths and alleys winding between spokes; she used them to sidestep the crowded merchant spokes on her way across the city to Gaurie's house. They moved swiftly, avoiding the dank shadows, intent on reaching home.

But Hanah's footsteps rang oddly apparent as she hit a section of cobbled street. She hesitated, looking for the bevy of drunks who often hung out on this corner…checking for the small group of tough young men who spent their wasted time one block down. Sharlie walked on tentative and wary feet, as though uncertain she should take the next step … but then, she often seemed just that uncertain these days.

The exchanged shouts of an argument rang loud against the silence where no skinny children played and no half-drunken lovers quarreled. "— Too dangerous!" cried an older woman, her voice quavering. The answering voice shouted something defiant and crude; a door slammed so hard it bounced back and hit the wall behind it. Leather soles slapped against dirt and Hanah pivoted in time to see a young man run the dirt path she'd recently crossed, snaking between sagging old houses to head for the merchant hub.

"Fool!" the woman shouted after him, but there were tears in her voice.

No one else reacted at all.

No one else seemed even to be here.

Sharlie looked back over her shoulder, brown-rimmed amber eyes rounded with worry. Hanah said absently, "We'll just see what's going on," and was gratified when with this, at least, Sharlie seemed to find accord. She even led the way, breaking into a little jog until Hanah called her back.

And so it was that Hanah was thinking of how she and Sharlie should have been moving with silent teamwork as they broke from the alley into a main spokeroad, and so it was that she burst out upon astonishing, insensible chaos without warning. *Flash chaos.* Where others along cross-spoke streets and alleys hung back, mouths agape, hands fisted, bodies poised to act but never quite moving, Hanah stood in the middle of the street and saw one block down to the next turning point in her life. *Where were you when —?* people would ask each other, and Hanah would never answer, because she was too close to pretend she hadn't seen the smallest detail and too far to have been any real part of it ... and she just wanted to forget every bit of it.

But she never would. She knew it in an instant, as Sharlie threw herself back against Hanah's thighs, cringing close for comfort. Hanah staggered back and then held her ground, gaze riveted on the conflagration in the middle of the street. Awnings hung ripped from their storefronts; outdoor displays lay scattered like toys. *People* lay scattered like toys, boneless cloth dolls in broken poses, or huddled against brick and stone in abject fear.

Flash creature.

Soundless lightning filled the street, blue and white and clouding the air; a spark of something floated to the ground by Sharlie's feet, and she pressed even harder against Hanah's legs. But Hanah couldn't look away from the center of the street, where a lone brace team stood their ground against that roiling nimbus of movement, a combination of flesh and energy. The human partner pulled on Flash-tanned gloves to compliment his leggings and vest; he and his similarly protected brace dog looked tiny against the looming bulk of living light so cool and sharp it hurt Hanah's eyes. She thought she saw the lash of a tail, then the spark of claw.

Another brace team ran in, already armored up. By the time another four teams arrived, lugging a net of rope so heavy it required a cart and mule, Hanah began to absorb the complexity of the scene— the deep rumble of the creature, fresh from the Flash and furious to find itself here. The stink, a dry crackle in her nose mixed with stone dust and burned air. The buffeting wind, itching fiercely against her skin and raising the flush of sudden sunburn on her cheeks.

Sharlie had somehow managed to push Hanah back against the cobbler's shop on the corner. The shop's gaily striped awning flapped and struggled in the unnatural wind; down the street the brace teams worked to contain the berserk, unworldly creature, hauling the immense Flash-treated net to the rooftops while the remaining brace teams used Flash powder delivered by hand-shot to inflict what damage they could … and to keep the creature's attention on the ground.

Hanah knew some of the Flash creatures could be canny, as smart as the best of brace dogs. This one seemed all fury and reaction, striking out mindlessly. It bowled a brace team up against a building, leaving the human too dazed to move and the dog scrambling to stand on three legs — still guarding its partner with ferocity as it leapt at the tail that struck at them.

The net dropped.

The street erupted into an impossibility of conflagration. Hanah ducked, crouching with her arms over her head. A dare of a glance showed her a building crumbling, taking those on the roof with it. A brace dog leaped to snatch the slack net, using jaws and spurclaws, snapping through the air like a whip until others found purchase and slowly weighed the net down. Balls of flash lightning rolled along the street; barely discernable flickers of solidity raced along the cobbles.

Sharlie gave no warning — she threw herself against Hanah,

snarling. Hanah cried out in surprise, bowling back against the cobbler's shop; her head hit brick, knocking her vision into splotchy, scattered darkness. When she blinked herself back into total awareness, Sharlie was only then bounding again to her side, her amber eyes crazed and wild.

Hanah shoved her away. "Godspoke, Sharlie, *be careful!*" She gingerly rubbed the back of her head, found blood, could barely focus on the sight of it smearing her fingertips. Beyond her trembling hand, the street spewed dust and screams and the roar of something mighty in deep offense ... but the net closed tightly around the struggling energies of the Flash creature, forcing it smaller, tighter ... brighter. A thunderstorm's worth of corruscating light flickered against details both too bright and dim to see, leaving only tantalizing glimpses to suggest the creature had any solid form at all.

But Hanah had seen its solidity ... could see the aftermath of it, in the lame brace dog and the human it still guarded. On the other side of the street a smithy had given up the fight to remain standing, crumbling in upon itself to scatter bricks along the cobbles. As the net drew tighter, condensing power into something suddenly small and manageable, the FlashGuard rushed forward with practiced teamwork. With rope and chain and mule teams, they hauled the restricted and squirming captive into a large flatbed wagon ... and then they hauled it away.

For a moment the street was silent. And just like that, the quality of the light, the sound, the very air Hanah drew into her lungs ... those things changed. Became lighter, softer.

Then those left behind began to gather their wounded. *Then* the world became real again. Hanah's head throbbed; her eyes didn't quite focus. She stuttered over the impulse to run in and help ... and then, looking at the capable efficiency, hearing the calm command in raised voices, knew that she'd only be in the way. At her side — *back* at her side, somehow, without attracting Hanah's attention — Sharlie whined. She lifted one paw, extending it beseechingly toward Hanah.

Hanah sighed. "You're right," she said, and touched the rising knot on the back of her head. "Neither of us belongs here." But she looked up at the lingering disaster down the cobbled street and added with grim determination, "*Yet.*"

And she thought ... after this, Stark will need us more than ever.

—•—

The Flash comes.

—•—

Guarie and Hanah spent the evening in subdued silence and murmured conversation, weighed down with the awareness of change. Never had a Flash creature of such size and strength invaded the spokes; it meant a new gate had bloomed nearby. The murmurs of impending disaster seemed not so much exaggeration as reality, and after Guarie's best friend — another seamstress for the Guard — came over and spent evening tea by lamplight reciting all the recent incidents of which she knew, Hanah crept away for an early bedtime, her head aching.

The following morning Hanah left early, heading for the steep, rocky training grounds that would be unusually abandoned this day. Both the academy and the guard would be turned inward, regrouping and coping and licking their wounds … as well as looking ahead. Hanah grabbed the chance to work the rugged terrain, careful to keep Sharlie beside her with body language and unspoken words — and ever caught unaware when Sharlie lingered in odd places, looking to Hanah with that beseeching paw extended.

Hanah's head ached fiercely in the bright, cloud-free sun of the day and finally she burst out, "Come *on*, Sharlie!" She was so heavy with the weight of looming change and the need to *do something*, to be the one who kept the next family from disappearing into the Flash even as another day of failure tightened her throat moment by moment until she couldn't even —

Breathe.

Take a deep breath, and another. Sit on the rough granite bench that cut through the short grass of this steep slope and look down on the neat pattern of the city below, the spoked wheel that bulged ever so slightly to the south as the landowners claimed more space in the only direction that would allow it. She thought she saw the dark, disturbing blot where the smithy had given way, the charred streaks against the brick that had remained standing. "Let's at least go back down into the city together." She blotted her eyes on her soft sleeve, surprised to find the need. "C'mon."

—•—

Oh, but I'm already here, my HanahPup.

—•—

Gaurie's inescapably troubled gaze greeted Hanah from the kitchen. Gaurie looked up from the deep bowl of the sink, taking her hands from the varied spring greens of their side yard garden to dry her hands on one of the towels she'd stitched from scraps at work.

"What is it?" Hanah asked, stopping just inside the sliding door, hesitating in the hallway that ran the length of their long, narrow home. Sharlie nudged her head under Hanah's hand, seeking the caress that Hanah gave without thinking.

"Come in and sit down." Gaurie patted the table, a half-circle slid tightly against the wall at the back of the kitchen. The cheerful touches of the room — flouncy curtains and lace wall-hangings and quilted cut-outs of bird and flower and the Wheel of Life — seemed to recede and disappear. "You had a visitor today. From the academy."

Hanah sat. *They need us now.* Maybe *right now*, even if they were still short on skills. Maybe Stark had no choice but to accelerate their training. Sharlie sat by her leg and rested her chin on Hanah's leg, folding her ears back against her head to give Hanah a worried eye. Hanah ran a finger from Sharlie's nose to the back of her skull, following the strength of that long muzzle, the dip at her stop, the strong dome of her head. Over and over. "The academy." *Finally.* She held her excitement to that one careful motion, stroking Sharlie's head.

Words came bursting out of Gaurie in a desperate, helpless flood. "They're letting you go."

Hanah blinked, unable to make the news fit that which she'd expected to hear, and therefore not quite able to understand them at all. "They're...what?"

"It's over." Guarie sat down next to her, and took Hanah's hands.

Hanah took them back, curling them into tight fists. Guarie sighed, a resigned sound. Now that she'd delivered the devastating message, she seemed more her normal self. Calm. Capable. Understanding. "They're out of time, Hanah."

"*Them?*" Hanah laughed, as bitter a sound as she'd ever heard. "You mean *us*."

Her cousin nodded, running a hand over the frizzy brown curls that escaped her work bonnet. "Yes." Her eyes were quiet. Not blaming. "After yesterday, they need to accelerate the students in training ... they need to focus on the teams that are working out —"

Hanah jerked around in the chair, full of anger and denial and unable to speak lest she take it out on the one person who'd tried to make up for her early losses. Never had Gaurie discouraged her, not even when the inevitable loomed.

And the inevitable was here. Just when Hanah had so stupidly thought herself on the verge of success ...

Failure.

Gaurie cleared her throat. "You know you can take up work in the kennels. You can even stay close to Sharlie that way. Former students always have first choice of those positions."

Hanah couldn't say anything. She squeezed her eyes closed, trying to clamp down on anger before she lashed out with unfair words. Sharlie nudged her hand; Hanah pushed her muzzle away. *If only you'd found your voice ...*

Gaurie's next words came a little more firmly. "The secondary who visited —"

Hanah turned to her in surprise, eyes flying open.

Gaurie nodded. "Yes. It was Roge. He's seen to a lot of your tutoring, has he not? He came in person. He was very sorry. He said they just didn't have any choice. He said he admired your determination and persistence ... but that it was also getting in your way. He wished he could give you more time."

"Give *me* more time," Hanah repeated numbly.

Another nod. "He said you'd been seen yesterday, near the hub. During the ... incident. He wanted you to know that Sharlie saved your life."

"I—she—*what?*"

Sharlie looked at Gaurie, cocking her head as Gaurie looked back at her and nodded. She extended a paw, spurclaw politely tucked out of the way; Gaurie took it, and then took Hanah's gaze, something in her pale blue eyes unyielding. "That's what he said. He specifically wanted you to know."

Hanah frowned against a whirlwind of confusing emotions, the startled confusion tangling with lingering anger and the sudden glimpse that things were not all just exactly as she'd thought they were. Sharlie had ... *when?* Hanah recalled only a few stray skitters of blue-white energy, the painful impact of her head against brick, the wild, frightened look in Sharlie's eye.

Gaurie folded her hands together, regarding Hanah thoughtfully. "I know you've been trying your hardest to prove your independence from me," she said. "To earn your place as a grown woman. To keep yourself from being a burden on me ... and to take up the fight against the Flash. I've tried to give you all the space you've needed — I'm not your mother, and we both know it. But I think you need to know, Hanah ... even a grown woman takes her strength from others sometimes."

Hanah had nothing to say. Nothing but words that Gaurie didn't want to hear — *I don't need anyone else* and *no, you're not my mother* and beneath those habitual snarls of defiance, a barely heard cry of grief for her family. Unless she became one of the FlashGuard, how could she make up for the loss? How could she make things all right?

"Roge said there'd be a delay in re-assigning Sharlie. They'll give you plenty of notice, you needn't worry about that."

Hanah gave Sharlie a startled look, another impossible realization piled on top of the others these past two days had wrought.

Of course they're going to take her away.

Hanah leaped from the chair and bolted down the hall, and made it to her small, narrow room just before the tears came.

Alone.

—•—

One day. Another. And another, until they piled on top of themselves and Hanah did no more than blunder on with her life, finding no new direction, no true acceptance of her own failure. Her student stipend would run out in a matter of days, but she had no patience for the detailed stitching work that Gaurie accomplished without second thought. She had no skills other than those she had so carefully cultivated — her agile swiftness through the rugged terrain she loved, the lands she'd memorized so she could later protect them, the care of the brace dogs, the long history of the Flash intrusions and the theory behind detecting and dealing with them.

The image of herself working the kennels for the rest of her life, always close to the dogs but never bonding with any of them, hurt so much she could not bear to contemplate it.

So as the city rebuilt its damaged section, as the people withstood a myriad of scares and cried out fearfully at every faint evidence of Flash activity, Hanah did what she knew best. She took Sharlie out into the city surrounds, always changing the terrain and swapping out sections, not moving with any real purpose.

Habit, perhaps.

Desperation.

She was fifteen years old, ready to start a new life … and could see nothing ahead. Nothing to keep her thoughts from wandering back in time. Nothing to keep her focus forward instead of constantly drifting over those moments the Flash had open before her, blue and white light expanding from a pinpoint to a tunnel of eerie lightning … and then close around her family, leaving her alone. Five years old, and alone.

Quite suddenly, Hanah's knees went out from beneath her, and she sat against the abrupt wall of the southwestern earth crack into which she'd come. She'd meant to leave Sharlie up top so the brace dog had the chance for independent exploration, but when she looked up in a dazed way she found Sharlie sitting nearby, head cocked. With slow understanding, Hanah said to her, "They're not coming back. They're never coming back. Now I'm never going to find them, and I'm never going to make up for what happened."

For being left behind.

For surviving.

And Hanah burst into great big noisy sobs. For every grieving tear she'd failed to cry over the years, for every sorrowful tear she'd hidden behind her determination, she now cried two. She cried endlessly. And the shadow from the high wall of the earth crack crept over her, leaving her in the chilly spring air; a territorial songjay got up the nerve to flutter in close and scold her for daring to be there at all. Sharlie wiggled in on her elbows and put her chin on Hanah's leather-clad toes and then after time and more time had passed, inched close enough to sit upright and wash Hanah's face with her tongue. Hanah threw her arms around those sturdy tan merle shoulders and cried all the harder.

Eventually she stopped. Her nose was stuffed and her eyes were gritty and swollen and her cheeks held blotchy heat. She groped around the hard, rocky ground for the velvet-soft leaves of the spike mullen she'd been beside, and made a messy job of blowing her nose. In a voice thick and full, she told Sharlie, "'Spokes, it's going to be a week before I can go out in public again."

Sharlie ignored Hanah's sarcastic tone and very carefully cleaned her face again. Hanah squinched up her eyes and nose and pressed her lips together under the washing, and then scrubbed her shirt hem over her face. But she dropped a kiss on top of Sharlie's head before she stood up. "Now," she said. "Good-bye to the past. I just ... have to figure out what's next." She gave Sharlie's big upright ear a slight tug. "For both of us."

Sharlie flicked her ear away, snagging Hanah's hand in a light, careful grip of teeth — not so much as to dent the skin, but not so Hanah could pull away, either.

"Yes," Hanah said. "Together. I don't know how ..."

No, that was a lie. She looked down into those kohl-rimmed amber eyes. "The kennels. I'll work the kennels, if that's what it takes."

And having said it, Hanah suddenly felt ready to move on — out of this diminutive box-end canyon and back to the city. Back to tell Gaurie what she'd decided. Back to the school, to look for new directions.

Sharlie unexpectedly tightened her grip, startling Hanah into a yip of discomfort. And then Sharlie's hackles went up, and she dropped Hanah's hand altogether, staring down into the end of the earth crack with the intense *eye* of a herding dog on sheep. When she glanced back up at Hanah her tail dropped, wagging fast and low in the apologetic manner with which Hanah was so well acquainted.

"'Spokes!" Hanah said, throwing her arms up. "I'm not even asking you to do anything! What's your proble —"

Sharlie bounded away. In mid-word, she bounded away, head low; she ran full speed toward the deep box end of the earth crack, three times as high as Hanah was tall and about that same width, and then she stopped short, weaving back and forth on her front legs. She ignored Hanah's call, moving aside to repeat her strange weaving motion — and then she ran back to Hanah.

— • —

Oh, my HanahPup, please listen! Listen now.

— • —

"Splinters, Sharlie, what the Flash is your problem?" And wouldn't Gaurie just wash her mouth out with soap had she heard that little outburst? But Hanah was beside herself, tired and wan from packing years of denied grief into one afternoon, still aching with disappointment for what she'd hoped would be. *Hanah and Sharlie, brace team.*

Sharlie didn't drop her gaze; Sharlie didn't drop her tail. Sharlie burst out with one uncharacteristic bark and threw herself at Hanah, shouldering her legs so she couldn't help but stumble back. Stumble and fall, astonished. And still Sharlie pushed at her, shoving with her head, with her shoulders, with the hardness of an amber eye gone ablaze — an expression Hanah had never seen.

A sudden tingle ran down Hanah's spine. Her eyes widened as an eerie flicker of white patterned her hand, her sleeve, and Sharlie's merle sides.

The Flash burst into existence around them.

Not before them, not beside them, but fully engulfing them. Cutting shards of blue and white light seared into Hanah's vision; she sat not on the ground but bounced in a turbulent, semi-solid footing that made her clutch for something — *anything* — solid.

"Sharlie!" she cried — and then screamed it, because her voice made no noise in this alien place, and she suddenly realized she heard nothing at all. Not the wind that whipped up her chronically short hair, not her own whimpers of fear. She'd been taught about the effect, and had been totally unprepared anyway. "Sharlie!"

Something solid filled her arms. Solid and a little musky and covered with crisp merle hair. Hanah clamped down tight, closing her eyes; her world seemed to stabilize. She held Sharlie without questioning, without second thought; she believed in Sharlie more than in her own weak legs and confused senses.

She *believed*.

In *Sharlie*.

::Hanah. Finally, my Hanah.::

The voice came not through ears that didn't function here, but deeply into Hanah's mind. Not with words so much as meaning and intent, a foreign communication that she could not help but translate to familiar form. She gasped; her fingers spasmed to clench down on Sharlie's coat.

Sharlie gave her a quick nuzzle. ::Leave this place,:: she suggested, with all the implication that they *could*.

"But how —" Hanah cut herself short. Could Sharlie even hear her? After a moment during which the buffeting of the Flash seemed to fade, she remembered to concentrate on her words so Sharlie might hear them within her mind. This, too, she had been taught — along with so many things that suddenly made a visceral sense. The silent language of hand signals between brace dog and handler. Blindfolded exercises. The assignments to develop sense of direction.

But none of these things had been done in excess — because no one, not even advanced, experienced brace team members — willingly chose to enter the Flash. And not everyone who did came back out.

::Leave?::

The novelty of Sharlie's voice struck Hanah all over again. She cracked open one eye, and found the spears of Flash-generated light to be bearable if she squinted hard. Sharlie stood before her, the black mottling of her coat reflecting a deep cobalt in the eerie lighting. A trace of Flash powder dusted her shoulder. "You found your voice!"

::Now you *hear*,:: Sharlie told her. ::Leave?::

Hanah heard Sharlie's thought without absorbing the meaning, knowing she'd have to return to such questions when they reached their own world.

If they reached their own world. For Hanah had not yet been trained to fight her way out of the Flash if the interfaced closed before she reached it.

Sharlie cast a worried glance Hanah's way. ::??::

"Leave!" Hanah agreed emphatically, trying to project all the confidence she could. Sharlie could hear the interface of Flash and normality; Sharlie could detect the way home. Would take them there. Hanah only had to believe in her.

Believe.

And then Hanah's head filled with a rushing noise, the sound of wind in trees, waxing and waning like a living, breathing thing. She looked at Sharlie with wonder. "That's what you hear?"

::We go.::

Hanah stood, one hand on Sharlie's back. They made their unsteady way toward the interface, quartering slightly to pinpoint the exact spot. Sharlie moved in silent grace, every step deliberate, never thrown off-balance in the heave and sway of the Flash. Her great amber eyes narrowed, focused inward ... concentrating for their lives. In moments she slowed, and her movement turned to a primal dance with the elements ... slightly crouched, a creature of contained power and grace. Hanah had a startling glimpse of the wild and untameable nature of Sharlie's ancestors, the ferocity that allowed the caydogs to face the Flash.

Until quite suddenly Sharlie straightened and looked back at Hanah, her expression tinged with the uncertainty Hanah knew so well, her foreleg lifted in supplication, reaching. Hanah bit her lip in an instant wash of disappointment and fear and frustration, knowing Sharlie had lost their way.

But the sussuruss of interfacing worlds came as loudly as ever. Louder. And Hanah had a flash of insight so great as to take her breath away: *she* had done this to Sharlie. *She* had created this uncertainty. Hanah's demands, her pushing, her inability to understand that all those times Sharlie had acted strangely and reluctantly, she'd been trying to tell Hanah those things Hanah was not yet able to hear.

That Sharlie had been sensing the rising Flash all along.

That all she needed now was Hanah's confidence.

And Hanah clapped her hands in silence and cried, "Brave Girl!" and sent it to Sharlie with all the confidence she could muster, awkward with the newness of it.

Sharlie's ears came up; her eyes sparkled. Instead of reaching out to Hanah, she pawed at a spot in the Flash — a fading, a thinness; a deep veil of scintillating fog with a faint landscape behind it. ::Here!::

But as they stepped toward it together, Hanah's new-found stability exploded, turned to slam-and-tumble, and scrambled her wavering orientation until she screamed silently into the confusion, shrieking fear and protest. A brief respite gave her time enough only to open her eyes and glimpse the same whirl of energy she'd seen in town, and then something snatched her up and tossed her through the air like a dog tossing a rat.

Playing with her.

Preparing to kill her.

::Nonononono!::

Hanah fell again, lost her breath on impact with the imperfect ground, bounced and rolled and clawed her way to a stop. She looked up in time to see Sharlie in furious battle with the Flash creature, jaws latched tight to a limb Hanah couldn't see, back legs braced as Sharlie ripped and tore that ethereal flesh, spurclaws raking fiercely — and then the creature lashed out with a barely visible limb and swept Sharlie away.

The tenuous connection between them snapped; Hanah's internal ear went silent, losing the sound of the Flash interface. She scrambled after Sharlie and she might have been screaming Sharlie's name and she might not.

But Sharlie clawed her way to her feet as Hanah reached her. Blood turned from red to black in this light, splotching Sharlie's naturally mottled coat; her whiskers seemed singed. Her foreleg dragged and her gaze drifted away from Hanah's as she staggered and recovered. There would be no voice between them, not now. Hanah pulled Sharlie against her, supporting her, searching for the creature that had attacked so suddenly and now coyly waited just out of perception, revealed only by the excited intensity of the Flash lightning off to the side.

But Sharlie resisted Hanah's support. She lurched away, and then she looked over her shoulder. Hanah hesitated, her gaze darting from Sharlie to the lurking creature and back again — and with the greatest of effort, Sharlie lifted her drooping foreleg a quivering fraction, her spurclaw twitching to offer a submissive gesture. Beseeching.

Too long Hanah had failed to believe in her companion. Too long she'd shut her out. And now Sharlie needed that belief even without voice between them … could only save them if she had it.

Believe.

Hanah ran to catch up, offering the hand signal of approval, mixing it up with the one for praise. It didn't matter. Sharlie barely kept her feet, but she still moved with purpose. She quartered only once, and then as the creature realized their intent and made a last furious sweep at them, Sharlie found the interface and took them home.

—•—

"It's a big breach." Hanah waited outside the brace dog infirmary, her nose full of odors both strong and raw. Roge stood beside her, a slight man with shoulders slightly bowed and a perpetual worry line over somber eyes. She added, "The way it sits in that earth crack, even if you were hunting it, you wouldn't find it."

"We *have* been hunting it." Roge rubbed the back of his neck, gaze betraying concern as it wandered to the infirmary door. "As far as we can tell, it was the source of the creature who wreaked havoc near the hub, not to mention half a dozen smaller incidents we've managed to keep quiet. No mistake about it, being able to patrol that area directly will save Sprenten untold loss." He gestured at Hanah. "You haven't been seen to. Let me take you to a medic."

Hanah had tumbled out of the Flash with a dozen deep cuts and a deep, rashy burn on her cheeks and forearms. She'd sacrificed the strap of her water skin to create a sling around Sharlie's chest, supporting her on the long, stumbling hike back to the city where the tower watch had seen them coming and sent out help and a padded cart for Sharlie. The cuts stung; the burns hummed like leftover Flash on her skin. But she looked at Roge's concern and shook her head. Firmly. "I have to see Sharlie first. And I have to know what will happen to her."

Roge briefly pressed his lips together, thinning them. "You know she was badly hurt."

"I was there," Hanah reminded him, more dryly than was respectful.

He gave a short nod, moving against the wall so a brace dog medic could pass more easily, her arms full of salve pots. "For the most part, she'll heal. But —"

"Her leg." Hanah thought of how lifeless the leg had been, how Sharlie could barely twitch it. How she didn't seem to feel it when the limp paw dragged on the ground, the top of the foot worn through to blood by the time they'd reached Sprenten.

Roge took a deep, bracing inhalation. "She might get some control back, especially if we brace it. But she'll never handle rugged terrain again. It's a damn shame."

His words seemed to imply more than the obvious, and Hanah gave him a quizzical look.

"She's got tremendous potential." He said it as though it were a given, and Hanah supposed it should have been. And he said it in a way that suddenly made her understand that the masters had never questioned Sharlie's ability to find her voice, but that they'd never been certain Hanah could clear her mind of obstacles — of her past — well enough to hear it. "We need her now more than ever." He rubbed the bridge of his nose. "The masters have already been in discussion. You need not worry about Sharlie, Hanah. Once she's learned to use her leg as best as she's able, we'll add her to the city teams."

"But —"

But the city patrols were for the older brace dogs, the ones who provided a presence among the people as opposed to those dogs who actively hunted Flash. They were for the dogs who never quite reached potential — the ones who barely detected Flash activity at all.

Roge smiled wryly. "Yes," he said. "There's a stigma attached. But things are changing. The attack in the city marks a turning point in our world, and we have every reason to believe the Flash activity will continue to rise. Sharlie's new position may seem cruel to you, but the

truth is, she will be the first of many. We need actively capable —
actively *outstanding* — brace teams here in Sprenten. We'll find her a
partner who's satisfied to work in the city. It would help if you would
explain this to her. She needs to know it's an honor, not a punishment.
And as you know ... she's extremely sensitive to disapproval."

Hanah winced. "I'll explain." But she didn't have any idea how she
could possibly explain *good-bye*. If Sharlie was on a city team, even
working in the kennels wouldn't keep them together.

Roge rocked back on his heels. "As for you ... your youth works
in your favor, as does the determination we've always admired. We'll
assign you a new puppy shortly. Given your previous experience, we
expect you to be one of the youngest teams out on active duty."

Hanah blinked. "But ... I've been dismissed!"

"And much has happened since then, has it not?" Roge raised one
eyebrow in pointed question. "You were too deep in your past and what
it demanded of you, Hanah. Do you think we left Sharlie with you
those extra days by chance? We'd hoped the dismissal would shock you
into paying attention to your *present*. It didn't work exactly as we'd
hoped ... but it worked. With your knowledge of the terrain and your
early experience added to your ability to hear voice, I expect you'll
make a strong brace partner for your next dog."

"But —!" Hanah said again, and this time she nearly sputtered it.
"Why didn't you *tell* me it was me?"

Roge smiled a quiet smile. "We did, Hanah. Any number of small
ways. You simply weren't ready to hear. And would you have believed
us if we'd told you outright? When you were trying so desperately, and
driving yourself harder than any student we have?"

Well.

No.

He must have seen the answer on her face. He nodded once, and
turned back to the door.

"*But*," Hanah said again, and he wasn't expecting that; he looked
at her in surprise. "If I'm not dismissed, can't I stay with Sharlie?"

For the first time he seemed at a loss for words. "We thought ...
the city stigma...your determination to be the best —"

"That," Hanah said firmly, "would mean staying with Sharlie."

And as Roge slowly smiled, Hanah heard a tired whisper deep in her mind.

::My HanahPup,:: it said. And then, ::Now… Just Hanah."

Companions Disguised

The Day Michael Visited Happy Lake

by

Matt Walker

The house was quiet when Michael got there. Mom was at the hospital for a late shift tonight and wouldn't be home until midnight, later if she picked up some overtime. And considering the money from Dad was late again this month, overtime was likely.

He ignored the supper she'd left in the fridge, instead nuked a frozen pizza. After he was done that and a can of Coke he watched some TV, did the little bit of homework he'd brought home, then got himself ready for bed. There was nothing else to do, no friends to see or talk to, and he liked reading in bed the best, anyway.

He'd found some old books at a rummage sale on the way home today, and something had made him buy them. Lucky that Grandma had sent him ten bucks a couple of days ago.

One was a tattered old sci-fi paperback, but the rest were books he remembered from when he was a kid, titles that Mom had likely tossed during one of her cleaning fits: *Tales of the Green Green Woods*, by Walter T. Haywood, a small hardcover, pretty beat up, and a bunch of other books by Haywood, including *Culpepper Frog's Big Day*, *James Jackrabbit's Exciting Race*, *How Randall Grizzly Came to the Woods*, and more. Just holding them had brought back warm memories, and he'd decided right then that he had to have them again.

The novel looked interesting, but Michael decided he would check it out tomorrow. Instead, he started to flip through the Haywood books.

There were fourteen in total, in varying conditions, all with illustrations on the cover and inside by someone named F.M. Davies. All of the pictures were of the creatures of the Green Green Woods, just as he remembered them. A distant memory cropped up, Michael sitting on the couch and wiggling because he had to pee so bad, until his mother in disgust had finally taken the book from his hands and sent him to the bathroom. He grinned as he remembered the look on her face.

Doubling up his pillow, Michael read *Culpepper Frog's Big Day* in less than a half hour. Yeah, it was a book for little kids, but the message about conservation was actually pretty decent; how Culpepper and the other animals kept Happy Lake from being drained would teach kids a lesson in a way adults couldn't.

He flipped to the front of the book, looking for information on when it had been published. On the inside of the cover he saw the words "This Book Belongs To," and a child had scrawled his name on the line below, "Willy Thornton." Curious, Michael picked up the other books and saw that all had once belonged to young Willy Thornton. One of them also had the date written in pencil under his name, 1938, in a more adult hand.

Tales of the Green Green Woods was next, short stories about all of the animals in the woods, and Michael skipped back and forth, reading some stories now, saving others for later. By the time he got to the end of the last story he was starting to feel pretty fuzzy. He read the last few sentences of one story out loud to try and keep awake, half-mumbling and once had even lost his place, then closed the book, laid it on his table, shut off the light. All in all he felt pretty satisfied, despite his day at school.

He didn't feel like he'd been asleep too long when the light came on again. Michael groaned and covered his eyes, then sat up, expecting that his mother was poking her nose in to tell him something of marginal importance. But when he managed to open his eyes to a squint he saw that the door was still closed. But he could hear something rustling around at the edge of his bed.

Before he could react to the noise a large rabbit poked its head up down by his feet, then with a huff it hopped onto the covers, followed by an over-sized frog. Both were wearing clothes, the rabbit in tie and tails, the frog wearing a yellow waistcoat and a bowler hat. Except for the fact that they were three-dimensional and very real-looking, they were exactly as F.M. Davies had imagined them in his illustrations for the books: James Jackrabbit and Culpepper Frog, in the flesh.

Michael searched for but couldn't find his voice. Culpepper Frog hopped over and sat on his pillow, then reached up and gently tapped him on the cheek. "You're awake, kid. This ain't a dream." The frog's voice was low and raspy, with something of a Chicago accent. And it smelled *musty*, which was a surprise; he would have expected it to have a moist odor, like a pond. Like Happy Lake, however that smelled.

James Jackrabbit hopped over and settled in on Michael's legs, its weight feeling very real. "What's your name, son?" asked the rabbit. It also had an accent, from New England, Michael supposed.

"Um, it's Michael." He wanted to jump out of bed and run, but with the rabbit sitting on him he was scared to move.

The rabbit smiled at him, an eerie, unsettling sight that looked even more unnatural than the fact that it was wearing tie and tails and was proportionally not at all like a real rabbit. "Nice to meetcha, Mike." It — he — shuffled up and sat on Michael's stomach. "I'm sure you've guessed by now, but as I remember my manners, I'm James Jackrabbit, and this is my compatriot, Culpepper Frog."

Culpepper tipped his hat and also smiled. His teeth were flat and white, very much like a human's.

"I'm... pleased to meet both of you," replied Michael. He closed his eyes and tried to take a deep breath, but only managed a series of slight gasps, he was shaking so hard.

James Jackrabbit arched an eyebrow and smiled again, this time at Culpepper Frog. "He's a polite one, ain't he?"

"That he is," agreed the frog. "It's nice to come back to a polite kid, Michael." He stood on his hind legs and peered into Michael's face. "But ain't you a little bit old to be needing us?"

Michael blinked his eyes. "Needing you? What do you mean?"

James Jackrabbit tut-tutted. "Culpepper, he may be a little older than our last friend, but that doesn't mean that he doesn't need help."

"Help?" Michael was beginning to feel stupid, but before he could ask more, the door swung open and in lumbered a bear on its hind legs with a crow on its shoulder. The bear was a smallish grizzly — although it still had to duck its head and turn sideways to come through the door — and wore checkered knee-length shorts, and, while the crow wore no clothes, it chewed on an unlit cigar. Randall Grizzly and Cameron Crow, joining James Jackrabbit and Culpepper Frog in Michael's bedroom.

"There ain't nobody else in the house," said the bear, his deep voice a rumble that penetrated right to Michael's heart. "Kid's all alone."

"Where's your folks, kid?" asked the crow; he had a New York accent and while he talked held his cigar between two wing feathers that he worked like fingers.

The frog reached over and grabbed a picture of Michael and his mother from his bookshelf and waved it at the others. "There's no father in this photograph, fellas," he said.

Michael finally managed to find his voice. "My Dad's gone. We don't hear from him too much. Mom's at work tonight, doing overtime." He looked to James Jackrabbit. "Listen. Can I get up and get myself a drink?"

"Absolutely, kid," answered the rabbit, hopping down to the floor.

Michael got up and pulled his housecoat over his pyjamas, shuffled out to the kitchen and got a tall glass of water, added a couple of ice cubes that he chipped out of the frost-ridden freezer compartment, then went into the living room and sat down on the couch, letting the kitchen light spill in rather than reach overhead to turn on the lamp. All four animals sat on the floor in a semicircle in front of him. He took a long drink, gasped when he was done, and sat there looking at them, turning the glass in his fingers and rubbing at the condensation forming on the bottom.

"I can see that you've decided we're real," said James Jackrabbit.

Michael nodded.

"It must be pretty scary having the lot of us just pop up the way we did."

"I would say—" Michael's mouth was suddenly too parched to talk, so he took another drink. "I would say that it wouldn't matter just *how* you popped up. I'd still be freaked out."

All of them chuckled at this. Then James hopped up onto the couch and sat beside him. "And yet we're here." He was smiling.

Michael smiled back, nodded. "Yes. Yes, you are."

James clapped a paw on his shoulder. "So in that case, let's settle down and figure out why you called us here."

Michael took another swallow of water. "But I didn't call you here. You just showed up."

"Kid, we've been flat and dry for a long time now, and the only way for us to come back out is to be called."

"But I *didn't* call you. I picked up some used copies of the books about you guys and read a couple before I went to sleep, is all. Just wanted to remember what it was like."

Culpepper hopped up and sat on the other side. "What *what* was like, kid?"

Michael hung his head, feeling a little embarrassed. "Um… being younger, when I didn't have any worries."

"Ah." All of the animals nodded.

"Are you saying you just got these books today?" asked Cameron Crow.

Michael nodded. "At a rummage sale."

James sat up straighter. "Randall, go get the books from his room."

The bear ran and fetched the books, dropped them in a stack on the couch beside James. "Which one did you read last?" he asked.

Michael pointed to *Tales of the Green Green Woods*. James slowly picked up the book, held it up to his face, nose quivering as he closed his eyes. "Oh my," he finally said, voice soft and sad.

"What?" asked Culpepper. "You know I can't smell anything. Was he rolling the book in carrots or something?"

James shook his head and held out the book for Randall to smell. From the bear came a growl that made the hairs on Michael's neck stand on end.

The rabbit then handed the book over to Michael. "We can't read," he said. "But we know, nonetheless. Still, I want you to read the name of the owner of this book."

Michael flipped it open and found the name the young hand had etched. "Willy Thornton."

Cameron squawked and flapped into the air, one feather coming loose and twirling to the floor. Culpepper's croak was almost a belch, and his eyes looked ready to pop out of their sockets.

"The young master must still be alive," said Randall. "He's the one who needs us."

The rabbit nodded. "Michael, do you have a map of your town anywhere in the house?"

"I think so." Michael jumped up and ran into the kitchen, opened the drawer underneath the microwave and rummaged through the papers. "Here it is," he said, opening it as he ran back into the living room. He spread it on the floor and the animals gathered around it.

James tapped at the map. "Blue means water, right? And green is for park or forest?"

Michael nodded.

"This ain't a town, guys," said Cameron. "It's a pretty big city." He sounded worried.

James twitched his ears. "With Michael's help, we'll be able to do this, don't fret."

"With *my* help?" Michael sat back on the floor. "Why do you need me?"

"You found the books for a reason, Michael," said Culpepper. "And you know this city better than any of us."

He frowned. "What do I have to do?"

James smiled and slapped him on the back. "Atta boy! Here," he said, leaning back over the map and poking at it with his other paw. "This is the biggest lake that I can find. How far is that to walk?"

Michael counted off the street numbers in his head; the park was clear across town. "An hour, maybe more." He shrugged. "I've only ever ridden the bus or gone in the car with my Mom before. Why?"

"Because that's Happy Lake, that's why."

"No it isn't." Michael peered at the map. "It's called Chester Pond."

James smiled, and all the other animals chuckled. "Tonight," said the rabbit, "it's gonna be Happy Lake." He stood up and folded the map. "Now get yourself dressed and maybe grab a snack to bring along. We get to pay another visit to the Green Green Woods tonight."

"And bring along the books!" shouted Culpepper. "We're gonna need them!"

—•—

It was close to one in the morning when they finally stepped out into the night air. Just to be sure nobody was watching, Michael shut off the porch light and then had them all go out the back door. He stood there for a moment, surrounded by these impossible animals, and then sighed and pointed. "This way."

They weren't even out of the yard when two cars drove by; all the animals froze, low to the ground, and Michael just stood there, shifting the backpack full of books and snacks, hoping they wouldn't be spotted. They weren't, but he started to wonder if it would be possible to even make it a block before someone called the police or the zoo or something.

"We have to go over right away," said James. "Michael, get *Tales of the Green Green Woods* and read the title and first line from page 37 out loud."

Michael sat on the grass and pulled the book and his flashlight from the pack, and opened to the first page. "'Bonnie Raccoon's Fishing Trip,'" he said. Then, "'It was a bright sunny morning when Bonnie Raccoon climbed from her comfy warm home in the side of the old oak tree.'"

A ripping sound came from the book, and with a flurry of grays and muted color a small patch of paper jumped from the pages of the book and unfolded itself in the air, stretching and rasping and twisting into a new shape. Bonnie Raccoon. She stood before a gaping Michael, and as she opened her eyes, the house behind her faded to darkness, and the light from the lamp in the street seemed to go out. Instead of his front yard, Michael was now standing on a dirt path in a forest, his surroundings lit by thousands of stars and a half-moon.

"Welcome to the Green Green Woods, Michael," said James.

"But, where —"

"You read the four of us out when you read our stories," said James. "Now you've done the same with Bonnie, but we're using her a different way." He turned to Bonnie. "The young master needs help, and Michael here's gonna lead us to him. You feeling up to carrying us for awhile?"

She nodded, eyes shining in the moonlight. "Thanks, Michael," she said, voice soft and high. She turned and hurried up the path, James Jackrabbit hopping beside her. Michael followed, and Randall Grizzly fell into step beside him, running on his hind legs and panting with every step, with Cameron Crow riding on his shoulder, still chewing on the cigar as he bounced along.

As they ran, the trees on either side quickly faded into the blackness, but what he could see in the moonlight showed them to be well-sculpted; just as an artist might envision trees in a forest. There seemed to be little or no undergrowth, and the path had no roots to jump out and trip him up.

After a time of silence, the only sounds of feet on the path and the heavy breathing of Michael and the animals around him, Culpepper asked, "How are you holding out, Bonnie?"

The raccoon, who had started off running on her hind legs, had not long ago dropped to all fours. She stopped to catch her breath, and the rest of them stopped as well. "Awful," she said, smiling as she bent over, breathing hard. "I haven't felt like this since Zacharia Coyote almost caught me at the edge of the Merry Brook."

"You able to go on?"

She straightened up. "Anything for the young master," and was off and running again.

For the next half-hour they alternated between a slow jog and a fast walk, mostly to allow Michael to keep up. Every once in awhile he had to stop and sit on the path, back against the solid trunk of a tree, while the animals paced or hopped about in worried circles. All the animals except Cameron Crow, that was, who took to perching on Michael's shoulder at those times, bemoaning the fact that he didn't have a light for his cigar, and Randall Grizzly, who would take the opportunity to lean against a thick tree and scratch his back as he grunted and made blissful faces.

At the end of their fourth stop Bonnie tried to run, but immediately pulled up short and stood there with a look of distress. James slowly hopped over and put a paw on her shoulder, and the other animals followed suit, briefly touching her before stepping back.

"You did a good job, kid," said James. "We're well along, and that's all thanks to you."

"Don't worry," added Culpepper. "We'll be seeing you again as soon as this whole thing is squared away. Right guys?"

The other animals nodded and made agreeable sounds. Then Bonnie walked over to where Michael was sitting on the ground. "Could you pull out your copy of *Tales of the Green Green Woods*, please?"

Michael fished in the backpack, found the book.

"Please turn to the end of my story and read the last line aloud."

Michael flipped the book to that page. "'From that time onward, Bonnie Raccoon was always careful to use her own fishing hole.'" After one last look over her shoulder, Bonnie leaned one paw against the book, and then instantly changed from three-dimensional to two, was flattened out and folded over, turned into a page and halved and quartered. Michael turned the open face of the book towards him, and watched as what had once been Bonnie Raccoon assimilated itself into page 49 of *Tales of the Green Green Woods*, accompanied by the whisper of paper on paper.

He looked up to James and the other animals, was startled to see that they were no longer in the Green Green Woods. Instead, they were resting on grass near the playground of an elementary school. "What's happening now?" His voice was barely a whisper.

Cameron jumped from his shoulder and floated down to stand on his knee. "We're back in your world, kid," said the crow. "Bonnie could only carry us so far, and when she was petered out, she had to go back to where she came from."

"The book?"

"The book." All the animals nodded.

"We're safer in our land than in yours," said Randall Grizzly. "But to go back there, especially when our final goal is in your land, it's an exhausting thing. It stretches us thin, and eventually we have to go back and rest with the words and pages, to recover our strength and wait for the next time we're called."

James thumped his right foot on the ground, four times fast. "Speaking of all that, we have to go on. Michael, turn to the next story and do your thing."

"'Captain Zacharia Coyote Returns From the War,'" read Michael. "'Of all his possessions, Captain Zacharia Coyote was most proud of his hat.'"

Again, the book seemed to tear and jump, and a piece of paper ripped itself from the pages and flew into the air, unfolding and reconfiguring itself into Zacharia Coyote. For a moment he stood there, eyes closed, dark blue uniform jacket and felt hat with crossed swords emblazoned on the front both looking impeccable. He opened his eyes and again Michael's world faded away, was replaced by the Green Green Woods. This time he wasn't quite so disoriented; if he could accept this visitation by a bunch of talking animals from a children's book, he could certainly accept being taken back to their home.

James looked about to tell Zacharia what they needed of him when there was the distant bark and then howl of a dog, and right then it occurred to Michael that he had not heard any other sounds when he had been traveling through the Green Green Woods before. The other animals all froze, ears cocked, looking anxious, and then the bark came again, sounding marginally closer, and now accompanied by a distant shout.

"It's Clem," hissed Culpepper, jumping up and down, eyes looking to pop out of his head.

Randall stood back up and grunted. "I'll go get rid of him," he said, and he bared his teeth in a vicious smile.

James shook his head. "Not yet, Randall. You heard Farmer Godfrey, and so did the rest of us. If he's carrying Old Lightning, then you're big enough to spot in the dark, and will likely take a tail-full of shot because of it."

"Then what?" Randall didn't look too pleased with this, but he also didn't try to argue his way around it.

"Right now, we run. Zacharia, the young master needs us, and we need to keep ahead of Clem."

Captain Coyote snapped a salute and off he ran.

As he ran to catch up Michael cast back his memory, trying to remember more of the stories. There had been mention of Farmer

Godfrey in the books he had read that night, but he had never actually made an appearance. He could remember scenes of the farmer trying to hunt down animals that had raided his gardens, often with the help of his hound dog — that would be Clem — but never with any success, although sometimes the animal being chased would be exhausted and would claim to have learned a lesson about thievery.

But why was he hunting them at night? The only time the animals had been here, in the Green Green Woods, was when they had been with him. No one had raided any —

There was a loud crashing in the trees to his left, and everyone froze. Tumbling onto the path came Miranda Whitetail, who wore a handsome diamond-patterned scarf around her neck.

"It was only a few vegetables at the edge of his garden, I promise," she said, seeing the looks on everyone's faces.

Randall huffed and James rolled his eyes. "Stay with us," said James, hopping on ahead. "How many stories did you read?" he asked Michael, looking back over his shoulder.

"I can't remember," Michael managed to huff out in between deep gulps of air. "Maybe more than I thought I had."

They ran again, and this time Michael tried to push himself harder, allowed fewer stops for himself and made sure he ran, or at least walked, a little faster. But even he could tell that the sounds of Clem and Farmer Godfrey were getting closer. The animals looked worried, but no one said anything until Captain Coyote finally dropped down to the ground, tongue hanging from the side of his mouth and a look of defeat in his eyes.

"I'm terribly sorry, all," he said, taking off his hat and fanning himself as he loudly panted. "I tried to carry us further. Really."

Michael was already pulling out the book and searching the table of contents for the end of Zacharia's chapter. He flipped it open and waited.

James saluted the coyote. "You did very well, Captain. Thank you for your service, and we'll see you when this is done."

Captain Coyote returned the salute, then walked up to Michael. Before he put his paw on the page, he said, "So much of this rests on your shoulders, son," he said, still panting. " Do your duty."

Michael nodded, then read the last line of the story; "'From that day forth, Captain Zacharia Coyote would always think of Anna Fox as his friend.'" Captain Coyote flattened and twisted, folded over and over and then melded with the pages of the book.

They were now sitting on the grass at the edge of trees that lined the freeway. All of the animals ducked down low as cars raced past, but no one would be paying attention to dark shapes by bushes that were thirty feet from the edge of the road. Michael held the book in his hands and waited for more instructions.

"We need to look at the map again, Michael," said James, slowly hopping over. His ears were slung low and every time a car went by his nose twitched.

Michael unfolded the map and peered at it, trying to make things out by the dim street lights. Finally he poked his finger at the paper. "We're here," he said, "and we're going here."

James nodded and stood up, turning his body to face the direction they would be headed. "Read us in at the start of the next chapter, then."

"Wait a sec," said Michael. "Where did the dog and the farmer come from? And where do they go when we come back to my world?"

James shrugged. "Same place, I imagine."

"But won't it be safer in my world? We could lose Clem easily with the roads an' stuff."

"We'll never get there in time in your world, Michael," said Culpepper. "And there ain't no way we'd be safer." He harrumphed. "Now read."

Michael nodded, cleared his throat. "'Anna Fox and the New Sweater,'" he started, squinting to read the words under the distant street light. "'One Friday morning, Anna Fox woke up to frost on the ground and on the yellow leaves of the tree, and felt a chill in her bones that reminded her how threadbare was her old sweater.'"

More tearing and jumping and unfolding, and then standing before him was Anna Fox, wearing her raggedy old sweater. She opened her eyes and the city again faded from view to be replaced by the Green Green Woods. Quite a bit closer this time, they heard Clem howl. All the animals turned to look, fear on their faces. Michael saw the fur standing up on the back of Randall's neck.

They went faster. Michael was really starting to feel it now, and his pack was slapping against the small of his back, digging at it with each step, so that after a short while he was running with a kind of limp, trying to let the pack wear at another spot, but eventually just slipped it off and carried it in his arms.

Clem howled again, the sound so close that Michael ducked his head. Miranda Whitetail stopped and turned, then with a look at James Jackrabbit, plunged into the trees, running toward Clem and Farmer Godfrey. No one said anything, instead they just carried on.

Minutes later Clem howled again, a little more distant, and then came the sound of angry thunder, Old Lightning being fired. Randall Grizzly growled and Cameron Crow let go with a small squawk, but they didn't break their stride.

They ran like that for another five minutes or so before there was a crashing in the trees nearby. Everyone froze, and Randall hauled himself up on his hind legs, shook his head and bared his teeth, then dropped back to all fours and ran towards the approaching sound. There was a streak of gray and brown, and Randall had Clem Coonhound pinned by the neck with his forearm, up against the fat trunk of an old oak tree. The dog whimpered and scratched at the bear's belly with his hind claws, but soon realized that he wasn't getting anywhere and just hung there, still but tense. "Is Miranda okay?" asked the bear, his voice a deep and threatening growl.

Clem slowly shook his head. "Farmer Godfrey got her in the backside. Don't know if she went down or not."

Randall Grizzly growled again, teeth bared and snout right up to Clem's eyes. The dog didn't bat an eye, just said, "Almost went for the scent of blood, I did, but there's more happenin' here, ain't there?"

James hopped over and looked up at the dog. Voice shaking, he asked, "Can you let him down and keep us safe?"

"I can try." Randall leaned forward, and both Clem and Michael cringed as he opened his jaws wide, but all he did was grab hold of the dog's neck with his big sharp teeth and then lower Clem softly to the ground, like a mother cat carrying a kitten. Once on the ground, though, he didn't let go, just kept his mouth in place.

"Onh oovh or I ite oo."

James cocked an eyebrow. "Did you understand that, Clem? Randall's talking with his mouth full, which I expect is kind of rude. But I'm pretty sure he was threatening you."

The dog didn't answer, just sniffed the air before turning his gaze on Michael. "Who's the kid? Don't look like Willy, sure don't smell like him." Clem had a southern accent and a deep, rich voice, with a trace of a quiver that was likely from his current predicament.

Culpepper smacked his forehead. "'Course he's not Willy, you dumb mutt!"

Clem growled briefly at this, but a slight tightening of Randall's jaws shut him up.

"Um, my name's Michael."

James hopped over and put a paw on Michael's forearm. "Clem, Michael here has Willy's old books."

There was a pause and then Clem's eyes opened wide. "How did *that* happen?"

The rabbit leaned forward until he was right in front of the dog's muzzle, one ear turned towards Clem, the other cocked back in the direction of Farmer Godfrey. "Only one way it could happen, Clem, and you know it. Willy needs us, and the magic that Walter was able to work has given us Michael." He stood up on his toes, so that he could almost look eye-to-eye with the hound. "So you tell me; what do you think we should do about this situation?"

Clem looked at Michael. "Lemme see the books."

Michael opened his pack and pulled them out, stepped over and showed them to Clem, who sniffed at them. Then the dog's eyes went wide, and after a few more seconds of silence he huffed, a sound almost like a sneeze. "Promise nobody else is gonna go raidin' the garden?"

James Jackrabbit turned in a slow circle, looking each remaining animal in the eye. In response, each one of them nodded their answer. James turned back to Clem. "Well?"

"I'll do my best," growled the dog. "Farmer Godfrey'll be anxious to teach you all a lesson, so I can't keep leading him astray. But long enough for you to get to Willy, hopefully I can do that."

"Give us enough room and let us worry about the rest," answered Cameron Crow.

Close by, they heard Farmer Godfrey holler for Clem. Michael instinctively ducked, but the animals didn't move a muscle. "Is the big lug gonna let me go?" asked Clem.

James nodded, and Randall Grizzly opened his mouth and stood. "Boy, you taste awful," said the bear.

"And I'm sure covered in your spit I smell real nice as well," answered the dog, who gave James a quick glance and then howled in response to his master before plunging back into the dark forest.

James turned his attention to Anna Fox. "You all right to go on?"

She nodded. They ran again, and over the sound of Michael's effort-laden breathing he could hear that Clem and Farmer Godfrey were getting further away. Did the man wonder about his world, about flipping back and forth between the Green Green Woods and the city that was Michael's home? He wished he had the time and the energy to ask, but didn't know if James or any of the other animals would be able to give him a satisfactory answer.

Soon the forest opened up onto a large, moon-lit meadow. They crossed through the tall grass and reached the other side, and were greeted by the sight of Miranda Whitetail, lying in the grass, blood caked and glistening on her back. "Hurts," she said. "But I got away." She stood up, looked to James and the others, and then turned and looked down, still breathing hard.

Michael followed her gaze, and saw that the edge of the meadow sat at the top of a hill, which led down to a big round lake with several islands in the middle, set in the rough outline of a smiling face. They were at Happy Lake. On the shore to the right he could see a small fire, but they were too far away for him to see if anyone was tending it.

Anna coughed. "I have to stop, James," she said. Michael dug out the book and found the end of Anna's story. "'Although she enjoyed every summer, Anna always looked forward the most to autumn, when the leaves were golden and the frost first escaped from Grandpa Winter's lips, and she could pull on her sweater yet again.'" Anna jumped through the air and into the book, folding over and over until she had become a part of the pages, and then Michael closed it shut.

They were near what Michael imagined must be Chester Pond. On one side there was a large low building, a few lights shining inside and out, vaguely institutional and threatening. Overhead, street lamps buzzed urgently, and moths and other insects circled them in large, swinging arcs, sometimes coming close enough to slam into one before bouncing off with a frustrated flurry of wings. Nearby, a car alarm sounded, and then Clem's howling joined the city's night time chorus.

"Last time to read, Michael," said James. "We're almost home."

"'Cassie Beaver Builds a New Home,'" read Michael. "'Nobody ever expected that a flood at Happy Lake would get the best of Cassie Beaver, but one year it did.'"

Again the book jumped in Michael's hands, and again there came a tearing sound, and Cassie Beaver unfolded before his eyes. "Lead us to Willy, Cassie," said Culpepper. A second or two later they were back on the hill overlooking the lake, and after one quick glance behind them, James Jackrabbit nodded his head and they were running and hopping down towards the lake and the fire.

Halfway down Clem howled, practically in their ears. All the animals froze, a beat ahead of Michael, and then Old Lightning roared, and Michael heard the shot slice through the air, barely above his head. James turned and looked at the rest, then took Michael's hand. "Write me a good story some day," he said, and with a shake of his tail he raced off towards Farmer Godfrey and Clem.

"No!" shouted Culpepper Frog, but Randall Grizzly growled and jumped in his way, kept Culpepper from chasing after James.

Two more shots were fired, and Clem howled again. "The young master comes first," growled the big bear.

They carried on down the rest of the hill, quiet and somber now, and stopped when Culpepper raised his hand, the fire and the lake on the other side of a small grove of trees. The mammals in the group sniffed at the air, but Randall shook his head. "Nothing but smoke," he said.

"I'll go," said Cameron Crow, and with a flap of his wings he launched himself into the air, circled their group twice before he disappeared over the tree tops.

There was silence for a few seconds, and then came a loud squawk, followed by laughter, and then a child's voice rose up out of the night. "The rest of you should quit skulking about in the dark and come join me."

All the animals froze for just a fraction of a second, and then with roars and squeals and cheers they rushed through the trees, catching Michael by surprise. He ran after them, and came out of the woods onto the rocky shore of Happy Lake, a comfortable and welcoming camp fire placed carefully in the middle of a circle of several old logs, a young boy sitting on one of the logs, Cameron Crow perched on the boy's knee and the other animals gathered around the boy, jumping and chattering excitedly.

The boy, no older than eight or nine, looked up at Michael with a smile. "You brought back my friends," he said. "Thank you."

Michael sat on a log on the opposite side of the fire. "You're welcome. You must be Willy."

The boy smiled and nodded. "I am." He leaned forward and enfolded Cassie Beaver in a tight hug, buried his face in her fur. "I'm sorry I ever let you guys go." He looked around at the rest of them. "Where's everybody else?"

All the faces turned sober. "Most of 'em are back in the book," said Culpepper Frog. "Except for Clem and Farmer Godfrey, who're chasin' after us."

"Most of them?" Willy stood up and walked over to Miranda Whitetail. "He got you with Old Lightning?"

She nodded, tears in her eyes. "He got James, too," she said, barely a whisper. "I don't think he's coming back."

Willy closed his eyes, pain written on his face. But when he opened them again, he smiled. "He'll come back, girl, don't you worry. He'll find us or we'll find him." He stroked her neck, then looked around at the other animals. "Who brought you all here?"

"I did," said Cassie Beaver. She stepped forward, and Willy reached down and scratched her behind the ears.

Willy turned to Michael. "Read her back into the book for me, will you?"

Michael pulled out the book and turned to the last page of Cassie's story. "'It was a fine home, as beautiful as any other in the Green Green Woods, and the next time a flood came to Happy Lake, Cassie Beaver's wonderful construction job held fast.'" After one loud slap of her tail, Cassie flipped and folded and disappeared inside the book.

Michael blinked against the sudden harsh brightness. They were in a kind of hospital room, fluorescent light buzzing and flickering overhead. An old man, one tube stuck in his arm and another leading into his nostrils, lay in bed, stroking Cameron Crow with wrinkled, papery fingers. Culpepper Frog sat on the foot of the bed, concern in his eyes, and Randall Grizzly and Miranda Whitetail stood at either side, Randall leaning his front paws on the mattress, which sank down several inches.

After a moment of stunned silence, Michael spoke up. "You're Willy, too."

The old man slowly turned his head, broke into a coughing fit before he could answer. "I am." His voice was a dry whisper, but Michael could hear a long-sought joy embedded deep inside.

"We're here for you now," said Culpepper. "We've missed you so." He buried his face in Willy's shoulder and his body shook as he silently cried.

Willy reached up and stroked the frog's back. "I'm sorry I abandoned all of you," he said. "I thought I'd grown up. Never knew how much I'd need you the rest of my life." He looked again to Michael. "Bring me the book."

Michael crossed the room and handed the old man the book. He slowly flipped through the pages, often grunting in amusement or with recovered memories. "Mr. Haywood and Mr. Davies were family friends, you know," he said to Michael. "Mr. Haywood was my godfather, too. When he gave me these books, he told me that they were special, but I was young enough when I first went to the Green Green Woods that I think I took the magic for granted." He closed his eyes. "And then the war came, and my Pop went away and died on some island in the Pacific, and right quick I had to stop being a boy." He reached out a tentative arm, rubbed Randall's head. "Time to be with my friends again," he whispered, and then he turned back to the beginning of the book and read, out loud, slowly and cautiously, "'Culpepper Frog's collection of flies remained the biggest at Happy Lake, and the jar he got to replace the old one was his pride and joy.'" Culpepper hopped over to the book and was folded in as he turned a somersault in midair. He read the ends of the stories for Miranda

Whitetail and Randall Grizzly next, slowly and carefully, making sure all the words were right.

That left Cameron Crow, Michael, and Willy. "What's going to happen to Clem and Farmer Godfrey?" asked Michael.

"Water," whispered Willy. Michael got him a glass and straw, helped hold up his head so he could have a sip. He smiled his thanks. "Better. Clem and Godfrey will go when this is done, since they never had a story in the book to themselves." He looked back to the bird sitting on his chest. "You ready, old friend? You were always my favorite."

"Ha!" squawked Cameron, holding his unlit cigar in one wing. "I always thought so."

"'Even though things had pretty much gone Cameron Crow's way that day, he remained in a *very* bad mood indeed, and until night fell he sat in the Old Papa Oak and yelled and screeched at everyone who walked by.'" Cameron winked at Michael and then flew into the air, folded as his wings flapped, and then Willy shut the book and set it on his chest. He kept his eyes closed for a minute, then looked back at Michael. "Sit with me. Pretend you're my grandson for a minute. That'll be the story you can tell the nurse if she comes in."

Michael pulled a chair across the room and sat beside the bed. He yawned.

"Do you have parents who will be worried about you?"

With a start Michael saw on the clock by the bed that it was already almost five in the morning. Hopefully his mom had just assumed he was asleep in bed and hadn't come in to kiss him on the forehead or anything. "My mom," he answered.

Willy broke into another coughing fit. "You'll see her soon. In the meantime, promise me you'll take care of these books for the rest of your life. Don't just put them on a shelf and forget about them, or worse, sell them for a quarter to some kid down the street." A single tear welled up in one eye, but dried up before it could follow a track down the wrinkles of his face.

Michael fought to hold back his own tears, unsure why he would want to cry right now. "I promise."

Willy smiled and closed his eyes, and Michael watched as his breathing slowed, then stopped. His mouth was half open, and the only sounds in the room now were the buzzing flickering lights and the steady hiss of an oxygen tank that was no longer needed. Michael searched in his memory for a prayer he could say for Willy, then he stood and pried the book from the old man's fingers. It felt a little bigger now, and when he flipped it open to the back he saw that there was a new chapter, and the first sentence read; *The day that young Willy finally decided to make the Green Green Woods his home was the day that saw the biggest celebration any of the animals could ever remember.* Just as important, the second sentence read; *And although he had a bit of a limp for all the rest of his days, James Jackrabbit was first to greet Willy that day.*

Michael smiled and dug into his pack, pulled out a sharpened pencil, and after flipping to the front of the book, wrote under Willy Thornton's signature: "And Now to Michael Cashman" followed by the date. He sat back down and had read all of the stories by the time the sun rose, and he looked out over Chester Pond — Happy Lake — and watched a family of ducks as they splashed in the early morning light.

Eggs for Dinner

by
Jay Lake

C ourtney's life had changed over time, though never for the better. Her father left for overseas when she was eight. "Oil," Mom always said in the years since, but oil came from the earth everywhere — Alaska, the Middle East, Texas — sucked up by pumps like giant mantises praying to the sun-burned grass. Dad left, and only his postcards came back from foreign parts.

After a while even the postcards stopped.

Much later, as Courtney was starting high school, her Grandmother McCandless came to stay. Mom needed to go spend a long time in a cuckoo hospital, talking to doctors about oil and Courtney's father. Grams didn't hold with doctors, or much else, but Courtney had nowhere to go. So she ate the same burnt-edged eggs every morning, rode the same bus to school every day, and came home to the same homework and prayers every night, wondering if life would ever get better.

Or when she could run away, too. She would escape, but like her father — free — not like her mother, wandering into crazy. Like him, Courtney would go over the seas, live her life on the water she'd never yet seen.

When Mom finally did return, she was different. Like a postcard of herself, sent in reminder from a distant country.

"Hey, sweetie," said the woman standing on the second step of the front porch.

The house hadn't been painted since Dad left. Seven summers had flaked the color away to silvered wood with long-grained cracks like the lines on Grams' face.

The woman on the porch had lines on her face, too, that ran from the corners of her eyes and mouth. She looked like Mom but was twice too thin to be Courtney's big, comfortable mother. She had on a crisp blue sundress that didn't seem like it could be hugged.

"Hi, Mom," Courtney said as she stopped in front of the porch. She knew what was expected of her.

"It's been a while." The woman's smile already looked brittle, sharp as the creases in her dress.

"Grams is inside, I expect."

"I wanted to see you first, sweetie. I...I..." The woman sat down on the old porch rocker. The chair creaked like the backyard larch in a windstorm, and Courtney could hear the baling wire that held it together popping free. "I got some things to explain."

"No." Courtney leaned forward and dropped her book bag on the porch. Loud. That was an extra ten minutes at evening prayer right there, but she didn't care. "You don't have nothing to explain."

The woman's lined face ran with tiny rivers of tears, but Courtney ran harder, faster, further than even her mother's sobs could carry.

—•—

Courtney hid under some cottonwoods in a place by the river that had been her secret even when Dad was still around. Maybe it was dumb, having a secret place now that she was a sophomore, but no one had ever known to call her stupid. Sometimes she needed the quiet.

The spot had grown with her, mud hardening to clay with the passage of years, rocks brought in one by to one to make an almost-floor. It always smelled of moss and mud and that faint whiff of river-rot. From here she could watch the herons stalk their way toward the death of fish, and hear the little frogs peep when they thought no one was around.

Only the mosquitoes were indifferent to her secrecy, rising up off the water to find Courtney whether she was hidden or exposed.

It was almost sundown. The riverbed was cloaked in deep, warm shadows, and summer pollen glittered in the air like fairy gold. The far bank rose in runneled lines of graveled clay to a drunk-walking barbed wire fence behind which Old Man Elliot ran his cattle. This bank was bottom land, as overgrown as anything in eastern Oregon ever got, with her at the bottom-most of the land, hiding in the shadows.

Something plopped in the water.

Big.

A footstep?

She peered out through the bushes. Grams never followed her down to the river. The old woman couldn't make the trip, really, not without fear of falling and losing her dignity. Grams stood on dignity the way some people stood upon the earth. That and fear of the Lord were her twin anchors.

Could it be Mom?

Not walking in the river.

Plop.

Courtney scanned some more, but there was still nothing, just mosquitoes and the failing light of day.

Plop.

"I see you," said a voice.

Male, female, Courtney couldn't tell. She spun, looking for an intruder in her secret place. She saw nothing but rocks and the cotton-wood trunk that always watched her back.

"I see you."

This time she was sure the voice came from the river. Courtney grabbed a stone that fit well within her fist and stepped out into the open.

"Where are you?"

"Right here."

And there, in the water, was a salmon long as she was tall. The gravel was so shallow that half its body was out in the air. It was ugly in the way of all salmon, with an upside-down mouth and fish-staring eyes and too long for its width.

"You?" A thousand stories leapt to mind — Indian lore, Grimm's fairy tales, that book of Chinese myths she'd read in the library — but somehow a talking salmon had never been among them.

"Me," said the salmon. "I see you, Courtney Summers Laing. You should see yourself."

With a flip of its tail, the salmon was gone, disappearing in water too shallow and fast to hide a football in, let alone a fish five feet long or more.

—•—

When she came back to the house, all the lights were on. Grams never left the lights on at night — for the waste — which meant Mom was really home.

Or the woman who looked like Mom, Courtney told herself.

She banged through the back door. The woman was in the kitchen, one of Grams' cardigan sweaters covering the shoulders of her sundress, cooking eggs on the stove. The burnt-butter smell of frying filled the little room.

"Eggs? At this time of the night?" Courtney didn't try to hide the scorn.

"Henfruit," her mother said. "Always a treat." She looked up from the pan. Her eyes were red with crying, and the tears had left faint tracks on her cheeks. "I've missed fried eggs. All we ever had was scrambled."

"Could have stayed here and fried eggs every night." Courtney opened the fridge and grabbed the milk carton. Then she went to the drainer for a glass. No drinking from the cardboard.

What had the fish meant, that she should see herself?

Courtney sat down with her milk, perching on the edge of the chair, and stared at her mother. Was that who she was supposed to be?

It was a scary idea.

"Grams worries," Mom said.

"Grams always worries."

Another red-eyed glance. "Some day you'll worry about a girl too. Then you'll understand."

Courtney already knew she'd never have kids. Not ever. Not with what people did to kids and kids did to people. She was going to have her tubes tied as soon as she was old enough to sign the forms herself.

Just in case.

Mom slid the eggs onto one of the chipped china plates leftover from Grandma Laing's wedding set, then sat down opposite Courtney. Courtney stared. There were six eggs on the plate, cooked so far past hard they made Grams' rubbery eggs seem delicious.

Her mother laughed nervously. "Out of practice, I guess."

Courtney sneered. "Six? What a pig."

Mom stared at the plate. From the way her shoulders moved, Courtney figured her mother was wringing her hands under the table. Mom had done that a lot, before Grams came to stay and Mom had gone off to talk to the doctors for a year and more.

"It was supposed to be better now," her mother said in a small voice.

"Better than what? Prayers all the time? Better than rubber eggs every day of my life?"

When her mother burst into tears, Courtney fled to her room. It felt good to run away from the sting in her own eyes.

—•—

Later, she said her prayers in case Grams was listening at the door. Sure as shooting God hadn't listened much lately. Then Courtney turned off the light and sat on the foot of her bed to watch the silver-bellied moon rise outside her window.

Something in the color reminded her of the salmon's scales. The longer she thought about it, the less Courtney believed in that talking fish. She'd been tired, sad, worn out — whatever. Imagination was a powerful thing. They kept telling her that in school.

"I imagine myself on the moon," she whispered to the window screen and the insects buzzing beyond it. "In a land of silver cities with a watery sky, where everyone is cool and no one leaves until they're ready for their journey, and the river always carries them home."

That night she dreamed of fish, tiny little fry lurking among the algae-fringed gravel while skinny dark bird's feet stalked past, death on tall sticks.

—•—

Grams made eggs the next morning. There was no sign of Mom. Courtney sat down at the table. Her book bag waited on the floor.

"Gave you your head yesterday, girl," Grams said. "Even though you showed no respect." She set the plate down in front of Courtney. Two rubber-whited eggs, two glistening, limp pieces of bacon and a slice of whole wheat toast, dry.

Just like every day.

"Eat up." Grams flicked her towel. "Don't get used to having things your way, neither."

"Thank you, ma'am," Courtney said, though Grams was already running the faucet to wash up. Then she folded her hands and prayed grace over her food. "Dear God who is in Heaven, watch over me as I consume this food, bless the hands that made it and the hens that laid it, and forget not the little fishies in the sea. In Jesus' name we pray, Amen."

Her grandmother rattled dishes in the sink — a warning in their little household code — but did not turn with a hard rebuke. Courtney ate and watched Grams clean.

She supposed her mother's mother wasn't old, not really, not like Mrs. Andersen down the street with the walker and the Pekinese. Grams' hair was still mostly black, and Grams was small and slender like a girl. The woman whom her mother had become looked a lot more like Grams, in fact, than like her Mom from before.

Courtney turned this over in her head. Everybody got fat. That was life, and a trip to the Wal-Mart showed the truth of it. You just tried to find a nice boy before your boobs swelled out and fell down.

But Grams wasn't fat. Grams was the opposite of fat. She wondered what it had been like for Grams as a girl. Had her grandmother's mother gotten lost in words, pining for someone who never came home?

"Get on to school, girl," Grams said over the rush of more hot water from the faucet.

Courtney headed out the front door with nothing more than a mumbled, "God bless."

There was no sign of Mom, the old or new version, that morning. Like the salmon, her mother could have been a dream.

—•—

School was school, same as ever. Math was more fun than Courtney would admit, and physical education was torture just like always. Fifth period was her study break and she found her way to the little frog pond behind the science gardens. A few nerdy kids were tending their radishes or whatever, but other than them Courtney had the place to herself. Everyone else was playing basketball out in the bus park or, God forbid, actually studying in the library.

"What did you see?" asked the salmon from the scummy surface of the pond.

Courtney shrieked, dropping her book bag to spill a small riot of pens, pencils and paper across the muddy grass.

"You okay?" asked Carleton Smoot from over in the radish patch. He was a skinny kid with pimples like an ape's butt and horky black glasses. Courtney actually felt more sorry for Carleton than she did for herself, but she wouldn't ever tell him that.

"None of your business, monkeyface."

"Okay." He smiled anyway and went back to work.

Courtney stared at the pond. Now there was nothing there but algae and slimy rocks, though ripples ran back and forth through the green water as if something had just dove. Which was idiotic — the pond wasn't two feet deep, and it was fed by a hose most of the year.

"I know you're in there," she said, hunched forward.

A crooked silver mouth broke the surface, fishy eyes staring like dinner from just under the water. "I'm here," the salmon agreed. "Did you see yourself yet?"

"No." Courtney wanted to throw her bag at the fish, or her books, but something stopped her. Sheer improbability, for one. She was no better than Mom if she went around talking to fish that weren't there.

Couldn't be there.

"You're not real."

"Maybe not. Maybe I am. But that's my problem."

"No, it's my problem. There's enough crazy people in my family. Grams is crazy-sick for Jesus, Mom's crazy-sick for Dad and his oil. I don't want to be crazy-sick for a fish."

The salmon wriggled in a way that suggested a shrug. "Crazy is as crazy does. You just need to see yourself."

Courtney thought about watching Grams in the kitchen that morning. She hunched over even further and began to weep. "I did look. All I saw was crazy-sick."

"Then you're not looking close enough," said the salmon.

With another plop it was gone.

—•—

Courtney skipped the bus and walked home. It was almost four miles, but she wanted to be alone in her head without Tom Reynolds grabbing her butt in the aisle on the bus, or having to listen to the cool kids from over on Ainsworth Street talk about *some* people's horrible taste in clothes.

She didn't believe in the fish, not really, but it was trying to tell her something. She wished she'd paid more attention in social sciences when they talked about Native American legends.

Were salmon supposed to be wise? Or were they just food, like trout?

The walk took some kinks out of her back and legs and cleared her head. When she got home, she decided to look more closely. She couldn't see the harm in following the salmon's advice.

She walked in quietly, like Grams wanted her to. Her grandmother sat knitting in an old wingback chair she'd brought with her when she'd first come to stay.

Grams knitted for the poor. God knew their household could barely afford the wool, but that's what Grams did. She didn't hold with television and she couldn't stand whatever was on the radio, so she knitted.

Courtney sat across the little living room from her grandmother, on the love seat with the bad spring. She set her book bag down and looked, really looked, at Grams and her work.

The wool was bright red.

Courtney had never thought about it before, but Grams always knitted in bright colors. The older woman never wore anything but blues, browns and blacks, mostly knee-length dresses or polyester pants suits from the Goodwill, but she knitted in colors that could frighten a hummingbird. Courtney watched the hands move with the needles. Grams wore two rings, on the ring finger of each hand. Her left was a simple gold band, her right was a silver ring with some chasing Courtney couldn't see from across the room, and a green chip of a jewel.

"What is it, child?" Grams finally asked, not looking up from her work.

What was there to see? Courtney knew she was the sum of this woman's hopes and fears, passed through her Mom like water through coffee grounds. Could she see herself in her grandmother? She reached for the thing she knew least about. "Grams...please tell me about Grandpa McCandless."

The needles clicked for a while without any answer to her question, but Grams didn't roll her eyes, or snort, or reprimand like she often did. Finally: "Child, why do you got call to ask that question?"

But her voice was soft.

Courtney tried again. "Because I...I don't know, ma'am. And I want to."

"Wanting to know has been the death of many." The needles clicked a while, then the older woman actually smiled. "It's your history, too."

She stopped then, staring into nothing. Then, "When I was a girl, William Roundtree McCandless was the most beautiful boy in Malheur County." Grams' smile mellowed into a sort of ease Courtney had never seen on her grandmother's face. "He had hair the color of a chestnut horse, and eyes gray as a summer storm, and his shoulders could have carried a brace of carpenters at their work and never jogged the level."

Courtney held her breath, afraid to distract her grandmother. She'd never seen Grams smile like that. Besides, she knew nothing about her mother's father.

"He took a shine to me when he was nineteen and I was fourteen."

Grams actually laughed. "Pawpaw was fit for a scandal and said he'd shoot Bill McCandless in the belly if he caught him sniffing around me." She glanced up at Courtney, their eyes meeting for the first time. "That was so Bill would die slow, you know."

"Uh huh," said Courtney. Who knew her Grams had lived such a life as this?

Then the smile clouded. "We wooed anyway, and when I was fifteen Bill and me run off to Idaho and got married. He never lost his beauty, I must say, but when President Johnson had his war there in the Vietnam, Bill signed up to go off. He was too young for Korea, and he'd grown up on stories of the big one. Your mother was born right before he shipped out to Fort Lewis for training."

The needles resumed their clicking. Courtney hadn't even realized they'd stopped. Grams was silent for a long time, sort of smiling, sort of frowning.

"He came home, didn't he?" Courtney finally asked.

"Yep. I reckon he did. Everything comes home in the end. Left the best part of him behind, though." The needles stopped again, her grandmother meeting Courtney's eye to stare intently. "Don't get me wrong, girl, I still loved him. I love him yet. But that beautiful boy came home with an anger in his heart that no amount of praying, no amount of drinking, no amount of fighting could close up or cast aside."

"Oh."

"Oh is right. When finally we laid him to his rest in 1976, it was time to have said good-bye. But I hadn't seen that beautiful boy of mine in ten years by then. Just the sad, sorry man he'd become. The good Lord didn't mean my Bill to have a happy life."

"How'd he die?"

The needles clicked once more. "Fishing in the river. Pulled in by something, big bull salmon maybe. Drunk off his head, drowned in a pool eight inches deep, wedged between two rocks."

"I'm sorry."

"It was the Lord's will, child, the Lord's will." Needles clattered as Grams slapped the arm of her chair. "Now go do some homework."

—•—

Later, over a language arts assignment on European folkways, Courtney stopped and stared out the window. It was near sundown and the Sheepshead Mountains glowered brown and gray in the distance, their ridgelines touched with a pinkish gold. The river wasn't visible from her room, but the tops of the cottonwoods were, poking up from where they grew down in the channel. Their unseen trunks would already be deep in shadow. A light breeze brought the stale water smell to her nose.

Had her grandfather died right here? Courtney's salmon had come up in impossibly shallow water to speak to her. She could imagine a handsome man, gone to age and drink, arguing with a big old fish.

The thought made her shiver.

—•—

After a while she heard the back door with that odd squeak from where the frame was out of true. Grams never went out at night. That had to be her mother.

Mom.

The thin woman, Courtney couldn't help thinking.

She closed her book on a picture of a smiling girl in a red dirndl carrying a tray of huge pretzels. Outside was dark, with just the yellow lights of town fighting with the stars.

Courtney liked taking her bike out into the country sometimes. It wasn't far to ride and she could lay down among the warm, stinky cattle for windbreaks and stare up. Away from the lights of town shooting stars were easy to count, and she could imagine sailing a sea that looked like the night sky. Being penned up just made her want to run. Her whole life was nothing but a pen, she a fish caught behind a dam.

"Mother," she whispered, then headed downstairs.

Grams' light was on under her bedroom door at the bottom of the stairs. The rest of the house was dark. Just the way Grams liked it.

Had she imagined the noise of the back door?

Courtney glanced into the kitchen, then turned to look in the living room.

Mom sat on the love seat, at the end with the busted spring. Courtney snorted. That figured. She walked over and sat down next to her mother, who smelled of butter and sweat.

There was silence between them for a while, broad and bright as the stars over a country field. Courtney didn't want to be there, didn't want to be talking to this woman who'd left and not really come back yet. But the fish had been right about her grandmother.

Maybe it was right about her mother.

Eventually, she cleared her throat. "Tell me about Daddy, Mom. Before the oil, I mean."

Her mom laughed. It was a dusty sound, rocks rattling in a dry creek bed. "I ain't supposed to talk about the oil."

"*Before* the oil, Mom. Before."

"Yeah." The couch creaked as her mother settled in a little further. "Maybe I'm supposed to tell you. You were beautiful, you know."

It was Courtney's turn to laugh. "Me?" Her boobs were too small, her butt was too big, and while she didn't have Carleton Smoot's zit farm, no one would ever mistake her skin for clear and clean.

"You're pretty now, girl, but when you were a baby…ahh." A sigh, years pressed out between chapped lips. "I was bound and determined to have you natural. Mercer, he kept saying, 'use the drugs, damn it.' His sister'd had two long, hard deliveries when he was still a boy, I guess. He didn't believe in natural childbirth. But I did."

"Mmm…" Even before Mom had gone away, there had been a long time when her mother had talked about nothing but oil and Mercer Laing. Hearing about herself was a new, or at least renewed, experience for Courtney. She didn't want to interrupt.

"So I went at it the hard way. Even Mama thought I was wrong, and she don't hold with much that ain't in the Bible. But I did it. Screamed and sweated and bit on one of Mercer's belts for seventeen hours until you came out. You took forever, but when you finally showed, you popped like a watermelon seed."

This time her mother's laugh was genuine.

"Midwife caught you and clipped you, then smiled to say you were the prettiest thing she ever did see. She put you on my chest and my God, you were a little blue-faced rat with a pointy bullet-head and covered with gray goop like some bird crap. I screamed. I don't know, I was thinking of one of those diaper-ad babies or something. Not the real thing. Nobody'd ever told me nothing about it."

Courtney's heart skipped with a cold shiver.

"Then…" Her mother stopped and drew a deep breath. "Then I looked at your squinty blue eyes and those two tiny fists and I knew that you were all the beauty in the world, and you'd come out of me. I made you and that was the greatest thing I ever did."

"And Daddy?" She had to ask.

"He laughed at my screaming, and he laughed at the midwife, then he took you in his arms and sang awhile." She sighed again. "You were the beautiful bridge to make things right between us."

Those words made Courtney's heart soar and sink at the same time, like she was two girls in one body. Mom cried then, but the tears were soft, almost gentle. A while later, Courtney heard her Grams' bedroom door snick shut.

—•—

Right before she went to sleep, Courtney read in her biology textbook:

Anadromous fish are those fish born in a freshwater stream that migrate to the ocean for their adult phase. Most salmon are anadromous. Some species' populations can be trapped by changes in water flow, or perhaps impounded behind a dam and still survive. Those non-anadromous populations are considered resident. Anadromous and non-anadromous forms of the same species can have different life cycles and even different morphologies.

Morphologies. That meant what their bodies looked like. Mom had certainly come home with a different morphology. A hundred pounds different. But no one could be more impounded than Courtney was.

No, she thought. Grams and Mom had both been more impounded. The dry mountains and high deserts of eastern Oregon were a giant dam behind which all the people struggled for escape.

—•—

She dreamed of the salmon that night. It sat in her little study chair in front of her desk, bent at an angle that looked uncomfortable. The upside-down mouth seemed cruel somehow, and the fluttering gills were wounds on its body, stigmata for a fish dying in air.

"You're supposed to be in the river," Courtney said. It smelled like the river, the river-rot in particular. She didn't remember that odor from before.

"I can go wherever there is water to hold me."

"There's no water in the house. Outside the kitchen and bathroom, I mean."

"Saltwater tears are enough for me."

Who had been crying? "I looked at Grams and Mom," she told the fish. "Really looked."

"What did you see?"

She thought about how to answer that question. "I don't know. More than I ever knew was there."

"You're growing up."

Courtney hated it when people said that. She always had. It didn't sound any better coming from a fish. "It's crummy enough being in high school. Don't patronize me."

The fish gave one of its not-shrugs. "Truth is truth. What is there for you now?"

She thought of the ocean reflecting all those summer stars, salmon swimming their long cold migration through distant seas only to finally come home again.

Why would anyone ever want to come home again?

But Mom had.

And Grams after her, when Mom got sick.

She knew then, in her heart and in her gut, something she'd never quite believed or understood. "They love me," Courtney told the fish. "They're trapped behind their dams, but they still love me."

—•—

The next day she went over to the King-Freeze after school and asked for a job application. Courtney figured if she could save enough money in the couple more years from now until she graduated, she could follow the river down to the ocean.

Carleton Smoot's oldest brother was the day manager. He was cute in an older guy sort of way, no pimples, and he grinned at her when he handed her the greasy sheet of paper. "Want come to drop some fries with the big boys, eh?"

"Keep your oil to yourself," she told him, but she smiled back at him.

She folded the paper into her pack and went down to her secret place by the river. The salmon wouldn't be there now — it had done its totem animal thing, right? But when she settled in among the bushes at the base of the cottonwood trees, the creature flopped up into the shallows.

"Ocean's cold, you know," it said.

Courtney thought of her biology textbook. "Life's a challenge for a fish. You've survived it."

"I'll never die. Not until I spawn."

"How long...?" In the middle of the question, Courtney realized she was being rude.

"No one's asked me that before," the salmon said. "I remember the biggest flood of all. More years ago than you've had days in your life. It tore mountains from their roots and pushed half the continent toward the sea."

"Missoula," said Courtney, memories stirring of a trip to a museum up in the Columbia Gorge.

"The Missoula Flood. That's what you call it now."

"What did you call it then?"

Somehow the salmon managed to smile. "Life."

"Life." Courtney laughed, the honest laugh of water on rocks and wind in the trees. "Why'd you wait this long?"

The fish wiggled, a sort of silver-scaled shrug. "Life. Waiting to see tomorrow. Waiting to meet you."

Courtney imagined the march of all those years, all the history of water and Indians and Lewis and Clark flowing by while the salmon waited for her. "Maybe," she said. Then she knew she wouldn't see the fish again, the same way she knew she was going to draw her next breath. "I got to ask one last thing."

The salmon said nothing, just smiled its upside-down smile.

"Was it you that killed Grandpa Bill?"

"It was time for the river to take him home. Everybody comes home in the end."

Sometimes, Courtney thought, if they were real lucky, people started out at home too. Then she waded into the water to kiss the fish before heading back to the house to fill out her job application. She thought maybe she'd practice by cooking eggs for dinner for Mom and Grams.

Dances with Coyotes

by
John C. Bunnell

"You dance very well, Elena," said my partner as the song ended. "Perhaps another?" He lifted my hand and bowed slightly as we stepped apart.

"And you picked up that foxtrot really fast," I told him. "But maybe later. I think I'd better find my date."

"Until we meet again, then," he replied. A moment later I lost track of his silver-gray tuxedo in the swirl of teen-aged dancers — and felt a tap on my right shoulder.

"Who was *that*?" asked Aaron Morris. As one of the half-dozen tallest seniors in Hood River Valley High's graduating class, he tended to stand out in a crowd, and his dark, chiseled Native American features made him even more distinctive.

I frowned thoughtfully. "Now that you mention it, I don't have the faintest idea. Which is strange, considering; our class isn't all that big." The music started again—a lively waltz number—and we linked arms and began to dance. The prom committee had gone seriously retro; the old-time swing band's music and the ballroom's vintage decor both dated from the "roaring '20s, when the Columbia Gorge Hotel had been built.

"I don't know what I'd be doing here without you," Aaron said, softly, matching my rhythm even more smoothly than the stranger had.

I restrained a giggle. "Yes, well, I have an excuse. Back in Boston we were on the social-elite circuit, so Mom and Dad made me learn all the ballroom steps. You, on the other hand —"

"As of a week ago, I'd never even seen the inside of a ballroom," said Aaron, chuckling. "It's a good thing the library had a couple of dance-lesson videos I could study."

"You don't learn to move as well as you do by watching videos," I retorted. "You're *good* at this — which is why you're so popular tonight."

A dark expression flickered across Aaron's face at my words, and he fell silent. Before he'd asked me to the prom a week earlier, he and I hadn't really known each other—but I was observant enough to realize that nearly every social clique in the school acted as if he didn't exist, most likely because he was the only Indian in the class. It wasn't an entirely unfamiliar situation. In the year since Mom had accepted the lead scientific job at the Bonneville Fish Hatchery west of Hood River, I'd made few friends, and the Greek coloring I'd inherited from Dad made me nearly as distinctive as Aaron was.

Prom night, however, had altered the equation a little. Aaron and I were very nearly the only people in attendance — chaperones included — who actually knew how to dance to the band's old-fashioned rhythm, and our popularity was growing in direct proportion to the number of times other people's toes were getting squashed. As a result, we both drew more would-be dance partners than we could gracefully refuse, whether we recognized them or not.

For me, it was refreshing; the crimson-and-gilt atmosphere reminded me of other gatherings back east, and when we finished the waltz, Aaron and I both acquired new partners for the swing number that followed it. But as our paths intersected again at the end of that song, Aaron scurried toward me like a deer caught in someone's headlights.

Not that he didn't have reason. "What did that girl think she was doing?" I demanded as we found seats at a side table. "She could out-cling a whole roll of plastic wrap."

Even Aaron's burnt-copper coloring couldn't hide his flush. "I don't think you want to know," he said, looking everywhere except at me. "Come to that, I don't think *I* want to know."

I blinked and took off my glasses, only partly because the lenses needed cleaning. "It's kind of early to call it a night," I said doubtfully, just barely touching my handkerchief to the corner of each eye before tucking it back into the tiny clutch that went with my emerald-green dress. Nor was the gesture purely for effect — I realized as the words came out that I was talking about our date as well as the dance.

If anything, Aaron's face reddened even further, but his eyes were amused. "So it is," he said. "Maybe ... I know. Let me show you something."

Taking my hand, he rose and led the way toward the ballroom's main entrance, then through the elegant hotel lobby and out onto the grounds. The late evening breeze was crisp, and Aaron paused to drape his tuxedo jacket over my shoulders. "This way," he said, waving his free hand at the strip of lawn running between the parking area and the wide expanse of the Columbia River. I quickly slipped my shoes off before following him along a cobbled walk, down a few rough steps, and into a little hollow flanked by clusters of venerable evergreen trees, with a low semi-circular wall guarding the steep drop-off separating us from the water's edge. Light from a nearly full moon and a liberal dusting of stars rippled and flashed across the river's surface, and the liquid *shoosh* of wind on wavelets echoed upward toward us.

"This was a gathering place even before the white man came," Aaron said quietly, leaning lightly against the little wall "The river people called it *Wah-gwin-gwin* — place of rushing water."

"It's — extraordinary." There should have been a better word, but my senses were too highly wound for me to come up with it. The wave-cooled breeze tickled mischievously below my hemline, which ran from several inches below one knee to several inches above the other— but at the same time, the air between me and Aaron pulsed with magnetic intensity. My subconscious had just time to whisper *like calls to like* before the attraction drew us together, my lips meeting his as his arms encircled my shoulders, tentatively at first but then with careful firmness.

All too soon, lack of oxygen — and practice — forced us to break the kiss. "I think," Aaron said in a dazed tone, "that I've been very, very lucky."

"That makes two of us," I replied, only slightly less muzzily.

"But it is not luck," said a third voice, rumbling out of the darkness, "if it results from wisdom and good judgment rather than from pure chance." We both whirled, detaching ourselves from each other's arms, as a coyote nearly the size of a Volkswagen Beetle trotted noiselessly out of the trees, its tail flicking back and forth while moonlight shimmered against its silver-gray fur.

Aaron was first to recover his wits. "*Koyoda Speelyi!*"

"At your service," replied the giant talking coyote, nodding at both of us in turn, "and pleased to be so. You have done very well."

My eyes — all I could seem to move reliably just then — flicked from the coyote to Aaron and back again. "Wait a second," I said, my voice gaining strength word by word. "You called it — him — Koyoda something-or-other. Who is he, and what's going on here?"

"Koyoda Speelyi," said Aaron, his voice a tangle of emotions I couldn't decipher. "Most stories now told or written down call him only Coyote or Trickster, but the oldest tales of the Klickitat — my people — name him truly. He is the voice and the will of Sahale Tyee, the Great Spirit, in the world below."

I regarded the grinning car-sized coyote skeptically. "If you say so. But if we're not about to become coyote chow, what is he here for — the prom?"

"Very perceptive," Koyoda said to Aaron, a touch of a yip behind the words. "And a skillful dancer as well. Wisdom and good judgment, indeed."

"A skillful dancer?" I echoed, mystified. "But how would you know … ?" My voice trailed off as I stared at Koyoda Speelyi, whose shadow flickered oddly in the moonlight as if it sometimes had two legs rather than four. And there was something else familiar — I abruptly snapped my fingers, recalling a certain silver-gray tuxedo whose color just matched a coyote's fur. "That foxtrot number, of course. Someone around here has a severely warped sense of humor."

Koyoda merely grinned at me, tongue lolling out. Then he tilted his head back toward Aaron, his yip growing more pronounced as he spoke. "I told you she was perceptive. Most commendable. You are in good hands — and you have earned what you sought, and more. Guard it well." He threw back his head as if to howl, but instead there was a flash of moonlight, a sudden rush of wind, and between one breath and the next, the giant coyote had vanished. And beyond where it had stood, resting on the ledge atop one end of the low stone wall, was a plump brown pouch no larger than my clutch.

Aaron reached for it with a slightly dazed motion and tucked it into a pocket, but not before I'd gotten a good look — and even I had read enough about Indian customs to have some idea of what it was. "But if that's a medicine bag," I said slowly, "then that would mean ..."

"That tonight was a spirit quest," Aaron said, all the life drained out of his voice. "And so it was."

I tried to wrap my mind around the idea. "Are you telling me that Koyoda Speelyi is your — what's the word, guardian spirit? — and that the spirit quest he assigned you was going to your high school prom? You have *got* to be kidding."

Aaron nodded unhappily. "I am not — although it is very unusual. Guardian spirits don't normally appear to anyone other than those who seek them, and then not until a quest is complete."

"But you must have seen He Who Foxtrots before tonight," I said, slowly, "in order to know not to do the usual fasting-and-camping-out routine. Except if that's what happened ..." Another mental domino fell over. "Then it was all Koyoda's idea for you to ask me out!"

"*No!*" Aaron said instantly. "The quest was only to come to the prom — *follow its customs and traditions, as you would follow your own*, he said."

"Bringing a date being one of them. All you needed was a warm body on your arm."

"That might have satisfied the form," Aaron said, "but not the substance. I had to ask someone — but I *wanted* to ask you."

"But you didn't tell me why you were really asking," I shot back. "And if He Who Foxtrots hadn't pushed you into it, you wouldn't have asked at all."

To that Aaron had no swift comeback. "I'm — sorry," he said after a long, drawn-out moment.

"So am I," I said, shrugging out of his tuxedo jacket and handing it back. "I think you'd better take me home."

The silence in Aaron's pickup as we drove through Hood River was thick enough to make soup with. Only when he parked in front of my house did he finally break it. "This isn't how I wanted things to turn out. Everything was going so well until …" He trailed off and tried again. "I meant for you — for both of us — to have a good time tonight. I had no idea Koyoda would be there."

I shrugged and opened the passenger door. "I'll give you one thing; it was definitely memorable. They say you never forget your senior prom — and Lord knows I won't."

"I don't suppose … ?" Aaron was still having a hard time finishing his sentences.

"That we could try again? With your friend the giant talking coyote playing chaperon? I don't think so," I said, slipping out of the pickup.

But the memories in my mind as I walked up the driveway had as much to do with the kiss Koyoda had interrupted as with the Klickitat spirit-being himself.

—●—

Mom, of course, insisted on a play-by-play rundown of the prom the next morning over brunch — though needless to say I omitted any mention of giant talking coyotes, and gave her a noncommittal "maybe" as to my prospects with Aaron. But Koyoda was very much on my mind, and after I'd loaded the dishwasher I headed for Dad's study and the shelf of local-history books he'd been accumulating since our move to Hood River.

Dad himself was away for the week, on assignment covering a trade summit in Montréal, so I was free to rummage undisturbed. There were at least a half-dozen volumes of legends collected from local Indian tribes, a good many of which mentioned Coyote—but only as Coyote, not *Koyoda Speelyi*, as Aaron had called him. And though the Coyote on the printed page might sometimes be part demigod, he was also careless, impatient, temperamental, self-centered, and by some accounts an extremely dirty old man in pointy-eared clothing. Worse, he had an alarming habit of turning people to stone first and asking questions later, and Coyote's statuary didn't revert to normal at the end of an episode, in the manner of modern cartoons or comic books. Instead, it stayed put long enough to graduate from antique to local landmark.

The more I read, the more the stories blurred together, not only with each other, but with my prom-night encounter — or encounters, if one counted both Koyoda's disguised turn on the dance floor and his later entrance as himself. Part of me wanted to believe I'd imagined the whole episode, but that theory had serious drawbacks. Somehow I doubted Aaron would consider Koyoda a hallucination, and the only other option was that I'd hallucinated the entire date, Aaron and all — a theory which failed to account for the emerald-green prom dress upstairs in my room, even now awaiting a trip to the dry cleaners.

I still didn't have answers when I stacked up the books, replaced them on Dad's shelf, and went to see what Mom was doing about dinner. But I had made up my mind on one point: no matter how good kissing Aaron Morris had felt, his faithful coyote sidekick was too high-maintenance to justify the risk.

—•—

It occurred to me as I pedaled toward school Monday morning that the last month of classes could be awfully complicated under the circumstances. I couldn't avoid Aaron entirely — we shared second-period English and sixth-period civics — and I wasn't sure how much sheer proximity might tend to cloud my better judgment about his taste in guardian spirits.

But at least for the first day or two, it wasn't much of an issue. We took seats on opposite sides of the classroom, ate lunch in different parts of the cafeteria, and went our own ways after classes let out. And if I occasionally caught Aaron casting wistful-looking glances in my direction, I ignored them as studiously as I avoided equally poignant reminiscences of the kiss we'd shared at the prom.

Tuesday afternoon promised ample time for self-reflection — or would have, if not for the sizeable load of homework I was carrying as I pedaled up the driveway after school. I had the house to myself for the afternoon; Dad was still in Canada at the trade summit, my barely-teenaged twin brothers had Little League practice, and Mom wouldn't be home from the hatchery till nearly six.

After stowing my bicycle and helmet in the garage and dropping my pack at the bottom of the stairs, I headed for the kitchen. Five minutes' work produced a plateful of sliced locally-grown apples — a staple of Hood River's economy, along with windsurfing — garnished with a handful of microwaved cocktail weenies and accompanied by a super-sized tumbler of iced tea. Carrying the plate, glass, and my school pack upstairs to my room was a balancing act worthy of a circus performer, and I was frowning as I pushed the bedroom door open with one foot, as I didn't usually leave it ajar.

Nor was there normally a Great Dane-sized gray coyote sprawled lazily across my bed, taking up almost all of its surface. *Well*, I thought, *there goes the it-was-all-your-imagination theory.*

The next few moments blurred, but somehow the only thing that ended up on the floor was my pack. When time unfroze, the apples, weenies, and iced tea were neatly arranged on my desk, but I couldn't have said whether I'd set them there myself or if they'd been rescued from free fall at a flick of Koyoda Speelyi's tail.

Besides which, I had other priorities, such as pulling a small cylinder out of my jeans pocket. "Give me one good reason," I said, "why you don't deserve a faceful of pepper spray and a one-way ticket out the window."

My visitor yawned toothily and eyed me with a pained expression. "Greetings, Elena Santorini," he said mildly. "Despite appearances, I am not the Coyote of your father's books. I am Koyoda Speelyi, and I mean you no harm or ill will. Besides, Midsummer Peach is hardly my color."

"Midsummer —?" I blinked at the object in my hand, which was — now, at least — a harmless tube of lipstick. What it had been a moment ago, I was no longer certain. "All right, then," I said, "you're not planning to live down to your — or Coyote's — press coverage. So why are you here? If this is about more dance lessons, the high school library has videos you can study."

Koyoda's voice deepened, acquiring just the hint of a growl. "You are a friend to Aaron Morris — perhaps more than a friend," he said. "Or so I had thought."

I opened my mouth — then closed it, not quite spluttering, before my first angry retort could escape. After three more failed attempts at getting out a properly scathing reply, I gave up. "I might have been," I said at last. "And I might even still want to be — not that it's any of your damned business. But the way *you* set this up, I'm just the door prize in a magic scavenger hunt with a peeping Koyoda hovering in the background. Sorry, but I don't do kewpie doll."

The tip of a pink tongue flicked past Koyoda's lips. "Your tiny sausages grow cold," he said, "and your tea grows warm."

With an exasperated shrug, I plunked myself onto the chair next to my desk and took a long swallow of tepid iced tea. "And your point?" I inquired, absent-mindedly tossing a cocktail weenie in Koyoda's direction before biting into one myself.

The far-less-than-bite-sized morsel vanished down his throat with a sharp-toothed snap. "Tasty," he said. "As for your question — you know something of Aaron's history, I think. Tell me this: left to himself, where will he go once he graduates from high school a month from now?"

"To the reservation up by Yakima, to live with his mother's relatives," I said at once. "Faster than a speeding roadrunner."

Koyoda gave the line the minuscule chuckle it deserved. "We are agreed. Now a more difficult question — *will he be happy there?*"

I resisted the impulse to snap back *How the hell am I supposed to know?*, and tried to wrap my brain around the problem. I didn't know much about the Yakama Reservation, beyond the fact that its leadership had changed the name's spelling a few years earlier so that it no longer matched that of the nearby city of Yakima. I knew a bit more about Aaron — most of it based on the past week's acquaintance and our eventful prom date. But I knew a bit more than that about myself, and I cast my mind back over the past year, thinking about my own adjustment from life in Boston and in Hood River.

"Peaceful," I said at last. "Peaceful, and safe. But happy? Somehow I just don't think so."

"Again we agree," returned Koyoda. "And so it follows that we must not leave Aaron to himself to make that decision."

"What do you mean *we*, He Who Foxtrots?" I demanded, paraphrasing a very old joke. "You're the guardian spirit; can't you just tell him where to go? Or where not to go, in this case?"

For once, Koyoda let the attempt at humor pass. "A guardian spirit does not impose its will on those it guards," he said. "It may advise, even influence, but not compel. Besides, some tasks are better accomplished by wit than by strength alone."

It was my turn to laugh. "In other words, I'm supposed to seduce Aaron for his own good. Sorry, but I don't do James Bond movies either — and I thought you said you weren't the Coyote in the books. Or is the voyeur bit part of the real you after all?"

Koyoda merely licked his lips in amusement, while my bedsprings squeaked under his weight. "The answer to that question is extremely tangled," he said. "To simplify it greatly, *coyote* and *Koyoda* are words from different tongues entirely, and *Trickster* and *Changer* very different aspects of spirit-power. Yet by accident or design — or perhaps both — all these things manifest in the same shape."

He paused. "But we digress. I seek no more than you have already given, in one coin or another, save your pardon for my indiscretion these four nights past. Your hopes and mine are not in conflict, and I do not wish to be the cause of ill will between you and Aaron." Stretching, Koyoda adopted a classically soulful hurt-puppy expression, gazing up from the bed at me with wide, liquid-midnight eyes.

I tossed another cocktail weenie at him, forcing him to give up the puppy-dog face in order to catch it. "Oh, all right," I said. "But if this is going to go anywhere, you have to stay on your best behavior. If I get even one hint that you're doing the invisible chaperon routine again, Midsummer Peach lipstick will be the least of your problems."

"You have my thanks, then," said Koyoda. "May Sahale Tyee smile upon you." Whereupon the curtains framing my bedroom window abruptly rustled — even though it hadn't been open earlier, either — the scent of evergreen blew into the room and out again, and somehow, between breaths, Koyoda Speelyi was no longer there.

Neither, I noted wryly, were the rest of the cocktail weenies.

I wondered for a moment if the entire conversation had been another hallucination. Then I took a good look at the bedspread and laughed out loud.

Not only was there a large rumpled oval where he'd curled up, but he'd shed traces of silver-gray fur all over the pale green fabric.

—•—

The school day had ended on Wednesday before I actually caught up with Aaron, as we both headed for the parking lot after a surprise civics quiz. "Hold on a moment," I said, lightly tapping his arm as he pushed open the door and started to step outside.

He glanced sideways, his posture stiffening as our eyes met. "Elena? I thought."

"I know," I said. "But we need to talk. I — said some things at the prom that I probably shouldn't have."

"Oh?" Aaron's tone was cautious, but he followed as I waved him toward the rack where my bicycle was locked.

"I didn't give you enough credit for what you actually did, as opposed to what you were told to do. And I let the end of the night count for too much compared to the beginning. Dinner at Skamania Lodge, especially — that was way beyond minimum prom-night requirements."

"Maybe so," Aaron agreed, "but it was what the occasion called for."

"I won't argue," I said, recalling smoked roast quail as well-prepared as any meal I'd ever eaten in Boston. "As for a certain giant talking coyote … "

Now Aaron chuckled. "Koyoda Speelyi can be — less than diplomatic, and his timing was atrocious."

"But it wasn't your fault — and I shouldn't have treated you as if it was."

"I appreciate that," Aaron said, his expression softening visibly. By this time I'd unlocked my bike and wrestled it out of the rack. Before I could mount, Aaron reached out, set a hand atop mine on one handlebar, and added, "Very much."

It was as if an electric charge had been simmering between us ever since we'd parted company Saturday night, and it was all I could do not to throw myself bodily over the bicycle and into Aaron's arms. But there was still a fair amount of people-traffic in the parking lot, so instead, I tried to lighten the mood while reining in my rampaging hormones. "Yes well, and it doesn't hurt that He Who Foxtrots can be surprisingly well-mannered when he puts his mind to it."

"*What?*" The magnetic current flipped inside out with an almost-audible *SNAP* as Aaron's face hardened and his hand recoiled from mine. "Koyoda Speelyi appeared to you again?"

I gave him a puzzled look. "We had a very productive talk."

"You had a talk," Aaron repeated slowly. "With Koyoda. And then you came to see me."

"Ye-es," I said, not sure where he was going.

"This from someone who objected when she thought Koyoda was using her," said Aaron, his tone flat. "You don't see the irony?"

"Damn it, this wasn't —" Aaron cut me off before I could finish the sentence.

"*Wisdom and good judgment,* he said. *Trust in your own choices,* he said. *Walk in the white man's world.* He did not say *and here is the path and someone to walk with you* — yet he set them out all the same, with markers to ensure I would not stray." The tirade wasn't really aimed at me; Aaron was acting as if I wasn't there. I tried to interject, but it was like waving a white flag in a blizzard.

"Very well, Koyoda Speelyi," he said, though the oversized coyote was nowhere to be seen. "I will walk in the white man's world — by following the advice you spoke aloud, not the path you marked behind my back."

And for the second time in less than a week, I stood in stunned silence while Aaron spun sideways, stalked rapidly across the parking lot to his pickup, and sped off with loose gravel rattling in his wake.

—•—

Even if I hadn't lost nearly a minute staring dazedly after him, I couldn't possibly have caught Aaron on two non-motorized wheels — not, as I thought about it, that going after him would have been the right idea anyway.

The thing was, he had a point about the irony of the situation, and storming off in a huff was all too much like what I'd done on prom night. Even Koyoda had left me alone for a couple of days before attempting to reason with me, and chances were that Aaron would be more amenable to further overtures after he'd had a chance to cool down.

So instead of tearing through the streets of Hood River trying to find him, I pedaled in the opposite direction — toward home, in our tidy new subdivision a mile or so south of the high school on the fringes of the Hood River Valley's serious apple-growing country. Time enough, I thought, to try again tomorrow, or the next day.

Which might have been a perfectly good plan, if only Aaron had been in school Thursday or Friday.

I didn't worry when he missed English Thursday morning. I simply assumed he was avoiding me as actively as possible — though it wasn't like Aaron to skip class. And the odds that he was ill were too low to contemplate; even a week's acquaintance was enough for me to recognize a titanium-plated constitution when I saw one. He didn't turn up at lunch, either, nor did he reappear to collect his graded quiz in civics — which had the teacher shaking his head, since Aaron's was one of the three As in the whole class.

Friday was another matter. When he didn't show up for English, I stopped in the office between periods, but the attendance secretary had no idea where Aaron might be. By lunchtime I was formulating wild theories about what might have happened to him — perhaps he'd been run off the road, or kidnapped, or eaten by a river monster out of one of the local myths. I thought seriously at lunch about calling the police, but decided against it — for all practical purposes, Aaron had been living by himself for the past several years, and that wasn't likely to sit well with the local authorities. (There was also the minor difficulty that I didn't actually know where Aaron lived.) I was utterly unsurprised when his place was vacant again in civics, and after class I simply stood next to my bicycle and stared into space while the parking lot emptied around me.

"Damn," I said aloud after the last car churned over the gravel shoulder onto the street. "Why isn't there ever a giant talking coyote around when you need one?"

This time, however, Koyoda Speelyi utterly failed to pick up the cue. I didn't bother trying again; the last thing likely to draw out a capricious demigod was someone wandering around calling "Come, Koyoda!" as if hunting for a lost puppy. Which left me with a problem — just how *did* one summon up the aforementioned capricious demigod?

I went to work on the matter as soon as I got home. Plugging the name "Koyoda Speelyi" into a Web search got nowhere at all, which I'd expected — especially considering that I'd never asked how to spell it. But when I tried each word separately, the search engines were more cooperative — and if most of the results weren't what I wanted, the few relevant hits were at least slightly encouraging. It was obvious almost at once that I wasn't going to find a tidy set of instructions online — not that I'd expected that, either — but within half an hour, I found a number of references to an old, locally published book, *Legends of the Klickitats*, whose descriptions sounded potentially intriguing. The good news: the local library's catalog listed a copy. The bad news: I couldn't get at it till they opened the next morning ... and the longer Aaron was gone, the less confident I was of ever seeing him again. Nor was there any guarantee that the book would have the information I wanted in it.

Actually getting hold of *Legends of the Klickitats* Saturday morning was the stuff of routine, though it involved being up and around at an hour I rarely saw on a weekend. The round trip to downtown Hood River via bicycle was long by my usual standards, mostly downhill on the way there and mostly uphill coming back. Luckily, the book was skinny and lightweight, but I was still puffing by the time I staggered through my front door with it half an hour before lunchtime.

Within the first few pages, I knew I'd hit the jackpot. The spellings were creative — not unusual, since there were no standard rules for translating spoken Indian names into written English — but the writer named and described Koyoda Speelyi in unmistakable terms. Now if only he reported a method for calling the Klickitat guardian spirit ...

Which he did — near the end of the book, of course, and when I got there I nearly fell off my bed laughing, because the ritual amounted, more or less, to calling for Koyoda as if he were a missing puppy. The details, however, were a trifle more involved, and I was abruptly grateful I'd skipped lunch as I headed for my closet, since fasting was one of the preparatory steps.

Several hours later, I crept as quietly as possible down the stairs. I was hoping to slip out of the house without being noticed — not a trivial feat, since it involved borrowing Dad's Thunderbird to get where I needed to go. Mom was washing lettuce in the kitchen as I tiptoed past her into the pantry, where we kept the spare-key rack, but she looked over her shoulder at exactly the wrong moment as I came out again, keys in hand.

"What in creation are you doing in that getup?" she demanded. "And where do you think you're going fifteen minutes before dinner-time?"

From Mom's perspective, it was a reasonable question. The white bridesmaid's dress I was wearing was trimmed with a terminal overdose of lace and left over from a cousin's wedding. I'd augmented the outfit with a drawerful of gaudily mismatched costume jewelry I hadn't touched since I was ten, twined a six-foot loop of barely-better-than-plastic pearls into my hair, and completed the ensemble with a totally inappropriate but comfortable pair of white high-top sneakers.

"Long story, short notice, dinner's covered," I said, trying to sound less rushed than I actually felt. "If I'd known this was coming up, I'd have said something."

Mom eyed my peculiar clothing choices as if trying to figure out the fashion statement they made. "I sincerely hope it's a costume party. Are you a runaway bride or a virgin priestess?"

I gulped, hoping Mom's prescience was purely accidental. "Priestess," I said, "and running late. Can I *please* get going before the twin terrors see me in this outfit?"

"Heaven forfend," said Mom, laughing. "As long as you've got your cell phone — and be careful with your father's car."

"Deal," I said, and ran for the front door.

—•—

Almost half an hour later, I turned off I-84 — the highway that runs along the southern banks of the Columbia — into the Memaloose

Island rest area several miles east of Hood River. As I'd hoped, the long parking lot was mostly empty. I'd seriously considered returning to the little viewpoint — Wah-Gwin-Gwin, Aaron had called it — where Aaron and I had first seen Koyoda, but the historic hotel and its dining room were sure to be be packed on a Saturday night, and the last thing I wanted for my upcoming performance was an audience. It was still a risk — the rest area was actually part of a sizeable state park — but as long as I stayed away from the park's campground, the chance of being disturbed at this hour was slight. The reason was straightforward: it was nearly sunset, and the ordinarily spectacular panoramic view was blocked by the dazzling glare of sunlight reflecting off the full width of the river. I blinked and tried to shield my eyes against the onslaught without much success as I walked from the car onto a wide strip of lightly landscaped lawn where a few scattered trees stood like sentinels, watching over the waters below the steep bluff atop which the park was situated.

According to *Legends of the Klickitats*, the Klickitat and Yakima (or Yakama, depending on whose spelling you preferred) tribes had once summoned Koyoda Speelyi by dressing their most beautiful maidens in white, decking them in other finery, and dispatching them to dance along the river's edge, singing and praying for him to appear. The book also said it had taken Koyoda many, many days to answer, but I avoided thinking about that passage — and how absurd I'd look if someone other than Koyoda happened along and saw me — as I concentrated on finding a suitable patch of ground on which to take up the call.

"Come, Koyoda! Koyoda, come! You are needed!" I began chanting softly after a few moments. My dancing consisted of a vague half-skip, half-sliding step, moving thirty feet or so back and forth along the grass. My eyes still half-closed against the fierce sun-glare, it was surprisingly easy to yield to the simple rhythm. "Koyoda, come! Come, Koyoda! You are needed!" A marching band might have paraded through the parking lot without my noticing, and the passage of time quickly dropped out of my consciousness.

Then: "Impressive," came a familiar rumbling voice from just behind me. "The costume needs work, but the execution is admirable. Someone should take a photograph."

I stumbled, barely catching myself before my face hit the land-scaping. My knees weren't as lucky, and I absently noted that getting grass stains out of the lace was going to be difficult at best. "Best I could manage on short notice," I told Koyoda Speelyi breathlessly, turning to where he lay curled lazily under a tree at his Great Dane size. "And if anyone did get pictures, I'm counting on you to fog the film."

Koyoda chuckled. "If you insist." Then he stood, stretching, and his tone grew more quiet. "However. You would not have not called on me without purpose — and you are here alone. Why am I needed, Elena Santorini?"

I returned his gaze with interest. "I gather you haven't talked to Aaron lately. He didn't much like your stage directions; the minute I mentioned you'd come to see me, he decided you were trying to manipulate him, and five seconds after that, he was heading for parts unknown trailing a cloud of gravel. And that was," I paused, counting, "three days ago now."

A coyote's face isn't designed to frown, but Koyoda's expression couldn't be called anything else. He made an annoyed noise that wasn't quite a growl, cocked one ear upward, and *listened* for several long moments. "West," he said at last. "A good distance west, at that; sixty miles, perhaps."

"Bright lights, big city," I said, nodding. Sixty-odd miles west along the interstate meant metropolitan Portland, with a total regional population of well above a million. "He said something about *walking in the white man's world*. Please tell me he's actually been there more than once in the past decade." Based on our dinner conversation before the prom, I doubted it. Between his Klickitat ancestry and his father's small-town upbringing, everything about Aaron signaled someone who found urban landscapes roughly as alien as the surface of Mars.

"That I cannot do," Koyoda said, a trace of humor returning to his voice. "But what would you have me do — fetch him back?"

"Damn right," I told him. "Aaron in the concrete jungle is like a salmon in a scented bubble bath — totally out of place. He's way out of his element — and besides, we need to talk, all three of us."

Koyoda's expression darkened. "You do not trust him on his own," he said, his rumbling undertone growing more pronounced. "Yet

without trust and self-confidence, Aaron cannot break free of the
limitations he has placed on himself. If no danger threatens him, he
need not be rescued — and if it does, it is his right to face it."

I glared into his beady coyote's eyes. "Are you telling me you're
not going to help your prize pupil if he happens to need you?" I
demanded. "I thought that's what guardian spirits were for."

"*Do not challenge me!*" Koyoda's eyes flashed obsidian-black, and
abruptly he was half again as large as he had been a moment earlier —
fully as tall as I was, and close enough that his hot, moist animal breath
puffed steam-like into my face — and to give me an intimate, dripping
view of fanged teeth big enough to make a velociraptor jealous. Just as
suddenly, I recalled another aspect of the legend that had described the
summoning ritual. The dancing Indian maidens had succeeded in
calling Koyoda — but they had been turned to stone for their troubles.
And if Koyoda's temper was any indication, I was about ten seconds
away from becoming a rock formation myself.

I wanted to shout right back at Koyoda, but instead I took a step
backward and a deep breath, keeping my voice as quiet and steady as I
could. "If you're going to do the statuary thing, go ahead — but answer
me one question first. If this is all about trust, *why didn't you trust
Aaron enough to ask him the questions you asked me?* You can't have
been up-front with him about all that, or we wouldn't be here now."

For a long moment, Koyoda Speelyi's eyes glittered like ebony
flame, and he inhaled as if preparing to blow someone's house down
like the big bad wolf. Then, as suddenly as he'd grown, he blinked
down to the size of a St. Bernard and regarded me with a remarkably
shamefaced expression.

"That," he said, "is an extremely good question. I was right a week
ago; you are uncommonly perceptive. Not to mention dangerous to my
self-esteem."

I relaxed muscles I hadn't realized I'd stiffened. "You just haven't
watched enough soap operas," I told him. "First rule for avoiding years
of messy melodrama — don't lie, don't keep secrets, don't dither. You
get to the happy ending a lot faster by stranding the hero and heroine
someplace together and making them fend for themselves."

Koyoda grinned wolfishly, his tongue lolling sideways. "Be careful

what you wish for. First, however, we had best go and find your hero."
And he trotted off toward the car.

"Just try not to shed on the seats," I told him, as I fumbled in a
pocket for the keys. "Dad's flying in tomorrow, and somehow I don't
think I'll have time to vacuum."

—•—

As it turned out, Aaron did need rescuing, though not of the sort I'd
anticipated. We found him parked outside a shopping center on
Portland's east side, trying to deal with two flat tires. "I was on my way
home this afternoon when a semi flipped over and scattered nails all
over the eastbound lanes; it sounded like a fireworks show." The kicker
was that he'd driven off without enough money to cover replacements.

"I just about cleaned myself out for the month covering the prom,"
he admitted wryly, "and when I went barreling out of town Wednesday,
I didn't have the card for our household account with me."

I'd been better prepared, though the Visa tucked into my purse was
attached to Mom's account. No doubt she'd have questions when a
charge for two new tires showed up on the bill, though Aaron promised
to pay me back once we got home.

Once Koyoda Speelyi had established to his satisfaction that Aaron
and I weren't likely to kill each other, he vanished with his usual silent
whoof — taking with him not only any trace of shed fur, but the grass
stains on my bridesmaid's dress. I also sprang for submarine
sandwiches from the shop next door to the tire dealer — having missed
both lunch and dinner — and related my quest for the summoning
ritual while Aaron's new tires were being mounted.

It was almost midnight by the time we'd caravaned back to Hood
River. Aaron insisted on following me all the way home, and parked on
the street after I'd pulled into the driveway. "You'd have made a
spectacular statue," he said, leaning into the Thunderbird's window,
"but I like you better this way."

"I'd have looked a hell of a lot better as a statue," I retorted. "All
this fake jewelry would be a lot more tasteful in basic granite."

Aaron laughed softly. "But much less colorful." As I opened the door and got out, he stepped back, brushing my cheek with a quick, almost cheerful kiss. "Call me tomorrow. We have things to talk about."

"With or without the giant talking coyote?" I asked mischievously.

"Without," said Aaron. "I think we've both had enough of dancing with guardian spirits for the moment."

We both chuckled — and then glanced out into the night, as a high, clear *yipyipyipARRROOOOO!* echoed softly somewhere in the distance.

Riverkin

by

K.D. Wentworth

A fter Luke buried his pa that morning, he lay on the river bank to soak his burned hand in the cold water. He'd scorched it reaching through the flames to pull Pa from the burning tent just after dawn. Evidently, Pa hadn't banked the coals properly the night before and the wind had whipped the flames into the tent's fabric. Luke, who'd slept at the other end, had gotten out, but he reckoned the smoke had already killed Pa at that point.

It was so unreal. The two of them should have been cooking breakfast and getting ready to work their claim. Pa had been turning up flakes of gold in the sluicing pan over the last week. Just yesterday, he'd told Luke that he thought they were close to finding actual gold nuggets. When they hit it big, they would move back to a city, maybe even St. Louis or Chicago, and live in a big house with servants.

The river's meltwater, born of the snow pack up in the mountains, had a fierce, swift current. As long as Luke kept his hand in the cold water, the pain was only a distant throb.

A brown head popped up out in the center where the light reflected in diamonds on the rushing waves. Eyes as black as jet blinked in the whiskered face. At first, Luke thought it was a beaver, then realized the teeth were too small, the face too narrow. It was a sleek river otter, staring as though it wanted something.

"What are you looking at?" he asked it angrily, but the animal just bobbed there, as though the current weren't racing past. He sat up and threw a stone at it with his good hand. With a chirp, it dove beneath the surface.

He lay back down, pillowed his head on his arm, and tried to decide what to do. He had no cash money. Pa had always used flake gold panned out of the river to pay on their account at the store. Luke could work the claim alone, but without Pa, it seemed pointless. Or he could go into Liberty, the nearest town, sell their claim and then try to find a job. Though he was just fifteen, he was strong for his age and Pa had always called him a hard worker.

At the thought of his father, he closed his eyes. The pain of missing him was much worse than the throb of his hand. Finally, the river's song carried him away into sleep.

—•—

The voices were thin-edged and yet bright, like sunlight on a winter's morning. "It does not move," one of them said close to Luke's nose. "Everything that is alive moves, even leaves in the wind. It must be dead!"

"But dead smells dead," the other said. "This smells quick."

"Bite it!" the first voice said. "See if it moves!"

He must be dreaming, Luke thought. He tried to turn over, but he'd lain with his burned hand in the icy water too long. He was cold, stiff in every part, and his body didn't answer.

A sharp nip on his ear opened his eyes and he jerked up. The narrow brown face of a river otter gazed at him. He edged back, cradling his injured hand against his chest. "Get away from me!"

The black nose twitched. "Quick," the shrill voice said.

The otter undulated toward him, sinuous as a snake. Its eyes were bright, its coat smooth as silk. A second one joined it, distinguishable from the first by a drooping ear. The two beasts studied him with cocked heads.

"The two-legged is sad," one said. "That is what you tasted in the water, its grief."

"Sad?" The other otter blinked. "What is there to be sad about? The air is clean from the morning wind. The river runs high and bold and is filled with sassy fish just waiting to be caught. The banks cry out for sliding!" It wriggled in anticipation.

He must be feverish, Luke thought.

"Slide with us," the otter said. "Then you will not be sad."

Luke pressed his forehead to his knees. He did not hear those thin, high voices! Folks who heard such things were crazy!

"To be still is to be dull," the otter said.

He looked up to see its companion slither on its belly across the bank into the rushing water. The otter disappeared with a splash, then its dark head popped up above the waves.

"See? Long-Tail is not sad," the remaining otter said, then dashed away and slid down the bank too.

"Otters can't talk," Luke told himself, staggering to his feet. "Only people can."

"We are a mighty nation," the otter said from the water. "Four-legged, instead of two, but busy and rich with the world." It dove, then its companion did also, and Luke was alone.

"Long-Tail," he said, but it hadn't happened. None of it had. His father was dead and he dreamed of otters as his mind tried to find relief from his sorrow.

He dried his wet hand against his shirt, then staggered to his feet to take stock of what was left after the fire. Most of what they'd owned had been in the tent — with Pa — all gone to smoke and ashes now. All gone.

—•—

He walked to Liberty in the afternoon, seeking work. The people of the little town gave his burned hand curious looks, but no one would hire him or advance credit for new supplies. His pa already owed for the last batch, they said, and Luke couldn't do much work with only one sound hand. It was a shame about his pa, but good men died up here in the mining camps every day, and that was a fact, though they wished him well.

No one wanted to buy an unproved claim either. Those folks who were inclined to pan or sluice for gold already had their own claims, equally unproductive.

Luke returned to the river in the late afternoon as the sunlight slanted down through the trees. It was August and, though the air was warm now, winter came early to the high places. He had to plan for the future, but his mind was mired in misery and he could think of no remedy for his situation.

When he'd asked at the dry goods store for work, Mrs. Eardly had given him two biscuits wrapped up in a piece of tattered gingham cloth, so he sat on a boulder by the stream and ate one.

Round and round, his thoughts chased each other. He had to make his way in the world, now that Pa was gone, but he didn't know where to go, what to do. Ma had died six years ago. His grandparents had passed away before he was even born.

"Food!" a voice as sharp as a knife said. A gleaming brown head popped up in the center of the swift river. "Share!"

Luke glanced down at the second biscuit, then wrapped it up tight in the cloth. "You might as well leave off yammering," he said. "I ain't listening."

Another head appeared and then another. Bright black eyes studied him. "Your kind never listens to the riverkin."

Luke brushed crumbs from his hands. "That's because people and otters got no business together."

The otters swam closer. "You chase the fish away and muddy the water."

"They'll come back," he said.

"They are a timid nation," the otter said. "It will be long before they forget."

"Look, I got worse problems than a few spooked fish," he said. Forgetting, Luke put his burned hand down on the rock, then sucked in his breath as pain rolled over him.

"You are hurt." The three otters swam to the shallows, then emerged onto the bank and shook themselves. Drops of water flew through the air and wet his face.

"My hand," he said, feeling foolish to be talking to a bunch of dumb beasts. If anyone from town happened along, they'd think he was crazy for certain. "I burned it in the fire."

The otter stood on its hind legs and sniffed. "Put aside your human self until it heals and swim with us," it said.

Luke stared at them.

"There is another you beneath the skin, a true-self," the otter said. "It is to that person we speak, not your outer seeming."

Luke didn't know what to say.

"We riverkin have a lodge under the bank," the smallest otter said, "a marvelous place." It put a delicate paw on his knee. "A thousand generations have labored in its making."

An otter lodge? A house? What would that be like? For a moment, he let himself wonder. Would it have halls and rooms like a human habitation? Chandeliers? Banisters and stairways?

"Do you not feel how loose that hurt skin is?" the first otter said. "Put it aside now and come with us."

Afraid, Luke lurched to his feet. "Go away!"

With soft plops, the three dove, disappearing beneath the back of the shining water.

—•—

When the sun dipped behind the mountains, the air cooled and Luke shivered, but he had no blankets. He lay down beneath an oak close to the river, huddled against the growing cold, and watched starlight dance on the rippling water.

No closer to figuring out what to do with himself, he only knew he could not stay here. Maybe in a few more days, things would seem clearer. Maybe tomorrow he would go back into town and borrow a fishing pole to catch one of those skittish fish the otters had spoken of. Maybe …

His eyes closed.

In the velvet depths of sleep, it seemed the three otters came back and showed him the trick of putting aside his skin. He just had to turn a certain way, drop his shoulder and shrug free. His discarded skin lay behind him in a heap on the bank.

In the starlight, this new body seemed light-bound, shining like the moon and undamaged. His hidden self felt the night wind as only a cool caress, not a chill misery, as before.

With chirps, the otters urged him into the river. It was so exhilarating, he dove in the racing current again and again, delighting at the sleekness of water. Beneath the waves, everything was green and mysterious. The water had a strange taste, though, bitter and unpleasant, as though something tainted the river.

"What is it?" he asked his companions.

The biggest, called Long-Tail, a fine, hearty male, swam in circles around Luke as though he just could not be still. "Greed," he said, "from two-leggeds standing in the river to claw rocks from the bottom."

When he wearied at last of swimming, the trio led him underwater to a hole in the bank just big enough to slither through. But, once inside, the entrance hall was huge, much bigger than Luke had ever dreamed. It should have been dark, since they were beasts and had no fire, but scattered clumps of fungus glowed a dim, ethereal blue.

The otters crowded in behind, then shook themselves dry. He gazed at the ceiling, which shimmered white as starlight.

"It is made from the lining of a thousand thousand mussel shells," Long-Tail said.

Low couches were made of woven reeds in beautiful patterns that never repeated, stuffed with dandelion down. Garnets and opal, jasper and amethysts were scattered about. And with a shock he saw gold, too, nuggets as big as his fist set into the walls in pleasing patterns. No wonder he and Pa had found only flakes. The real find was all down here.

He touched one with wondering fingers. "Why have you gathered all this gold?"

"It poisons the minds of two-leggeds," an old female said, "and makes them crazy, so we bring all we find down here. That way, we hope they will go away and leave us to our seasons once more."

He walked from wall to wall, touching the nuggets, marveling.

"I am Sharp-Nose," the she-otter said, her black eyes glittering. "How are you called?"

"Luke," he said. "Lucas McCrory Hamlin."

"Those are just sounds," Sharp-Nose said. "When we know you better, we will give you another name, one that means something."

"I can't stay," Luke said.

"Why not?" Sharp-Nose asked, her whiskers quivering.

There must be a reason, he thought, but suddenly he couldn't remember it.

He heard singing, far-off but sweet, and walked toward it, passing through a soaring gallery lined with gold flake, then a little nook floored in garnet. There were walls of jade and opal and topaz, each room more fabulous than the last.

The otters trailed after him, apparently content that he should explore. After a room of gleaming black onyx, he found the source of the singing: a pair of otters, their muzzles gray with age. They sat before a wall partially covered with silver.

"It is not finished," Long-Tail, the male otter, told him.

The hand of this true-self was not burned, like his human hand, so he helped the otters pound silver nuggets flat, then smooth the fragile sheets onto the wall so that the chamber shimmered like the heart of a star.

The song was so sweet, he thought sometimes it would melt his bones. But he worked along with the otters and the night passed. When the last of the silver was in place, he lay down and closed his eyes, letting the otter song carry him away.

—•—

He woke on the bank, his hair wet with a heavy dew, shivering and hungry. Overhead, clouds hung heavy and low, dark with promised rain.

The memory of the otters' house was already fading. A dream, he thought. Beautiful, but foolish, as though wild beasts had the wit to gather precious metals and gems.

He sat up and saw otter tracks on the river bank, both coming out of the water and going back into it, and a scrap of something shiny. He teased it out of the mud with the fingers of his good hand. It was a thin, shining flake of silver.

With a shudder, he flung it into the river.

Later, when he'd quit shaking, he gathered up a few of Pa's mining tools, hiked back into town and sold them. They didn't bring much, having been used hard and not of the first quality to begin with. But he used some of the coin to buy bacon, matches, a loaf of day-old bread, and beans, all tied up by the clerk in a bit of checkered cloth. He could survive on that until he decided what to do.

He asked after work again, and of course no one would hire a one-handed half-growed boy. Boys, as a woman explained to him, worked only half as hard as men, but ate twice as much, since they were still putting on height and bone. "Go home to your people," she advised him.

He hadn't the heart to admit he had no people.

In the afternoon, he wandered down the river and watched men work their claims. It was noisy, dirty work and everyone worked in a furious hurry since the good weather would hold only another month. The snow would begin up here much sooner than in the low elevations. The steep pass back over the mountain would close, the river ice over. Anyone who didn't want to freeze to death would have to leave and not return before late next spring.

Just before dark, the rain finally came, turning the banks to a muddy slurry. Luke slogged back to his own claim, despondent. He had no shelter and no way to make a fire in all this wet.

An otter surfaced out in the middle of the river and effortlessly kept pace with him, even though he was walking upstream. Its black eyes seemed to be asking him a question. He glared at it. "What?" he shouted. "What do you want?"

The otter's head disappeared under the white-crested waves.

Luke curled up to sleep under a pair of close-set pines that grew not too far from the burned-out tent. The carpet of needles underneath them protected him from the damp ground to some degree and smelled fragrant, like the sachets his ma used to slip between clothes back when they lived in Missouri.

Sleep rushed over him like the black current out in the river when he had swum with the otters. But that, he chided himself, was just … a … dream.

"Bright-Skin, get up!" Long-Tail's cool nose nudged his sleeping body. "We have much to show you."

It was easier to put aside his human self this time, just a quick twist and it was done. His body lay behind, curled in the nest of pine needles, burned hand against its chest. The rest of him was free to go wherever he wanted.

In this form, the rain was no longer cold and dismal, but sweet with a soothing rhythm. The otters led him back to the river where they played a merry game of tag, almost human-like. At first, he was slow, always behind, but then his secret body learned the trick of it and he was arrowing through the star-struck water almost as fast as his otter companions.

When they wearied of the game, they led him back to the otter lodge with its soaring galleries and gem-encrusted nooks. "This house has endless doors," Sharp-Nose told him. "Not just the one through which you entered, but on every stream and river and ocean throughout the world where otters fish and play."

That made as much sense as anything else down here, he thought. They showed him other entrances. One opened on a towering waterfall where spray hung in the air like jewels, the plants were an odd, brilliant shade of green, and the sun still shone, even though it was night elsewhere. Then the otters took him through another door to a deep blanket of snow, a night sky that shimmered with red light, and huge white bears that played lumbering savage games.

Afterward, they went into a vast opal chamber with gleaming white walls that shimmered with blue and pink. Slides of packed dirt soared high above the floor, ending at the bottom in deep pools. Otters climbed to the top, then slid down steep curves and over sharp drops. Luke romped with them until his true-self was pleasantly numb with exhaustion.

Finally, he tumbled into a heap beside his otter friends. "I wish this weren't a dream," he said.

Long-Tail turned over on his back and squirmed to get comfortable. "This is real as the stars, Bright-Skin."

"You're just my dream talking," Luke said. He stroked Long-Tail's velvet brown fur with one finger. It was the softest thing he'd ever touched. He closed his eyes. "Tomorrow, when I wake up, I guess I'll have to start back over the pass. No one up here will give me work. I have to get down into civilized country where there's jobs for even a one-handed fellow like me."

"Do you want to go away from us?" Sharp-Nose asked. He could feel the old otter's warm breath on his ear.

"No," he said, surprising himself. "These are the best dreams I ever had. A fellow could put up with almost anything in the hopes of such dreams."

Sharp-Nose snuggled close, fitting her supple body under his chin so that her fur tickled. "Sleep, child," she said. "You swim with us now. Your riverkin will provide for you."

—•—

He woke, of course, under the dripping pines, not in the sprawling magnificence of the dream-time otter lodge. It hurt, though, to know none of it was real, as though he had lost something wonderful. And every morning now, when he woke, he had to realize all over again that Pa was dead. Luke was alone in the world, and perhaps he always would be.

Turning over, he felt something knobbly clasped in his good hand. He sat up and opened his fingers, then exclaimed aloud at the sight of a gold nugget, the size of a robin's egg.

His heart pounded. Where in the blazes had that come from, he asked himself. But then he knew. Sharp-Nose or Long-Tail must have plucked it out of a wall in the otter lodge and left it with him while he slept.

It was all real. He couldn't fit his mind around that in the light of day.

Something splashed in the river and he lurched to his feet. It was a pair of otters, swimming out in the center of the current.

"Thank you!" He held up the nugget.

Sharp-Nose gazed at him, her black eyes knowing. "That is our gift, since you two-leggeds set great value upon such things. Use it wisely."

With a splash, both otters dove and, though he waited, did not return. Finally, he pocketed the nugget and went about the dreary business of seeking wood dry enough to burn so he could make breakfast.

After he'd eaten bacon and toast, he cleaned up as best he could in the cold river, washing his clothes and draping them across the bushes to dry. Funny how the river seemed so silken and inviting at night when he swam with the otters, but so cold and unwelcoming in the light of day.

And he was oddly uncomfortable, as though his skin didn't quite fit anymore. It seemed too small and chafed him under his arms and across the small of his back.

When his clothes dried, he tied the rest of the bacon and bread in the gingham cloth and hung the bundle up in a tree, so chipmunks and other scavengers wouldn't get at it. Then he walked back into town to sell the nugget.

The teller at the bank looked at Luke sharp when he laid it on the counter. A gnarled man with a straggly beard, he picked the nugget up and then used a tool to scratch it. "You and your pa made a strike?"

"No, sir," Luke said. "My pa's dead. All I have is this one nugget. There won't be any more."

"How do you know that?" The man's brow wrinkled as he set the nugget back down on the counter. "If I'm not mistaken, this is pure gold. Did you perchance steal it off a growed man's claim?"

Luke stiffened. "I'm not a thief!"

"Well, maybe I'd just better hold onto this," the teller said, "until we're certain exactly who has the right to it." He reached for the nugget.

"That's mine!" Luke grabbed it before the teller could touch it again and then thrust the gold back into his pocket. "If you don't want to buy it, then I'm sure someone else will." Ears burning, he hurried out of the little bank.

The teller followed him into the street. "No matter where you go, boy, folks will want to know where a nugget of that size came from," he said as Luke walked away. "You might as well set your mind to that."

Long-Tail had been right, Luke thought miserably, as he made his way back to Pa's claim. Gold did make two-leggeds crazy. His fingers turned the cold lump of metal over in his pocket. And what good was gold anyway, if you couldn't exchange for it something like clothes or food or shelter? Maybe he should just give it back to the otters.

He heard feet on the path behind him, which wasn't surprising. This was the way back to the river and at least thirty other claims lay within walking distance of the little town. There was bound to be a certain amount of traffic, although most folks were busy panning or working their sluices this time of day while the light was good.

With a sudden hunch, he slipped off the path and hid behind a boulder about twenty feet back.

Several minutes later, two men, whiskered and dirty, came hurrying down the trail. "We should have caught up with the little wretch already," the shorter one said. "He didn't have that much headstart."

"Keep your voice down, Rance," the other said. He was ginger-haired and lean as a starved dog. "Don't want to spook him before we get our hands on that gold!"

They plowed on down the path, swearing when branches caught them across the face or their feet tripped on the rocks, until they passed out of sight.

Luke sagged back against the huge gray rock. Bushwhackers, he thought. Pa had told him about such folks. Lazy and good-for-nothing, they waited for other men to make a strike, instead of working a claim of their own. This pair must have seen him at the bank.

There were two of them, to his one, and even worse, he was one-handed. Fighting them off wasn't an option. He might as well just give them the blamed nugget and be done with it. Otherwise, they'd creep up on him when he wasn't looking.

He pulled out the nugget and stared at it. There was no guarantee they wouldn't kill him anyway, just so he couldn't say who'd robbed him. Wind rustled in the trees and for a second, he could hear the river's sweet rushing voice. He got to his feet, then left the path, so they couldn't backtrack and find him, and worked through the woods back to his camp.

The water was running high from yesterday's rain. Fish jumped out in the current. He wished he had a fishing pole. Fresh fish for supper would have been nice.

He sat on a rock down by the shallows and listened to the rush of water over stone. It was sweeter than the best music he'd ever heard, he thought, better even than —

A stick cracked and he half-turned, then a hand seized his shirt and hauled him to his feet.

"Got you now, you little gutter rat!" The taller of the two bushwhackers stared at him triumphantly. "Hand it over!"

Luke struggled to get free, then froze when he heard the unmistakable click of a gun being cocked.

The second bushwhacker stepped out from behind a pine tree. "Give us the gold!" he said. He was missing two of his front teeth and Luke could smell the stench of his unwashed body. "That is, if you know what's good for you."

Luke pulled out the nugget. The taller man snatched it, then shoved him to his knees. "Where'd you find it?" he said. "And how much more do you have?"

"I-I found it up by the waterfall," Luke lied. "And there ain't no more."

Plainly, they didn't believe him because they wasted a good bit of time searching his meager camp, even hauling down his food bundle and opening that. They jeered when they saw what little he had to eat, but then stole that too and used the cord to lash his hands behind a tree.

"We're going to the falls," the taller one, who seemed to be named Rance, said. "But we'll be back. If you're lying to us about where you got that gold, you'll regret the day you was born!"

Laughing, they set off upriver.

There was of course no gold up there, so he had to free himself before they returned. But the cords were tight, biting especially bad into his burned hand. The already-raw flesh throbbed every time he even moved. Panic raced through him. He couldn't think what to do.

A small cool nose bumped his knee and he looked down. "Long-Tail!"

But it wasn't just Long-Tail. A wave of sleek brown bodies surrounded him. It was Sharp-Nose and at least a dozen more. "Hold still, Bright-Skin," the otter said.

The cords soon parted before their sharp teeth and he pulled his hands back around where he could support the burned one against his chest. "I can't stay here," he said. "Those men will be coming back for me."

Sharp-Nose sat on her hind quarters and gazed up at him with her wise black eyes. "Come and bide with us."

It was tempting, but when he swam with the otters, his human self was left behind on the bank. It would be helpless when those claim-jumpers returned. What if they killed it as they'd threatened?

"No," he said. "I'll go into town. They'll protect me."

—•—

There was no sheriff in Liberty. It was far too small. When he asked at the bank and dry goods store and the saloon, they each told him the same thing: Law could be sent for, of course, from the nearest town of any size, but it would be a long time in coming, and at this point most likely no one would come at all before spring. It was already snowing up in the heights and no one wanted to be stuck here for the winter.

"Best thing you could do is take on a growed partner," Hovey Sorenson, owner of the saloon, told him. "One good with a gun."

But even his eyes, normally preoccupied with the details of business, looked at Luke with speculation. "I heard about that nugget," the man said. "Let me see it."

Luke backed away. "The bushwhackers took it," he said. "And there ain't no more."

"Now, that seems almighty strange." Hovey patted him on the shoulder as though they were friends. "Any time a piece of gold that size breaks out, there's usually more to be had."

Luke touched his hat to be respectful, like Pa had taught him, then ducked back out into the dirt lane. Everyone stopped for a moment, looking at him, and it was as though he could hear their thoughts. Got a big strike but can't protect it, they seemed to say. Just a kid, don't know what he's stumbled onto. Too big for his britches and dumber than dirt. Someone should take him — and that gold — in hand.

Suddenly, he wanted to be with the otters, wanted to dive in the cool green-black of the river at midnight, romp with Long-Tail and slide with Sharp-Nose.

The town, with its rickety shacks and tents, populated by grubby people, stank of garbage and unwashed bodies. Where before it had looked interesting and full of life, now it seemed ugly and confining. The feeling of greed here was so thick, he could taste it. He wanted to get back to the stars and the sky and most of all the clean bright song of the water.

Thunder rumbled up on the heights as he headed back down the trail toward the river. The wind gusted with the sharp chill that usually heralded a storm.

He decided he was sick of running away from his problems and even more tired of trying to get other people to help him. A man helps himself, Pa had always said. No good ever came out of trying to get other folks to do your portion.

Thinking long and hard, as he made his way back, he discarded first one idea on how to deal with the bushwhackers, then another and another. They wanted gold and he didn't have any to give them. The only gold he'd seen belonged to the otters, and, no matter how much he gave them, they'd only want more.

Night was closing in and the trees were whipping in the wind now. Thunder rumbled again, this time much closer and lightning flashed up over the mountain tops so that for a second, everything was clear as daylight.

As he neared his camp, he saw a fire burning in the rock fire-pit he and Pa had built. The bushwhackers had returned. He backtracked and then cut over to the river. The water seemed even swifter, flying over the rocks, so he knew it had been raining up in the heights.

He lay on his belly, thrust his good hand into the river and waited. Once, when he had lain like this, the otters had tasted his grief. Would they taste his need now?

The trees tossed. Thunder rolled. The storm was nearing. He closed his eyes and waited for the riverkin to come.

A forepaw touched his wrist and he jerked awake. A narrow brown face regarded him. "Long-Tail!"

"You called us," the otter said with a flick of his ear. "Are you surprised then that we came?"

Luke sat up and dried his hand on his shirt. "No," he said, "and yes. I didn't know if you would be near."

"All water is the same water," Long-Tail said. "It dances up in the air, plummets to the earth, and then races down small courses toward ever larger ones until it reaches the vast singing ocean." His whiskers twitched. "What is known in one part is known in all. Wherever you are, you have only to call."

"I have an idea, but I need help," Luke said, "help that only my riverkin can provide."

"If the riverkin can aid you," the otter said, "we will."

—•—

Long-Tail swam upstream and Luke tried to keep pace on the rocky bank until they reached his old camp. The two bushwhackers had fallen asleep before the coals of the fire. Each slept with a pistol in hand, most likely in fear that Luke or someone else would jump them.

But that wasn't what he had in mind at all. His plan involved a more enduring solution. He crept close. "Come and swim," he whispered in their sleeping ears, working his way into their dreams. "Don't you hear the water, how it calls? Put aside those dirty human skins and come into the river."

The taller one, Rance, stirred, his mustache twitching as he mumbled in his sleep. "Not — possible."

"You want gold, don't you?" Luke said, his voice no louder than the whisper of wind against leaf. "Well, the gold is down at the bottom of the river where the otters live."

The short one turned over, taking the gun with him. Luke could see the crusted dirt in the creases on his neck. "Dumb beasts." The thief sneered through his filthy beard. "Not even good eating."

His eyes fluttered and for a moment Luke was afraid the older man would wake. Then he settled back, hand curled around the pistol's barrel.

"Gold," Luke whispered again. "Nuggets as big as my fist, thousands of them, all waiting down there for the man bold enough to go after them."

Long-Tail watched him from the bank, pacing up and down with that peculiar flowing stride common to all otters. Then he seemed to lose patience and dove back into the river, disappearing under the sleek black water.

"Think of what you could buy!" Luke said, growing more desperate. "Mansions and fine horses, carriages and servants!"

Rance smiled in his sleep. "Rifles," he mumbled. "Imported tobaccy. Likker."

"Yes, all of that!" Luke looked from man to man. "Just slip out of your skin and follow me into the river. I'll show you where it is."

Rance's eyes opened just a slit, but he was still mostly asleep. "Why?"

"I'm tired of being hunted," Luke said. "Are you coming?"

"No one can put aside his skin," Rance said, closing his eyes again. "T'ain't possible."

"Yes, it is!" Luke risked touching his shoulder. "Here, watch me!"

Rance's eyes opened a fraction. Luke twisted, as the otters had taught him, sliding what he really was out of the human flesh that merely contained it. *"See?"* he said, holding up his shining hands. *"Like that."*

The bushwhacker bolted to his feet, fear contorting his face.

"I was scared the first time too," Luke said.

"I ain't scared of nothing, you little weasel!" Rance's gaze turned to Luke's discarded flesh and he raised his gun.

With a plop, Long-Tail reappeared out of the river, shaking water from his dark fur. He held a golden nugget in his mouth. Two more otters emerged beside him, also bearing gold.

"See!" Luke said. *"It's all true. If you want gold, you have to go down to the otters' lodge."*

The other thief was awake now too, staring at the otters and the gold. He pointed his gun at Long-Tail. "Drop it!"

Long-Tail turned and splashed back into the water, gold and all. The other two followed. Both men fired, but too late. The smell of burnt powder filled the air.

"There's plenty of gold," Luke said. *"Down below."*

Rance paced the bank, mumbling under his breath, kicking stones and branches out of his way. The storm was drawing closer and a few fat raindrops pelted down.

Suddenly he whirled on Luke's light-bound form. "Show me the trick of it again!"

With a sigh, Luke went back and stood over his flesh. It lay curled up on the ground, breathing softly, apparently asleep. He leaned down and shrugged back into it, struggling to make it fit. It was tighter than ever, pulling so that the bones shone white through the skin.

Rance's gun was aimed straight at his heart. "What in the blazes are you?"

"Human, same as you," Luke said. The rain was coming down harder now and lightning snaked across the sky. "Only the otters showed me the trick of this. Do you want the gold or not?"

"T'ain't natural!" the other bushwhacker said. "Plug him now and let's get clear of this place!"

"Wait a minute, Hector." Rance lowered his gun just a mite. "Just how much gold is there?"

"The walls of their lodge are covered with it," Luke said. His heart pounded.

"Then show me again," Rance said.

"No!" Hector cried.

"Shut up," Rance said. "You know as well as I do, there ain't no gold in this here claim bigger than a flake. We looked hard enough this afternoon to be sure of that. No one up or down this valley has found even a small nugget, much less one as big as an egg. A strike of that size could set us up for the rest of our lives! We could go back east and live like kings!"

"But —!" Hector shuddered. "You seen what he did. He slipped plumb out of his skin!"

"If he can do it, then we can too!" Rance said. He turned back to Luke. "Show us!"

Luke turned in the special way the otters had taught him, dropping one shoulder, twisting his head to the side. Rance copied his every move.

With a shake, Luke stepped free of his loosened flesh and it crumpled to the ground. His other self, bright as a newly risen moon, gleamed in the darkness.

Rance tried to copy his movement, but couldn't shed his human body. He tried again, more violently, but remained as he was.

"You're trying too hard," Luke said. *"Turn your head, drop your shoulder and shiver as though you stepped into an icy wind."*

Rance did as he was bid to no avail. Then he tried one more time and his flesh slipped free. A different man stood there in his place, though his form was not bright like Luke's. Instead, it glowed dimly like a shaded lamp. Some parts, including his face and hands, were splotched with dark and didn't shine at all.

Hector sank to his knees. "No!"

"'Bout time!" Rance said, staring in satisfaction down at his body. *"Now you."*

The shorter man was shaking his head, his eyes staring.

"If you want the gold ..." Luke said.

With a muffled cry, Hector dug through the pockets of Rance's discarded trousers and came up with the stolen nugget. "This here's enough gold for me!" he cried, then snatched up his pistol and ran into the darkness.

Long-Tail reappeared from the river, sleek and wet. Thunder boomed again, this time much closer.

"Follow Long-Tail," Luke said.

"It feels — so — different," Rance said, gazing up at the sky.

"That is your true-self," Long-Tail said. "Not the dirty pile of flesh you left behind." He turned and slid back into the water, leaving only a ripple.

As though in a trance, Rance followed, leaving Luke on the bank.

Luke waited until he was sure Rance wouldn't balk and come right back, then put on his human self again. This time he could barely make his flesh fit at all. His fingers and toes hurt and even his jaw and ears. It was like he had become bigger inside than out, like he grew somehow whenever he was not in his body.

Sharp-Nose, the old female, appeared with a splash and regarded him with piercing black eyes. "Dark-Hands is below, going from room to room. He cannot decide what he wants."

Luke reached down and seized Rance's shirt with his good hand. Now he had to drag it off to someplace where the bushwhacker would never find it, or Rance would plunder the otters' gold until the day he died. But it was hard, especially one-handed. Rance was heavy, even without his inner self, and Luke's fingers ached from being crammed into a body that seemed too small.

Rain pelted down. He was cold and tired and hungry. Sharp-Nose followed but could be of no help. This was something Luke had to do alone.

Through the rest of the night, he labored, sliding Rance through the forest, leaving him finally in the trees at the edge of the town just before dawn. What the town-folk would make of the man's empty flesh, he had no idea. He just knew he could go no further, nor would his conscience let him dump the body somewhere isolated where it would starve and die.

The rain had faded to a light drizzle, but he couldn't be any wetter or colder than he already was.

"Come," Sharp-Nose said. "We must go back to the river." She nudged him with her muzzle.

He knelt and smoothed his palm over her sleek fur. "I wish I were an otter," he said. "This business of being human is hard."

"To each of us is given a *form*," she said, going ahead and leading the way down the muddy trail. "And we must make the best life we can in it."

He found a little wooded hollow, close to the river and curled up in the wet leaves to sleep. Sharp-Nose curled against his chest, head to tail, and together they slept.

—•—

In his dream, it seemed that the bushwhacker Rance came to him, angry and perplexed. *"My body done wandered off without me!"* he said to Luke and the otter. *"What am I going to do now?"*

"Maybe it don't like the way you've been living," Luke said. He gestured at the gold nuggets the size of hen's eggs that Rance clutched in each hand. "Maybe it wants something better than the low kind of life you've been giving it of late."

"It's plumb beautiful down there," Rance said. He closed his eyes. *"All that diamond and jade, silver and turquoise, not to mention gold. I never seen anything so all-fired pretty."*

"The world is full of beauty," Luke said. He felt cross and tired and completely out of patience. "If only you take the trouble to look around you once in a while."

"I have to get back to my body," Rance said.

"Promise you'll give up thieving," Luke said, "and I'll tell you where it is."

"Thieving is all I know!" Rance said.

"Then the world is better off without you in your flesh," Luke said. "Go away and let me sleep!"

—•—

When he woke, the sun was just rising above the trees. The bushwhacker's inner self sat close by, watching him. His form hardly shone at all. The two gold nuggets were perched on top of a rock. *"All right,"* Rance said, low and angry.

Luke sat up, rubbed at his eyes. Sharp-Nose stirred beside him, half covered in leaves. "All right — what?" he said.

"All right, I've looked through the night, but I can't find it. I'll give up thieving, like you said. Just show me where in the blue blazes my body is!"

Sharp-Nose nudged him and Luke knew what she meant, plain as if she'd spoken. "How do we know you'll keep your word?"

Rance held out his splotchy hands. *"I seen your true-self last night, all shiny and bright, but look at these dark patches. There's something wrong with me."*

"There's sure enough something wrong with the life you lead," Luke said.

With a rustle, Long-Tail appeared, followed by a dozen other otters, all black-eyed and expectant. They flowed into the hollow and pressed against Luke, joyful to see him again.

"Look at the way them critters fawn over you," Rance said, *"but they don't care a jot for me."*

Luke thought about the gun. "Why should they?"

"No reason why they should," Rance said, *"and that's a fact."* The older man looked tired and puzzled.

"Okay, I'll show you," Luke said, "but you have to give the gold back to the otters."

Rance stiffened. *"It's mine now!"*

"It was never yours," Luke said, "no more than any of the other things you've thieved over the years."

"But what am I to do, then?" Rance said. *"Thieving's all I know!"*

"You could work a claim like everyone else," Luke said. "You could work with me on my pa's." He blinked, surprised at himself.

Rance's mouth twisted. *"And what would your pa have to say about that?"*

"He's dead," Luke said, "and I need help. I'll go equal shares with you."

"Reckon I might just be interested," Rance said, *"if I had my body."* He gestured at the gold nuggets. *"Take them pretties back where they belong before I change my mind,"* he told the otters.

Long-Tail and Sharp-Nose seized them in their mouths and dashed back to the river.

Then Luke led him to the woods at the edge of the town, where the thief's empty flesh lay. Rance put it back on, though it took him ten tries and the thief was badly frightened he wouldn't make it until the last.

After that, they went into town and Rance bought supplies with what coins he had in his pockets.

—•—

That night, Long-Tail came to Luke in his sleep, emerging from rushing black water struck by starlight. "The river is full of fine sassy fish and fat frogs!" The otter wriggled with excitement. "Come and swim!"

Luke held up his hand, the fingers swollen and sore from being crammed into flesh that could barely contain them. "I can't," he said sorrowfully, "not if I want to remain human."

Long-Tail blinked at him.

"Each time I come back to my body, it's harder," Luke said. "I thought I would never get back into it last night. The next time, I might not manage it at all."

"You could bide with your riverkin forever then," Long-Tail said.

"I could," Luke said, "and part of me wants to, but I was born to the world of men."

"What of your companion?" The otter glanced at the snoring former bushwhacker. "Do you truly trust him?"

"No," Luke said. "You must seal the door to your lodge in this river and never come back. That way, even if Rance slips out of his skin some night, he won't be able to get in."

Long-Tail sat very still, which otters rarely did. "Then you will be alone."

That he would. Even in his sleep, Luke felt the desolate chill of that fact. He stroked Long-Tail's silken pelt. His dream-throat was tight. "I won't forget my riverkin."

The otter pressed his narrow head against Luke's hand in a fleeting caress, then was gone, disappearing in the dream-river with a splash.

— • —

So the days passed. Luke and Rance worked the claim until cold weather settled in, coming to respect one another, though they would never be friends. He learned that Rance had been orphaned young too, but had taken up thieving to make his way.

They wintered down in the low country and then returned to the claim the next spring. They never spoke of the otters, but sometimes Luke would find the former thief sitting on the river bank at night, gazing at the swift, dark water with troubled eyes.

In the end, through hard work, they accumulated a fair amount of gold flake, enough to split and go their separate ways. Luke used his share to open a dry goods store in Aspen Valley, married himself a sweet-natured red-haired girl, raised three rowdy children, one of whom broke his heart, but on the whole counted himself a fortunate man.

And when he lay down to sleep, every night for the rest of his life, the riverkin came into his dreams, sleek and playful, wise and daring, always in motion, frolicking with him down in their jewel-encrusted lodge that had a door on every river in the whole wide wondrous world.

Companions
of Power

Wings to Fly

by

Fran LaPlaca

Rezzi knew something was wrong the day Eda's crow showed up her doorstep. Well, flew through her window and landed on her kitchen table, actually. It was baking day, and as much as Rezzi hated the chore, she was kneading dough for bread while the heavier journey cakes baked in the large brick oven.

The bird looked tattered and bedraggled, but its eyes were bright and alert as it stared at Rezzi until she stopped kneading the dough and stared back.

"Well?" she finally asked impatiently, and the bird cocked its head to the side and cawed harshly. So Rezzi put the dough in a large bowl and covered it with a clean cloth, and then she followed the crow back to Eda's house.

Eda had died painlessly, Rezzi was glad to see. She still sat on the old wooden bench on her front porch, a bowl of snap peas in her lap. Rezzi gently removed the bowl and covered Eda with one of her handmade quilts, kissing the old woman's cheek lightly before she went back to town for the Healer.

Though Eda was past any help from him, Rezzi thought as she wiped the tears from her face. She was surprised to find herself crying, and then surprised at her own surprise.

Eda was more of a mother to me than my own mother, she told herself. And she was my friend. Of course I'm crying. The crow rode on Rezzi's shoulder and cawed softly. His claws were sharp, and Rezzi remembered the padded cloths Eda had sewn onto all her garments.

If this bird stays, I'll have to try that, Rezzi decided. *After all, I can't very well let him go back into the wild. He's so old he probably doesn't even know how to hunt anymore.*

The crow took off, his claws digging in harder as he pushed off, and his cry sounded mocking to Rezzi's ears.

Fine, then, she told the bird as it flew off. *Saves me having to take care of you.*

The crow was back the next day. The men had dug a grave for Eda, and Rezzi was pleased to see most of the villagers show up for the burial. The crow landed on her shoulder as the first shovelful of sod hit the plain wooden casket, and Rezzi reached up and absently stroked the bird's feathers as the hole filled. The bird stayed with her until she reached her own home, and then hopped indoors.

"Have you chosen me?" Rezzi asked the bird glumly. "Well, I suppose it's better than if she'd left a mewling brat behind. What I'd do with a child is beyond me." She slumped down in the twig rocker by the cold hearth. "For that matter, what I'll do with an ancient old corby is beyond me."

The crow cawed once, sounding smug, and flew to the low rafters and settled in.

After a few days it no longer seemed strange for Rezzi to return to her cottage and find the bird waiting for her.

"Some people who live alone prefer dogs, you know," Rezzi told the crow conversationally. "Or cats. Shall I get a cat as well?"

The crow turned its back to Rezzi as if indignant, and Rezzi laughed for the first time since Eda had died.

"What's your name?" Rezzi asked suddenly. "I don't remember if Eda ever called you by name. I can't keep calling you 'the bird'." She stared at the crow in thought. "Nothing much comes to mind other than 'Featherbrain'."

The crow flew out the window.

When it returned a week later, Rezzi was waiting apologetically.

"Sanchez," she told him.

The crow cocked its head to one side, and then bobbed its beak once, as if accepting her naming.

"Very well, Sanchez. What shall we do today? I have baked enough for three families, my laundry is drying outside, the kitchen is spotless, and the schoolmaster does not need my assistance today. I feel at loose ends."

Sanchez hopped to the doorway and looked back. Rezzi nodded slowly.

"All right. Lead on, bird. Sanchez," she amended as he looked back at her.

Sanchez led her to Eda's deserted cottage. Rezzi had meant to take care of it, to pack up the valuables in case unknown relatives materialized, to sort through the clothing and take them to the poor, and she fell to reluctantly. This seemed more final than burying poor Eda's body in the ground.

Late in the afternoon, at the bottom of a chest of drawers, Rezzi found the books. A dozen or so, books that Rezzi had never seen. In fact, she'd never seen the old woman reading anything, and she ran her fingers gently over the spines in wonder. Leather-bound and old, she could tell, but no titles showed on the outside. Rezzi opened one at random and fell inside.

Time passed. Bewildered, dizzy with unnamed fears, Rezzi wandered through a kaleidoscope of colors, of sounds and scents, voices deep and loud and soft and whispering. Dry, dusty air filled her lungs, and she groped for a way out.

"This way."

The voice was familiar, yet Rezzi knew she'd never heard it before.

"Where?"

"Come with me," the voice told her, and Rezzi tried, but the voice soared into the airs above her and she couldn't follow.

"Wait," she called frantically, and the voice was beside her.

"Use your wings," it told her.

"I have no wings," Rezzi said in confusion, but suddenly realized she did, indeed, have wings. "I don't know how to use them."

"They are a part of you."

Rezzi's fear grew, but her voice sounded cross. "They are not. I did not have wings this morning, and even if I do have them now, which I am not altogether sure I do, I do not know how to use them. I cannot follow you."

"Then you cannot get out."

"But where am I?"

"In the book," the voice said, and with that Rezzi was released.

She sat still in Eda's loft, the book on the floor in front of her. The voice in her vision still echoed in her mind, and she used her long skirt to close the open book, her eyes fixed firmly on nothing. One by one she removed the rest of the books and placed them in her basket, carefully gripping both front and back firmly, until the drawer was emptied. Dusting her hands, she stood, took up the basket, climbed down the ladder to the one room below, and headed briskly back to her own cottage.

Later that night, her supper dishes cleaned and put away, the fire neatly banked for the night, Rezzi climbed into her own bedroom loft and slipped under the blankets piled there. She could see the bird's shadowed form in the ebbing firelight as he perched on the cottage beam.

The moon was high in the sky before she broke the silence.

"I do not have wings."

Sanchez shifted on the beam, his feathers rustling in the silence.

"What is that book?" She waited, but there was no answer. "Is it magic?"

Sanchez launched off the beam and landed next to her, walking in circles on her quilted blankets as if making a nest.

"Are the books for me?" Rezzi asked finally.

A faint nip on her ear was the only response.

Sanchez was still there, sleeping next to her, when the sun hit Rezzi's eyes the next morning. She paid no attention to him, washing herself in the cold water she'd left out the night before, heating more water for tea, and putting together a breakfast of bread and cheese.

Finally she pulled the basket to her.

Sanchez fluttered over and perched on the table as Rezzi lined the books up in front of her.

"Which one first, Sanchez? Smallest to largest? Or the other way round? Not this one," she touched one finger quickly, almost fearfully, to the book she'd opened the day before, and the bird cawed in agreement. "Oldest first? Newest? Help me, Sanchez. You were Eda's bird, and these were Eda's books. Which one first?" Her voice turned stern, hiding a shakiness she felt inside. "I don't wish to be lost inside. I do not have wings."

Sanchez tilted his head and observed her with his bright eyes, then slowly stepped forward and lowered his beak to one of the books. Then he stepped carefully back to his original position and waited.

When Rezzi came back to herself the sun was high in the sky, and her stomach cramped with hunger. The crow stood in the same spot, his eyes on Rezzi unmoving until she stood and stretched her arms high over her head.

He cawed once, harshly, and she turned to him.

"No. I didn't understand it all, but I didn't get lost this time, either. It will take a while, I think."

Sanchez cawed again, this time softer, and he flew out the open door and began scratching in the dusty grass as Rezzi chopped vegetables for stew.

He slept on her bed again that night, and she only spoke once.

"Why did I have wings in the book, but I don't have them now?"

The dark bird in the dark night did not answer.

As the weeks passed Rezzi found her confidence growing. After a while the villagers didn't bother her anymore, seeming to realize that a transformation was taking place. They dropped by now and again with food, or just to see if she was all right, but they quickly learned not to interrupt if Rezzi had a book open in front of her.

"What do they think I am becoming?" she asked Sanchez. "I wish they would tell me, because I don't have a clue what is happening."

She had finished four of the books before she realized that she could use the things the books were teaching her, the things that Sanchez was showing her.

She knew her place in the world, small as it was, and she knew the world's place in her, which many people never learned.

She knew of the plants, some rare, some quite common, how they lived and died, who they fed and eased.

And she was beginning to learn of water, fickle, wayward water, in all its many ever-changing forms. She thought she could call it, but she hadn't yet tried, and then the headman's baby fell into the river.

She wasn't a baby, really, near to two years old, and she'd been walking for over a year. Her mother had looked away for only an instant, but the door was open, and when she looked again, the little curly-headed girl was gone.

She toddled out the door, through the village, past the blacksmith's shop (which later Rezzi was grateful for, for she hadn't learned fire yet) and down the bank into the river.

The blacksmith looked up from his work just then and saw the child go under, and his bellow brought the entire village on the run, including Rezzi, who had been deep within the book.

The little girl clung to a rock in the middle of the river. It had rained for three nights, and the river was to the top of its banks, fierce and angry. How a two-year-old knew to hold on was never understood, but as the men, the blacksmith in the lead, began to battle the strong current to rescue her, her tiny hands lost their purchase and she was swept downstream.

Her mother screamed, and many of the other village women as well, but Rezzi screamed loudest.

They told her later her words were nothing they'd ever heard before, but to Rezzi the commands were clear, concise and firm, and the water obeyed.

The river held the child, as if a cradle of water had somehow formed around her, and it lifted her above the current. Those watching were somehow not surprised to see Rezzi's crow flying above the child as the river fought itself, pushing against its own current to return the child to shore. The bird's wings moved slowly, too slowly for a bird to stay in the air, yet he paced the water-child until the blacksmith's large hands grasped her firmly, removing her from the water's hold and taking her back to her sobbing mother.

Sanchez flew then to Rezzi's padded shoulder, and his one harsh cry made them all look. Rezzi's arms were out-stretched as if beseeching, but her hands were steady, commanding.

She had called the water, and it had answered.

"What did I do?" she whispered to Sanchez in the dark. "I read a book and now I can make the river obey me? What's next?"

The next day Sanchez indicated another book, and Rezzi spent several weeks bathed in flames, learning the heat and chill of fire, the anarchy and the control. She lit candles with a look, and finally, the day she closed the fifth book, she went down to the smithy, closed her eyes, and stepped into the blacksmith's giant forge barefoot.

He tried to go after her, but the immensity of the heat drove him back. He tried again, tears of terror streaming down his face, but Sanchez flew at him, pecking him mercilessly, until the big man fell to his knees keening in grief. When Rezzi stepped out unscathed, and Sanchez perched himself immediately on her shoulder, the blacksmith put out his fire and walked into the fields and did not return for three days.

"He'll be all right," Rezzi told Sanchez. "I promised him I wouldn't do it again. Thank you, my friend, for allowing me to prove it to myself."

Sanchez nipped her ear in affection.

Autumn was upon them, and Rezzi was almost done. She had read all the books but two; the smallest, barely large enough to fill her hand, and the first one, the one she'd opened in Eda's house. The one that had taken her prisoner.

The next morning Sanchez tapped on that one with his beak.

"No." Rezzi shook her head. "I am not ready for that yet." She stroked the bird lovingly. "I have told you many times, Sanchez, I have no wings out here. If I am to put myself in that place again, I will not do it until I have learned to fly."

Sanchez bobbed his head again, slowly, as if in reluctance, and tapped his beak on the other, small, book.

Of course, Rezzi told herself as she fell inside. *I have studied the earth and the beasts that live upon it. I have become a tree and a blade of grass, and the very ground they grow on. I have been a badger and a bear. I have called water to my command and walked through fire. Now I must learn of the air.*

This smallest of books had within it almost more than Rezzi could take in.

Water was fickle, but was bounded on all sides by riverbanks and seashores, lakefronts and rock cliffs.

Air had no boundaries but the earth.

Fire roared and spat.

Without air fire was nothing.

The earth was solid, firm and steady, but air was wind and breeze, storm and fair skies, and led everywhere and nowhere.

Rezzi learned air, but she had no wings, and air nearly destroyed her. She felt her control slipping, her grasp loosening, and fear filled her throat.

"Friend." The voice was back, and Rezzi knew it now for who it was.

"Sanchez, it's too hard. I can't control it. Help me." Rezzi knew she was close to panic, and she groped for Sanchez with eyes shut tight against the sweeping winds.

"Use your wings," Sanchez told her.

"I have no wings," she shouted, and she did not.

"Then use mine," he told her, and he perched on her shoulder. His feet gripped her hard, the talons digging deep into her skin. Blood trickled down her shoulder, she could feel it, but she could feel as well Sanchez beating his strong wings, and slowly, so slowly, her panic receded.

When she opened her eyes she sat at the same wooden kitchen table, Sanchez in front of her, his bright eyes unwinking in their concern. She laid her head down on her arms and cried, for she had no wings.

The next day Rezzi did not take out the books, going instead to the schoolhouse and teaching the youngest children sums and spelling while Sanchez sat on a tree branch outside the schoolhouse and cawed. Rezzi ignored him.

The day after she spent baking and scrubbing. Sanchez refused to enter the house, and she refused to ask him in.

After that she traveled overnight to the next village, bartering for the villagers, bringing back cloth and threads and dyes for the womenfolk, a pack horse laden with metal ingots for the smith, leather and tack for the innkeeper's stables, and sheet music for the school-master's pianoforte.

Sanchez was nowhere around when she finally got back to her own cottage, and she went to bed that night and refused to look at his empty place on her blanket.

On the fifth day she took the last book out of the basket and laid it on the table. She stared at it a long while, then raised her head and gave the air a message.

"Tell him I will try."

Then Rezzi opened the book and fell inside.

It was nothing. It was everything. Wind and rain, snow and flood, reds and greens and blues. Children laughing, cows lowing, sand between her toes. It was bewildering and exhilarating, and Rezzi's fear was blown away as she wandered far and near.

"Where am I?"

The air swirled around her, and brought Sanchez to her side.

"You are in the book."

Fire and water came, and Rezzi held them in her hand.

"What is in the book?"

"Magic."

A long time passed.

"Who are you?"

"Your friend."

Rezzi took a deep breath.

"How do I use my wings?"

"I will show you," Sanchez told her.

The villagers watched in wonder as Rezzi's large crow flew high above, circling and calling, and when he was joined by another, smaller, sleeker, crying in a joyous voice, they knew Rezzi had found her wings.

Last of Her Kind

by

Janny Wurts

Everyone knew the king's tribute officers seldom visited the remote villages, high in the mountains.

"A crown rider hasn't set foot through Sky Notch for more than five decades. Late snowfall and hard travel keep such as them in the comfort of taverns, down-country." So the wizened grandmothers said, who were of the age to remember. Smiling, they pressed the spring milk into cheese, or folded the heavy weight woolens away into the winter clothes chests. "Why should a rich courtier trouble himself, or lame his fine horse in the passes?"

The gossips agreed, nodding over their spinning. Under their gnarled and tireless fingers, the goats' silken fleece became twined into yarns, which brought them a hard-earned prosperity. "The crown officer spurned our candidates, then. Left empty-handed, complaining."

Certainly no courtier would brave these rough roads, with just two in this vale of an eligible age to be appointed to foster homes. Beside Katlynne, a silent girl with wind-tangled hair whom everyone humored as a simpleton, only the woodcutter's son had turned fourteen since the snowmelt.

When he, who was wishful, suggested the improbable, the merchant who weighed out the yarns for the dyer broke off his haggling to laugh. "You have no idea, boy. None whatsoever. What use would you be, with your dialect not understood barely twenty leagues

down the road? The young people sought by the king's tribute are well
born, always the brightest and best in the land. They have learning, neat
manners, and understand style, things needful for a court fosterling." A
smile followed, kindly meant, as the merchant balanced the weights on
his scale. "Not mentioning, boy, in those quaint mountain clothes,
you'd roast yourself crimson, at seaside. Be sure of this, you'll grow
old shearing goats. The honor of being placed under the crown's
wardship is unlikely to be visited upon anyone born in this backwater."

Yet as the brooks roared underneath melting ice, cascading white
spray off the cornices, the merchant's musings and the grandmothers'
remembrances came to be wrong. A royal officer arrived in fact, bearing
the white staff of tribute. He was attended by four liveried guards,
mounted upon lathered horses whose legs were muddied up to the hocks.

Katlynne was the only one in the village oblivious to their arrival.
As the party straggled up the switched back trail to tie up at the
ramshackle guest house, she was in a high glen, flopped on her back,
watching the streamers of cloud that plumed off the rims of the snow-
fields. The twine tie on her braid had already unhooked, lost on a
runner of briar. She also had snagged a rip in her cuff, sure to set her
mother to scolding.

"Ah, daughter, again? No matter. Soon enough, it's my sister will
be sorely tried, asked to foster such feckless temperament." The
chiding would end with a tolerant smile. Few stayed angry with
Katlynne for long. "Under Aunt's roof, child, do you think you can
mend your careless habits and not treat your clothing like rags?"

Content at the moment, Katlynne rubbed a smear of dirt from her
cheek. She rolled over, chin propped on cupped palms. Torn cuff
forgotten, she gazed down and got lost, immersed in the miniature
forest of moss, caught between sheltering rocks. The wind off the
peaks hissed over her head. Freed hair lashed her cheek, as her braid
came undone, unkempt as the fleece on a goat.

Whose roof came to foster her seemed a meaningless detail, of far
less concern than the puzzle, that no two clumps of moss, or two
clouds, or two stones in a stream, were ever exactly the same. Every
day of her life, Katlynne pondered that riddle. As though she drew
breath by the born need to know what made each separate thing

different. She frowned, lightly chilled, as a cloud blocked the sun. All
the moments she remembered had brought her no nearer to finding that
fiercely sought answer.

Until now, as a stir of awareness rippled into her mind. Change
touched her. Katlynne shivered all over, as though newly awakened.
The smell of the moss became dizzying. Every sense sharpened.
Colors and sounds became richly alive, filled to bursting with an
indescribable nuance. As though a door had suddenly opened, she saw
and heard with a crystalline clarity beyond every familiar perception.

Then a shadow swept over her, not cast by a cloud. Katlynne
looked up, astonished. Her wide, dreamer's glance met another's, not
human. A huge spotted cat padded onto the ledge, and sat down with
majestic composure. The creature was nothing born in these
mountains. A ruff of silken, black mane robed its neck. Stiffer, dark
hairs ran the length of its spine, and tufted the tip of its tail. Its eyes,
locked with hers, were as burning a green as the emerald jungles that
grew over the southern sea. Unafraid, Katlynne stared in absorbed
fascination. Her widened gaze stayed reflective with thought, filled yet
with the drift of the day's silent clouds, and the wordless tints of small
flowers. Her calm held the same stilled patience found in the buds of
the twigs, furled tight under slow-melting ice.

As though visitations by exotic predators were quite natural, she
offered a tentative hand.

The cat blinked, hunkered down, then shoved its triangular head
under her fingers. The touch was a welcome. Without any words, but
as pictures and feelings, the great cat extended an invitation. Katlynne
laughed for joy. She curled against the beast's warm side, abandoned
to impulse, and made secure through the wonderment of a shared
communion.

—•—

The royal visitors' mounts had to be stalled in a cow shed, since the
village guest house did not offer stabling. The king's riders accepted the
setback, resigned. Informed, as well, of the dearth of child candidates,
the court-bred young man with the tribute stave shrugged. "Two, or

twenty, I'm charged to be thorough. The search has already taken me up and down this whole country. No fosterling we have encountered so far suits the foreign envoy we've brought for the choosing."

"No joy for you here, then," said the talkative woman who made up the beds. "The one boy is dead lazy. The other girl, Katlynne, is touched in the head. She'll be tucked up somewhere, leeside of a crag, staring at clouds like a lackwit."

"You say so?" The tribute man sighed. "The settlement at the last cross roads insisted their eligible daughter was a cripple. She wasn't, as though lying would matter. Crown obligation says every child of age gets presented."

The king's riders clomped into the guest house kitchen, intent on hot food and chilled beer, while the matron grasped the crown officer's sleeve and badgered him with one more question.

"What, the envoy?" The tribute man raised his eyebrows in reproof. "He's behind us, on foot. The horses won't bear him. He doesn't speak, either, maybe can't, in our tongue. The reason he walks is a tale in itself. You'll see why, the moment he gets here."

While the king's riders sprawled at the trestle to shoot dice, the tribute officer attended his duty. The villagers were summoned to hear him review the old law, that granted crown right to name the foster home when any child reached fourteen years of age. "You will realize," he informed the uneasy parents, "today, we escort an envoy from the southern court of Tahira. If your child candidates should suit his request, and be favored with a selection, they will be admitted into the household of a foreign state for the traditional term of five years. Once grown, they will be free to choose. Some return to our royal court, and serve there. Some come home to their families. Others prefer to stay with their foster home, to assume a post in foreign employ. Thus, has our nation promoted the understanding and good will that enables the peace across borders."

Inside an hour, the boy was presented in his best clothes, prepared for the envoy's inspection. For Katlynne, the delay would be longer.

"Easier to wait until she straggles in," her embarrassed relations apologized. "Why wear ourselves out, climbing the crags? A search is unlikely to find her."

"No matter." The tribute officer laid down his white stave and claimed the best chair by the fireside. "Tahira's envoy will arrive before sundown. He's treated each low country town the same way, and every shanty and farmstead. Never speaks a word to the candidates, besides. Infinite grace only knows if there's a living soul anywhere who will see his fool's errand satisfied."

—•—

The envoy made his appearance at dusk, a strange, silent man with distinguished features, and elaborate robes patterned with silver shells. He came empty handed. His quiet approach would have passed unnoticed, but for his dark eyes and outlandish clothing. As the king's man forewarned, he addressed no one. Never acknowledged the gathered villagers, or the boy candidate his whim had kept waiting. Though the steep climb had winded him, he took no moment to rest. On his feet in the rising, chill wind of evening, his restless glance combed over the darkening peaks, and then stopped with resharpened attention.

High up, where the afterglow rinsed the rocks red, a doll-sized figure descended. Windblown and rough in her thorn-tattered clothes, Katlynne picked her way down the goat track that led from the barren heights. She was not alone. An enormous cat paced at her side, exotically maned, its silver coat spotted with black and gold markings. Its chest was as wide as a stout man's arm, and its paws, large enough to slap down a yearling bullock. Should it bare its teeth or unsheathe its claws, a grown man would be less than a morsel. A lethal predator out of its element, the feline padded in step with the girl, who walked at its shoulder, fearless.

"Grace above, we are saved! Our cat's found his match!" exclaimed the Tahiran envoy in his home language. Faced away as he was, no one saw his tears of naked relief. Then he made himself understood, slowed by his stilted accent, "That girl is our chosen. As your king's custom of amity permits, your Katlynne is the one that our line of princes would beg leave to foster."

—•—

She was a gift, a reprieve, and a miracle, found a desolate generation after the fire, set ablaze by the malice of enemies. That calamity never forgiven, or forgotten, had seen the last of the court's guardian-seers slaughtered. The close secret of their ancient knowledge had been lost to ashes along with them. Without living partners, one by one, the maned cats who survived pined and died. No one expected to find one such as Katlynne, able to link with the only survivor: a last, forlorn kit nursed to an uncertain maturity in the wake of the horrific carnage.

Discord fanned the deep-seated intrigues that riddled the ruler's council. The fire's aftermath had left gaps and contention, as ambitious lords chafed to seize power. Frightened officials decried the last hope, that the old lines of the guardian-seers, whose infallible vision enforced a just peace, would not fade away into legend.

Yet the doomsayers were wrong. On the first morning the northern girl and the cat were welcomed to Tahira's royal palace, Katlynne's unwavering, candid gaze stripped the masks from the courtiers' posturing. She needed no words. When confronted by the mere presence of falsehood, her clarified senses responded. She would flinch at first sight, or frown and shrink back. Petitioners who presented themselves in dishonesty were exposed, while the cat at her side laid back black-tipped ears and snarled his uncanny warning.

Soon enough, the crown's councilors learned sharp respect. In gestures, in expressions transparent as glass, Katlynne traced the sources of discord and treason. As guardian-seer, she verified equity.

While she sat at the right hand of the throne, no man, not even Tahira's crowned sovereign, might use the law of the realm to impose corrupt sanctions and tyranny.

The girl with her odd, northern name became legend. If she never spoke, if her manner stayed simple, the sensitivity of her gift, bonded with the last cat, surpassed every seer come before her. While the peace restored by the court's fostering led the realm back toward settled stability, the time set by her king, and the custom of northern tradition was limited.

Four years passed by with dizzying speed. Next spring, before witnesses, in accord with the law, Katlynne would be free to name which of two realms she would prefer to call home. The last of the maned cats born among humans, as her partner, would stay or go at her side. Troubled over that very question, Tahira's rulers gathered in private to share a distressed round of council.

"Sky above!" the Queen whispered, her head in her hands. "If our seer goes, we're going to be eaten alive by the predation of the eastern empires."

The princess, heir apparent, clasped her delicate ringed hands, without consolation to offer. This had been the desperate risk they had shouldered, when Tahira agreed to a foreign alliance, and recovered the seer's gift through the sacrosanct custom of sealing amity through outland fosterlings.

"We daren't try to keep Katlynne by force!" the aged chancellor said, just as disheartened. "Aside from the wrong imposed on the girl, our breached trust would mean war with the north."

"We'd field the war, anyway," snapped the crown's craggy advisor. With no seer's talent to forecast the winds for first warning, the eastern fleet would renew their past pattern of surprise attacks. "Lose Katlynne, and we'll see our port towns set ablaze before summer. Until the peace lasts long enough to recover, our strength relies on her gift." Gems gleamed like sparks to his stabbing, quick gesture. "Without her, what choice? We'll go down by conquest. If our country falls, I say that the north will suffer worse unpleasantness yet. Without our secure boundary, Katlynne's people would face a more ruthless foe than any muster raised by Tahira!"

While the polished lamps burned low in the old hall of state, and the great of the realm thrashed out Katlynne's fate, a much smaller concern dodged the vigilant guards assigned to the young seer's protection.

Lui paused in the darkness, breathing too fast. *He dared not be seen, here.* The bet made to impress his wild, young friends had been nothing less that dead foolish. Of course, his faint hearted companion had deserted him at the gate. Probably wisely — caught within palace grounds, seen by the crown's guards, boy or not, he would be condemned as a spy or a traitor. Lui knew what he risked, more than any. His grandfather and his father, killed in the fire, had served the titled Warder of Cats. Now alone, and regretting his boastful dare, Lui crouched, shaking with terror.

The footstep of another armed guardsman crunched past the bushes that masked him. He could be struck down on sight. Katlynne and her cat were kept closer than royalty in these times of uncertain alliances.

For she was the last of her kind. The seer's tradition, old as Tahira's history, would fade once Katlynne took ship for the north; and she would. Who would stay, kept under lock and guard, and confined as though held as a prisoner? From the quayside, each day, she could be seen on the ramparts. The maned cat at her side dwarfing her shoulder, she would gaze over the walls toward the jungle outside the town gate. A young fool who occasionally ran with bad company, Lui had watched her with sadness. What ridiculous impulse had made him ponder aloud, and wonder what she might be thinking?

"Think? That's a hoot!" Kuarl had scoffed. "Everyone knows our seer's a mute. Dumb and simple. Last month, she picked the pearls off her state clothing and tossed them into the poor quarter streets!"

"Gave them to the hungry," Lui denounced, against his companions' sniggering taunts. "Katlynne may not speak. That doesn't mean that she's stupid."

"She's stupid. You're soft. Mushy sweet as a lisping ninny." The bystanding boys from the craft shops had laughed. Kuarl always challenged to pick a fresh fight. Like his rough older brother, he won his esteem by gaming and forfeit. To prove him wrong without blacking an eye, Lui had taken the idiot's wager: to break in using his father's old key, and bring proof of Katlynne's intelligence. Which game of madness now landed him here, shivering in a cold sweat.

Lui took a deep breath. He had made it this far. Night hid his presence. No wakeful birds called out in alarm. He gripped the key in his clammy palm, slunk out of the bushes beside the barred gate, then raced on bare feet down the gravel path and up the open stair to the seeress's quarters. There, no guard or lock had ever been needed. The solitary trespasser who meant Katlynne harm, and who escaped the tight cordon of sentries, was a fool and a dead man, both.

The uncanny maned leopard would sense his approach. Lui wondered how the great cat would react, in empathic communion, to warn her: as thought, shaped in pictures, or as distinctive sound, precisely tinted with his stranger's scent and his jaggedly anxious emotion. Bonded as one with the cat's keener senses, the young girl would see how her partner perceived him. Rash, Lui may be, but his prankster's fears posed no one a lethal threat.

Unlike others, who sometimes came skulking by night. Did Katlynne know how many assassins had been paid bribe-price for her life? Kept in cosseted luxury behind guarded walls, *did* she realize how vitally important she was, and how cherished? Did she understand that her gift as companion to Safali-leopard was the influence that defended Tahira's sovereignty?

Lui reached her balcony and paused with respect. Flicked to shame by his father's memory, he would brave a soft knock and ask polite entry. But the door swung open before him.

Katlynne stood there. Up close, she was delicate, a porcelain still figure with a serious face and haphazardly tumbled hair. The maned leopard, Safali, loomed at her back, the towering image of sinuous grace and scarcely restrained ferocity. The intrusive visit had not surprised anyone. The royal fosterling was dressed. Not in the glittering finery of court style, but a belted tunic and trousers plain enough to belong to a servant. Guardian, seeress, she and her cat fixed Lui with a probing glance that demanded, as though his scapegrace thoughts could be peeled out of his breathing flesh.

The contact scalded. Unprepared for that presence, Lui was struck dizzy. Hand clamped to the rail to save his reeling balance, he felt the cat's eyes, like lamps, burning him down to a spark that held nothing but candor. The contact shocked his being, consumed him until he stood reduced to one moment: *a memory made poignant by piercing emotion, when he had looked up at the rampart and wondered what Katlynne might be thinking.*

"Honored," he gasped in traditional greeting. Rushed breathless, drained white, he sank as his knees gave and bowed until his forehead touched the painted boards of the balcony. Then, as though moonstruck, he extended his opened hand with the key.

He heard Katlynne's soft cry. The cat coughed, reacting to the unworldly rapport shared between them. Then a rustle of movement broke the stunned pause. Lui felt Katlynne's fingers snatch up his offering. He had no chance to redress his insanity. His palm was left trembling and empty. Witless or mute had become a moot point, he had just given Tahira's last guardian-seer her means to step past every sensible, guarded protection.

As she rushed to thrust by him, Lui scrambled upright. "Honored, I'm with you. If you're going out, I beg you, don't try this alone!"

For answer, her anxious, hot grasp snagged his wrist and tugged him headlong down the stair. The rumors were true, then. Katlynne used no speech. Whether she was simple, or not, her single-minded desire to flaunt safety was terrifying. Lui stumbled awkwardly at her heels, rocked by the knowledge that he alone was responsible, to the lasting ruin of his family.

"Honored!" he protested. "Stop! This is no less than suicide."

Now on the path, pulling him forward, Katlynne did not so much as turn her head. Her cat partner gave him a predator's glare, angry and warning him, both.

Lui shut his mouth. Call out, raise the guards, surely he would be mistaken as Katlynne's abductor. The maned leopard's claws posed as dire a threat, if he tried to cross Katlynne's set will. Already in trouble over his head, Lui had to trust the pair's keener senses could steer all of them clear of disaster.

Together, the three fugitives raced through the lush palace grounds. Danger sharpened the dew-laden fragrance of foliage, and gave each step the thrill of adventure. Already, Katlynne's exuberant eagerness raised Lui to exhilaration. *Who understood what her life had been like?* How many times had she been called in the night, summoned from bed and asked to dress for court, then whisked under guard in a shuttered carriage to strange places, where her gifted sight as a maned leopard's bonded had been asked to serve Tahira's need and verify truth on a touchy point of diplomacy? Had anyone ever dared the brash risk, or invited her out to experience the land for herself, through Safali's unleashed senses?

Did anyone know her, Lui wondered? Without speech, could her foster-family ask if she was offended, or tired, or whether her heart would rather be elsewhere? Lui could not venture the first wild guess. Born but a short time ahead of the fire, he had little recollection of his father. No experience could match the force of Safali's size and power, ranging in sinuous strides through the shadows alongside the path. The animal flashed him a stripping glance. Lui hunched his shoulders, feeling exposed. The cat's senses made him feel naked. Worse, the beast watched because Katlynne stared also. Hers was an unruffled, fearless interest. Those blue, northern eyes perceived him in ways that a fellow human could never imagine.

The maned cat turned its head and coughed warning. As fast, Katlynne caught hold of Lui's shirt, and hauled him into the shrubbery.

Lui flushed. She was no longer child. He, a young man, crouched next to her in close quarters, an embarrassment that could not escape the reach of her gifted awareness. He sweated with unease as the sentry tramped past. Katlynne herself scarcely waited. At one with her restless, quivering cat, she rushed for the gate before Lui recovered his breath.

Her trembling, quick hands already twisted the key in the lock.

"Grace above," Lui whispered. "Will you be careful? We'll cause an uproar and worse, if you're noticed."

She glanced over her shoulder in scalding contempt. Then punched his arm in vexed irritation. *Couldn't* her bonded gift read his dismay? *Didn't* she understand he was betraying the realm, if he made no effort to stop her? Katlynne *must* realize what her presence meant. Honored, beloved, revered as Tahira's savior, she also had earned many dangerous enemies through her stay as a royal fosterling.

Her link with the maned cat's empathic senses had averted bloodletting disputes. Had spared crops, and eased famine, and held ships safe from storms, by finding and naming the source of imbalance, and so giving the Tahiran magicians the precise, safe direction in which to apply the double-edged forces invoked by their mastery. Any ten petty factions in league with crown rivals would rejoice to see her talent removed from the court.

She was not replaceable.

No one knew how Katlynne's bonding had happened. The beast at her side had no mate. The ancient legacy of her kind already trembled on the brink of being irretrievably lost.

Yet Lui had no chance to voice such concerns. Already, Katlynne sprung the locked gate. The cat bounded beside her, all oiled grace. Then both had slipped through, running amok down the darkened thoroughfare, while the gapped panel swung open behind them. Past stopping what folly had set into motion, Lui shoved off and raced after. He dared not delay to ease the lock shut, or recover the heirloom key. A nation's future lay in his hands, if cat or girl came to harm in the streets.

The slap of his sandals fell loud as a shout in the windless night. Katlynne and Safali streaked far ahead, a furtive flicker of movement crossing the glow of the precinct lanterns. Lui gave chase. Pressed by nightmarish thoughts of assassins with darts, and his dread of pursuing crown guardsmen, he sprinted after. Through several turns, they plunged off main streets, pounding through a maze of back alleys. Once, skinning his shins and knees, he scaled a garden wall and tripped, splashing, through someone's fish pool. Lights flared in the windows. A shutter clapped back and a disturbed matron screamed. Lui ran, stubbed his toes and ripped his sleeve on a hedge. He crunched over a pile of basketry. By now, cat and girl flew at breakneck speed through the backyards of the craft quarter. Lui panted, wrung with fatigue, eyes tearing under the coal fumes thrown off by the forges. He heard clanging hammers, even this late. Ever-present, the threat of war had the armorers working all night. Once or twice, through the pound of his heart, Lui thought he heard the tumult of crown riders, following.

Katlynne and Safali knew better then he, if they had aroused armed pursuit. The pair hurtled on, the great cat's mottled pelt gleaming like tossed gold, onyx, and platinum under the thin gleam of starlight.

"Stop this!" Lui gasped, folded over, a stitch in his side, and each panted breath he drew aching. "I can't go any farther."

Eyes watched from the dark, northern blue, and pale emerald; Katlynne and the maned cat had circled back to retrieve him. Lui swiped his sweat-dripping hair from his forehead. "Slow up, can you please? If you won't turn back, at least stay uphill! The waterfront's poorly guarded at night. You could run headlong into trouble enough to get any one of us killed."

Katlynne shook her head, adamant. Touched his cheek, *an apology*? Then she twisted his fingers into the thick, silken hair of Safali's sable mane. His sweating grasp held in place with her own, she tossed her head, and again, they were running. At her behest, the massive cat towed Lui's tired strides at speed toward the darkened quay.

Dockside was where Katlynne intended to go. No warning word, and no rational argument held any power to stop her. Nor did squalid shacks and confining, black bylanes blunt her determination. She crossed reeking puddles and rat crawling middens with no sign of hesitation. Ducked past the raucous noise of the cheap wine shops, that served blowsy women and sailhands and the bleak, shifty blackmarketeers. Katlynne and Safali slipped past unseen, on set course, who knew where, in the darkness. Past the stacked crates by the custom house, now limping and bruised, Lui skidded over the slippery cobbles of Fish Monger's Lane, and wondered if she had a waiting boat.

Was there a conspiracy? Had he been cozened by her arcane gift to help with a covert escape? Breaking into the open, slapped by drying fishnets, Katlynne skirted the reeking sand where the day's catch had been gutted for salting.

Distressed, forced to rein back blind panic and *think*, Lui understood that her movement was purposeful. He felt the tensioned ripple of muscles under the maned cat's shoulder. Each step taken now held wire-strung wariness. Whatever else moved abroad in the dark, Katlynne and her leopard were stalking. Unguarded, alone, a servant's boy should have run. Surely ought to yank free and summon the guard, as Tahira's most irreplaceable asset crept toward the ramshackle sheds at the waterfront. No lamps burned, here. The desperate poor lived and squabbled, packed in the tumbledown shacks of the alleys, and the inbound tide stank of garbage. Safali's pointed ears were pinned back, while unsavory vermin chittered and scuttled from underfoot. Lui clung to the cat's mane, held in thrall and drawn on by the animal's raw power. Its uncanny warmth, and the grace of its presence braced the boy's quailing nerve, as step after noisome step, at its side, Katlynne advanced, self-contained in her eerie composure.

She surveyed each rock and cracked board, each cornered and ravenous rat. As though joined to the cat by an unseen current, her attention directed the leopard's. Astounded, Lui realized that she noticed
everything. The maned cat's senses followed her focus. She moved, not
as others, but as though wrapped in trance, while Safali's expanded
sensory range amplified her human awareness. Whatever she experienced, the cat shared, and to its response she *listened* in turn, with an
acuity that shattered reason. Katlynne saw from moment to moment,
not what was expected to be, but the detail of what was before her.

Through partnered senses the wind and the water, each sound and
each movement, and the stunning, stilled presence of stones, spoke to
her in a separate language.

He was the one, mute. His mind, the one simple.

Lui stared, set aback by his shocked understanding. Alone in the
dark, at one with her bonded companion, the guardian-seer was
hunting. The moment he had surrendered a key on a balcony had been
no fool's prank gone amiss. By the uncanny powers fused with a maned
leopard, more likely *he had been called to serve Katlynne*.

All at once, the cat paused, hackles lifted. Lui was snapped out of
furious thought, as his wrist was seized by the girl's icy fingers.

"What do you see?" he mouthed at a whisper.

Katlynne tipped her head. He could feel her shivering, now, not
because of the misty damp. Safali uttered a rumbling, soft growl,
eyes like lamps in the gleam slicing through the gapped door of a
warehouse. Angry voices arose from inside. Several rough men were
arguing. Although Lui could not make sense of their words, the gravel
tone of the one who demanded obedience was distinctive enough to be
recognized.

"Grace above!" Lui whispered, "That's his Lordship of Dacque!"

Katlynne glanced back at him, questioning.

"You know what's been claimed?" Lui rushed on at a whisper.
"That his lordship's lies and his double dealing are what's straining the
fifty year treaty securing our eastern border?"

The guardian-seer frowned. She was not puzzled. Though his
speech had likely gone over her head, she knew of the hatreds that
smoldered tonight in the dark. Her link with the cat read the heart, and

Safali, hackles risen, was an infallible gauge of the deceptions that unbalanced the peace. Katlynne had been drawn by the desperate awareness that *something* here threatened the realm.

"Why me?" Lui entreated, far more than afraid. "Why didn't you call the crown guardsmen?"

He would not receive answer. Katlynne's wordless beckoning hastened him urgently onward. Masked by low tide, shadowed under the hulk of the dock, she and the maned cat crept up to the warehouse and snatched shelter under the pilings. The ramshackle floor had cracks in the boards. Wormed underneath, soaked by tide-washed sand and rank heaps of flotsam and weed, Lui peered inside.

Dacque's hired brutes had caged a maned cat. Not only locked inside a barred crate, a magnificent, near adult kit had been chained by the neck, that the rake of its paws could not reach through the slats and maim its unscrupulous handlers. To molest such a creature, far less poach in the jungle to snare it, was an offense more heinous than treason. Worse, as Lui eavesdropped, he realized the dispute concerned the complaints of the sailors whose task was to load the trapped kit on a boat.

"They are smuggling a maned cat out of the realm!" gasped Lui.

Katlynne nodded. There were tears on her face. Beside her, ears flattened, Safali loosed a rumbling growl, too low for human hearing. Girl and cat, such sharp grief hurled Lui to intuitive understanding. Katlynne blamed herself. *If not for her, no foreign land, and no traitor, would have expected that a gifted match might be sought outside Tahira's borders.*

"I can't stop them," Lui whispered, wretchedly helpless.

But Katlynne and her leopard already moved, edging out from under the warehouse. Inside, Lord Dacque's ugly threats had ended the argument. Sullen mutters, an oath, and a bump on the boards meant the sailors were shifting the massive crate. At the end of the dock, a shackle and sling waited to load the contraband animal into the hold of a ship flying flags from the east.

Lui went cold, seeing that. If Dacque's plan succeeded, there would be war, and worse. Last free outpost, Tahira held the old line against the four empires that endorsed slavery.

Silent, her tears falling, Katlynne looked to Lui. Safali's shivering rage filled the air, as its younger, caged cousin yowled protest.

Yet even the maned cat's grown strength could not hope to salvage the situation. "Send Safali out there, he'll just be killed! Each one of those handlers carries a spear. Lord Dacque is armed, also. Word on the street claims that his blades are poisoned. The royal guard ought to handle this, Katlynne. An hour ago, you would have had time. Why did you bring no one but me?"

Lui might never know. Katlynne could not tell him. Her tearful glance met his fear, in the dark. Then she raised her hand and placed her spread fingers over his soiled shirt, at the heart.

"I have to fetch help," Lui begged, wrung frantic.

She caught his sleeve, held him back. When he moved to jerk free, she clamped stubborn fingers, her pale eyes open and anxious. Already, the men dragged the crate to the dock. Lord Dacque paid off a bald man holding a candle lamp, while cursing sailors fumbled to fasten the sling, and draw up the block and tackle.

"You want me to wait?" Lui snapped in disbelief. "Once they have that kit loaded, we'll be too late, even if I could talk the king's guards into listening." *Did* she understand? He was a servant's son, born to a man whose name would be long forgotten. His accusation would carry no weight, set against a powerful noble. Once that ship set her sails, he'd have no shred of evidence to prove the maned kit's existence. The animal would be lost to unknown shores, with who knew what fate set in store for it.

Whatever she felt, whatever she knew, Katlynne tightened her feverish grip. While she threatened to rip the sleeve off Lui's shirt, Safali flashed him a warning glance that forestalled every question of moving.

Seeing him trapped by that dire accord, Katlynne released him. She crept toward the dock, slipping through the thick darkness. Safali followed with a whistling lash of his tail, the black hackles raised on his back. Then he coughed. His tufted ears pricked. Katlynne shivered, and Lui heard the tramp of running feet, then the horn calls of a crown officer. Either his prank with the key had been noticed, or Lord Dacque's plot had been sold by an ambitious informant.

"Katlynne?" Lui gasped.

She did not answer. Could not. Whatever had alerted the soldiers, the sailors heard their approach, also. The caged kit was hoisted, dangled above the dock, when the party of men bracing the tackle gave way to shouting and panic. They dropped the rope. The cage fell with a crash and a splinter of wood. The trapped kit screeched. Its frantic rage yanked the staple holding its chain. Freed, hazed wild, it charged through the smashed gap in the slats.

Safali answered its keening challenge. His roar split the night. Reared on his hind legs, fore claws raking the air, he towered above Katlynne, while the escaped kit streaked like a molten thunderbolt over the boards of the dock.

Lui did not see the men scatter and run. The shouts of armed guards, and the clatter of horses — all passed him by, so much meaningless noise and commotion. He had no thought to spare beyond the loosed kit, now bearing down in a savage charge, dragging a clatter of chain.

Katlynne stood her ground, Safali at her back. She would be killed, and Tahira's hope with her, while the jungle-wild kit and the last, bonded male tore themselves to ribbons before Lui's eyes.

No one alive could separate the two cats. But Lui was close enough, and the only one able to shove the last guardian-seer clear of the carnage.

Before thought, he moved, thrust in front of Katlynne with intent to throw her to safety. Knock her sideward, the crown riders might react fast enough to pull her out of harm's way. Save her life, and someone might learn how she had accomplished her mystical bonding with a maned leopard.

Lui moved, but without accounting for the cat. Safali dropped back on all fours, fencing him between clawed forepaws. Katlynne, now pinned behind Lui's back, braced her trembling hands on his shoulders.

"Here, boy!" a man shouted. "Toss the Honored one free!"

Yet no time remained. Lui could not turn, catch her wrists, or fling the royal fosterling to safety. A trapped shield before her, he was faced by the rival kit's charge, bounding in and now all but on top of him.

He met the cat's eyes, wide open and burning. Saw into the flaming core of a rage whose blasting, raw force consumed him. The maned kit's charging presence filled all the world. *And the moment froze.* Lui saw, with the utmost, terrible clarity, the fate a rash wager had bought him.

He saw himself, again, *staring up at the ramparts, wondering what Katlynne was thinking.*

That one branding instant, he sensed Katlynne, still behind him. With her, he acknowledged the shattering roar of the maned leopard who was her companion. Bonded male, and fear-maddened kit, the two cats matched stares, with Katlynne in gifted communion, between them. And Lui, who had once pondered with singular will, was unwittingly wrapped, caught up in the stream of electrical *force* between cat and cat, and partnered human girl, as their linked awarenesses blended. Thought stopped. Terror was dampened. Lui was rocked off balance, thrown back as though wracked by a silent explosion. Katlynne's grip held him upright. Slammed through, overset, a whirled mote in a current, he lost his awareness to dizzied confusion.

Then the pressure burst through. Some inner barrier snapped in his mind, and he sensed, not rage, but a *welcome.*

The maned kit broke from her headlong charge, skidded in stride, and crouched on her haunches before him. Lui matched her golden stare, unafraid, lost in wonder. And the world opened, as though he had stepped through a door, into a realm undreamed of.

She: her warmth cradled his in protective, fierce custody that blanketed him, as inseparable.

Katlynne laughed. Slapped his shoulder, while the clarity of her emotion ran through him as singing thought. *'One of us, now.'*

Shattered by that truthful awareness, Lui stood, beyond speech, as the maned cat before him bent her proud neck, and shoved her triangular head under his fingers. Her touch opened gateways. Beneath his feet, the very stones sang. The air glimmered, laced with pearlescent light. The sea wind in his hair spoke with scent. Wherever he looked the cat's senses turned also, drowning his in ecstatic communion.

He saw the world as reborn. Guardian-seer newly partnered to a maned cat, he received the name of his companion. "Hafest," he whispered, then felt, like the burn of dawn's sunlight, the shimmering wave of astonishment emanating from his surroundings.

Men looked on in wonder. The crown riders, who had taken Lord

Dacque into custody, now gathered about in a ring. To the last, they dismounted, saluting as though to royalty with bent heads and speechless, stunned reverence.

Before Katlynne, the king's fosterling, so Lui thought. They honored Safali, her leopard companion. Yet Hafest all but bowled him off of his feet, with her blast of her amused correction.

Where one cat and one seer had defended Tahira's future, now, on this night, there were two. The forgotten secret that brought maned cats and humans to achieve active bonding was lost no longer.

Left breathless and terrified that his change in perception might have undone his memory of speech, Lui groped for words. And language came. "How did this happen?"

He heard, '*We are called.*' The clear thought, arisen from Katlynne and her cat, was a marvel of singular harmony. '*You heard us, first. After us, we'll find others.*'

She had gone before. Alone, with no guidance, a northern girl had bridged the gap between human and cat on her own. No help from her kind had led the way, but only the dauntless depth of her listening. For that courage, Lui would always hold her in awe. Not least, he knew rising joy, that come spring, when her time as a fosterling ended, she might freely chose to go home to her kin and the freedom of her native mountains. Now, if Katlynne left for the north, the realm of Tahira would not be without a guardian-seer's protection to keep the peace after her.

Blood Ties

by
Sarah Jane Elliott

Kayla gasped as the force of the blow rang through her body. She shifted her weight and struck, but she was tiring and her opponent knew it. Nearing desperation, she barely managed to fend off the next round of blows and found herself wishing for help. Lyssia perhaps — surely an enchanted blade would make her more than a match for —

Another stinging blow sent her sword flying from her hand. A heavy boot swept her feet out from under her and she fell to the ground. She braced herself, ready to lunge back to her feet, but halted abruptly as the point of a sword settled at her throat. As she glared up through the sweat-dampened fringe of hair that obscured her vision, her opponent threw back his head and laughed.

"You're dead, Princess."

Kayla Cestril Aliyah t'Meladon, Youngest Daughter of the royal house, ninth in line for the throne of Meladon, found herself glowering up from the dirt. Again.

"That's the third time today!" Huffing, Kayla raised her hand and shoved the sword aside. "I still say you're cheating somehow."

The noise of derision Rylan made clearly told her what he thought of that accusation, but he sheathed his sword and held out his hand. "You're still letting me get to you." He hauled her to her feet. "It makes you sloppy."

Kayla raised a brow and went to retrieve her blade. "How do you avoid getting angry if someone is trying to hack you to pieces with a sword?"

Rylan grinned. "Practice."

Kayla rolled her eyes. "Not again."

"You were the one who wanted these lessons, Cestril."

Kayla grinned. Most of the court called her by her formal name of Aliyah, if they called her anything at all. Her common name, Cestril, was used only by those closest to her. Her true name, Kayla, was known only by her parents and the priestess who had given it to her, and it was used by no one save herself.

It had taken months to get Rylan to stop calling her by her formal name, but as soon as he had started calling her Cestril, the lessons had changed from toil into fun. It was almost like having one of her brothers back, before they had gotten old enough to start taking up their duties in court.

"Lessons," Kayla emphasized. "Not sessions of torment."

"In fight training, there's little difference." But rather than drawing his blade again, he reached out and ruffled her hair. "Though I think you may have had enough for one day. You're definitely improving."

"Thank the Lady!" Kayla collapsed, limbs splayed, and stared up at the sky. "I think my arms are like to fall off."

She heard the soft footsteps in the grass before Rylan dropped with easy grace down next to her. "Now if that were true, we'd have a garrison full of men without arms." The sunlight set his golden hair to gleaming. It was a mark of his peasant stock — most of the nobility had pale eyes and hair that ran to dark — but Kayla found it charming. And that made it all the more difficult to pretend to be angry at him.

Kayla moved just far enough to stick her tongue out at him. "Brute. You're going to be a terror when you're Captain."

"Who said anything about me being Captain?"

"No one had to." Kayla pushed herself up, drawing her knees to her chest and resting her chin on them. "You're good, and there's no one my brother trusts more than you." She nudged him with her toe. "Why do you think he asked you to teach me swordplay, even though the court will have a fit if they ever find out?" She nodded in assurance. "When Aeron is king, you'll be his Captain."

Rylan laughed. "I don't think so. I have no formal name, for one, and no one would be led by a Captain not of the nobility. And you've heard my attempts to use the court cadences."

"Formal speech can be learned. Formal names can be given. Nobility can sometimes be a gift, rather than a birthright. And it will be yours. You will be Captain."

Rylan tilted his head to regard her. "You seem very sure of yourself."

"I always am when I'm right. You'll see." She paused, and grew solemn. "Rylan, when you're Captain, will you be too busy to teach me?"

"What, and give up our clandestine meetings on the sward? Never!"

Kayla grinned her elation. She knew she had much to learn, but ever since Aeron, her eldest brother, had wearied of Kayla's pestering and given her to his friend's keeping, she had been sure she would be great some day. Great enough, perhaps, to lay claim to the ancestral sword …

"What's going through that devious little brain of yours?"

She pushed herself to her feet. "I was just wondering when I get to try for Lyssia —"

Without warning, she found herself on the ground again, staring up into Rylan's solemn face. "I said you were improving, Cestril, not able. I wouldn't trust you in combat with an ordinary sword yet, much less your great-great-grandmother's enchanted one."

Kayla glowered up at him from her sprawl. "No one's really sure it's enchanted."

"Only because the spell protecting it has either killed or banished everyone who's tried to draw it." He folded his arms. "I'm not going to put myself into the position of explaining to my future king why his baby sister has vanished without a trace."

She pushed herself up on her elbows. "I'm fourteen years old. I'm not a baby!"

"And I'm nearly twice your age." He grinned. "You are to me."

Kayla had already opened her mouth to retort when the high, clarion call of a hunting horn shattered the easy stillness of the day. She froze, and felt the blood drain from her face. "Oh, no."

She bolted to the edge of the clearing, stripping off her vest and tunic as Rylan turned his back. "No, no, no …" She dragged her gown off the branch over which she had flung it and tugged it over her head, struggling to get her arms in the sleeves. "Lace me up! Lace me up!" Freeing her hands, she attempted to redirect her tousled hair back into its long braid.

"Cestril —" Rylan's voice was weary as he tightened the laces of her gown.

Kayla shook her head. Snatching up her discarded clothes, she bundled them up with her sword and pelted up the path back to the castle.

She tossed her bundle behind the woodpile and rushed into the courtyard, up the stairs, and across the ramparts until she could see the procession winding up the road to the gates. Nausea swept through her and she sagged against the wall. "Not again."

Sunlight glinted off the pikes and armour of the knights in the procession. At the head, a solitary figure rode in triumphant splendour. Her father's face was bright with satisfaction as he led the train through the palace gates.

The anguished cries from the enormous cage at the end of the procession carried clearly up to her.

"When you're Captain," she said quietly, "will you put a stop to these hunts?"

Rylan sighed as he leaned against the wall next to her. "Cestril."

She pushed away from the wall to glare at him. "Well?"

"It's been killing our people, Cestril. It slaughtered entire families, in case you have forgotten. Those were innocent townspeople. Did they deserve to die?"

"Of course not," she snapped. "But those people didn't die until Father brought that first one in."

Rylan rubbed the bridge of his nose. "So are you saying it's His Majesty's fault those people are dead?"

"No, but —" Kayla let out a huff of frustration. "I don't have time for this. I have to go do my duty before someone gets offended."

She couldn't explain to Rylan what had upset her so. She didn't quite know herself. But from the moment her father had returned with the other creature, two weeks earlier, something had seemed to break inside of her. She knew they were predators. She knew they would kill anyone who ventured into their hunting grounds as easily as they killed deer or boar. And yet something within her had wept at the sight of the creature, broken and bleeding inside its cage.

Her chest tightened as she emerged into a scene almost identical to that first. The yard brimmed with denizens of the castle crowding close for a glimpse of the creature. To one side, a young kitchen maid pushed forward, calling for her husband, only to be caught up by the Captain of the Guard. Kayla couldn't hear what he said to her, but it hardly mattered. The girl's tears revealed the truth as clearly as any words. Dozens had set out after the creature. Only half had returned.

"Make way for Princess Alyiah!"

Kayla recoiled inwardly at the call, but she kept her head high as the crowd parted before her. At the end of that corridor stood the king.

The ebony hair and giant stature that stood as the hallmarks of the royal line made him seem more like a statue of some long-forgotten hero than a man of flesh and blood. But he turned his eyes to meet hers, those vibrant eyes of a shade trapped between green and blue, and he was once again her father. For she knew those eyes. They were known as Meladon eyes. And they were the one feature she shared with him.

Kayla made her way to her father and dropped into a deep curtsey.

"My Lord Father," she said. "The castle rejoices at your success. We shall rest easy this night knowing that our children are safe once again."

She saw Rylan wince out of the corner of her eye, though he was probably the only one who knew her well enough to hear the edge she fought to banish from her words. It was her duty as Youngest Daughter, after all, to express gratitude to the king on behalf of the palace. Even if that gratitude tasted bitter on her tongue.

"My thanks, Daughter." King Teague rested an affectionate hand on her head, but his attention lay elsewhere. "Come! This calls for a feast!"

A great shout arose from the assembled throng — those who weren't mourning the loss of the fallen — and they followed her father into the keep.

Kayla remained behind, breath caught in her throat.

They've learned.

The other had been a pathetic specimen, weak and dying, scarcely enough to awe the people of the kingdom with her father's hunting prowess. This one was bloody and bedraggled, its feathers askew and its fur filthy, but it was not mortally hurt, and the expression in its eyes was anything but pained.

Talons as long as her forearm dug into the floor of the cage, gouging deep furrows into the ironwood, as the creature fought against the shackles binding each limb. Massive golden wings strained against the walls, feathers gleaming as bright as polished gold. Then the great head swung 'round, the razor edges of the beak barely clearing the bars.

The griffin rose to its full height, and Kayla had to stifle a gasp as those enormous golden eyes fell upon her. The force of the creature's malice struck her so hard that she stepped back. Its eyes burned with anger and hatred, the lashing leonine tail betraying the creature's barely contained rage.

"Father," she breathed. "What have you done?"

"Hush!" Rylan's harsh whisper in her ear startled her. "Someone will hear you."

Kayla didn't care. She couldn't tear her eyes away from the griffin's unblinking gaze. It was so different... The first had been smaller, the fur duller, the feathers a muted tan with brown patterning the wings and head. The only time she had ever seen feathers near as brilliant as the ones this one bore were on some of her mother's songbirds ...

Kayla gasped. Rylan's hand was instantly on her shoulder. "What's wrong?"

"It was his mate," she said. The golden eyes bored into her, stripping her down to her soul as realization spread through her. "That first one. She was his mate. He was killing our people because we killed his mate."

"Cestril." Rylan tugged her away from the cage. "You forget, you are speaking of an animal. An unintelligent beast."

Kayla couldn't look away. "Am I?" But she allowed Rylan to drag her into the warmth and light of the great hall, away from those eyes so deep she felt herself like to drown in them.

And so Kayla did not see that the griffin continued to stare long after she had vanished into the keep.

—•—

Light, dazzling golden light everywhere. Touching her. Blinding her.
Wind rushing past, gentle fingers against her skin. Then the light fled.
She was falling. Too far, too fast, the ground impossibly far away
but coming on too fast, hungry to meet her. She threw out her hands, a
vain attempt to stop the fall, and screamed.
She held a blade in her clenched fist. A blade stained bright red ...

—•—

Kayla woke to pain, and opened her eyes to see the floorboards a
hairsbreadth from her nose. She attempted to roll over with little
success, finding herself hopelessly tangled in her bedsheets. Finally,
after a desperate battle with the quilt, she managed to free herself and
rested her back against the bed. She didn't want to get up off the floor
yet — she wasn't entirely sure she'd stay in bed if she managed to
climb back into it. Slowly, her breathing began to calm, her heart to
slow, as the sweat cooled on her brow.

This wasn't the first time she had endured such a dream, so vivid
it had thrown her violently into wakefulness. She had endured such
dreams before. And yet, few dreams had possessed such a sense of
urgency. In fact, there had been only two — this one, and the one she
had dreamed two weeks ago. The one that had ended with Kayla
standing awake and frightened, shivering and barefoot in front of a
cold iron cage in the courtyard. Standing with a blade clutched in her
hand ...

Kayla buried her faced in her hands, fighting to control the tremors
that wracked her body. "Not again," she whispered, her voice
trembling, to whoever or whatever might be listening. "Please. I don't
want to do that again."

She wanted to curl up and hide, bury herself beneath the blankets
where she had always felt safe. But she couldn't bear to stay in her
room, lest she fall asleep and back into the dream. So she climbed to her
feet, wrapped a robe about her, and made her way down to the temple.

Kayla paused to genuflect at the gates before entering through the

Western Door. She kept her eyes meekly averted from the east side of the temple, and the golden statue of the Bright Lord that dominated that end of the hall. It wasn't until she was standing before the pale marble statue of the White Lady that she realized she was holding her breath, and she let it out in a rush.

"Now you're being silly," she chided herself, but kept her voice hushed as she knelt before the Goddess.

Kayla stayed there, head bowed and eyes downcast, until the last of the skittishness of the dream faded, replaced by the gentle lassitude that the presence of the Lady always evoked. A little more at ease, she rose and delivered the proper obeisance to the statue.

Ordinarily, she would have turned and left. But something this night was out of place, grating upon her nerves. Casting the Lady a wary glance, Kayla edged around the dais and through the archway all but hidden behind the statue.

She could feel it as she drew closer. It reached out to her, tracing over her skin like velvet, thrumming as it rubbed over her, smug as a purring cat. She halted at the end of the hall, and worried her lip with her teeth.

The blade lay on a cushion of blue velvet, illuminated only by the braziers placed on either side. The scabbard was old, worn and plain. The hilt had once shone brightly, silver inlaid with some sort of odd white polished stone. Now the three ringed crescents of the Lady were all but obscured by the grime that tarnished the pommel.

Lyssia. Her great-great-grandmother's blade.

Kayla's blood pounded in her ears as she raised a trembling hand. Common sense screamed at her to stop, to run, but another part of her refused to listen. It was the part deep within that always wanted to reach out and touch the dancing flames of the hearth fire, to jump from the top of the highest parapet, just to see what it might feel like.

Sensation intensified as her fingers neared the pommel. The hairs on her arm lifted as the power slid, catlike, across her skin. She had only to touch it …

It seemed that she hung there an eternity, a breath away from discovery, before her hand dropped limply to her side. She couldn't do it. She never could. In the end, the fear won. As always. Defeated, she sagged against the wall and slid down it, wrapping her arms tightly around her knees.

A seeming age passed before the light of a lantern pierced the dimness of the hall.

"Who's there?"

Kayla started, her head oddly heavy as she lifted it to look at the priestess.

"It is only I, Mother Elorah," said Kayla, her voice lapsing into the formal court cadences.

"Aliyah?" The priestess squinted in the dim light. "Lady bless, child, not again."

Kayla didn't meet her gaze as she got to her feet. "I am sorry, Mother."

Mother Elorah smiled gently. "All right, all right. I'll not tell your parents about this time either, provided you hie yourself back to bed this instant."

"Yes, Mother."

A tug on Kayla's arm halted her as they passed back into the temple proper. She turned, bewildered, to meet the priestess' concerned gaze.

"Child," she said gently, "if something troubles you, you may talk to me about it. Or if not me, the Lady will always listen." She inclined her head toward the statue. "I do not like these shadows I see in your eyes."

With great effort, Kayla forced a smile. "I thank you for your concern, Mother, but I assure you, I am fine. A little tired, perhaps, and restless. But I am better now." She genuflected briefly to the Lady.

The priestess eyed her for a moment, but could find no fault in Kayla's demeanour. Reluctantly, she stepped back. "Off with you then. But remember, the Lady is here should you have need of Her."

"I will, Mother." Kayla genuflected once more to the priestess, and had to hold her steps to a walk, so great was her urge to flee from the temple.

The hair on her arms didn't settle again until she reached the courtyard. Shivering a little in brisk wind, she rubbed her arms and frowned. She couldn't talk to the priestess about what was bothering her. Nor could she address the Lady. Not while there was a chance someone might overhear.

A low whine at her heels broke her out of her musings, and she knelt beside the dog at her feet. "Hallo, Digger. There's my Merry —" she turned her attention to Digger's mate "— how are my fine babies?"

Kayla giggled softly as the wolfhounds — two ferocious beasts that had been chained next to the great iron cage and set to guard it — collapsed in a wriggling heap beneath her hands. Dropping his dignity, Digger forgot that he was a wolfhound and not a lap dog, and attempted to climb into Kayla's lap. She fell beneath him with a smothered laugh. As she scratched behind Digger's ear, to his great joy and ecstasy, she glanced beyond them to the cage they guarded, and found the grin slipping from her face.

Giving them one final pat, Kayla braced herself and she shoved the dogs aside so she could rise. The griffin watched her, its gaze unwavering. Ever so faintly, the hair at the back of her neck began to prickle. She took a tentative step forward, and then another, moving toward the cage until she was a step away from being able to reach out and touch it.

The griffin hadn't moved. Hadn't made a sound. Just continued to watch her with those eerie golden eyes.

Memory flashed through her, of another such pair of eyes. The pain, the anguish reflected by the amber orbs had been bad enough, but it was the surety of knowledge, the depth of comprehension shining in the depths of those eyes that had stabbed like a dagger into her heart …

Kayla staggered, and caught herself just before she reached for the cage. She raised her head and found herself lost in a field of gold.

Slowly, she drew back.

"For what it's worth," Kayla said quietly. "I'm sorry."

The griffin remained motionless. Tearing away from his gaze, which was more difficult than she would have expected, she made her way back to the keep. With luck, she would be able to get at least a little sleep this night.

"Perhaps if you just told us what you're looking for?"

"I don't *know* what I'm looking for, Miara!" Kayla winced at the petulant whine in her voice, and attempted to bring it back under control as she addressed her sister. "Just anything I can find about the Old Blood."

Miara shook her head. "Honestly, Cestril, I can't understand this sudden obsession you have. The only indications we have of the Old Blood at all are that rusted sword in the temple and Aunt Fillia."

"And hunches on what weekends are best to bring in the harvest are hardly stunning evidence for the Blood."

Kayla glared at her red-headed brother, seated on the other side of the library table. "You could be a little more interested in our history, Bryce."

He shrugged. "Why should I? It's only ever supposedly shown itself in the female line." But he was grinning as he pulled another book off the top of Kayla's pile.

Kayla fisted a hand in her hair and tugged, returning her attention to the volume before her. "I just want to find out what it's supposed to *do*."

"Why?" Miara asked, toying with the end of her ebony braid.

Kayla cast her a look. "What else is there for me to do?"

Neither sibling could argue that. The duties of Youngest Daughter were few and trifling. They exchanged a knowing glance and returned their attention to the aid of their little sister.

"… but I don't understand. He's the *king*."

Kayla looked up as the voice drifted in from the hall, growing louder as her brother Ren entered in the wake of Aeron, the eldest. Both were dressed in their good court clothes, which made Ren look just like a copy of their father. Aeron, however, shared Kayla's earthy hair, which softened and warmed his face and made him imminently more approachable than King Teague. It was one of the reasons all the siblings brought their troubles to Aeron. His patience and generosity when dealing with those problems were what told Kayla he would be a great king.

"That's precisely why he must adhere to the laws," Aeron attempted to explain, crossing to one of the shelves and pulling down a volume of history. Kayla winced. She'd read it. The grammar was atrocious and the handwriting even worse. "Because he *is* the king."

Ren huffed as he dropped into a chair by the fireplace. "But what's the point of having a royal family who can't do what they want?"

"That's the difference between a king and a despot." Aeron turned to his brother. "Or did you even read the section on the Thirty-Year War?"

Ren yelped as Aeron dropped the heavy volume into his lap. "You know I hate the histories."

Kayla rolled her eyes. "The Thirty-Year War started because the people rebelled against King Brayle, who decided that the laws against murder, theft, and treason didn't apply to him. The war didn't end until Brayle's son killed him and swore that from then on, no member of the royal family would be above the law."

"If our house were to break faith with that," Aeron leaned against a shelf, "we'd risk plunging Meladon into war again."

Miara yawned, leaning back in her chair and stretching. The voluminous sleeves of her gown trailed across the table as she did so and knocked a sheaf of papers to the floor. "Cestril, I can't understand why you learn such things."

"It's more interesting than the things I'm supposed to be learning."

"Well, it's far too dull for me. Here, see what you make of this, I'm off to get some embroidery done by the end of the day." Miara dumped the next volume in her pile in front of Kayla and swept out of the room.

"So," Aeron continued, ignoring Miara's somewhat spectacular exit, "if someone like … oh, say, Cestril were to break the law, Father would have no choice but to try her as he would a peasant who broke the same law."

Kayla giggled. "What law would I break?"

Aeron reached over to tug her hair. "Knowing you? Inciting anarchy."

Still smiling, Kayla shook her head and turned her attention to the book Miara had left behind. She frowned a little as she traced her finger over the letters etched into the old leather.

"'*Lhiavan K'Ahressan…*'"

Bryce leaned over, still keeping an amused eye on Ren and Aeron as they bickered over the propriety of the laws. "What?"

"These words." Kayla indicated the book. "Do you know what they mean?"

He frowned, turning the book slightly. "'*Lhiavan K'Ahressan* ...'
Odd. What language is that?"

"I have no idea," Kayla murmured. "None of the ones I know."

"Then they'll be of no help." He jerked his thumb at Ren and
Aeron. Ren was trying to get at his eldest brother, but Aeron held him
off easily with a hand planted on the top of Ren's head. "You know as
many languages as Aeron does. Why don't —" He broke off as a knell
sounded throughout the halls. "Bother. There's the afternoon bell." He
pushed away from the table and followed his brothers to the door.
"Good luck finding what you're after, Ces."

She nodded absently as she opened the book and attempted to
decipher the script. It was a very old hand, and it appeared the scribe's
pen had been cut too sharp, so it took a moment to puzzle out that all
the 'b's looked like 'l's, the 'o's like 'a's, and the 'd's like a 'q' with an
extra tail. But when she figured it out, something in her went very still.

Lhiavan K'Ahressan: A Chronicle of the Blood of Meladon

There was something odd about the way 'Blood' was written. The
'B' in 'Blood' had a horizontal bar through it. An annotation scribes
used only rarely, in this particular script, for added emphasis.

Hand shaking, Kayla turned the page.

—•—

Kayla didn't stop reading until she was in danger of smudging the
pages with her nose. Rubbing her eyes, she stretched, blinking in the
lantern light. They'd be expecting her for dinner any moment. She
placed the book back on the shelf and hurried to her rooms to change,
chewing on the pad of her thumb as she went.

Oh, she'd learned about the Blood, all right. Learned that it had
once manifested in her ancestors as Dreams — the 'D' had been
emphasized with a horizontal bar as well. Dreams that were at once
cryptic and true, and had an alarming tendency to drive the recipients
mad. There had been other effects of the Blood mentioned as well,
though the author had grown vague at that point, as though he hadn't
really understood it either.

But the author had been very clear on one thing. Every member of the House of Meladon who had shown some strong connection to the Old Blood had had died young. And often badly.

A wave of dizziness swept through her as she left her rooms, and she clutched desperately at the doorframe. For a moment, she almost thought that the hand clenched against the stone was stained with something … dark and red …

She squeezed her eyes shut, shaking her head. "I don't want this," she whispered. "I don't want any of it. Please, Lord and Lady, take it back …"

"Cestril?"

Kayla started visibly as Rylan appeared at the end of the hall. He'd laced a vest over his rumpled shirt in an attempt to dress for dinner — normally, it would have made her smile, but her mood was far too dark for levity. Her hand against the wall trembled.

Rylan's brown eyes darkened with concern and he came closer, reaching out to support her. She quickly shook him off and turned away.

"Everything all right?"

Kayla didn't quite look at him, hiding instead behind the brown curtain of her hair. She wanted to tell him. She wanted to tell someone what had happened to her two weeks ago. What was happening to her again. She wanted to cleanse the blood from her hands. But she couldn't. Rylan's first duty was still to the throne, and what she had done was tantamount to treason. She straightened and gave him a smile. "I'm fine."

"One of the guards on night watch said he saw you going into the temple at an ungodly hour."

Kayla stiffened. "And? Am I not allowed to pray? I do not think —"

"Is praying all you were doing? At several hours past midnight?" He braced his hands on his hips. "You weren't trying for a certain sword?"

"Do you take me for a fool?" Kayla hugged her arms to her chest, fingers digging in to her skin. "None but the best and brightest might the sword choose, and I am but an unimportant daughter of an unrepentant house. Your advice is neither desired nor necessary; I have no great wish to die."

Rylan's face was a study in concern. "Hey, now. Don't go getting all formal on me, Cestril. I'm worried, that's all." He took a hesitant step forward. "You haven't been yourself, really, not since they brought that first griffin here —"

"I do not wish to discuss it."

Her royal cadences hurt him; she could see that much in the way he drew back from her. But he simply straightened and offered her his arm. "Then might I escort you to dinner, Your Highness?"

Kayla flinched. When it came to quarrelling and veiled insult, Rylan could give as good as he got. And that, somehow, was enough to make her smile. Her heart lighter, she slipped her arm through his. "You may. I'm suddenly rather famished."

He glanced at her, and matched her grin with his own. "I'd best move slowly then, till the others have had their share. There won't be anything left after you get through with it."

"Spiteful man!" Kayla cried, reduced to helpless giggles as she tried to pull away from him, but he refused to release her. "I'm tall, not overindulgent."

"Ah, and that's why you tore the sleeves out of your best dress yesterday."

"Who told you that?" She couldn't stop laughing. "That was because the swordwork is making me muscular!"

"Yes, Princess, of course it is." He tugged on a lock of her hair.

"I can have you beheaded for that."

"Ah, but since all my swordplay lessons are locked in my head, I know it's safe."

"I can have other things cut off, then."

"Cruel girl. No wonder half the world fears the house of Meladon."

"'Fears' indeed. There's a world of difference between fear and respect, I'll have you know. Perhaps I'll start with your tongue."

"Oh, do my ears first. Then I'll not have to listen to you pestering me for a new lesson."

Kayla was helpless with laughter by the time they entered the dining hall, her concerns at long last set aside.

Set aside, but not forgotten.

—•—

Every part of great dining hall had been built to impress. Around the edges of the room, just below the commencement of the ceiling vaults, some long-forgotten mason had carved an elaborate forest scene. Myriad creatures peered through the foliage of the stone-carved trees, as gallant kings and elegant ladies rode after them in a spirited hunt. Kayla had lost many hours of her childhood to examining these carvings. As she stared at them now, she realized that not once was there the image of a griffin.

Kayla stifled a sigh and pushed her food around on her plate, wishing fervently that she wasn't seated so prominently. The rest of the court assembled at long tables that spanned the length of the hall, but the royal family and their favoured attendants shared the great table on the raised dais that crossed the width of the hall. King Teague had the honoured centre seat, with his queen on his left. To his right sat Kayla and her sisters, while her brothers sat arranged to the queen's left. Seated at her father's right hand as she was, there was no hope of a quiet and unnoticed departure.

Her lack of appetite made dinner tedious enough, but her father insisted on reliving the hunt yet again with his Captain, and since Kayla and her sisters sat between the two, Kayla was forced to share in the shouted conversation in its entirety.

It was with no small amount of relief that Kayla set aside her barely-touched dessert. All that remained now was the cup to be shared by the family, and she could escape. At last, the doors at the end of the hall opened and a servant bore in the cup.

"Daughter."

Kayla started at the sound of the king's voice, and cast a quick glance in his direction. "Yes, Father?"

"You've been uncommonly silent this night. No ripping tales from your latest book? No scrapes with the kitchen steward this morning?"

"No, Father." She studied the plate in front of her.

"Are you ill, youngest?"

The concern in his voice struck her more powerfully than any blow could have. She squeezed her eyes shut for a moment before forcing herself to look at him. "No, Father. A little tired, perhaps, but I am sure I will be well in the morning."

A smile stole across King Teague's features. "Good then. But a sip from our new cup shall aid you. Come, you shall be the first to drink."

"New cup?" Kayla frowned as her father turned to take it from the servant. When he turned back, Kayla went cold.

The goblet had been removed from its former base. Now the bejewelled golden cup sat clenched between stubby claws. The talon had been shorn off halfway down the foreleg, the bone set into a sturdy jewelled base so that the talon held the cup aloft.

The talon was far too small to be that of the female. Horror crept over her, wrapping icy fingers around her heart as she realized what that meant.

Her father held the cup toward her.

Unable to stop herself, Kayla lurched back, covering her mouth as bile burned her throat.

That one act was enough to bring every gaze in the hall to rest upon her. Her father's brows drew together in a scowl. "Something displeases you?"

"I can't drink from that," she whispered.

The scowl deepened. "Nonsense. Griffin talon is ward against poison and conveys strength. It won't harm you."

She gazed up at her father, tears welling in her eyes. "It's not that. Papa, please don't make me drink."

He leaned closer to her. She pressed away from the cup, but she was trapped in her chair, unable to get away, unwilling to let the talon touch her skin. Her father forced her chin up with his free hand until she met his eyes.

"You would dishonour your family by refusing to drink with us?"

"No," her voice shook. "If you would but find another vessel I will drink, I swear —"

"This vessel is a mark of honour, taken with skill and pride in the protection of the kingdom." His fingers tightened. "You *will* drink."

"No!"

The volume of her scream startled even her, but it surprised her father enough that she could jerk free of his grasp. The crash of her chair against the dais echoed throughout the silent hall as Kayla leapt away and fled.

Her father was going to be furious. Kayla would most likely be beaten for this — something that had not happened since she had disrupted delicate peace negotiations when she was seven. But as terrified as she was of what her father was going to do to her, she could not have forced herself to drink from that cup.

The talon was too small. It could not have come from the female. It could only have come from an infant. One the griffin had been carrying when she died.

When she had been slaughtered.

She held a blade in her clenched fist. A blade stained bright red ...

Kayla made it as far as the stables before she was violently ill.

—•—

Kayla hid in the loft when her father sent her brothers to look for her, and remained there long after the midnight bell, until she was sure everyone but the guards had gone to bed. She couldn't escape punishment, but at least she might delay it a while.

Try as she might, she couldn't settle her thoughts. Her father was responsible for the deaths of not only the griffin's mate, but also its unborn child. Everyone was wary of griffins up in the mountains, and occasionally lost part of a flock to them in the outlying villages, but none had ever attacked a village — until her father had gone, in the name of protecting the kingdom, and taken the griffin's mate in her den. Only then did the griffin attack, slaughtering men and women alike.

"But not the children," Kayla whispered. "When they spoke of this griffin's rampage, they never mentioned the children."

The image of that little talon swam before her. Choking on a sob, she buried her head in the straw.

—•—

When Kayla had finished crying, she made her shaky way down from the loft, stopping by the kennels to pull some dried meat from the stores. Then she went to the courtyard.

Secure in the knowledge that Digger and Merry would raise the alarm if anything was amiss, there were no guards set to patrol the courtyard this late at night. No one, save perhaps Rylan, knew that the wolfhounds didn't view Kayla as a threat. And Rylan would never expect her to be here at this hour.

Calling out softly, Kayla greeted Digger and Merry with a few morsels. Digger, glutton that he was, inhaled his first and began to whine at his mate, who growled and shifted to guard her portion. Kayla knelt, wrapping her arms around the dog's neck as he pressed his massive head against her. "Do you love her, Digger?" she whispered into one silky ear. "What would you do if anyone hurt her?"

Digger whuffed softly and made a dash for Merry's treat. Kayla shook her head, and rose.

The griffin was watching her, something alien and unreadable blossoming deep in its fathomless eyes. Its blood-matted golden feathers and tawny fur, which had been raised and bristling, began to settle. Inexplicably, that only unnerved her more. Tears stung at her eyes.

"I am not brave."

The words startled her, and it took a moment to recognize the raw, trembling voice as her own. Her empty hand clenched in the fabric of her skirts. "I do not know what to do anymore. If I were brave, I might do something. I might claim my grandmother's sword and confront my father and get him to stop doing this whenever he feels he must appear strong and noble for his people. But I am not brave." Tears burned across her skin. "I am afraid of what he is going to do to me now. I am even more afraid of what I have already done. I do not understand what is happening to me. I do not want to. I want it all to go away. To go back to the way things were before." She glanced down at her hand, opening it slowly to reveal the meat clenched within. "But in a way, I am as helpless as you. So once again, I take the coward's road." She tossed the meat into the cage, and fled.

It took a long time to cry herself to sleep.

—•—

"I don't understand why you didn't just take the cup."

Kayla peered over her shoulder at Rylan, wincing as the movement pulled the bruises on her back. "I don't expect you to understand." She turned back to stare across the courtyard.

She had been banished from the hall for a month, her return dependent on her acceptance of the cup. Her family was forbidden to speak to her until her father broke the silence. And she had been soundly beaten by her father.

She supposed she ought to be grateful for that much. Since she had refused the use of a whipping boy, it fell to her father, as the only man of greater rank, to administer her punishment. From the tales she heard amongst the guardsman, she was much better off with her uncertain father than with the practiced hand of the Captain or the armsmaster.

Still, that didn't mean it didn't hurt.

Rylan's gentle touch at her elbow roused Kayla from her thoughts. "Cestril, why won't you tell me what's wrong?"

"Everything."

Rylan moved in front of her. "I never thought I'd see the day you'd go this far just to get out of sword practice with me."

Kayla glanced up at him in incredulity, and despite herself, began to laugh. She shook her head. "My, but we think highly of ourselves."

Rylan grinned as he sat next to her, gently tousling her hair. "That's better."

In the courtyard, one of the pageboys ventured too close to the cage. The griffin lashed out, coming up sharp against its bonds. The terrified boy leaped away, bringing him within range of Digger and setting the wolfhound off in turn. Barking and snarling, Digger lunged to the end of his chain, sending the pageboy fleeing for his life.

"Digger," Kayla admonished, though the hound was too far away to hear.

"Hush you, he's doing his job." Rylan cast a smug grin the hounds. "There's a reason we set them there and give them the keys to guard. I'd be most displeased if they started letting everyone and their pageboys come near." He glanced at her. "Come to think of it, I'm none too pleased by their acceptance of a certain princess, either."

Kayla blinked at him innocently. "I helped raise them."

Rylan glanced skywards. "And for the life of me I still can't figure out how you talked me into that."

Kayla was saved from having to respond by the approach of another guardsman. Kayla recognized him — he was a friend of Rylan's, and had also had a hand in the raising of Digger and Merry.

"Forgive my intrusion, Highness," he said, his face growing paler as she watched.

"It is no trouble," Kayla said gently.

He bowed and turned to Rylan. "Have you noticed that the dogs are a little more on edge late —" he caught himself with a wary glance at Kayla "— of late?"

Rylan frowned. "Not particularly." He gave Kayla a questioning glance.

"I do not think it particularly serious," Kayla said. "I have come across mention in my readings that the scent of a griffin may unsettle even the steadiest of beasts. The beasts, at least, are wise enough to recognize that they stand in the presence of a greater predator. Perhaps it is this that has unnerved them."

The young guardsman nodded and bowed. "Of course. Thank you, Highness."

"Be well." Kayla watched him go, and turned to meet Rylan's look. "What?"

"Lord and Lady, Cestril, would it kill you to drop the formality, even for a little? You can see how nervous he is around royalty. Moren's a good man, and he just lost his father and brother to the griffin. The least you could do is settle him with the common speech. I know you're not supposed to, but couldn't you just … I don't know, let it slip?"

Kayla just stared at him, and this time it was Rylan's turn for discomfort. Kayla shook her head. "My brother has been lax in your instruction, it seems."

A furrow appeared between Rylan's brows. "I don't know what you mean."

"He took in the peasant boy and trained him to speak to nobility, but he failed to teach you why such distinctions are important." At his blank look, Kayla sighed. "You've learned the courtly speech, but it's still strange to you. It's different when you're born speaking it." She toyed with a strand of her hair. "The formal cadences are automatic, it's the common speech that takes effort. It's … very personal. Intimate. Amongst nobility, it's used only when greatly at ease, in the company of very close family or friends. I could no more inadvertently let it slip than I could inadvertently disrobe in front of someone."

Rylan was silent for a long moment. "But … you use the common speech with me."

Kayla turned to him, her pale eyes locking with his brown. "Yes. I do."

A deep blush blossomed on Rylan's cheeks. Dismissing it with a cough, he stood and offered Kayla a hand. "Now then, it's getting late, and certain young princesses really should be getting out from under my feet and back into bed."

Kayla stuck her tongue out at him, but let him pull her to her feet. "I let you off easy today. Mark my words, you'll fear my sword tomorrow."

"I'm quaking in terror." He gave her a gentle shove. "Off with you."

Kayla made her way back to her room and curled up beneath the covers with the novel she had filched from the library. But though she had always adored the tale of the brave farmer's daughter who had ventured forth to honour and glory, it brought her no comfort this night. Finally, when she heard the midnight bell, she gave up and set the book aside.

Unable to rest, she slipped from her bed, pausing only long enough to wrap a walking-gown around her. Sure enough, her feet led her straight to the courtyard. She paused at the threshold, safe within the little pool of light cast by the lantern on the wall. Shivering a little in the brisk night air, she stared at the cage at the other end and tried to banish the knot of dread in the pit of her stomach.

"Cestril?"

The soft voice from the darkness nearly sent her out of her skin. The moon had chosen this night of the month to hide her face, so that only the stars illuminated the night. "Father?"

He moved toward her, and as the torchlight illuminated his features, Kayla was shocked at how haggard he appeared. He stopped at her side, glancing over at the cage. "Why aren't you in bed?"

"I couldn't sleep," she said.

His eyes finally met hers, and she saw guilt within them. "Does it hurt?"

"Yes." Her voice was soft.

Teague was silent for a long moment. "Your mother reminded me of something tonight. Of last time I found it necessary to strike you."

Kayla glanced down at her feet. "When I disrupted your peace treaty with Jeletha."

A smile tugged at the corner of his mouth. "Indeed. It was your mother who reminded me that you burst in upon us crying because the cook was killing the chickens you'd had a hand in raising." He laughed softly. "King Liran was amused by that. He said that if my children got that upset over chickens, it was obvious we weren't raising you to carry on with war."

She'd never heard that part. "Really?"

He leaned against the wall. "I was furious with you. Because you'd disrupted something of such importance for something so trivial, and because you'd had a part in such a trivial thing in the first place. I was mortified that Liran found out a daughter of the house of Meladon was raising chickens."

"I thought they were sweet," Kayla murmured.

"I know. I had forgotten that. But your mother hadn't. And it was she who pointed out to me that you still have trouble bringing yourself to eat meat when you can recognize the animal." He turned to her, and took her gently by the shoulders. "I didn't know the cup would upset you so. You should not have refused it, but for what it's worth, I regret forcing you to make that choice."

Kayla glanced past him to the cage, and the golden eyes burning deep within. Shuddering, she tore her gaze away. "I'm sorry I disappointed you, Father."

"No matter. There will be other chances to make up for it." He patted her shoulder. "Get to bed, youngest. Leave the worrying to those old enough to have earned it."

Kayla delivered a brief curtsey to her father before gathering her skirts and fleeing back to her room. She collapsed on her bed, shaking with exhaustion. Her father never apologized — to hear him do so should have been great comfort to her. But somehow, it only served to make things worse. At the end of her strength, she let herself slide into the welcoming embrace of sleep.

—•—

Darkness surrounded her. She blinked, turning, but there was no light to relieve that horrible emptiness. A cool draft swirled around her, tracing over her skin like long, clammy fingers. She shuddered, pulling her arms close around her. "Hello? Anyone?"

But there was no answer from the blackness.

Kayla fought to keep her breathing calm. She couldn't remember how she'd gotten here. For that matter, she had no idea where 'here' was. "Anyone?"

Something in the darkness gave a deep scream of pain.

Kayla cried out and began to run, not sure if it was toward or away from the sound, but unable to keep still. Unable to ignore that cry for help.

"Lady, please," she gasped. "Help me."

At long last, as though in answer to her prayer, a pinprick of light appeared before her. Choking back a sob of relief, Kayla quickened her pace and raced toward it.

Without warning the light was around her, and she found herself in the temple, staring at the statue of the Lady. But the Goddess could not hold her attention long. Kayla could feel the power coming from the alcove behind Her, wrapping around Kayla's heart and drawing her forward. She slipped around the statue, and her breath caught in her throat. At the end of the hall, Lyssia pulsed with dazzling light, calling Kayla forward, daring her to take up the blade.

Folly, *whispered voices from the dark within her.* Only one whose hands have bathed in blood are strong enough to wield this blade.

"There is blood on my hands." Kayla's voice was choked. Her hands were trembling.

Come to me, *the sword seemed to whisper in her mind.* Are you brave enough to take up my legacy? Are you truly a daughter of my house? Or are you simply a coward?

"No," Kayla breathed. "I am not afraid." She reached for the sword.

She froze, staring at her hands. They were coated in fluid, thick and red, that ran down her arms and dripped into the puddle at her feet. Her breath laboured, coming in gasps. The blood ... the blood was everywhere.

"Kayla."

The sound of her true name ripped through her, numbing her, bending her will to its wielder. She turned, nearly slipping in the pool, and stared at her father.

"Papa?" She held out her hands, shuddering as the warm liquid poured from her fingers. "Papa, I'm scared."

"Then drink, child. All you need do is drink, and you will have the strength to be brave. You can take up the sword and slay the demons that plague you."

He held the cup toward her, and she found herself reaching for it. The golden cup clenched in the talon of the infant griffin. The one that had died with its mother ...

"No!" Unable to stop herself, she lashed out, knocking the cup from her father's hand. She stared as it fell, impossibly slowly. The ruby droplets of the blood within the cup fell like rain against the smooth floor of the temple, flowing in rivulets toward her.

A sound like thunder rent the air, and the floor began to crack along the bloody lines. Kayla lurched, unable to keep her balance as the stone broke up beneath her, and she fell.

She was still falling. Impossibly high, so high that the air was ripped from her lungs and the wind etched lines of frost along her skin. The ground stretched out inconceivably far below her, so vast that she could see it laid out like the great map of the world on the wall of the library.

She was falling. Too far, too fast. The ground that had awed her a moment before was rushing toward her now, greedy to meet her. She was going to die.

She didn't want to die. Kayla screamed, reaching out as though she could push the ground away. Her heart thundered in her ears, so loud that she almost didn't see that her hands were finally clean. So loud, that she almost couldn't hear that her voice sounded not like the cry of a human, but of a great raptor.

She saw her shadow upon the ground now, growing larger as she fell. As she watched, the silhouette of great wings blossomed from the human form etched upon the hungry ground. And then she felt a great pain as talons sank into her chest and pierced her heart ...

—•—

She was falling.

The scream died in her throat as Kayla hit the floorboards next to her bed. Thrashing to be free of the blankets that pinned her limbs, she finally managed to extricate herself from the mess. She was on her feet and running before she had time to think about her destination.

All those nights spent wandering the halls came rushing back to her. Kayla knew where the guards were and how they moved during their shifts. She knew where to be to avoid their notice. Her bare feet were almost silent as she flew over the cold stone, down the stairs, and into the courtyard.

The night was impossibly dark, the moon hidden, but the dogs didn't need light to know who approached them. Kayla followed the eager whine to Digger's side. She dropped down next to him and buried her fingers in the silky fur, digging through his ruff until her fingers brushed against metal. "Easy, Digger," she whispered. "There's my good boy. Who's a clever, clever dog?"

She could feel him shaking as his tail waved wildly back and forth. She finally managed to work the leather through the buckle. She hugged him tightly to her, sending him into another frenzy of tail-wagging, and slipped the collar from his neck.

"Good boy. Stay now."

Kayla's trembling fingers curled around the cold metal of the keys, and she tugged them free of the collar.

The griffin was awake and alert. It watched her as she approached, its golden eyes luminous as they caught the light from the lanterns set about the cage. Kayla stood before it, shaking so hard that she could barely keep her feet.

"No more," she whispered. *"I will have no more blood on my hands."*

Drawing a deep breath, Kayla reached out and touched the bars.

The creature made no sound. It stared at her, unblinking, as she used the first key to unlock the cage. She drew back the door slowly, lest the hinges give her away. At last the door hung open, and she found herself facing the griffin.

A surge of panic coursed through her as she took in the razor edges of the griffin's beak and talons. She glanced down at the remaining small key that would unlock the manacles that secured the griffin at the limbs and neck. There was no way to reach them that would not take her within striking distance. She looked up once more to meet those enormous golden eyes, and held them with her own.

"I know you can't understand me," she whispered, "but I'm only trying to help." Her fist clenched on the key. "I must be mad." Then, with a final breath, she pulled herself into the cage.

She didn't die. Kayla let out the breath she had been holding, and the scent of griffin overwhelmed her.

She froze for a moment. There was something about that scent, beneath the stench of waste and blood, that sent every instinct in her clamouring to run. It was rich and heady, almost like spices, and the prey in her knew better than to expose herself to it. But she had a job to do. A sturdy chain had been bolted to each corner of the cage, those chains riveted to thick manacles bearing sturdy locks. There was no removing them without the key.

"Pray, excuse me," Kayla said, and dropped to crawl beneath the griffin in order to reach the manacles on its hind legs. Finishing quickly, she crawled back out again and turned her attention to the chains on its forelegs.

She got one open, catching it carefully and lowering it to the floor of the cage. Shifting back, she turned to the other one. It was going to be more difficult to reach. She would have to —

The griffin moved. Kayla threw herself back, only to come up sharply against the foreleg the griffin had placed in her way. She gasped and braced for the killing blow as the griffin lifted its other talon.

It didn't come. She blinked in amazement at the foreleg offered to her. Glancing up, she found the griffin watching her almost expectantly. Catching her lip between her teeth, she reached out and took the talon in her hand.

It was an odd sensation. The large scales on the upper surface were cold and hard, but those on the inner surface were smaller, soft as fine leather, and warm. She started as the talon curled ever so slightly around her hand, the muscles within shifting over her palm. There was an impossible strength to it. She knew that if the griffin chose to hold her, it would never let her go. But it didn't. It just waited.

She drew a deep breath and, though her hand was shaking badly enough to make it difficult, she turned the talon, fit the key in the lock and released the shackle. The griffin instantly pulled the talon from her grasp, and Kayla got unsteadily to her feet.

The curve of the beak hung directly over her head. She tried very hard to ignore it as she reached for the final lock that held the massive iron collar around the griffin's neck.

A final turn of the key, and the griffin was free.

Kayla struggled to catch the collar as it fell, lowering it carefully before regaining her feet. Raising her head, she felt her blood turn to ice. The look in those golden eyes was anything but patient now. Kayla now knew how a mouse might feel falling prey to an eagle. Helpless, she watched as the griffin gathered itself, preparing for the strike. She could do nothing but meet the griffin's hypnotic gaze.

And it hit her.

Age and power both. Claws that dripped with the blood of ages. Judgment and condemnation. The world from heights no human had ever seen. And wings, great golden wings, stretching above her to blot out the sky ...

Kayla gasped as that wave of ... of whatever *it* was abandoned her, and she collapsed to her knees, fighting for breath. She felt worn, stretched, as though something impossibly-large had filled her for a moment and gone. Two weeks earlier, she had felt something similar as she dreamed. But that had been only a hint of what had just ravaged through her. She raised her head.

The griffin was pressed against the back of the cage, staring at her with what could only be horror shining in its eyes. Before Kayla could move, it leapt.

The girl ducked, clasping her hands over her head as the griffin soared above her, its wings snapping audibly to catch the air. Pressing her hands against the talon-scored floor, Kayla went weak with relief. The weight that had been pressing upon her for two long, intolerable weeks was finally gone.

Digger and Merry let out a frenzied chorus of howling.

Kayla felt her mouth go dry. She had just robbed the king of his prize. She had just released the greatest threat that her kingdom had faced in years.

She had just committed treason.

She had to run. To hide. No one would ever suspect her, if only she could get clear. She shoved herself away from the cage and bolted across the courtyard, lungs burning. She just had to reach the doorway ...

She was only steps away from it when something moved in the shadows. Unable to stop herself, she collided with it and sprawled back against the cobblestones. The keys flew from her hand, ringing impossibly loud as they hit the ground. Shaking the stars from her vision, she looked up, and her heart caught in her throat.

Her father stood above her, his eyes wide with shock. "Kayla ..."

Her true name hit her, ravaged through her, bound her and held her fast as the guards appeared in the courtyard. Rylan stood among them, staring at her in disbelief. It was too much. The world spun and blurred, and Kayla fell back into darkness.

—•—

There was nothing anyone could do. The tribunal took three days to complete, but though her father and Aeron had sat in the library for hours with Ren and Bryce and her brother Daren, and two of the five justicars, it came to nothing in the end. Half the castle had seen Kayla sprawled in the courtyard with the keys next to her hand.

And the true bitterness lay in the fact that, had she not been who she was, they might have let her go. She was only a child after all, perhaps too kind-hearted for her own good, and had seen only a creature in pain and not a threat to the kingdom. But she was also Aliyah t'Meladon, the youngest daughter of King Teague of Meladon. To let her go would invite the rumours and unrest, charges that the family of the king held themselves above the law. And so, in the end, there was no choice at all.

Before her family, her court, and half the kingdom, Kayla was condemned to die.

—•—

High in her cell in the north tower, Kayla could hear the shouting of the people below her. Some were sympathetic to her plight, others celebrated the decision, but all were vocal and extremely angry. She curled on her side, letting her tears soak into the straw beneath her. She ached from the days spent on the cold, unforgiving floor. In accordance with the laws, she hadn't even been permitted to change her clothing — prisoners were given no opportunity to gain a means of escape, and they were accorded no courtesy.

The once fine fabric of her nightgown was absolutely ruined. The filth that years of neglect had left on the stone floor had soaked through the thin fabric, and it itched abominably. Her wrists chafed beneath the manacles she wore. The grime from the floor coated her flesh. Never in her life had she felt such complete and utter despair.

She raised her eyes to the tiny window. The moon still hung in the sky, a pale crescent fleeing before the light of the morning sun.

"Where are You now, Lady?" Kayla wrapped her arms tightly around herself. "I was so sure it was what You wanted of me. Why else would You have been in my Dreams?" Anger, quick and sharp, stabbed through her. She pushed herself to her knees, weak from hunger and despair. "Where are You now? Where are the forces that guided me? Where are the Dreams that drove me, that prompted my hand and my step? Where are those that demanded I give of myself? Where are You? I gave up everything that I might do Your bidding, and now You are nowhere to be found. I did everything You asked of me! Why do You not protect me now? *Why have You forsaken me?*"

But though her heart ached with the force of the words, there was no answer. She remained as she was, cold and empty, and utterly alone.

The key turned in the lock.

Kayla struggled to her feet, grabbing at the wall for support. One look at Rylan's expression as he entered was enough to kill any faint hope that she might still emerge from this ordeal. With a soft moan, she sank back to her knees and buried her head in her hands.

"Cestril ..." She heard his footsteps come toward her.

"You couldn't stop them," she said. "I know."

"Why, Cestril?" His voice was raw, the edge in it cutting her deeply. "Why did you do it?"

"Because it had all gone wrong." She drew a shuddering breath. "I just wanted to make things right again."

Her words were met with silence. In her darkest hour, even her truest friend had forsaken her.

She heard the soft sound of metal being set upon the floor next to her. Peering through her fingers, she found herself staring at a basin of water and a washcloth. She summoned the courage to look up.

Rylan held out a bundle. "I couldn't get into your room, and your mother and sisters wouldn't speak to me. But I had this." He set it before her. "You deserve your dignity."

Tears welled in her eyes as she gathered up the small bundle of her practice clothes. "Rylan ..."

"I wish there was more I could give you."

Somewhere deep inside her, she found the strength to smile. "It's enough."

Rylan released her from the shackles and stood with his back turned. Kayla washed as best she could, using the comb he had brought to straighten out her tangled mass of hair. She braided it and secured it with the bright length of ribbon Rylan had brought. Then she rid herself of the ruined nightgown and drew on her breeches and shirt, laced up her vest, and pulled her boots on her feet.

From the courtyard below came the deep call of a horn.

Rylan turned, sorrow darkening his features. "It's time."

Kayla nodded. "I'm ready." But she reached out and clung fast to the hand Rylan offered as he led her down through the keep.

—•—

Rylan paused at the door to the courtyard and accepted the length of rope one of the guardsmen held out to him. As he bound Kayla's hands behind her back, he leaned close and whispered softly into her ear.

"No sister could ever have brought me as much joy as you did. I will always love you, my princess."

Kayla throat burned. She cried out, trying to turn as the guardsmen pulled her from him and swept her out into the turmoil of the courtyard.

The noise washed over her, threatening to sweep her away. Before her stretched two lines of guards, forming a living barrier against which the tide of people strained. On all sides people crowded against the guards, screaming, reaching past the linked arms of her father's men to tear at her. Kayla shied away from the grasping hands, but the corridor the guards cleared for her was not terribly wide, and each recoil brought her within range of another pair of hands. They were everywhere, grabbing at her, scraps of her clothing tearing away beneath their fingers.

Heedless of her distress, her escort continued to push her toward the dais that awaited her where an iron cage once sat.

Eventually, impatience overwhelmed the screaming dissenters who could not quite break past the guards to reach her. Something soft and rotten struck her temple, odorous fluid oozing down her face and into her collar. That unleashed the tide, and the missiles began to fly — some threw flowers, but most were not of such charitable mind. When the guards finally reclaimed her and dragged her up the stairs, Kayla was covered in gobbets of rotten fruit and saliva.

Three hooded men stood upon the dais, and one took her from the hands of the guards. Kayla peered up beneath the concealing folds of his hood, and gasped.

She found herself face-to-face with her father.

"Kayla." He gently wiped her face clean. "Please, forgive me."

Kayla's eyes widened as the first tear spilled down his cheek, and widened further as he pressed a kiss to her brow. In all her years, she had never known that kind of affection from him. But then he was gone, descending the stairs to be swept away by the waiting guardsmen. The corridor closed, and the path of escape vanished beneath the seething mass of people.

"Father?" Kayla breathed. "Papa? Papa, wait!" She lunged after him, but hard hands caught her and drew her back. Though in her heart she knew it was useless, she struggled with all her might. She didn't want to die. "Papa, *please*! Please don't let them do this. Papa, please, make them stop! *Papa!*"

Someone caught at her, and she found herself staring at a face she knew, though Moren's features were so darkened by fury that she barely recognized the shy, stammering young guardsman who had once sat with her amongst the wolfhound puppies. A sharp blow struck her, and she doubled over as the air drove from her lungs. The crowd erupted, some cheering and others hissing their displeasure as she was bent over the block. Hands seized her and bound her feet. One of the hooded men stepped before her and stretched another rope over her shoulders, securing her fast to the bloodstained wood.

Kayla looked out over the crowd, past the jeering faces, and found her family on the raised dais across from her. She scanned the weeping faces of her mother and sisters, took in Bryce's distress, Ren's fury, Daren's anguish, and Aeron's cold anger. But there was no sign of her father.

Something within her snapped. She began to scream as the tears poured down her face. She struggled against her bonds, but they held fast. She couldn't think, couldn't speak, couldn't breathe as terror seized her, reducing her to a helpless wreck.

A shadow loomed behind her. In a horrible parody of the shadow-plays that were so popular with the court, Kayla could see her executioner raising his sword. Her sobs rose to a high, keening cry, and she squeezed her eyes closed.

There was a shriek from someone in the crowd. Then another. And then all other noise was suddenly drowned out by a cry from above; a deep, resonant scream that turned Kayla's blood to ice. She thought at first that one of the castle falcons had escaped the mews, but the sound was too deep, too large, to be that of a bird. Her eyes snapped open.

There was a shadow over her. It was not that of the executioner, for he was on his knees next to her, staring up in horror. Around her, the people trampled over each other in their desperation to get away from the dais. As she watched, the shadow grew larger until she lay within a vast field of darkness.

A sudden gust of wind buffeted her and a weight drove into her back, pressing the breath from her body. Long claws dug into the wood a hairsbreadth from her nose, parting the rope and the solid ironwood beneath as though it were no more unyielding than butter. And then those impossibly long, impossibly sharp talons wrapped tightly around Kayla's chest.

She felt a single great lurch as massive golden wings beat the air around her, and then she was staring down as the block dropped away. The tiny forms of guardsmen swarmed the walls, growing smaller by the minute. She saw the dark cloud that chased her as they loosed their arrows, but they fell far short of the mark. She was much too high for them to reach her. Within seconds, the castle was only a tiny grey dot on the landscape.

At last, there was no fight left within her. Kayla surrendered to oblivion and let the wings of fate carry her where they would.

—•—

Slowly, Kayla became aware of the cool grass that pressed against her cheek. Of the birdsong that filtered through the air around her. Of the scent of earth and flowers. And of spices. Rich, heady spices that set her heart pounding in fear. She opened her eyes and rolled onto her back.

Deep golden eyes stared down at her.

Only three days ago, the griffin had been battered, bloodied, and covered in filth. Now, though a few of the feathers were broken, and its hide was still marred by deep welts and gashes, most the blood and dirt was gone. The change was remarkable. Its feathers shone in the sunlight. Tawny gold fur rippled like silk over powerful muscles as the griffin flexed its gleaming talons. It was truly the most magnificent creature she had ever seen.

"Ah well," she whispered. "At least it's a much grander way to die. I hope it won't hurt that much."

The griffin cocked its head at her, and one of the cruel talons lashed toward her. Kayla's breath left her in a sob. It took her a moment to realize that her head was still attached. She raised a hand to brush aside the hair that had fallen over her eyes, and only then realized that her hands were free. The griffin lashed out once more with a talon, slicing effortlessly through the bonds at her ankles.

She hardly dared to breathe. "I don't understand."

The great beak parted. Kayla cringed, but was entirely unprepared for what emerged from the griffin's mouth.

"We are now even."

The griffin's voice, deep and melodic, and unquestionably masculine, rang through her like a bell and left her gasping for breath.

She blinked, shaken. "You —"

"I have fulfilled my debt. A life for a life." It — he — regarded her with unquestionable scorn. "Now you are on your own."

"Who are you?" was all she could think to say.

"My name is my own, *kichani*," he said, his voice cold and cutting as midwinter snow, "and not given lightly."

The great wings stretched. Kayla threw up her arms to shield her eyes as a blast of wind struck her. When she opened her eyes again, the griffin was gone. Kayla was alone.

—•—

Growing up, Kayla had always been sneaking adventure novels in with her texts. When her tutors had believed her to be memorizing who had married So and So in the kingdom of Too Far Away to Matter to Me on the day of Too Far In the Past to Have Any Meaning Now, she had instead been absorbed in the tales of poor abused orphans who fled their cruel homes to find fortune and glory in the deep wilds of the forests. Kayla wished she could have the idiots who had penned those stories before her now, so she could prove to them how utterly ignorant they actually were.

For instance, those brave orphans in the tales never ran into stinking, unkempt robbers mere hours after venturing in the woods. Kayla stared up through her tears at the one crouched over her now. She seemed to be defying convention at every turn.

"I ain't gonna ask y' again," the man snarled. "Where's yer gold?"

Kayla flinched as the stench of him washed over her. The layers of grime would have told her from a distance that he hadn't been acquainted with a bath in several months, even if the stink hadn't first clued her in.

"I already told you," Kayla sobbed. "I do not have any!"

She cried out as his foot connected with her ribs. Her cheek was already swollen, and her lip felt thick and hot from the other blows he had given her. She struggled to breathe through the pain in her chest.

"Don't lie t' me, girl." He shook her violently, baring what remained of his teeth, and his ragged companions laughed at her distress. "Where'r y' hidin' it?"

"I do not have any!"

Behind him, one of the others stepped forward. "Mebbe she's tellin' th' truth," he said.

Her captor spared him a glance of disgust, and struck Kayla so hard that her vision filled with stars. "Don't be stupid. Listen t' her talk. She's noble, no doubt, and I dunno of no noble what goes out wi'out gold."

Kayla froze as the man drew a knife.

But the blade didn't fall. A distant scream of deepest rage ripped through the forest, a sound Kayla had heard only once before. The men around her paled. In an instant, they were running, leaving Kayla forgotten on the forest floor.

Half blinded by tears, she gained her unsteady feet and stumbled through the dark woods, her only thought to put as much distance between herself and her attackers as possible. Terror fueled her bruised and shaking limbs, pushing her farther when exhaustion threatened to overwhelm her.

Kayla couldn't stop crying. In those same books that told of the remarkably fortuitous orphans, she had read tales of princesses left for dragons who had screamed and wailed and fainted at even the slightest hint of danger. She had always looked rather scornfully upon them, thinking that she would never act quite so silly should she be in their positions. Now she felt nothing but sympathy for them.

She hurt. She had never hurt this badly before. She was lost, alone, and terrified, and she was gradually becoming aware that she had no idea how a person was to survive in the woods with no food or shelter. It was beginning to dawn on her that the griffin might not have done her as great a favour as she had first thought. Perhaps he had only exchanged a quick death for one that would be slow and lingering.

If only she'd claimed Lyssia. The blade would have made her strong. Had she only taken the blade, she could have stood up to her father, to the court. She could have taken control of her destiny. Now she was doomed to blunder about the depths of the woods until she starved to death.

She should never have expected otherwise. Without the strength of her grandmother's blade, she was weak.

She was nothing …

As these dark thoughts continued to draw Kayla's spirits further and further downward, the silence of the forest was shattered again by the scream of a griffin, filled with fury still — but this time laced with pain.

Clarity returned to her with a jolt. Unable to help herself, she began to run. Then she broke into a clearing, and all rational thought fled.

The griffin lay on his side, thrashing against the confining strands of a net. Men gathered around it, throwing coils of rope over the massive form and lashing them tight. Men with familiar faces. Men wearing the livery of Meladon.

The man standing before the griffin she recognized all too well.

"Kill it," said her father. "Kill the beast that took my child."

Face cold and impassive, Rylan stepped forward and raised his sword.

A shriek of outrage and fury rent the air, freezing the men in their tracks. Even the griffin stopped fighting long enough to stare. Only dimly did Kayla recognize that the sound was coming from her. She slammed into Rylan, tearing the sword from his hands as she knocked him off his feet. Planting herself before the griffin, she turned and faced her father.

He was white with alarm. "Kayla …"

Shock, terrible numbing shock as Kayla's true name slammed into her.

At her back, the griffin screamed.

No! Her inward cry echoed through every inch of her as she steadied her grip on the sword. She could not fall. Would not fall. It was not just her own fate that she held in her hands.

King Teague reached for her, trembling.

I will have no more blood on my hands.

"Don't!" she shouted. "Don't you dare! You started all this, and now you seek to begin it all again? This creature saved my life, and I will not let you harm him!"

Tears shone on her father's cheeks as he stepped closer. "You live …"

"No." She stepped back, shaking with fury and with alarm at the pain in her father's eyes. Behind him, Rylan staggered to his feet, staring in astonishment at his former pupil. "Your daughter is dead. You killed her when you turned your back and left her to die on the block. You have only three daughters now, Your Majesty. I shall never be yours again."

Her father opened his mouth to reply, but Kayla never heard him. Something struck her from behind, but she did not fall. Instead, strong talons wrapped tightly around her waist. The sword slipped from her numb fingers as the ground dropped away once more.

The flight was not as smooth as it had been before. But it was enough. She watched the river pass beneath them, a deep gorge that was impossible to cross. The nearest bridge was leagues to the north. The hunters couldn't reach them now.

—•—

The trees rushed up to meet them, branches slapping at her face as the griffin plunged into their midst. Kayla dropped rather ignominiously to the ground, rolling for a moment before she fetched up against a tree. She lay unmoving for a long while, content to stare up at the green canopy above her and marvel at the fact she was still alive. Then, slowly, she rolled over and pushed herself to her feet.

The griffin lay a few lengths away from her, panting a little. His wings were spread, and Kayla could see where more feathers had broken off. It was a wonder he had been able to fly at all. He turned his head, bringing the full force of that golden gaze to bear upon her, and she took a hesitant step back.

"Shendriel's wings," he said at last. "What *are* you?"

Kayla raised a self-conscious hand to toy with the lacings of her vest. "Cestril Alyiah t'Meladon," she said.

He spared her an incredulous glance before he lurched to his feet. Kayla stepped back, but there was a tree in her way. She pressed up against it as the griffin approached her, bringing the sharp edge of his beak to within a hairsbreadth of her nose. "You saved me. Why?"

"Because," she said. "It was the right thing to do." Lady bless, but he was huge. Now that he stood before her, she could see that her head didn't even clear his back.

He gave a derisive snort. "It was not simply conscience that drove you. Not now, and not when you released me. Why did you do it? Did you think you could use it to control me?"

"No," Kayla protested. "I just..." She let out a frustrated cry. "I don't know why. All I know is that it was something I *needed* to do."

The griffin regarded her unblinking, long enough that she began to fidget, before he stepped back and sat, wrapping his tail about his talons. "I do not understand you. You are a princess of this realm, are you not?"

"Yes," she said.

"I killed your people. Why would you free me?"

Kayla shrugged. "I hoped you would stop if I were the one to let you go."

"You put a great deal of faith in me." The talons flexed, cleaving great furrows into the earth. "I thought your kind believed mine to be no more than dumb beasts."

Kayla swallowed, her throat gone dry. "No one who looked into your eyes could believe that."

The griffin snorted. "There were many eyes that stared at me while I enjoyed your father's hospitality. I spent much time staring back and imagining how those eyes would feel beneath my talons. I saw no comprehension there."

Kayla shuddered, forcing away the image. "Then they weren't truly looking."

"Eloquent words," the griffin purred. "So very much like your father's. Did they comfort you as you watched me suffer? Did they start you off on your little game to set me free? Did they reassure you when you were caught out at it? Did they berate you when instead of being forgiven for a childish whim you were punished instead?"

"It wasn't like that!" The outburst startled Kayla as much as it did the griffin. She drew an unsteady breath and forced her fists to unclench.

"It was my father's fault. He started it when he took your mate." Kayla's gaze dropped to her feet. "I was only trying to make things right."

The griffin had gone very still. "Ilaea," he said softly. "You saw her?"

"Yes."

"Before her death?"

Kayla forced herself to swallow. It was a long moment before she could answer. "Yes." She looked up at him. "I am sorry."

The griffin sighed. "Don't be. You did not kill her."

She held a blade in her clenched fist. A blade stained bright red ...

"Yes," Kayla whispered. "I did."

For a frozen instant, all the griffin did was stare. Then Kayla found his claws, each as long as her forearm, embedded in the tree next to her head.

"You had best explain yourself," the griffin hissed. "Quickly."

Kayla closed her eyes, as though it could block out the memory. "She was so hurt when they brought her in. She was dying. And she knew it. I could see it in her eyes. I couldn't stand to watch, so I fled to my room. But the Dreams took me. There is Blood in our family, Old Blood, and it did something to me ... When I woke, it was as though something was driving me, calling me, like it did with you. But I knew I could not save her." She drew a shuddering breath as the memory brought her tears to the surface. "I'm not even sure when I got the sword. All I remember is standing before her cage with the blade in my hand. I thought she was already dead, but she opened her eyes and ... and she just *looked* at me. And then... I thought I heard her say something."

"Shaskaea," the griffin breathed.

Kayla's eyes snapped open. "How did you —"

"Continue."

Nodding, Kayla wiped the tears from her cheeks. "I didn't think she had enough strength left to move. But she pulled herself to her feet and then … she … she presented herself to me. And waited. It was as though she wanted me to end it. She was hurt so badly I knew they'd never notice another wound. So I did it. I took my sword, and I killed her." She stared at her hands, flexing them. She could still feel the hot, sticky mess on them. "There was so much blood."

When she looked up again, the griffin had moved away. Somewhat shocked that something so large could have moved so quietly, Kayla took a tentative step toward him.

"Shaskaea," he said again.

"What does that mean?"

He glanced over his shoulder. "She is the Daughter. Shendriel and Udraea are the Father and Mother; Shaskaea is Their firstborn. She is the one who attends the fallen. If their souls are pure, if they have lived with honour, She slices open the body to release the spirit within."

Kayla went cold. "She is Death."

"Yes." Those golden eyes met hers, pinning her in place. "And She has used your hand as Her talon, it would seem."

Kayla's knees began to tremble, and she sat before they could give out entirely. "Why me?"

"I do not know," he said. "But there was something in your eyes then …" He shuddered, a ripple chasing from his head down to the tip of his tail. "No matter. I must think for a time. Pray be silent while I decide what I am to do with you."

"What —"

"Be silent, *kichani*, lest you wish to die. I am not in a particularly charitable mood."

Kayla considered for a moment that the griffin ravaged the villages and slaughtered half the guard before her father's men had at last captured him, and concluded that antagonizing him was probably not the wisest of ideas. Quietly gathering her tattered dignity around her, she removed herself a small distance and curled up in the grass, shivering with cold.

She was asleep moments later.

—•—

Kayla awoke to find herself alone. A large impression rested in the grass next to her, still carrying the faintest hint of spices. Not knowing what else to do, she set out to find the river.

It wasn't far. She stood at the edge of the gorge, listening to the thunder of water rushing past below. There, to the east, was a range of hills she recognized. Had there not been a forest in the way, she might have been able to see the castle, her home, nestled at the foot of those hills.

Her legs became suddenly weak, and she dropped to the ground. It wasn't her home any longer. She would never be able to go back there. She really was alone.

Kayla buried her head against her knees and wept.

She wasn't sure how long her tears continued, but it was some time before she found she had nothing left to cry. Spent, she rested her cheek against the top of her knees and hugged her legs to her chest.

"How did you come by those bruises?"

Kayla shrieked, tumbling sideways as the resonant voice came out of nowhere. From her sprawl on the ground, she found herself staring up into a pair of golden eyes. *Sweet Lady, how does he move so silently?*

"There were men," she said weakly. "In the woods."

"Ah." He cocked his head at her. "So you are not always the little warrior who faced down her father and his brace of knights?"

Her cheeks burned as she pushed herself off the ground. She turned her face away. "No."

The griffin settled next to her, shifting his wings as he stared out across the river gorge toward the heart of Meladon. "When you came to me, you claimed you were not brave." Kayla started a little, only belatedly realizing that he had understood everything she had said to him that night. She turned to find him watching her. "I think you were mistaken."

"But I'm not," she said. "I never did find the courage to take up the sword."

"Sword?"

Kayla reddened. "My great-great-grandmother's sword. Lyssia. She placed a powerful enchantment on it when it was forged. I knew that if I could take up the sword, it would make me strong. But I was too weak to do it."

"Ah. You *are* mistaken."

Kayla's brow furrowed. "What —?"

"You believe you require a sword to make you strong. Yet in the short time I have known you, I have seen you free a griffin acting upon nothing but faith and then face down a regiment of armed knights with your bare hands." He reared up, spreading his wings as he towered over her. "You may take up a blade. You may even return for this Lyssia someday. But the sword will not give you strength." His wings stretched further, enveloping her in their shadow. "You have more than enough already."

Kayla gaped at him. "But...I've never been so frightened in all my life as I have been since the night I set you free. And that I only did that because the Dreams were calling me."

The griffin shifted closer and closed his talon over her shoulder. Kayla stiffened, but though she could feel the strength in it, he kept his grip light. "And yet," he said, "you did free me. And you didn't need an antique sword to do it. Mark me, Kichani. I could scent the fear in you. You were not under the thrall of those Dreams." He released her. "No. I think the Dreams merely showed you the path. It was you who chose to follow it."

Kayla hugged her arms to her chest. "But I was so scared."

"And what of it?" He stretched, extending his wings to their fullest. Kayla ducked as the golden mass spread over her head. "Courage is not the absence of fear. It is the ability to act in the face of it."

She couldn't think of a thing to say. She remained still, listening to the river while the griffin settled his wings against his back.

"What happens now?" she asked.

"I don't know," the griffin said. "I hadn't thought that far." He lowered his head to rest on his crossed talons. "You must understand, when I returned home to find my mate gone and our aerie burned, my world came to an end. I had nothing left to me but vengeance. My only thought was to kill the one who had taken my mate and paint the skies with his blood. My world became the red haze of bloodlust. There was nothing else but the chase and the kill. No rest until it brought me to him."

Kayla shifted uneasily. The griffin raised his head, and Kayla found herself rocked by the pain in his gaze. "That is how they managed to bring me down. I gave no thought to defending myself. Not once I had my quarry in my sight. But even when they snared me, even when they filled me with their darts that dulled my senses and weighted my limbs, even when they chained me in a cage too small even to let me spread my wings, all I could see was the red. It wasn't until the second night that my vision began to clear. I began to see again." Kayla sat frozen beneath the attention of those golden eyes. "And what I saw was you."

Her mouth was very dry, and it almost hurt to speak. "What does that mean?"

The griffin snorted and looked away. "I was hoping you could tell me."

Unable to help herself, Kayla began to laugh. "When the Gods see fit to inform me of their plans, I assure you you'll be the first to know."

Before she could move, one of his talons lashed out to catch her around the wrist. She froze as he lifted it, increasing the pressure until he stopped just short of pain. "They are so fragile," he murmured. "I could snap these bones without a thought. And yet these hands of yours were strong enough to take my life into them." He released her, and she jerked her wrist back. But he had refocused his attention on the horizon.

"I have spent a long night thinking, Kichani. You truly are a bafflement to me. You are the spawn of the one creature for whose death I long more than any other, and yet I find I have already spared your life twice and given you the name of my mate."

"It wasn't her true name, surely," Kayla said, startled.

The griffin turned his head to glare at her, and she found herself wishing she could sink into the ground. "You humans and your mucking about with names."

"But the true name opens the path to the self," said Kayla. "It gives others power over you."

The griffin snorted. "Do you really see me as the type to do anything simply because someone calls my name?"

She glanced at the talons, currently engaged in carving absent patterns into the bedrock. "Not really, no."

"There are no strangers amongst griffin, so we give our names freely to one another. And few members of other species encounter a griffin long enough to call him anything." He considered for a moment. "Save 'dear Gods' or 'help.'" He turned his unsettling gaze upon her. "We keep our names close not because they give power over us, but because we grant them only to those whom we feel are worthy of the honour of knowing them."

Kayla stared at the ground. "I see."

"My clan is Shenareth," he said. "My name is Variel."

She found herself falling into his eyes. He was wrong. His true name did hold power, but it was not the same as that which Kayla's held over her. She tumbled, lost in the gold, as the weight of his trust settled like a mantle over her shoulders. When she at last returned to herself, she found that those golden eyes were no longer cold. They shone like the sun, enveloping her in their warmth and filling the emptiness inside her until she thought she might burst.

"Variel," she repeated quietly. Then she rose to her feet and delivered him her best curtsey. "I am Kayla."

Variel muttered something in a strange language, and she saw a wary amusement cross his features. "It suits you," he said, and inclined his head toward her. "I am honoured, Kayla."

For the first time in her life, the sound of her true name did not feel like the tug of a lead. It felt instead as though a warm hand had closed over her own.

"Well then," Variel announced, "it seems we must make a decision." He rose to his feet. "There are tales among my kind, and I have spent a long night remembering them. It is said that once, long ago, the griffin dwelled in Tarenath, where Shendriel and Udraea first spread Their wings. But there came a day when griffin set forth into the greater world, led by an ancestor of mine. I had thought the idea mere nonsense, you see, because the tales told of something else. That my ancestor led them in the company of a human." He turned his head to regard her. "It does not seem quite so nonsensical now."

A strange urgency began to fill Kayla, and she found it growing difficult to breathe. "Is that so?"

"It is." He turned his gaze to the skies. "I had thought Tarenath only a legend. Thought myself to be alone now that Ilaea is gone. And yet now I find hope that such a land might exist. That I might find a place where I can belong." He glanced over his shoulder at her. "But it will be a long journey, if such a place exists at all, and I find myself suddenly loathe to attempt it alone."

Kayla laced her fingers together to stop them from trembling. "Do you think, if Tarenath does exist, there might be a place there for a human girl?"

"I think that any creature Shaskaea deems worthy of Her notice will be welcomed gladly by my people." He moved toward her and ducked his head, preening back a loose strand of Kayla's hair with the lightest caress of his beak. "What say you, Kichani? Will you come with me?"

"What is it that you keep calling me?"

"Kichani?" He tossed his head. "Loosely translated, it means 'little one.'"

She frowned. "It sounds like an insult."

"To a griffin, it would be." He peered down his beak at her. "But you *are* very small."

Kayla couldn't argue with that. But something was nagging at her. Something about the sound of the language he kept using. "Do you know what '*Lhiavan K'Ahressan*' means?"

Variel jerked back a little, and stared at her. "Without the atrocious accent? 'Core of light.' It refers to the spirit that dwells within." He turned thoughtful. "I suppose, in layman's terms, it might mean something more akin to 'heart of the griffin.'" His wings arced, cupping her within their shelter. "How did you —"

"It's something I read somewhere." Hesitantly, she reached out her hand. Variel stiffened, but held his ground as she ran her fingers along the gleaming feathers of his wing. After a moment, the wing relaxed, pressing back against her hand as she stroked it. It was the softest thing Kayla had ever touched, and its warmth spread up her arm and through her like an embrace.

"I have lost my mate and the kit she carried thanks to your father," Variel said. He was so close that, though his voice was gentle, she could feel its resonance down to her bones. "And you have sacrificed your family for me. But we needn't be alone." He flexed his wings, closing the circle until Kayla was trapped within the downy warmth. "Come with me."

She looked up into the golden light of his eyes. Really, there was no other answer. She smiled. "I will."

The griffin drew back his wings, and Kayla blinked as the sunlight washed over her. She felt different somehow. Changed. And as she met the warmth of those strange golden eyes, she knew she was not the only one.

She was going to be all right. True, her only friend in the world now appeared to be a bloodthirsty predator with a decidedly twisted sense of humor, but in the grand scheme of things, it wasn't so bad. Whether or not Tarenath actually existed, whether or not they ever found it, the journey was sure to be remarkable. And, at long last, she had found a companion to whom she could give her name.

"So. Where exactly is Tarenath?"

"The stories are rather vague on that point. All they indicate is that it's somewhere to the north."

"Very well then. North it is." A newfound lightness in her step, Kayla struck out toward the trees. Yes, things were going to be just fine.

"Kichani."

Kayla turned, and found her new companion staring at her with a mixture of amusement, irritation, and wry tolerance. He jerked his head to gesture over his shoulder, toward the river gorge and the boundless green wilderness that lay beyond. "North is that way."

Dragon Time

by
Ruth Nestvold

I collect time. My grandfather always said that because I'm a girl, I have no business fixing it, but there's no harm in me collecting. Squirrels collect, girls can too.

What he doesn't acknowledge is that not only do I collect, I watch. Even though I am not supposed to fix time, I am good enough to be his assistant when he does. I watch while he takes apart the pieces of time and puts them back together again, watch as he cleans each small part, a magnifying glass in his eye and a neat row of tools on his workbench which look like those fashioned to build a house or fix a cabinet, only barely big enough for a doll. But my eye is good, and I can give him the jeweler's saw or the collet tool before he even asks.

Because I collect time, I noticed before anyone else when time stopped. It was winter, and the Dragon Queen still had not returned to the capital of Maresburg, when she should have returned at harvest. The hills rising up on either side of the river were dusted with snow, the vineyards below the trees looking like a patchwork of lines, plaid in shades of white and gray. In the valley, the brown of the turned fields was barely visible beneath the thin layer of snow.

So why hadn't the queen returned from the King of Dragons?

People worried, but not overmuch. Queen Dagmar had overspent her summers with her dragon before. Still, she had never stayed with him until the snow fell.

I was at my illicit worktable, a fine watch with designs of the signs of the zodiac embellishing the numbers spread out in pieces in front of me, when I noticed that all the clocks and watches and other timepieces on my table and walls and shelves had ceased to tick. I had several broken timepieces, certainly, but most of those in my collection worked — I had fixed them with my own steady hands, hands not good enough to work the magic of time. Women can be queens and warriors, but they cannot be magicians.

I ran down from my room to my grandfather's workroom. He was bent over the face of a large clock designed for a mantelpiece or a wall, its hands ornate and its numbers dark and commanding. Here too, time had stopped, Opa just had not noticed it yet.

He looked up as I entered, his frown of concentration fading only slowly. "What is it, Katja?"

"The clocks. Look at the clocks."

Opa took the magnifying glass out of his eye and glanced around, cocking his head to one side. The ever-present ticking had stopped, pendulums hung still, and the clocks with hands for seconds were unmoving. His gaze fixed on a fine upright of oak with an inlaid design of beech. "I just fixed that one this morning," he said, a frown adding even more creases to his heavily lined forehead.

"All of mine have stopped too," I said. "Something is the matter."

"But what?" Opa asked. "I am the best time-maker in five valleys. Even the Dragon Queen comes to me."

He was a good man, even if he would not let me fix time. That was more our world's decision than Opa's. At least he let me have my own room with a door that closed and had not yet forced me to choose a husband. In his own way, he was allowing me to practice his magic while still forbidding it, teaching me by letting me be his assistant, telling me which tweezer he needed when I didn't notice myself.

I took one of his dappled hands in both of mine. "I will go down to see Petra, see if time has stopped for her family too."

Opa nodded. "Thank you, Kati."

I took my heavy winter shawl down from the hook by the door, draped it over my head and around my shoulders, and let myself out of the front door of the shop.

My grandfather's shop was perched halfway up the hill on the edge of the village with a perfect view of the dragon hill on the other side of the valley. Beyond our land and everywhere above the houses of the village, crisscrossing lines of snow-blanketed vineyards covered the hills. Opa had once had a shop in Maresburg on Queen Street before I was born, which he sold to one of his assistants to buy the land here in Unterdrachenberg. But even though he was no longer in the capital, people still went out of their way to bring time to him.

I had barely made it down the path to the road through our winter garden of rapunzel and leeks and chard when a handsome young man with a wide smile and even wider shoulders stepped into my path. Georg, the blacksmith's son. I sighed. He had been courting me persistently and with a surprising lack of subtlety since early spring.

Like now.

"Kati!" He reached into his coat and held out the pocket watch he always wore. "My watch has stopped. Do you think your grandfather would have time to fix it?"

At least this time I had to believe his excuse to seek me out. I shook my head. "Time has stopped for us too. Everything. I was on my way down to the Wengerters to see if it is so for them as well."

Georg gazed at me for a moment without speaking. "Everything? All of your timepieces?"

I glanced across the valley at Drachenberg — the seat of the king of dragons, the beings who controlled us and had given us time. What did it mean that Queen Dagmar had not yet returned?

"Everything," I repeated quietly.

"I will accompany you to the vintager," Georg said, the tone of his voice expecting admiration for his gallantry.

I continued to walk, allowing him to fall into step next to me. Why did I find him so uninteresting, now that he had begun to court me? As children we had played together, and while I had often been irritated at his sulkiness when he did not win a game, he and Petra and I had been like siblings the way we fought and loved and hated each other.

Now I only loved Petra and avoided Georg, mourning the playmate of my youth.

I was relieved when we reached the house of Petra's family, and I could say goodbye to Georg. It was a fine, low building of wood and stone with the vineyards that had made them prosperous rising up behind it. Petra Wengerter was not only the daughter of the richest vintager in Unterdrachenberg, she also had the blood of the Valkyries in her veins. With her heritage, she should have been in training for a warrior, but she was much more interested in the grapes growing on her father's hills and improving the quality of the Riesling or the Trollinger her family produced. Since her lineage was that of the Dragon Queens, though, if a new one needed to be chosen, Petra would be among those she would be chosen from.

The house servant (something Opa and I couldn't afford, despite his many loyal customers) answered the door and led me to Petra's laboratory at the back of the house. I suppressed a brief feeling of envy — there were no social sanctions against women running vineyards as there were against women fixing time.

Petra looked up with a smile, her reddish-gold hair catching the winter light from a high window. "Kati! I'll be right with you." She added some drops of something to a vial that appeared to hold a sample of red wine, placed the vial in a wooden frame made for the purpose, and turned to me. "What brings you here?"

"Time has stopped in my grandfather's workshop. I wanted to see if you had the same problem."

Petra gave me a sharp look and rose from her stool. "Stopped?"

I nodded.

Together we went into her family's sitting room and stood in front of the mantle clock of cherrywood. "Stopped," she repeated.

If it was what I thought, my grandfather and I might not be fixing time for a while. The dragons had given us time; they could take it away again.

"I think I will go to Maresburg, see if anyone knows anything," I said.

"I'll come with you. I wanted to consult with the alchemist about some of the experiments I have been attempting to test the sugar and acid content of our wines." She was a true friend. She knew we could not afford a servant to accompany me to the city, and the roads would be safer with two than with one.

We took the valley route, following the path above the road and next to the first terrace on the hills of vineyards. It was a fine winter day, the sun warm on our faces and the snow crunching beneath our boots. The bare trees on the opposite side of the road were dusted with snow, whiter towards the crown than on the lower branches, and in between, darker clumps of pines. Maresburg, the residence of Queen Dagmar when she was not with her dragon, lay down the hill and on the other side of the river below our small valley, perhaps an hour's walk when the wait for the ferry wasn't too long.

We were on the path beneath the vineyards of Petra's family when a huge shadow fell on the snow at our feet, and a horrible screech rent the peaceful morning air. I instinctively pressed myself flat against the rock wall of the vineyard terraces, dragging Petra with me. She seemed to have frozen in place when the dragon winged over us.

The dragon — huge and red, terrifying and beautiful, darkening the sky — gave another loud screech and let loose a wanton belch of fire on the nearby hill, setting the stand of trees at the top in flames and destroying a section of the vineyards in one breath. Petra cried out and I pulled her into my arms, putting a hand over her mouth. If I wasn't mistaken, it was the king of dragons himself, and he was in a foul mood.

I had never seen a dragon so close in my life. As a child, I used to watch for them from my upstairs room in Opa's house, loved to see the way they would circle Drachenberg before landing and disappearing into their lair, but as I grew older and had to help Opa more on our plot of land or in his workshop, there was less time for lying on my bed and gazing out the window watching for dragons.

But this one wasn't just a beautiful silhouette on the horizon. I prayed to the gods of thunder and fire and the goddess of battle that he would not see us. The winter day had grown warm, and even in the shade of the terraced hills I was sweating, while Petra in my arms shivered with terror. Through our thick clothing, I smelled the tangy stench of fear.

Another petrifying screech tore through the sky, lower and louder, and I looked to the south where the dragon call had come from. A huge black dragon was winging its way toward us, larger even than the red, its cries filling the air. With one part of my mind, I had to wonder if we would survive this morning, but with another, I could only stare in awe at the beauty of the creatures in the sky above us. As long I could remember, dragons had never flown in the direction of the city, and now here was not just one but two of them. The dragons, only male, had to take human form to mate with women, but since the times of the Dragon Wars and the attempts by Siegfried and his warriors to wipe them off the face of the earth, they avoided men. Once, it was said, dragons had lived among us in their human form and only taken on their dragon form if needed, but now the opposite was true.

The black dragon flew straight toward the red dragon and past him, stopping in mid-air and blocking his path. Keeping him from continuing on to the city with his murderous breath and his bad mood.

The two dragons hung in the air above us, darkening the morning sky. I had never seen anything so beautiful in all the sixteen years of my life. Red and black they hung, their huge wings outspread, almost translucent in the winter sunlight. Their smooth, scaly bodies glinted and danced as they faced off, graceful and huge.

The screeching became deafening, and Petra slumped in my arms, fainting from fear. I staggered and leaned against the stones of the terrace, trying to protect her as much as I could; it could draw attention to us. But the dragons seemed very caught up in each other, extending their necks in what looked like a threat, wings flapping in the sky to stay in place. Then all the energy and anger suddenly seemed to go out of the red dragon. His head slumped to his chest, and he allowed the black to herd him back to the dragon hill, both of them silent.

All the energy went out of me as well, and I slid down to the ground, snow and all, no longer able to hold Petra upright. I took her shoulders and tried to shake her awake, when that didn't work, even slapped her face. No response. I didn't know what to do. I found myself crying, my friend's head nestled in my lap, my toes and backside growing cold.

Luckily, another traveler heading for Maresburg found us before we had to freeze to death next to the road.

"Ho! What are you doing sitting in the snow?"

I looked up, my heart beating rapidly. A finely dressed stranger was approaching us on the path. He was tall and dark, but at that moment, I couldn't see anything threatening about him — the sight of another person who could bring help was too much of a relief. "My friend fainted when the dragons scorched that stand of trees above us."

The young man's gaze followed the direction of my gesture, his amber eyes narrowing. "Dragons, you say?"

"Yes, there were two fighting in the sky here, one black and one red. Petra passed out at the noise they were making."

The stranger looked down at Petra, a faint smile turning up his lips. "Then we will have to wake her, won't we?"

Before I could react, he pulled Petra up and shook her so hard I thought her head would come off.

"Wait, stop!" I scrambled up and stumbled. I wondered how long I had been sitting next to the stone wall — my feet were numb.

Petra whimpered and opened her eyes, and my anger turned to gratitude, that fast.

"No!" she squealed when she saw the man holding her. I had to say, I didn't see any reason in his countenance to squeal "no" that quickly, and I knew from many long, giggled conversations in her father's attic that Petra wasn't instinctively prudish. The alchemist she wanted to visit in town seemed to be her latest conquest.

She pulled away from him and put her arms around me, leaning her head on my shoulder. The dark-haired man gave me a lop-sided grin.

I returned it and stuck out my hand around the cringing form of my friend. "Thank you. I'm Katja of Unterdrachenberg, and this is my friend Petra Wengerter."

The stranger took my hand in his own warm, strong, capable hand and smiled at me — a smile I felt down to my freezing toes. "It's nice to meet you," he said. "I'm Lothar."

"Are you from Maresburg?"

"No."

"What brings you to these parts?"

The smile left his face, and he glanced at Petra's back. "Business," he said shortly.

Which reminded me that I shouldn't be trusting a stranger on the road. I released the hand I was surprised to notice I still held. Under my cloak, I felt for the dagger in the pouch at my waist.

"We need to return to Unterdrachenberg to tell Petra's father about what has happened to his vineyards," I said.

"I'll accompany you," Lothar said.

I shook my head. "No need. It's not far. We'll be fine the rest of the way home. Thank you again for your help."

He nodded. "Perhaps you can help me in return — I'm looking for a clockmaker. Can you tell me where I can find one?"

A stranger who wouldn't state his business? No, I wouldn't lead him to Opa. "There is a shop on Queen Street, close to the livery. But they probably won't be able to help — time seems to have stopped. My friend and I were on our way to Maresburg to see if anyone there knows more when the dragon singed her family's vineyards and scared her half to death."

At my words, Petra straightened up and pulled out of my arms. "I'm fine now, Kati," she said.

"But we would still be sitting in the snow if it weren't for Lothar."

"She would have come to herself soon enough." Lothar graced us with a slight bow. "Well, ladies, I must be on my way. It was nice to make your acquaintance."

"Good luck with your *business*," I said, not without a hint of sarcasm. Lothar only smiled.

—•—

That afternoon, we learned that a messenger had come from the dragons of Drachenberg with the news that Queen Dagmar was dead. Petra brought the news to me, in tears as she ran up to our house between the rows of winter vegetables. I saw her from my upstairs window, where the pieces of time were spread out before me, and hurried down the stairs and out the door to meet her. As she threw herself into my arms, the bells of the dragon shrine in the middle of the village began to toll, and I knew what she was going to tell me before she got the words out.

"The queen is dead!"

All day, ever since time had stopped, I had been afraid of something like this. If a new queen was needed, Petra was one of the candidates.

"I can't be Dragon Queen," she sobbed into my shoulder.

I held her tight, maneuvering her into the house where the walls were thick and a fire burned. "Think, Petra," I said when I had Opa's door closed behind us. "How likely is it that it will come to that? Maybe the dragons don't want a new queen. Besides, you're not the only one with the blood of the Valkyries in your veins, it could easily be another unmarried woman chosen."

Petra hiccoughed a few times while the linen of my blouse grew damp from her tears, and then she raised her head to look in my eyes. "You're right. I shouldn't panic. I haven't been myself since we came so close to being eaten alive by dragons this morning."

But as it turned out, she had every right to panic. The news of the queen's death was soon followed by the news that the elders of the city had decided a new queen needed to be found for the king of dragons, and all the unmarried maidens older than fourteen descended from the Valkyries — fit to be a dragon bride — were to come to the Queen's Castle in Maresburg the next day.

—•—

I had never been in the Queen's Castle before, and despite the circumstances, I couldn't help staring. Petra had begged me to accompany her dressed as her servant. I had been more than happy to go along with the scheme; not only did I want to be with her if she needed me, I was curious.

The walls were thick and high, higher than the height of three men, and covered in gleaming tapestries that shimmered like the scales of a dragon. Here too was magic, even if it wasn't deemed such. No smells of onions and cabbage lingered in these halls; instead, they were perfumed with incense and the luxurious scent of burning wax candles. Here there were no simple tubs of fat with a wick, and the cooking and eating was done somewhere far away, not like in the small house I shared with Opa.

Petra clung to my arm, and I suspected she was seeing little of her surroundings.

We were led to a huge audience chamber with long, thin arched windows allowing the winter sunlight to pour into the room. The city elders were seated at a table at the front of the room, but the young women from whom they would choose their future queen were left to stand. Most of the girls looked as scared as my friend; it appeared that the fear of dragons outweighing the honor of being Dragon Queen was widespread. My own hopes that Petra would easily be able to decline the honor to a maiden more eager plummeted.

Once all had arrived, Mayor Creglinger rose and cleared his throat. "As you all know, a great tragedy has befallen our land with the death of Queen Dagmar. While we must mourn, for one of you it also means the opportunity to become the Dragon Queen in her stead. It is our hope that with a young woman to take the place of the queen, the king of dragons will see fit to give time back to us and refrain from randomly destroying the property of the citizens here in the land of the Seven Valleys."

I looked around me at the words and saw no smiles of anticipation. Instead, these girls looked like they were being led to their execution.

They weren't the only ones who weren't happy. To my surprise, a member of the council rose, an objection on his lips. "Honored Mayor, after the wanton destruction by the King of Dragons, there are those who question the wisdom of always appeasing the dragons."

"And what would you suggest, Councilman Roth?" Mayor Creglinger rapped out. "Attacking them?"

A huge sigh of dismay arose from those present, but Roth, a broad man, obviously strong, didn't cringe. He looked like the kind of man who would have wanted to join the ranks of the Valkyries if bearing weapons were not forbidden to men.

Councilman Roth drummed the side of his fist on the edge of the table. "He destroyed valuable land ... "

"And we need to calm him down before he destroys more." The other members of the council nodded enthusiastically. "We will proceed."

One by one, the maidens of Valkyrie blood were called forward to the table at the front of the room and questioned. Very few had actually trained as warriors — given the peace enforced by the dragons in the land, there was little need for soldiers. After the Dragon Wars, men had been banned from taking arms by order of the dragons, and only

Valkyrie women were allowed to work the Watch or the city defenses. But with the dragons strong enough to destroy any army breaching the peace, few chose to be Valkyrie in deed as well as in blood.

"Petra Wengerter of Unterdrachenberg."

The friend I had played with since before I became aware of time stepped forward, even paler than normal, her freckles standing out on her white skin. She was brave enough; probably only I knew how near to tears she was.

When I heard the direction of the questioning, my heart sank. They knew all about how the two of us had witnessed the king of dragons putting a corner of her family's vineyards in flames, knew that she was the heiress of those vineyards, and they were quite ready to see a significance in that beyond a confused dragon made mad by grief. By the time she returned to me, I was near tears myself.

These "wise men" thought it was a sign; they were going to choose my friend.

I don't know what I thought at that moment. I was little more than no-one; the granddaughter of a magician, it was true, but in my own right, nothing. It didn't matter to me. I started forward, ready to tell the city elders what I thought of their signs and portents. I had made it halfway to the long table when Valkyrie hands — trained Valkyries — grabbed my upper arms, pinching painfully. At the same time, the carved double-doors of the audience chamber crashed open. Between my guards, I craned my head around. It was Lothar, our suspicious savior of the day before.

He wore a black cape which swirled around his ankles as he walked, and his glistening dark hair curled at the collar of his fine linen shirt. He strode to the front of the room, as I had wanted to do, easily shaking off the Valkyrie guards who trailed him.

Mayor Creglinger rose, his expression irritated. "Yes, Messenger of Dragons?"

I started. Messenger of Dragons? Why would a *man* be acting as messenger to the dragons?

Lothar placed his hands flat on the table opposite the mayor. "I heard you intend to choose a new queen for the king of dragons. Let me assure you, the king of dragons does not ask for such a boon."

Mayor Creglinger, tall and thin and homely, drew himself to his full height and looked down his nose at Lothar of Oberdrachenberg. "Why would you think such a thing?"

Lothar removed his hands from the oak table and straightened to his full height, several inches more than that of the mayor and more substantial. He seemed to be steeling himself not to recoil at the mayor's nearness. "When the dragons asked me to bring the news of the queen's death, no mention was made of seeking a new queen."

"But we must appease him," the mayor insisted.

Lothar shook his head, his expression pained. "If the king of dragons loved his queen, how is some young woman, a complete stranger, going to help?"

I saw quite a few looks of incomprehension on the faces of the male council members and had to suppress a very inappropriate laugh of bitterness: obviously, most of the men here in the audience chamber thought it would help quite a bit.

Lothar's voice changed, filling the large room. "You must put an end to this farce."

It was a huge voice, almost a roar, and I looked at him more closely. Shining dark hair, amber eyes, an air of command; much more than any simple messenger. As long as I could remember, it had only been the queen or one of her handmaidens who delivered messages from the dragons — never a man.

"You!"

Now all eyes in the audience chamber were upon me, including those of Lothar.

"Ah, it is Katja Uhrmacher, the granddaughter of the greatest magician of time in the Land of the Seven Valleys."

I stared. "How do you know that?"

"There is a portrait of the two of you on the wall of the clockmaker's shop you directed me to. You must have forgotten."

I had. And he had very effectively taken the march on me. But how could I voice my outlandish suspicion anyway — that here in our midst we had a dragon himself?

"The king of dragons is much more in need of a clockmaker than a new bride," Lothar said now slowly, his gaze fixed on me. "Tell me, do you have any talent in the magic of fixing time?"

Mayor Creglinger gave a blustering snort. "She's a girl!"

The "messenger" ignored him, but I thought I saw him flinch at the sound of the mayor's voice. "Do you?"

I felt myself pursing my lips before I answered the question with one of my own. "Why?"

He gave me a lop-sided smile. "You must admit, a female with the ability to fix time would be much more appropriate for my purposes than a male."

Dragon or not, he wanted to bring back a clockmaker to the dragon's lair, where human men were not welcome — to fix the time they had given us and that *they* controlled?

When I didn't answer, his gaze wandered slowly to Petra, still standing in front of the long table with its collection of city elders in their long robes and long faces, serious and full of themselves. His gaze drew mine, and again I saw the dearest friend I had ever had, pale, an expression of frozen fear on her face.

He turned back to me. "Of course, we could also allow the honored mayor and elders of Maresburg to chose a new dragon queen and hope that would solve everyone's problems." He cocked his head to one side, a single dark eyebrow arched and a calculating smile on his fine lips. He was blackmailing me.

I swallowed. "You want me to go to the dragon's lair?"

He nodded.

I admired the dragons from afar, but visiting their cave was another matter entirely. How did I know one wouldn't singe me by mistake, as the King of Dragons had singed the hill behind Unterdrachenberg? The queen had come and gone as she pleased, it was true, and no harm had ever come to her, but the handmaidens she had taken with her had not all survived the experience well, returning to Maresburg weak-minded or hysterical.

"Well?" Lothar asked.

I swallowed again and licked my lips. "How am I supposed to help? It is the dragons who control time."

He shrugged. "Yes, but we don't *fix* it."

A gasp went up from the crowd in the room at his unintentional admittance that he was a dragon.

"Just one minute!" the mayor called out, striding around the table to Lothar's side. "You claim to be a dragon?"

Lothar shrugged. "I didn't want to, but I'm afraid I just have."

"How do we know you are what you say you are? It's well known that dragons cannot stand the company of men."

A huge, unholy grin spread across Lothar's face. "You want me to prove it?"

Before the mayor could protest or demand, the air around the dark-haired man began to shimmer and vibrate, and those of us near him stepped back instinctively. Then Lothar himself began to transform, growing larger and darker. Men and women both began to scream, hide under the tables, and run for the doors and the farthest reaches of the room.

For my part, I felt frozen to the spot, and could only stare at the metamorphosis. Soon, a black dragon over twice as tall as a man stood in the middle of the audience hall, its incandescent scales glinting in the winter sunlight pouring in through the high windows. The creature — Lothar — was so beautiful up close it almost hurt me to look at him. To call him "black" was much too simplistic: his scales shimmered with a kaleidoscope of hues, like diamonds bedded on black velvet. His long neck was graceful, his wings were folded tight against his body, and a long tail curled around his legs. The bright yellow eyes in the triangular head regarded me seriously. My breath caught in my throat.

After the screamers had fainted or run away, it was eerily silent in the room. The dragon and I stared at each other, and I thought I recognized the Black that had herded the King of Dragons away from the vineyards of Petra's family yesterday.

Lothar had proven his point, and the air around him began to shimmer and pulse again. The shiny, scaly blackness that had filled the room faded and shrank, and soon he once again looked like a normal man.

"By Fafnir," I said, hearing the catch in my own voice.

The black dragon looked around the audience chamber and then nodded. "Yes, you will do."

Around us, few were still left standing. I caught a glimpse of the mayor cowering behind a statue, while the young women who had surrounded me had either disappeared or lay on the floor like leaves scattered by a fall wind. Some stood flattened against the walls, eyes wide, as if Lothar were still a huge, black, scaly monster.

Then my gaze caught on Petra in a puddle of wool and linen on the floor. I ran over to her and knelt down.

"You bully!" I railed at Lothar. "You know how afraid she is of dragons!"

He nodded. "That's the point. They were about to try to marry her off to my — the King of Dragons."

His verbal slip didn't escape me. "My — the? Who are you, *Lothar*?"

The dragon's gaze didn't falter as he completed the sentence he had originally started. "My father."

We stared at each other until he looked away. "I need help. My father tried to turn back time, and in the process, he stopped it, broke it, I don't know. He's mad with grief over the death of my mother, no longer responsible for his actions." He looked back at me, his amber eyes suddenly terribly sad. "You have to believe me."

In his human form, he resembled Queen Dagmar, although he was dark where she had been fair. But his regular features, the high bridge of his nose, the cleft in his chin, those were from the queen his mother, given a masculine cast. With a wrench in my chest, I suddenly realized I found him as beautiful as a man as he was as a dragon.

I drew in a deep breath. "You kept the King of Dragons away from the city, away from Maresburg, didn't you?"

He looked down at the floor, past Petra's prone form, to some undefined point between us and the council table. "But I didn't keep him away from the vineyards of Unterdrachenberg."

He had protected the city from his own father. He was good, he was beautiful, and he was a dragon. The Prince of Dragons.

Meant for one with the blood of Brynhilde in her veins.

My chest was feeling tighter and tighter, and I couldn't look at him. "I believe you," I said. "But before I can help you, I'm afraid I will have to ask you to help with Petra again."

—•—

Many people fear the dragons, many people resent them, many even hate them. Despite what they have done for us, there are few who love them. They're too powerful; it makes us cowardly and rebellious. Take the name "Siegfried" for example. You would think, given the fact that he led the unsuccessful wars against the dragons, no one would give their child the name of the most famous loser in history — but the opposite is the case. It's a small, harmless rebellion, the kind we humans are good at and that makes us feel better.

Petra belonged to the vast majority that feared the dragons, and now that she knew who Lothar was, she refused to travel with him. When we returned to Unterdrachenberg to get my tools, we left her in the care of her aunt in the city.

On the way, Lothar explained to me what had happened.

"He thought he must be powerful enough to bring my mother back to life again," he said with a catch in his voice as we left the ferry. "Shouldn't controlling time mean being able to turn time back? But when he tried to manipulate the World Clock, he found that it wouldn't go backwards, and in a fit of rage, he destroyed it."

"Destroyed it? How destroyed is destroyed?" While I was proud of my abilities in fixing time, a clock smashed by the force of a dragon's tail could well be beyond repair.

"He twisted the hands of the clock back and back and back until something broke. Then he pushed the clock over. The side is smashed, and the hands hang limply at a quarter to nine."

I breathed a sigh of relief. "He was in his human form when he did this?"

Lothar gave me a sardonic look. "He had to be. He couldn't manipulate the hands of a clock with his dragon claws."

In the distance we could already see the singed hilltop where his father had vented his sorrow. What was left of the snow in the rutted road crunched beneath our boots.

I had never *loved* the dragons until now, but I had always admired them, their grace in flight, their freedom, the shimmering scales of their bodies. And that had always made me wonder why our worlds were so separate when they had once been so close.

"Tell me." I wrapped my arms around my body under my cape and felt the sting of the cold on my cheeks. "You and your father are men, at least sometimes. Legend has it you used to be men most of the time. Why do you hate human men so much?"

"Hate? Fear is more like it. Siegfried and his heroes almost wiped us off the face of the earth before we killed him and won the Human Wars."

I stopped in my tracks, despite the nip in the air and the frozen snow and mud beneath my boots. "*You* fear men?"

Lothar looked at me as if I had gone mad. "Of course we do. They are our natural enemies."

"And why not women?"

"They never hunted us," he said simply. "Besides, it was Brynhilde's alliance with Fafnir which brought about our victory in the war." He grinned. "And we need them to propagate."

I blushed and turned away. My stomach cramped at the thought of Lothar "propagating" with another woman. For my own peace of mind, I shouldn't be going with him to the dragon lair, shouldn't be doing anything with him.

My feet were cold and I began walking again, not looking at him.

"Time was a part of the treaty," he continued now. "That's why we have to fix it, give it back to humans. If we don't, men may begin to hunt us again."

"Do you really think so?" Of course, I knew the history, but the effect on the dragons themselves had never occurred to me. I thought of them as superior and unafraid of anything; the view of Drachenberg from our modest house was a view of the seat of power.

The Prince of Dragons gestured to the hill ahead of us. Near the top, scorched trees and a corner of the vineyard were clearly visible. "After what my father did? Yes. Peace and time, that was the deal, for the promise never to attack dragons again. But now time has stopped and peace is endangered."

"Because we no longer live together and fear each other as a result," I murmured.

Lothar shot me a sharp look but said nothing.

When we reached the outskirts of Unterdrachenberg, I knew the news had traveled faster than we had, rushing here while I took Petra to her aunt. Everyone stared at us as we walked through the village, not daring to come forward.

All except for one.

When we were almost to Opa's land, Georg stepped into our path, his usual smile for me absent from his face. Beside me, Lothar flinched.

"So, you're consorting with dragons now?" Georg said.

I shook my head. "I'm going to try to fix the World Clock. The dragons don't want human men in their lair."

"You? Fix time?"

I cut him off before he could say the damning words, "but you're a girl." "I don't know if I can, but I have watched Grandfather do the work for many years. And if no men are allowed in the lair, I may be the best hope we have."

"Helping the enemy," Georg muttered.

"No enemy," I said. "Good day, Georg."

I took Lothar's elbow and stepped around Georg to open the gate to Opa's small piece of property. "Would you wait for me outside while I get my tools? My grandfather is old and I don't know how he would react if I told him I was going to the lair of the dragons."

Lothar nodded and stepped over to the protection of the hedge on the eastern side of our property.

I let myself in the door on the side of the house and crept up the stairs making as little noise as possible. Most of my tools were laid out in a neat row on my worktable. I took a leather satchel from a hook on the wall; in went the magnifying glass, the hairspring tweezers (even big clocks have small parts), the sleeve wrench, the winder, the calipers, and everything else I thought I might need. The heft and the weight of them comforted me. I wasn't afraid precisely, but how was I to know what awaited me in the den of dragons?

No, it was a lie — I *was* afraid. Afraid of the unknown, afraid of being one small human surrounded by creatures who could toast me with a cough.

And especially afraid of how I would feel when all this was over.

I was stepping out of the side door of the house, when Opa came out of his workroom and saw me.

"Kati, my dear, I didn't know you were home! Where is Petra?" Then his gaze caught on the satchel slung over my shoulder, and his eyes narrowed. "Where are you going with my tools?"

"Opa, you don't understand, I'm not running away ..."

Then out of the corner of my eye, I saw a small army led by Georg at the bottom of the valley, armed with pickaxes and hoes and pitchforks.

I should have known that Georg had the makings of a dragon slayer.

There was no time to argue with Opa. I spun around and raced down the stairs, ignoring the shouted obscenities following me, my heart breaking. Opa never swore at me.

"Lothar!" I yelled. "Be careful! They're coming for you!"

He glanced down the hill, and even as I ran to join him, the air around him began to shimmer. "You must get on my back, Kati!"

As he spoke, he was transforming, and my name turned into a roar. By the time I reached him, he was huge and black and threatening, the dark silver scales of his neck glittering, and the would-be dragon-slayers stopped in their tracks between the rows of leeks and chard.

I clambered onto his back and clutched him tightly around the neck. "Don't hurt them, Lothar, please."

I thought I saw him nod, before he turned to gallop down the hill towards Georg and his band. I closed my eyes.

Then the air was whistling through my hair, tearing strands from my braid, and I opened my eyes again. Below us, Georg and his heroes had scattered before the charge of the black dragon and trampled our leeks in the process.

And we were flying.

As we climbed into the sky, Unterdrachenberg grew smaller and smaller, turning from a collection of doll houses to a collection of blocks, to a pattern of shapes between hills of snow and trees and barren vines. I clung to Lothar's neck with my gloved and freezing hands, my ankles locked around his back below his wings and my cheeks tingling cold from the wind.

But I was flying. *Flying.*

In a matter of minutes, we had crossed the valley and were circling Drachenberg as I had always seen the dragons do from my upstairs window. Lothar touched down next to the mouth of a cave; I slipped off his back, my knees weak, and clung to his neck for a moment. I felt a moist nose against the back of my neck, like a friendly horse, comforting, and I lifted my head and sighed.

"Thank you," I murmured and released him.

Lothar trundled away from me, ungainly on land in his dragon form, and the air around him began to shimmer.

"Thank *you*," he said, a man again, his voice low and quiet. "I hadn't noticed the men coming."

He took my hand and led me into the cave. It was dark and narrow, but ahead I could see light. Lothar's palm was warm against mine, and his fingers curled around the back of my hand.

Towards the back of the entrance passageway, a blue dragon lay curled, and his head went up as we approached.

"All's well, Hilmar. I bring a clockmaker."

The blue dragon nodded and laid his head back down on his front legs. I swallowed.

We came out into a huge chamber, much lighter than I would have imagined in the middle of the mountain. High up on the right side were a series of wide slits which let light in, and torches burned along the walls at regular intervals.

But the size and the light didn't surprise me as much as the women.

Women weaving, women cooking, women looking after small children — eight of them altogether, apparently living in the dragon's lair.

"Wives of some of the other dragons here," Lothar explained to me as we made our way through the chamber.

"And they all live here?"

"Where did you think they would live?" Lothar asked.

I blushed. "But, the stories ..."

Lothar gave a very dragon-like snort. "That we impregnate village women and then come and steal their babies?" He shook his head. "The truth is much more mundane. We dragons tend to be a loyal bunch. Most of us would be quite happy with one woman for a lifetime, if it weren't for the fact that we normally live twice as long as humans. The root of my father's grief," he added quietly.

We passed through the large chamber and entered a smaller one the size of Opa's house. On the far side lay an impressive clock, which upright would have stood taller than a man and over four times as thick. It was the most beautiful clock I had ever seen in my life, with a huge face with twenty-four hours rather than twelve and an intricate system of inner dials for the minutes. In the center of the face was a vivid painting of the dragon Fafnir defeating Siegfried, and the hand that counted the hours was in the shape of the sun.

I laid my satchel on the ground and knelt down next to the broken glass of the clock face. Carefully, I removed the cracked pieces and laid them aside so they wouldn't come loose and cut me while I worked. Then before I could move around to the back of the clock and remove the plate to check the condition of the gears, I found myself in tears on my knees.

Opa surely thought I'd stolen his tools to run away with a dragon — the lowest of the low. But wasn't it what I had done? Yes, I was to fix the world clock, but if Lothar had asked me to run away with him …

No, I couldn't think about it. For as long as I could remember, Opa was the only one I had.

Then there were two strong arms around me, pulling me against a wide chest, and the shock and fear of the last few hours — including my fear of the man who now held me — took their toll and I was sobbing, wrenching sobs that hurt escaping my chest.

"Shhh, shhh, Kati," Lothar said, rocking me. "If you can't fix the clock, we can do without time. It's not important. We still have the days and the seasons and the sun in the sky."

He murmured like that for a while until slowly I quieted. I wiped my face and sat up, not looking at him. I was terribly ugly when I cried, not elegantly ethereal like Petra: my skin turned blotchy and my eyes were red and swollen.

"It's Opa," I said. "He thought I was running away with you, I know it." I rubbed my eyes to try to keep the tears back.

"Any everyone knows what becomes of girls who run away with

dragons." Lothar's hand found my chin and he turned my face to his, blotches and all. "Do you want to try to fix the clock, or should I bring you home?"

I drew a deep breath. "I want to try to fix the clock."

Lothar gave me a fleeting kiss on the lips and rose. "Thank you. Do you need my help?"

I shook my head and gave a last hiccoughing sob. "Having you around will only make me nervous." The memory of his lips on mine, however short, was distraction enough.

With Lothar gone, I dried my face and set to work. Not that I knew what I should do: this was the World Clock, after all, and while I knew the principles of time we humans used, the springs and verges and escapements, I didn't know how dragon time worked.

At least Lothar had given me the freedom to fail.

The most logical thing to do would be to see what it looked like inside, if the mechanism was anything like I was used to. I pried the plate on the back off and was confronted with a construction vaguely like some of the larger clocks I had collected on my shelves. But the dragon clock had a long, heavy metal piece that made no sense to me — it was totally different from the springs or chains I was used to. It had a wheel, but where were the balance and the verge which kept the wheel in motion?

Perhaps the long metal piece was what moved the wheel. I examined the piece and the wheel, and sure enough, there was a place at the bottom of the wheel to connect them. I screwed the long, heavy piece back on with the tools I had brought, but it did no more than lie there.

To fix it, I would have to get the dragon clock upright again. I sat back on my heels. I couldn't lift this thing by myself, even if I were the most brilliant magician of time in all the Seven Valleys.

No, I wouldn't cry, not again.

I squeezed my eyes shut until the temptation passed and then rose, smoothing out my skirts. Out there in the main hall of the dragon lair were quite a number of beings who could help me right the World Clock.

—•—

Hilmar's wife Gerlinde burped her baby on her shoulder while Rudolf and the King of Dragons himself looked on as I tried to bend the upper part back into what I hoped was its correct shape. Hilmar was still guarding the entrance to the lair and couldn't help me right the clock, so Gerlinde had fetched the other two.

When I saw the clock upright again, it occurred to me that the long heavy part was a kind of pendulum, and the Dragon Clock must draw its magic from the power of the earth. But how did the rest of it work?

"You must forgive me for stopping time," the king murmured in his sad voice. "I was not myself."

I shook my head. "There is no need to ask my forgiveness. But you might want to reimburse the Wengerters of Unterdrachenberg for the damage you did."

The king nodded thoughtfully. He didn't seem the least offended that I, the mere granddaughter of a clockmaker, had just told him what he should do. I could hardly believe my own impertinence, but the normal rules of the world seemed to be suspended today.

"We've lost the craft," Rudolf said, watching me carefully as I worked. "It's good that you humans have kept it alive."

"But we still need your magic." I clicked the strange verge part that looked like an anchor into the teeth at the top of the wheel and pushed the pendulum to start it moving. When the clock began its regular "tick tock, tick tock," I nearly burst into tears in relief.

I sighed and leaned my head back on my shoulders, closing my eyes. Thus I felt Lothar before I saw him.

"You fixed time!" he said, embracing me.

I smiled at the feel of the hard chest behind me — smiled and almost cried again. He felt too good, and I was not of the blood of the Valkyries. "I fixed a clock."

I turned away, back to the clock, something I loved, something to do, something to keep me from thinking about what I couldn't have.

"Katja." Lothar's rumbling voice forced me to turn in his direction, my heart cramping in my chest. I took a deep breath.

When my eyes met his, he spoke again. "I am going to request the council of Maresburg award you official status as a magician of time. Drachenberg obviously needs a clockmaker."

"Me?"

"Certainly you. You fixed time, didn't you?"

"I fixed a clock."

Lothar took my elbow. "You will excuse us?" he said to the others and led me out of the cavern where the clock stood.

"Where are we going?"

"We need to talk." Lothar walked with me to the entrance of the cavern and out into the daylight again. In the valley below us, the bells of the dragon shrines were ringing, and we could even hear the singing and shouting of the people. The magnitude of what I had done finally struck me; I couldn't remember ever having been so happy in my life. I *was* a magician of time!

Beside me, Lothar drew a deep breath and I glanced at him sharply. He almost seemed nervous. "I've been thinking about what you said about fearing each other, and I think you're right."

"I'm right?"

"With dragons and humans living apart as we do, the fear and hatred will only grow. I have decided to take a house in Maresburg. Will you share it with me?"

I looked away, tears starting in my eyes. Again. I wiped them away angrily — how dare he destroy my moment of happiness? "I know I don't have blood of the Valkyries in my veins, but I can't shame my opa."

Lothar took my shoulders and turned me to face him. "Kati, as my wife."

I didn't have an answer for that one. "Oh. But Opa ..."

"While you were working, I returned to Unterdrachenberg to speak to him and explain. He asked me to apologize for his behavior, but I would have to get your permission to marry you, not his."

Lothar must have seen the answer he wanted in my reddened eyes, because he smiled.

I still collect time. I love the way the parts fit, large and small, the precision of it, all working together, like magic. Of course, no matter how much time I collect, it won't give me more with my Prince of Dragons. We will just have to make do with what we have, whatever that ends up being.

I'm just glad I'm not the dragon in this relationship.

Companions
Unexpected

Robes and Wands

by

Janet Elizabeth Chase

Purvis hurried to catch up. He often let himself fall behind to avoid stepping on the heels of his master. At seventeen, Purvis towered over Minden's sparse frame by a foot. The last time his master had brought him to town was two seasons ago. Minden was a fine master but when your life consisted mainly of chores and studies, you missed talking with other people.

It wouldn't be long now before he would rise to full mage. The thought excited Purvis but scared him as well. He trusted that Minden would not let him go until he was ready. Minden's subtle voice grabbed him from his daydreaming.

"Name them." Minden's voice was calm.

"Uh, um." Purvis lapsed back into silence. He hadn't heard the question.

"Daydreaming again, Purvis?"

"Uh, well." It was no good lying to Minden. "Yes, master."

"It is a beautiful day for it." The old mage chuckled quietly. "But come now. Name the five wands of the first level."

"First level." Too easy, Purvis thought. "Water, air, earth, fire, time."

"Fourth level." Minden responded without missing a beat.

"Fourth," Purvis paused to sort them in his head when the rumbling of a loaded cart jolted him and he leapt to the side of the road.

"Ah. We've arrived." Minden said, sounding mildly surprised. He straightened his robe, brushing imaginary dust from it. The warding spell kept the garment perfectly clean. Purvis followed at a respectful distance, as his master headed for the tea shoppe.

—•—

The jingle of doorbells announced their arrival. The shopkeeper, Trinna, poked her head out from the back room. She gave an enormous grin when she saw them. Truth be told, everything about Trinna was enormous. Purvis braced himself for the inevitable hug.

"He brought you!" Trinna said joyfully as she embraced Purvis. When she released him, he let out his breath. Trinna turned to his master and said, "Fa Minden. I have your packet ready. But first, a new mix I think you will like. Sit, relax. I'll check the water."

Purvis watched as she went to the back room, making sure she was gone. He fell into one of the four overstuffed chairs Trinna had in the front room of the shoppe. "Oof. I swear she's getting stronger."

"She's very fond of you." Minden smiled, turning to gaze out the large front window. His smile quickly fled. "Purvis, go help Mistress Trinna in the back room." It was not the calm, pleasant voice Purvis was used to. Purvis stood and hesitated. "Go. Now." Minden took a purposeful step towards him. The look in his master's eyes told him not to question. Purvis went.

A moment after he had left the room he heard the doorbells chime again, then he heard voices. Trinna held him back and peered into the front room. She pulled back quickly and shook her head. Her meaning was clear. Purvis stood just on the other side of the doorway, listening. Minden spoke first.

"Our conversation is long over, Breen."

"*Fa*. Please," came an eerily quiet voice.

"When you've earned the title." Minden spoke evenly. "Speaking of titles. Grimmel. Where is your novice wand?"

Purvis heard a hiss from a third man. "You were always picking on me, old man." His voice had a distinct whine to it.

"Now, now, Grimmel. He doesn't know you've risen," Breen said proudly.

"Risen? And who finished your training? Certainly not you, Breen." Minden had a slight chuckle in his voice. "You haven't the patience."

"I have many things you are not aware of, old man." Breen said.

"You will address me as Fa Minden. I *have* earned the title." Minden's voice was cold. Purvis fought not to look into the room.

Breen was momentarily silent. "I didn't come here to fight." A slight pause. "Fa Minden. I wish to finish our conversation."

"The conversation is finished. I don't have the wand. I won't make the wand," Minden said flatly.

"But you could." Breen let the implication hang in the air.

"You are wasting my time, Breen," Minden hissed. Purvis heard the doorbell chime ever- so-slightly as if someone were trying to leave.

"And what of your novice?" Breen asked. "I saw him follow you in here." Purvis steadied himself. He heard the front door shut.

"An errand boy for the shoppe keeper." Minden's voice was dismissive. "I don't take on novices anymore. Not after such a disappointment." The tone in Minden's voice told Purvis it was aimed at one of the men.

"You churlish old fool!" The one called Grimmel spat. Purvis heard some scuffling. He thought he heard Minden start an incantation but then a piercing noise made both him and Trinna drop to the floor in pain. Lying on the floor, fighting for consciousness, Purvis heard the voice of the one called Breen.

"See, old man? I no longer need to wield the wand to use the magic. I have earned the title Fa. It is a pity I will never hear it from your mouth."

Purvis heard more movement before passing out.

When Purvis finally opened his eyes, it was dark. Night had come while they lay unconscious on the floor of the hearth room. He attempted to stand again, this time leaning against the wall as he rose. His head pounded. He knew of no wand that could do that to someone that far removed. He could well imagine what it would do to someone in the line of fire. Minden! He stumbled into the front room. Lying there on the floor was his master.

Purvis threw himself down next to the old mage. Minden's face was white, his skin cold. He was dead. His mage's robe gone. Purvis laid his head on his master's chest and wept.

— • —

The clearing glowed with light from the pyre. Shadows flickered on the trees. Purvis stood and watched. When the fire had burned down to coals, Trinna rested a hand on Purvis' shoulder. It gave him no comfort.

"Purvis," Trinna began. He just shook his head and walked away. He settled himself at the base of a tree and stared at what was left of the pyre. Trinna turned, leaving Purvis to his thoughts.

Long after the coals had died Purvis rose and searched the ashes. He found a small sharp bone that must have shattered from the heat. Carefully he brushed the ashes from it and held it to the hem of his tunic. He removed his novice wand and opened the hem. Tenderly he slid the bone fragment into the hem and sewed it up with a flick of his wand. He rose and left the clearing without looking back.

It was early morning when Purvis arrived back at the tea shoppe. Trinna opened the door for him. He slumped into one of the chairs he'd found so comfortable the day before. Trinna brought him a steaming cup of something smelling vaguely of cloves. Purvis drank it absently.

"You're welcome to stay here," Trinna offered. "I know a tea shoppe isn't much after Fa Minden, but —" Purvis cut her off.

"Thank you. But I can't stay. I have some things I need to take care of."

"You aren't thinking of going after them?!" Her voice faltered. "If they did that to Fa Minden, think what could happen to you!"

"They stole his robe. His wands. That is unforgivable," Purvis said through clenched teeth.

"You don't even know who they are! Breen has been on Fa Minden's bad side for years. And Grimmel, don't even get me started about that bad seed. They're dangerous!" She waved her hands in finality.

Purvis stood and paced a moment then looked down at Trinna. She was still sitting, staring into her rapidly cooling cup. "Why lie about having a novice? Who was such a disappointment?" he asked.

"Grimmel. He was bad from the start. Fa Minden tried but it was no use. Grimmel wanted what he could not have."

"Which was?"

"Talent. Grimmel simply lacked the talent for the wands. He could do some of the incantations but he had no real feel for it. When Fa Minden tried to explain this to him he went crazy, took off, probably straight to Breen. That was years ago."

"Breen." Purvis whispered. "It was he who killed my master? Who is he?" he asked.

"Ah, Breen." Trinna rose to refill her now-cool cup. "Breen is a wand mage, much like your master was." Trinna paused in the doorway, looking back. "Oh, I'm sorry. I didn't mean to sound uncaring."

"It's all right." Purvis said quietly.

Trinna continued speaking from the back room. "The difference between the two was priorities. Fa Minden saw everyone, everything as a priority. He used to say 'without everyone and everything there would be nothing.'" Trinna chuckled to herself as she returned to the front room with a fresh cup. Purvis smiled to himself. He remembered Minden saying that as well.

"Breen's priority is himself. Always has been," she finished.

"What of the wand they spoke of?"

"That I don't know." She shrugged her shoulders.

"Would you mind?" Purvis held out his cup.

"Certainly." Trinna, once again, headed to the back room. Purvis could hear her speaking as she poured more tea. "You know why your master lied about you, don't you? Purvis?"

Purvis left the door ajar. He felt badly leaving like this but it was something he had to do. And yes, Mistress Trinna, he said to himself. He did know why Minden had lied. But Minden wasn't here to p.otect him anymore.

—•—

By sheer luck, Purvis caught a glimpse of Minden's robe. He was passing in front of an inn and glancing through the doors he saw the thief sitting at a table alone. Purvis began to rage inside. How dare this fraud steal and then wear the robes of a Fa mage! It took all of his will to continue on down the walkway. While physically Purvis had no doubt he could take the thief, he wasn't sure of the small man's abilities as a mage. He couldn't take any chances. Then again, he had no place else to go. He turned around and went into the inn. Trying not to stare, he took a stool at the bar. No sooner had he sat down than the robe thief rose. Purvis acted out of pure emotion. He slammed head on into the thief, knocking him flat on the floor.

"My apologies." Purvis mumbled as he roughly pulled the thief off the floor.

"Watch yourself, you impudent brat." The thief's face was red with anger. The whining voice told Purvis he was the one called Grimmel.

Grimmel attempted to brush the robe off. Giving up in a huff, he headed for the stairs. Purvis pretended he was leaving then quickly followed once Grimmel had reached the boarder's floor.

As he reached the top of the stairs, Purvis saw a door shut. He walked up to the door and listened, ready all the while to run. From inside he heard Grimmel ranting. It sounded as if he were talking to someone. He heard no response though and assumed Grimmel was talking to himself. The door handle began to move then stopped. Purvis made it to the back of the hall in two bounds. There he stood in the shadows and waited. Finally, the door opened and Grimmel emerged. His hair was wet from splashing water on his face. It hadn't helped. Grimmel's face was still nearly the same shade of red. What was different, Purvis noticed, was that Grimmel wasn't wearing the robe anymore.

Once Grimmel had descended the stairs, Purvis took a deep breath. He silently crept towards the door. He heard no voices inside the room. He gently tried the handle, but it resisted. That was no surprise. He tried a little bit harder. The handle came loose in his hand. Purvis just stood there and stared at it. A noise from down in the main room woke him from his astonishment. He quickly pushed open the door and entered the room. There was the robe. Purvis grabbed it without hesitation.

As he exited, he closed the door as best he could, replacing the handle carefully. Now, how to escape? Going back down through the main room was out of the question. His nose led him to his way out. At the far end of the hall was a small side corridor he hadn't noticed while hiding. It contained the toilet. With the robe draped over his shoulder, Purvis climbed through the air vent that made up one wall of the little room. From there he worked his way down to some crates. They held long enough for him to lower himself to the alley below. He immediately headed back to the tea shoppe.

—•—

What's got into your head, boy?!" Trinna balled her hands into fists and thrust them onto her ample hips. "I feared you'd gone and done something —" she stopped when her gaze fell on the robe in Purvis' hands, then continued "— stupid." She shook her head as if to make it not so. "You didn't. Tell me you didn't."

"I have nothing, no one. Just Minden's robe," Purvis pleaded. Trinna bent forward and gently rubbed the collar.

"The wands?" she whispered, hoping.

Purvis looked down at the crimson robe. He hadn't had the chance to check. He walked over to the bed and laid the robe out carefully. He opened one side then the other. Inside were long, slender pockets made from the same textured material as the robe though black in color. They were all empty.

"Gone." Without the wands Purvis knew he was truly left with nothing. He picked up the robe with the intention of throwing it. He stopped, looking closely at the silver thread. The warding spell must have worn off. The robe was already beginning to look dirty. Threads were frayed. He held it close to him. It still smelled like Minden. Absently he checked the large front pockets.

"Aye!" Purvis dropped the robe on the bed and jumped back. Trinna looked at him and then the robe. It began to move, or rather something in it began to move.

"Really, Grimmel. Is that any way to treat a mage's robe?" The small voice came from under the heavy fabric. Purvis and Trinna merely stared as whatever it was worked itself free of the material. Suddenly, a satiny black, furry head appeared from under a sleeve. "Oh. You aren't Grimmel." It seemed surprised but calm beyond that.

"It's a rat." Purvis said, stating the obvious.

"A rat. Yes," it replied. "Name's Folderol." The rat cleaned his whiskers briefly.

"A talking rat." Purvis added.

"To be more precise, yes," came its response.

"Are you, a — a familiar?" Trinna asked.

"Minden didn't have a familiar," Purvis said quietly to Trinna without taking his eyes off the animal.

"I'm not a familiar. I'm a rat. And I'm not Minden's. I'm Grimmel's, or rather, I am in the service of Grimmel." Folderol returned to his grooming.

"In the service of Grimmel?" Purvis asked.

"Yes. Does it help you to repeat what I say?" Folderol said brusquely.

"What?! Why you little vermin." Purvis moved to swat the animal off the robe. Trinna's hand stopped him.

"You are yelling at a rat," she said, turning her attention back to the small animal sitting on her bed.

"Yes. I thought we went over that." Folderol seemed tired of the conversation. "And because of you." A paw motioned towards Purvis. "What is your name, boy?"

"Purvis," he said through clenched teeth.

"Purvis? Too bad. Anyway, because of you I am now unemployed and without means."

"What do you mean 'without means?' You're a rat."

"There you go again. Listen carefully, will you? I was instructed to guard this robe. I failed at that because you decided my naptime was a prudent time to steal it." It was all the little rat could do to muster a yell of sorts. "You think I'm going back to Grimmel now? Without the robe? Are you daft?"

"Wait, wait," Trinna interrupted. "How is it you can talk if you aren't a familiar?"

"Ah, yes. An intelligent question. At last." Folderol tried to make himself comfortable on one of the sleeves. He pawed at a particular spot just below his stomach.

"Stop that!" Purvis said firmly. "You'll ruin the fabric."

Folderol pawed it again as if he hadn't heard, then turned his attention to Trinna. Purvis threw up his hands and sat down in the nearest chair with a thump. Folderol gave him a glance and continued. "As I was saying. I was once in the service of a potions mage by the name of Frezi. I was his experimental." The rat paused and gave his left ear a quick scratch.

"Experimental?" Purvis asked haughtily.

"Yes." Folderol quickly scratched his right ear before continuing. "Frezi would make a potion and I would drink it. Being just an average rat then I didn't think much about it. I always got a nice bit of cheese afterwards. I remember once he tried to give me wings. I ended up with the most beautiful black feathers." He ran his little claws through his jet-black fur. He paused and looked up. "No wings mind you, just the feathers. They eventually fell out. Just as well, terribly awful to keep clean."

"So he was the one who gave you speech?" Trinna asked. She had pulled up a chair and was leaning forward to be more at eye level with the rat.

"Yes. After that he didn't see much point in experimenting on me anymore. Didn't want to mess with a good thing I guess." He turned his attention back to his whiskers.

"A talking rat is a good thing?" Purvis muttered.

Folderol ignored the comment, again talking to Trinna. "Anyway, that was, oh, at least ten years ago." He turned in his spot, pawing at it again and then settling down.

"Ten years?" Purvis sat up. "How old are you?"

"Well, by my reckoning, I'd guess around twenty three."

"Lordes," Trinna whispered.

"Somewhere in the mix he slipped me a longevity potion," Folderol added. "Anyway, I came to be in the service of Grimmel." The rat started in on his tail and paused. "Or rather, was in the service."

"Because," Purvis urged.

"Because you stole the robe," the exasperated rat exclaimed.

"No. Why are you, were you, working for Grimmel?" Purvis said evenly, his temper contained for the moment.

Folderol finished grooming his tail and said finally, "Because Frezi, the daft old fool, fell off the roof while fixing a leak and broke his darn fool neck." Folderol shook his head sadly. "No way for a mage to die. I said my goodbyes and set out on my own. Grimmel found me a couple of months later." He sat up and sniffed the air. "Excuse me, is this by chance a tea shoppe?"

"Yes." Trinna said warily.

"Would it be possible to get a cup of sweet tea?" Folderol blinked his onyx black eyes. "Just a small cup, mind you."

Trinna nodded slowly. "I, I suppose." She rose and went to the hearth, leaving the two somewhat alone.

"What did you do for Grimmel?" Purvis asked, sitting on the floor by the bed.

"A little of this, a little of that. Mostly go into places he wasn't able. Hearing things he wasn't there to hear. You get the idea." The rat readjusted himself in the fabric of the sleeve.

"Yes, I can see how you'd be good at that." It was as close to a compliment as Purvis could manage.

"Thank you." Folderol sat up and pawed at the fabric again. Purvis wondered if all rats were this fidgety.

Purvis paused briefly before changing the subject. "Do you know what happened to the wands?"

"Oh, yes. Fa Breen took them. He made quite the deal out of checking each wand carefully. Looked over all five runes."

"Five? You only saw five wands? Are you sure?" Purvis was back up on his knees.

"Well, I wasn't there when Grimmel acquired the robe but, yes, I'm quite sure. Grimmel came back to our room with the robe and removed the wands carefully, laying them out on the bed. He was muttering something about being Breen's experimental. I assumed that meant he was checking for protection spells. Breen arrived a little while later."

Purvis rose. "Minden kept six wands in his robe." He dropped back into the chair across from the bed. Trinna came back just then with three cups of sweet tea. She set Folderol's on the small table next to the bed.

"Ah, that smells wonderful." The little rat sniffed the aroma coming from the cup. He dipped a paw, licking it off. "Quite possibly the best I've had." He stuck his small pointed head into the cup and lapped up the tea. After a few moments of this, he sat back on his haunches and began a thorough cleaning of face and whiskers.

"Grimmel still has a wand," Purvis said softly.

"Just one?" Trinna stopped her cup half way to her mouth.

"Minden carried six. The rat, I mean, Folderol," he nodded to the little rat, "saw five go to Breen. That means the thief still has one."

Folderol, having finished washing, went back to the sleeve of the robe. Before settling himself down this time he pawed at the spot with both front feet.

"Hey! Stop that!" Purvis jumped up and nudged the rat off the robe. He inspected the area closely. "You're going to ruin it." He stroked the fabric gently, looking for any tears or snags. His fingers went over something hard. He pushed gently. Definitely something hard. Purvis opened the robe, looking for anything he might have missed earlier. He saw nothing.

"What is it?" Trinna asked, now standing next to Purvis. Folderol sat on the bed watching.

"I felt something in the robe, but I can't find it," Purvis said as he continued to search.

"Yes, there was something underneath me. Couldn't get comfortable because of it," Folderol said, interested.

Purvis held an area of the robe in his hand. He felt along a seam. There was something sewn in between the layers of heavy fabric. It had been done quickly; the sewing was coarse. He felt the shape and his eyes lit up.

"It's a wand." He continued to feel the shape through the fabric. Purvis took out his novice wand and opened the seam. It opened easily without the warding spell. It was indeed a wand.

"It's one of Minden's." Purvis handled the thin polished wood lovingly.

"Which one?" Trinna asked.

Purvis checked the rune on the base of the wand. It was a square with a dot in the middle. "Immobility," he answered quietly. He rubbed the rune with his thumb. "So Grimmel was going to keep one of the wands for himself."

Folderol sighed. "Grimmel isn't very smart. Even by rat standards. Keeping something from Breen is not advisable." He found a nice spot on the bed to set himself down. Folderol curled up as if sleeping though both black eyes remained open. Purvis stood and addressed Trinna.

"I'm going after the wands."

"You're what?" she gasped. "You have the robe and one of the wands. Shouldn't that be enough?"

"But I've nothing else," Purvis said. He turned to Folderol, who was sitting up and now listening intently. Purvis turned to face the little rat. "Will you help me? Do you know where Breen is?"

"Believe it or not, we rats are a loyal bunch. But staying with Grimmel after what he's done to Breen does not seem wise." The rat scratched his ear. "Of course what you are about to do doesn't seem wise either."

Purvis felt his chances fading away when Folderol sat up on his rear haunches as if to proclaim something.

"After brief consideration, you seem like the better choice for allegiance." Folderol sat back down. "Yes, I know where Breen went. But before I agree to help, have you taken into account that Breen will be even more dangerous now? I mean he does have all those wands."

"He can't use them. Not my master's anyway."

"Then I agree." Folderol nodded his small head ever so slightly.

Purvis placed the found wand into its pocket inside the robe. He reached for his travel bag and gently packed the robe, then adjusted the bag on his shoulder. He walked over to the bed and held out his hand for Folderol. The rat climbed onto it. Purvis lifted him up to his shoulder where Folderol made himself comfortable in Purvis' shoulder length hair.

"You don't even know where you're going!" Trinna nearly yelled. "You've got one bloody wand and you're not a mage. Not yet." The last she said with some restraint.

"Two wands. And without Minden my only hope of becoming a mage is to find the rest of his. Besides, our friend here knows where we're going." Purvis tipped his head towards the now hidden rat.

"You're trusting a rat to take you Lordes knows where?" Trinna stood there. Her fists were balled up and on her hips again. "You're so all fired up to go you aren't thinking. You don't even know if the wands are still with Breen. Or if they're even still together."

"I'll find them. All of them." Purvis sounded the most confident he'd ever heard himself sound. He hoped it would last. Trinna paced briefly, never taking her eyes off Purvis. She let out a huff and went into the back pantry. A few minutes later she came back with a small bag and handed it to him.

With a sigh of surrender she said, "here, food." She started to put her fists back on her hips when she suddenly stopped. "Oh, and just in case." She pulled several coins out of her apron and held them out. Purvis slowly took them and tucked them safely away in his breeches.

"Thank you."

The shop keeper shoved her hands into the pockets of her apron. Purvis adjusted his pack again, feeling the awkwardness of the moment.

Then Trinna whispered, "He was a good man."

Purvis nodded. It was the simple truth.

"Which way?" he asked his new companion.

"Northish," came the reply.

"Northish?" Purvis repeated. "You sure?"

"You're repeating again. And, yes. I'm very good with directions. Frezi must have given me a —" Purvis hushed the rat, gave Trinna a smile and headed northish.

—•—

Soon after leaving town they passed through thin forest and green grasslands, finally emerging onto a road. There they were able to catch a ride on the back of a market wagon heading in their chosen direction. With little else to fill the time Purvis struck up a conversation with his traveling companion.

The noise of the wagon assured Purvis he could not be heard by the driver. "Where did you get the name Folderol?"

The little black rat emerged from Purvis' pack and swallowed his mouthful of cheese before answering. "Frezi. He seemed to get a chuckle out of it."

"Do you know what it means?"

"No. Frezi never said and I've never looked it up as I can't read." Folderol held on with his front paws as they traversed a particularly bumpy part of the road.

"Oh," Purvis said by way of changing the subject. "What other potions did Fa Frezi give you?" Purvis assumed any mage with enough talent to give speech to a rat must surely have obtained Fa status. His body swayed along with the motion of the wagon.

"I don't really know. I don't have many memories before he gave me the speech potion. The feather incident sticks in my memory of course. You don't soon forget something like that happening to you."

"No, you wouldn't," Purvis agreed.

"As for the longevity potion, well that became obvious as the years went by."

"I wonder why Fa Frezi didn't take it himself," Purvis mused.

"He may well have. It was a longevity potion, not an immortality potion. If that were the case Frezi would still be alive."

"I suppose."

"If you ask me, I think Frezi was just lonely. Even before the speech potion I remember him talking to me all the time. Constantly. Sad really when you think about it. I mean it wasn't like I could answer him or even really understand him. Just a lot of noise. I got the distinct impression he just wanted someone to talk to."

Folderol dug in the pack for another hunk of hard cheese. "And what about you?" he asked, poking his head from out of the food bag. "What's your story? You hadn't always been with your master, had you?"

"No, I was given to Fa Minden as a novice when I was eight. I was raised by the Na Do Nae in their orphanage. I don't know my parents." Purvis held the pack by a strap and steadied himself as the cart rose up a steep incline.

"Na Do Nae?" Folderol peered out of the bag. "Really?"

"Yes, I know. I've heard the stories too. They really aren't as odd as they say."

"But don't they do strange things with their dead? And eat live animals? And —" Folderol was cut off by Purvis.

"I don't remember a lot of meat on the table but what there was, was well-cooked."

"And the dead? I've heard strange stories about that." Folderol had forgotten his hunt for cheese for the moment.

"They have their ritual. Just like any other religion. There's nothing strange about it. I attended a funeral while there, for my former housemaster. They use a funerary pyre like most people. Afterwards those closest to the dead take away a memento."

"A memento?" Folderol cocked his head to one side. "What kind of memento?"

"Well, since Na Do Nae are burned with all their possessions, which aren't many, there isn't usually much left. I saw some take ash, others pieces of bone."

"Really? Interesting," Folderol sniffed absently. Purvis looked past Folderol in a kind of daydream. "What are you thinking about?"

Purvis grinned and blinked the dream away. "I guess they kind of rubbed off on me. After Fa Minden's pyre burned down to ashes I took a piece of bone." He looked down at his tunic hem thoughtfully. "I guess I didn't want to let him go entirely."

"I understand. I miss Frezi still," Folderol said as he went back into the bag for another look. Purvis smiled. As much as he hated the way they'd come to meet, he was beginning to like the little creature.

When the wagon reached a crossroads, they bid the driver goodbye. Purvis walked on with Folderol navigating from his shoulder. They continued this way until darkness made it too dangerous. They were surely not the only travelers in this area but they were probably the most honest. They made camp in a small stand of trees. There was no fire and therefore no sweet tea. Folderol was not pleased but said he could make do with extra portions of apple. Purvis gladly obliged.

"A question, if I may," the rat asked as he chose a piece of fruit.

"Yes?"

"When you said that Breen couldn't use the wands, what did you mean?"

"They are keyed to the one who made them or for whom they were made,'" Purvis recited from memory. That was first year novice stuff.

"So how do you get any training? You can't go far just mending hems," Folderol said matter of factly. And he was right. Wands were not easy to make. A master would not make a set of wands for his novice. The novice wand was granted after third or fourth year.

"If the maker is touching the person using the wand it will work for that person. Fa Minden needed only to lay his hand on my shoulder to enable the wands."

"Interesting," the little rat said as he bit into his third piece of fruit.

—•—

Come morning the two were off again, heading for the keep of Breen. Folderol, having been there, gave Purvis a rundown of the grounds. The wands, Folderol surmised, would probably be in the grand hall where Breen kept his trophies. While knowing where the wands most likely were was helpful, being told they were trophies was not.

"Trophies?! He's made Minden's wands trophies?!"

"That temper. You really should try to control it. Frezi had a lovely potion for temper. If I could only remember the ingredients," Folderol rubbed his nose thoughtfully.

"I don't need a potion," Purvis said through gritted teeth.

"As you say," Folderol said complacently.

—•—

By early afternoon, Purvis and Folderol reached the rim of a valley. Down on the far side, Folderol told him, was the keep of Fa Breen. Purvis winced at the title given to his master's murderer.

Purvis set his pack down and rested against a large boulder. Folderol climbed down from his shoulder and sniffed about.

"So. What are you going to do once we reach the keep?" the little rat asked.

"Uh, I don't really know." Purvis hesitated as he pulled a small apple from the pack and set it before his companion. He didn't have a plan.

"May I make a suggestion? I know the man. Force will be of no use. He's too powerful. And trying to slip in unseen would be unwise," Folderol said between bites.

"Then what? We didn't travel here for nothing did we?" Purvis carefully removed the robe and laid it out on his lap. He'd been thinking more and more about Minden. Removing his novice wand he began to mend the robe. He started with the silver flowerettes on the collar.

"Flatter him. He is extremely vain, egotistical and, I hasten to add, sadistic." Folderol climbed onto Purvis' lap to examine his work. "Very nice. Ever thought of becoming a tailor?"

"No." Purvis nudged the rat off the robe. "Any suggestions on how I flatter him?"

"Well, you could ask advice," Folderol paused "— or perhaps —" he sat up on his hind legs excitedly, "— ask to become his novice!"

"You're joking. This is the sadistic murderer that killed my master!"

"Yes, but I happen to know that he thought it very clever of himself to take Grimmel on as a novice. He'll take all the credit if you ask him. Not that I would. Grimmel is mediocre at best."

"Say I do this. I ask to become his novice. What then? How do we get the wands?"

"First things first. We get in. We stay alive. Then we figure out how to get the wands."

"But he's the one that —" Purvis was cut off mid sentence.

"What's done is done. You can't change that. What you can do is get back your masters' wands and wound that ego of Breen's by taking away his prize." Purvis could have sworn there was a smile on the little rat's face.

A quick drink from the water bladder and they continued their walking. Soon enough they came upon the opening of what looked like a small tunnel set into a rather tall rocky cliff.

"We go in?" Purvis asked.

"We go in," came the reply from his shoulder.

"Great." Purvis took a few steps into the tunnel and paused. "How do I see where I'm going? There aren't any torches."

"Just wait a minute. They'll wake up."

"They?" Purvis was about to ask just who 'they' were but stopped suddenly. All along the walls of the tunnel little lights started to shine. Slowly, and in pairs. The small tunnel grew into a large passageway. "And — and — wh— — what are all those things?"

Folderol sniffed in the general direction that his companion was pointing. "Eyes."

"Eyes? What do you mean 'eyes?' Look, there's more of them. They're all around us." Purvis spun around in the dim light of the entrance. In every direction, glowing eyes were staring at them. Occasionally, they blinked.

"I mean eyes," Folderol snapped back. "Calm down."

Purvis slowly walked up to a pair that were fairly close to the opening. He got his face as close as he dared and stared until his eyes adjusted. The eyes on the wall blinked at him.

"See. I told you. Eyes," Folderol said triumphantly. And indeed, they were just that. Glowing eyes. Nothing else. No body, no head. Nothing except eyes. The walls were covered with them. They lit up the cave well enough to walk by.

"What do they do?" Purvis asked as he stuck a finger out towards the pair he'd been inspecting.

"Do?"

"Yes, what do they do?" As his finger neared the eyes, they snapped shut, shutting out their little bit of light.

"They light up the cave," Folderol said as if that was all there was to them.

"That all?" Purvis stepped away from they eyes and they slowly opened again.

"What else do you suppose they could do?" the rat said sarcastically.

Purvis adjusted his pack and started through the passageway. After a few minutes, he spoke.

"Folderol?"

"Yes?"

"Why are you doing this? I mean, why are you helping me?"

Folderol didn't speak right away. "Grimmel was, well, temporary."

"Temporary?"

Before Folderol could answer, the passageway opened up onto a meadow. Having been in the semi-dark tunnel made the waning sunlight look twice as bright. Purvis blinked several times before he noticed a very large man with an equally large sword.

"Are you sure those eyes don't do anything else?" Purvis hissed.

The swordsman straightened from his relaxed position as Purvis exited the cave as if he had been waiting for them. Somehow they had been expected.

"Like what?" Folderol said, staring at the approaching behemoth.

"Like spy!" came the clenched response.

Folderol slid behind Purvis' hair, peering out cautiously.

Purvis let the man approach, though he was primed to run back into the tunnel. When the man was within speaking distance, he simply motioned for Purvis to follow him. The man easily weighed twice as much as Purvis with arms the size of small tree trunks. Purvis didn't argue. He didn't say a word except to Folderol, whispering "Stay hidden. Maybe you weren't seen."

On the far side of the meadow, a small stand of trees separated another, smaller clearing. There, Purvis saw the keep. The swordsman led him right through the open portcullis. Once inside he was led into a formal hall. At the far end was a darkly colored tapestry. Purvis could make out some sort of historic battle scene. Before he was close enough to determine what battle it was, the swordsman stopped. Purvis stopped too. Looking about he could see numerous items that might be considered trophies. It seemed Breen was a collector. There were items from other mage disciplines.

Purvis didn't notice the figure who appeared from behind the heavy tapestry until he spoke. "Who are you?"

Purvis recognized the voice. It was Breen. Minden's murderer. Purvis was startled but somehow kept his composure.

Breen held his chin in his hand. Purvis was startled to see that the mage was much younger than Minden. His straight blonde hair was tucked away behind his ears. His face was hairless.

"Wand Novice Ninth Year." He left out his name and bowed with his head only as was the custom.

"Wand novice? And so far along? What is it you want? Who is your master?" Breen's voice remained quiet, as if he knew he was in control.

"I am masterless. I require a new master to further my training so that I may rise." Purvis bowed his head again.

"A new master? What became of your master, ninth year?"

"Dead." Purvis nearly choked on the word. "I was —" he

swallowed hard. *Lordes forgive him for what he was about to say.* "I was told that you were a Fa among Fa. I had hoped you had time to share your knowledge. I am an apt student."

"We shall see. I don't often take on novices." Breen had started to walk around the room. His eyes never left Purvis. Purvis continued to look forward, towards the tapestry. Folderol, to his credit, did not move. He was well hidden in Purvis' hair. "You seem familiar. Have we met?"

Purvis could feel his legs go weak. He realized he was holding his breath. He exhaled and took a deep breath to regain his strength. "I do not believe so, Fa Breen." Purvis did what he could not to search the room with his eyes for the wands.

Breen continued to circle him. He finally came to rest in an ornate chair to the side of the tapestry. "Ninth year," he said more to himself than to anyone. Purvis could see he was mulling the idea over, looking for anything that might feed his ego. "I will give you temporary sanctuary. I alone will decide if you are worthy to be my pupil."

"My gratitude, Fa Breen." Again, Purvis bowed his head. Breen waved the swordsman out of the room. No sooner had the hall doors closed behind him than they reopened. To Purvis' surprise and terror who but Grimmel should enter, head bowed. Purvis turned quickly to face the tapestry.

"Grimmel. What have you done now?" Breen did not sound happy to see his risen pupil. It appeared no one was fond of the mediocre mage.

"Fa Breen. I've come to request your help."

"As usual. What is it now?"

"The robe. It was stolen."

"Stolen?!" Breen's quiet voice boomed through the hall. "How could it be stolen? Did you leave it in some bar? Or perhaps you draped it over the branch of a tree while you slept!"

"It was stolen from my room, Fa Breen. I had Folderol guarding it." As soon as the last word left his mouth Grimmel knew he'd said the wrong thing. Breen thrust himself from the chair.

"You left that ridiculous excuse of a companion to guard the robe?! I see now why Minden cast you out." Breen turned with a sweep of his own robe and headed back up to the head of the hall. "I will not help you."

"But, Fa Breen!" Grimmel pleaded. He was about to continue his useless whining when he suddenly stopped, having spotted Purvis. "You! You stole it!" He pointed and screamed. If there hadn't been a table separating them, Purvis felt sure Grimmel would have launched himself at him. Purvis said nothing. The small movement on his shoulder reassured him. He kept his temper.

"What are you ranting about?" Breen stared at the half crazed mage. "Have you gone mad?" Breen was about to sit when Grimmel ran up to him.

"It's him! He was at the inn. He insulted me just before the robe was stolen!"

"You are mad," Breen dismissed the rantings with a wave of his hand. Still Purvis said nothing.

"I swear it!" Grimmel was trembling with emotion. He turned to Purvis. "How did you know to come here? Who showed you the way?" He thrust his finger towards Purvis with each question asked. Purvis said nothing. He stared at Grimmel, making sure there was no expression on his face.

"Answer the questions," Breen said, falling back to his soft voice.

"I had a guide," Purvis said clearly. The truth was about to be seen. He had to continue playing his role.

"A guide? I saw no one else with you in the cave," Breen said unbelieving.

"If you will pardon me, Fa Breen. I did have a guide."

"Name this guide."

Purvis gave a small smile towards the now pathetic looking Grimmel. "Folderol."

"See?! It is him!" Grimmel began to gesture wildly. "He stole my robe!"

"I simply retrieved what was stolen in the first place, Fa Breen."

Breen's eyes lit up. He had made the connection. "So. Minden did have a novice." He clapped his hands to emphasize his pleasure. "You are Minden's novice."

"Was, Fa Breen. My training ended when Fa Minden died." Purvis' mouth was dry. He took a slow deep breath. "I retrieved the robe and now wish to continue my training." He bowed his head slightly.

Breen said nothing for a moment then: "It was gallant of you to want Minden's robe. But what am I to think? I need absolute obedience. Your connection with your dead master is unwelcome."

"If I may, Fa Breen. I retrieved the robe out of —" Purvis paused as if searching for a word "— a fondness for my former master. He is gone."

"Don't listen to him! He's here to take the wands!" Grimmel leaped at Purvis only to be knocked out of the way by a wave of Breen's hand. The mage fell to the floor, the wind knocked out of him. He sat on the floor, panting for breath.

"Do not tell me what to do, Grimmel." Breen stepped back towards his chair, sitting slowly.

While Breen sat and Grimmel slowly rose, Purvis inclined his head ever so slightly. He knew how to gain Breen's trust.

"If I may, Fa Breen." Purvis bowed his head and waited for permission to speak.

"You may," Breen said warily.

"How many wands did you receive?"

Breen's eyebrows rose ever so slightly. "Five. Why?"

Purvis allowed himself another smile towards Grimmel. It was enough to send the mage into a frenzy. He launched himself at Purvis again, this time hitting him square in the stomach. They both tumbled backwards over one of the long tables.

"Stop it! I will have order in my presence!"

Purvis threw Grimmel's wiry frame off of him and stood, straightening his tunic. He no longer felt Folderol on his shoulder. Where was he? Purvis knew better than to look for the little rat.

"Fa Breen. Fa Minden always carried six," he said catching his breath. Grimmel remained on the floor.

"Did he?" Breen's voice took on the eerie quiet it had just before Minden died. He rose slowly, adjusting his robes. "Where is the sixth wand, Grimmel?"

"Sixth? There was no sixth wand, Fa Breen. I swear it! I gave all of them to you! He's lying!"

"Somehow I think my new novice is telling the truth. You never did lie well, Grimmel. It was a fault I could never correct in you." Breen slowly approached the panicked mage. Purvis stepped back, out of the way. He stopped when he felt the tapestry behind him. With a slight flick of his wrist Breen caused Grimmel to writhe on the ground. Whatever wand he had on him was more powerful than Purvis had seen. The sounds coming from Grimmel sounded like gurgling.

Without looking away from Grimmel, Breen spoke to Purvis. "This is your first lesson, ninth year. Dealing with the unworthy." Breen made a movement with his fingers and Grimmel screamed. Purvis noticed that Breen was smiling. Suddenly Purvis felt the tiny claws of Folderol climb up his leg and under his tunic. He appeared on Purvis' shoulder, hidden in his hair.

"I don't think we should stay longer than we have to," Folderol whispered into Purvis' ear.

"Any ideas would be appreciated." Purvis hissed back. Grimmel's cries drowned out any other sounds.

"The wand," came the reply.

"What would you like me to do? Drop the hem in his pants for him?" Purvis kept his eyes on Breen. The mage's attention was fully on the man squirming on the floor.

"Not that wand. Minden's wand."

"I can't use it. It's keyed to Minden, remember?"

"You said if he was touching the person using it that it would still work."

"Yes." Purvis waited.

"The bone."

The bone! Of course! The shard from the funerary pyre. All that was left of the mage. Purvis reached down and ripped the hem from his tunic, removing the bone. He quickly pulled the robe out of the pack and slid out the wand. He dropped the robe and pack back behind the tapestry. Holding the bone and the wand in the same hand, he concentrated. Minden had allowed him to use this particular wand only once before on a butterfly. The delicate insect had fallen to the ground in mid-flight.

Through Grimmel's cries Purvis could hear Breen chastising him. He concentrated harder. Suddenly the cries stopped. Purvis lost concentration momentarily.

"What's this? Might this be the wand in question? And how thoughtful of you to bring it to me." Breen wrapped his robes about him and chuckled. "Bring it here, boy." He held out his hand. "I expect obedience, boy!" The quiet voice grew into a rage. "Bring me the wand!"

"You gave me sanctuary," Purvis stuttered stupidly.

"Temporary sanctuary. It has ceased." Breen made a movement with his hand but before he could complete it something small and black leaped from the table at his face. Breen fell screaming onto the table then stood up, hitting himself all over.

Purvis suddenly realized Folderol no longer sat on his shoulder. Breen wasn't hitting himself. He was hitting at something inside his robe. Folderol was attacking the mage!

Purvis steadied himself and concentrated. He spoke the words. A numbness went up his arm. He concentrated harder, speaking the words louder. This was no butterfly. Suddenly Breen froze then slowly fell over, landing hard onto the floor.

Purvis dropped his arm to his side. It was completely numb. The wand and bone fragment fell to the floor, the sound echoing through the hall. He ran to Breen's side. Carefully he searched the immobile mage until he found what he was looking for. Purvis gently removed the rigid rat and slipped him into his tunic pocket. His numb wand arm was beginning to tingle.

Once Purvis had Folderol safely tucked away, he began his search. There were many mage objects set about the hall, but none were the wands. Then for no other reason than the fact that Breen appeared from there, Purvis searched behind the tapestry. He found an ornate cabinet with an even more ornate lock on the doors. Being more concerned with time than subtlety, he kicked the cabinet doors with the heel of his boot. The doors shattered. Inside he found scrolls, several bottles of liquid, and a velvet pouch that resembled a wood carver's bag. He grabbed the pouch and unrolled it. Inside were the five wands. Purvis sighed in relief.

Returning to the hall, he grabbed the robe, wand, and bone shard and quickly put them inside his pack, placing the robe on top. He gave his wand arm a quick shake. He could move his fingers now.

Straightening his tunic and adjusting his pack, Purvis headed out the hall doors. The sun had nearly set over the trees. Several men glanced at him. No one hindered him. The swordsman must have spread the word that he was Breen's new novice.

Only after passing back through the portcullis, did Purvis remember to breathe. As soon as he felt safe, he cut over to the trees and made a run for it. With any luck at all, he could be well away before anyone realized what had happened.

—•—

The eyes blinked slowly at first, then more rapidly.

"Here you are. Take a sip." Purvis set a tiny thimble next to the resting rat. "Mistress Trinna says it helps hasten the healing." Slowly Folderol rolled onto his feet. He moved his head ever so gently. Attempting an ear scratch sent him rolling back onto his side.

"Take it easy, Folderol. You've been out a long time," Purvis said, making himself more comfortable.

"How long?" the rat asked.

"A couple of days. I ran the way back to Dorwich. I figured if anyone knew how to help with the spell it'd be Mistress Trinna." Purvis placed a piece of hard cheese next to the thimble. "Now drink. She made it extra sweet." Purvis smiled.

Folderol made his way to the thimble and sipped without sniffing. Instantly his nose was deep inside the container. Just then, Trinna came in.

"Ah, I see our hero has woken up." She set a small plate of food next to Folderol.

The rat raised his head, gave a quick shake, and said slowly, "Hero?"

"Yes, Purvis told me how you attacked Breen. Quite a story," she said as she made herself comfortable in one of the nearby chairs.

"Hero," Folderol said as if to himself. He appeared to like the sound of that. He absently took a bite of cheese.

Turning to Purvis, Trinna's tone changed to concern. "Breen will look for you. Have you given any thought yet as to where you'll go?"

Purvis only shook his head.

"Have you considered Dahn Tru Plet?" Trinna said between sips of tea.

"The Mage's Castle?" Purvis said in astonishment.

"Why not? You have misuse of a discipline to report, not to mention the need to find another master."

"Dahn Tru Plet," Purvis said quietly. "It would be a long journey."

A small furry head perked up. "I know the way."

Uncle Ernie Was a Goat

by

Kent Pollard

Uncle Ernie was a goat.

Ernie, not Uncle Ernie to me. When I was a kid, Dad told me, "Neighbours won't say anything about you naming a goat Ernie. They probably won't even say anything if you talk to it. But if anybody hears you calling that goat 'Uncle Ernie,' that one they'll talk about for the rest of your life."

Actually, Ernie was my Dad's uncle, my great uncle, and really, he was never as bad as Mom made out. She'd wrinkle her nose about the smell, then go on forever about the garbage and how he was always losing hair on the furniture, but really, he was pretty good. Gramper, Ernie's younger brother, had even rigged a bell by the back door and Ernie would happily ring it whenever he needed to go out to do his business.

It's not like Mom had anything in particular against goats, us raising them and all, but when you come from a long line of carnivores, there's this kind of snootiness towards the food animals. Since the rest of the family are all proper panthers in our natural form, a lot of the old folks have a hard time dealing with a goat in the family. When you add in that Ernie didn't even take his human form anymore, it was a bit of a stress on the whole clan.

I remember we were sitting in the yard one day when Nan Lou suggested that we "Just git it over with and eat 'im."

There was a shocked silence around the yard, but Dad spoke up, "I told you before, Lou, no matter how much I love your daughter, you're not eating Ernie."

"As you say," she looked as though it were no matter either way to her, "but mistakes will be made, and frankly, I can't tell him from the other goats around here. Are you even sure that's really your Uncle Ernie?" Which I always thought was a fair question. I'd wondered that many times myself, since the last time he'd been seen in human form was at a box social in the village, more than 20 years before I was born.

Dad grumbled at Nan, but the two of them really got along pretty well, so these things always seemed to end quickly with everybody still friends. I was young enough, then, that I'd always watch Nan close when this went on, wondering if we really needed to keep an eye on her, but there'd be a twinkle in her eye when she finished. She'd wink at me later and say "It's hardly worth trying, Ben. It's no work at all to get your old-man's goat." Then she'd laugh like she was coming to pieces, and bang her cane on the ground.

It always settled down and conversation would get back to the ranch. Gramper and Dad raised goats. Yeah, sure, you wouldn't believe how many times I've heard, "some of the finest goats for a thousand miles in any direction." They were still goats. They paid well. We always had enough money, and that was nice, but goats! Nan Lou would give me the nastiest looks when I complained. "You should be grateful we have those goats. That's where your spending money comes from. How many of the other kids get to ride their own horse to school? Huh? You ever think of that? You've got it darn easy, you live pretty high off those goats!" Then I'd have to dodge her cane. Long, hard, diamond willow with a big knob just inches from the bottom. For a ninety year old, she was wicked with that stick and I'd got it in the ankle more than once.

Not that she ever touched the goats, except when we had them for supper, and even then she'd get a pained look when they appeared on the table. I think that was when we got to look at the real Nan. We always got to eat the tough old goats that were hard to sell. Every time they showed up on the table, she'd give that little wince and her mouth would tighten for a second. Then she'd sigh and lift her plate. "More gravy!" she'd speak up. "Lots more gravy, Ben. And she'd wave the plate under my nose till I did as she said. She certainly hadn't complained very long when Mom told her she didn't need to help with the spinning anymore. And she wasn't about to volunteer to go watch them in the pasture either. I think if anything, Nan hated goats more than I did.

Anyway, watching them was my job, not hers, every day after school, and all day on Sunday. Our pasture was a meadow on the north side of a large, rolling hill at the east foot of the Cragspire Mountains. The holding had been in the family since the very first human settlers came over the mountains nearly a thousand years ago. Truth be told, my ancestors had hunted this range before the humans thought about coming over the western sea, let alone across the mountains. We'd come across the east sea to escape the qorg long before humans came to this land. Though we were settlers here ourselves, we were of the land and very proud of it. Bad enough the qorg had crossed the sea after us, this was our home now and we certainly wouldn't be driven from it by the humans.

There'd been a lot of trouble when they first came, a lot of misunderstanding and bloodshed, but my people had quickly understood that the humans weren't going to stop coming. When the next wave came across, we'd learned to hold the human form as though it was our own, and we had our favourite land clearly marked. Not all in one place, rather we were dozens of small families spread over hundreds of miles. Always with one side against the mountains, on land so rough the humans would never want it. It looked like we'd been there for years and that's what they told the humans, that we'd come from further south, and settled just a few years ago. If any questions were asked, it wasn't enough to cause any more trouble. From that time, we became humans. Living and working among them as though it had always been that way.

—•—

I think my first real connection to Uncle Ernie was the summer I got the hiccoughs. I was 15 years old and out on the hillside tending the goats. A quick hiccough and there I was — the finest, blackest goat on the hillside. For an endless second or two I was paralyzed, I had no idea what to do. I was humiliated. I felt like I was an inch tall as I looked around desperately, certain someone would have seen. I'd been born a pure black panther, the apple of Gramper's eye. Even Nan Lou couldn't find anything to complain about when I went back to form. Why a goat? Without so much as a thought on my part, I'd transformed into a food animal. I couldn't help but think of Nan running after me with a butcher knife, threatening to eat me.

And there I was, as obvious as a missing piece from a pie, a goat. I shivered, imagining myself turning into a goat in the middle of class. I'd had bad dreams about it before. Trapped in panther form. The whole school terrified of me and running in circles screaming before dad came to stop me. But a goat! I might as well die right now. I imagined running around helplessly in the schoolroom as the older kids laughed and chased me. Bad enough being a goatherd — if you've never had to tell your classmates that you herd goats after school, then I can only advise against it and hint at how hard I worked to avoid the subject at school. I must have heard every possible goat joke in the world by that time. From a faint "Baaaah" as I passed to "Ain't they a little horny?" And man, if there was the slightest hint of anything on my shoes when I got to school, the day was a washout, I might as well go home and start over. Now, here I was. I'd turned into a full-fledged goat without even trying. My stomach felt like it was full of lead at the thought of turning into a goat in class. Before I could work myself up more, another hiccough, and I was human again — and beet red with embarrassment.

Fortunately, the only one who saw me was Ernie and he wasn't talking to anybody. It never happened again and I never said a word about it. Though I lost a bit of sleep for a few days, I soon put it out of my head and practiced shifting forms, to make sure I never did it again. A couple of months later I'd pretty much convinced myself that it never really happened. A dream, I'd been asleep on the hill and imagined the whole thing.

—•—

A year later, a lot of things had settled down in my life, but others had gotten worse. On the plus side, in spite of frequent nightmares, and a few near misses, there'd been no "accidents" since that first one. Also on the plus, I was developing a serious interest in Victoria Taggart. She had these soft grey-blue eyes that seemed to look right through me, and a quirky smile that always seemed to be saying, "I know what you're up to." The attraction seemed mutual, but in our small community, there was just enough competition to make me nervous. That was the big minus. In a school where there were no girls older than Victoria, and the next in line was barely 11, any competition was enough to make me nervous.

Summer was nearly over and I was up on the hillside, still doing you-know-what. To break the monotony, I was practicing with my slingshot, firing up hill at a rock about the size of my head. Not that I'd had to chase off a predator in all the time I watched the goats, with big cats wandering around the hill, the smaller stuff just seemed to avoid our land. Anyway, I'd just scored a hit on the target rock, when I heard the town bells going wild. For a second, I looked for smoke, but then I realized it was the wrong pattern. I'd never heard this one except in tests. It was the double-clang-pause of trouble, men and horses needed. As I looked north and east down the hill to see if I could pick out what was up in town, I heard the sound of a horse approaching fast. With a thunder of hooves, it burst from the trees on the east side of the meadow, a large horse, with a qorg on its back. One of the raiders that'd been pestering the plains farmers to the east of us lately. They'd been getting bolder and bolder of late, often seen poking around farms at dusk. They were shorter than us, but massively wide and muscular. Foul creatures that painted their exposed skin with blue and red mud. Covered themselves with wild designs to frighten others. The qorg didn't used to press this far west, but from what we were hearing, there were few if any of our eastern cousins left. The qorg had a fierce appetite for flesh, and having run out of my people, they'd recently discovered they especially liked human kids.

The goats scattered away from the noise of the horse, and I was about to do the same when I noticed the load on the horse behind the qorg. There was a person up there, bound tightly and hung across the horse's haunches, behind the rider. It was small, almost certainly a child. Though I couldn't make out the face, the tunic was one of the ones that Victoria's mom made for her brother Jason, who was about eight.

I didn't have a lot of time to think. With the horse's speed, the qorg would only be in sight for a couple of minutes. I slipped a few feet over to one of the caches of stones I'd been building around the meadow over the years. I quickly loaded one in my sling, spun up, and let fly — and missed. Fortunately, the qorg didn't even seem to notice, so I got a second chance. It would be pretty close by the time I loaded, so I had to make this one count. Rather than try for a head or arm, I took a slightly bigger rock and aimed for the belly. I took an extra second or two, because there'd be no third chance, and it'd be close enough to know I'd fired, whether or not I hit. I wound up and let it rip again.

The stone connected solidly, with a loud thunk that let me know two things. One, that I'd hit, and two, it was wearing a thick hide shirt so the most I'd managed was a bad bruise. The snarl it made let me know that I was in trouble. I scrambled for another stone and loaded as the qorg jerked the horse's head around toward me. I was barely aiming as I spun the stone as hard as I could and readied to let fly at its face. My arm came forward with a feeble lurch as the sling went limp with the cord broken. My gut clenched with fear as the stone flew off down the hillside in the wrong direction.

The raider was close enough now that I could not only tell it was female, but could also see the sickening grin spread across her war-painted face as she slid her sword out of the scabbard. The dark blue covered what little was visible of her face as well as the thick matt of hair on top of her head. Most of her was hidden under the heavy hide armor she wore, but what did show was solid, with the thick arms that made the qorg so feared when they held a weapon. She pulled the horse up beside me and holding tight to the reins with her left hand, she spun up the large blade and leaned over the right side of the horse toward me as she brought it forward for a down-stroke.

There was an explosion of activity. A huge rattlesnake cut loose with a rattle that sent shivers up my spine. The horse reared and kicked out toward the snake with its front legs. Because of her lean and swing, the raider's center of gravity was too far off to stay on her seat. She rolled off the side of the horse in front of me, as the boy fell off the back of the horse and lay in a lump facing the other way. The qorg was forced to release the reins as the horse bolted away from the snake. I backed away from both snake and qorg as her mount tore off west across the hillside.

The qorg made as if to chase the horse, but then turned to me with such a look of anger that my stomach dropped like a stone. Again she swung up the sword, high over her head and then down at me in a shining arc of reflected sunlight. Braced, I tried to dodge out of the way, but pain shot through me as the heavy blade sliced through my left shoulder. The force of the blow combined with my dodge caused me to go down and roll completely over. I came up on my butt now, with nowhere to move, as pain ate through my brain from the ruined arm. I could feel the shredded tunic flapping loosely over my bloody shoulder as the qorg lifted the sword again. She spit on the ground between my feet and got a nasty smile on her face. She waved the sword in my face and gave a short guttural speech that told me nothing and everything at the same time.

Again the brilliantly shining sword came up over her head. Straight on this time, aimed to come down and slice me in two from the shoulder down. I froze and could think of nothing but the end. My eyes locked on the glinting steel that hung unwavering over me. With a final growl, she yanked it down toward me. I couldn't even close my eyes as began to pull it forward.

There was a howling like I'd never heard before in my life, and the qorg was rolling away from me, wrapped in a tangle with a huge cat. The two rolled about five feet away and the sword flew with them. The growling, yelling and snarling finally penetrated my frozen brain and I stood to look.

The qorg was locked in a wrestling match with an enormous panther I'd never seen before. It reminded me of Dad, but was bigger and its coat was mostly grey rather than dad's sleek, dark black. The cat was raking at the qorg, but its thick hide shirt was absorbing almost all of the damage. I was sure the panther would win, given time, but the raider had pulled free a boot dagger with its left hand and with a growling shout drove it deep into the cat's right thigh. Another mighty snarl issued from the cat as it twisted and took the dagger hand in its large jaws. There was a loud crunch of teeth in bone and the dagger fell to the ground near my feet. The cat rolled away and rose, its leg was definitely damaged, but it still seemed in control. It prepared for another launch, tail rippling as it dropped in preparation for a spring. I saw the qorg's right hand move and I shouted a warning…but it came too late. As the cat sprang, the large sword came up to meet it. Not enough to stop the attack, but it made a great slice down the cat's left side and deep into its haunch as the animal crashed into the qorg and sank teeth into the left shoulder.

It was over for the cat now, it had completely ruined the qorg's left arm, but it was panting on the ground and losing a lot of blood from both sides. The dagger wound had been bad, but the sword's slice was far worse. The qorg slowly got to her feet and began raising the sword again. I could see a look of sadness in the cat's eyes at it faced me from behind the raider. I felt like a million thoughts went through my head in a second. I knew that if the qorg won, she'd turn back for me next.

I fought the blinding pain and stood, scooping up the dagger as I did. I moved quickly to behind the qorg, surprised to realize I was slightly taller than her. I took a deep breath and raised the dagger quickly, using both good and bad hand together to drive it down into the back of her neck. I let go immediately as fire shot up my wrecked shoulder and into my neck. The qorg gave a surprised grunt and started to turn toward me, sword still raised, but never completed the move. With a gasping sigh, she dropped the sword and tumbled to the ground.

I felt sick now. Pain, fear, shock, all running through my body and then the spray of hot red blood that had magically appeared on the back of my hands. My brain kept trying to connect the blood to the qorg, but another part of me just shut it down. I turned away and heaved my lunch onto the ground. I wanted to fall to the earth and cry, but my head and heart were still racing with fear that it wasn't over.

When I turned back, the panther looked bad. Weak now, and panting shallow breaths. I didn't know who or what it was, but it had certainly saved my life. I was afraid to get too close because I didn't know anything about it. It was probably pure blind luck that it picked the qorg instead of me, though there was something not quite right about a panther I'd never seen before wandering onto our hillside. I wanted to help it, check its wounds, but there was little I could do for it anyway. Maybe Dad could help it, but first I had to make sure that Jason was OK. I couldn't very well leave him tied up alone on the hillside with an injured wildcat and possibly more qorg wandering around. Trying to keep an eye on the cat, I went over to get Jason loose. He was petrified. Even after I had the gag off his face and the ropes untied, he sat perfectly quiet with wide eyes, saying nothing. It took a fair bit of effort on my part to get him standing, my intention being to take him back to his folks' place. Then a little part of my head said I couldn't just leave the goats. When I turned back around and remembered to check on the panther, it was gone.

Through most of this, the bells in the village had continued to peel. Now that the whole world was silent, I realized the bells had stopped, too, and I began to make out the sounds of a large crowd of riders moving towards me along the east side of the hill, from where the qorg had ridden. A dozen or so men on horses burst from the woods and rode toward me. Jason's father, Mr. Taggart was at the front of the group and leaped from his horse so rapidly he nearly fell to the ground. He took Jason in his arms and held him tightly, trying to hug him and check him for injuries at the same time. He looked from me to the bloody sword and his eyebrow raised.

"What happened?" he demanded.

My head was spinning. It was hard to think straight, but we'd lived all our lives with secrets and I knew I needed to be careful what I said. I clutched my head as though struggling with the pain as I sorted though what to say and what to leave out. I knew Dad wouldn't want me to put too much onto a panther. "A wildcat spooked the qorg's horse," I paused again. "They tangled together for a minute. After the cat injured the qorg, and the qorg hurt it, it ran off after the horse into the forest. The qorg was nearly dead, so I used its own dagger to finish it off." I gestured at the dead raider a few feet away. As I told my story, Dad got a shocked look and I saw him searching the hillside closely. I looked over, but all I could see was the goats, wandering aimlessly now that they'd calmed down. After a moment or two of searching, his eyes got a twinkle in them and I saw his head nod a tiny bit.

When I finished, I knew there were gaping holes in my story. Fortunately, with the qorg dead, the crowd were more concerned with Jason and his safety. After someone checked my cut and told me to get down to the house to have it looked at and bandaged, the members of the group turned their attention to Jason, leaving me a moment to collect my thoughts. Jason was still speechless, though stuttering, a few minutes later when a larger group of men caught up with us. These men had no horses, but were carrying some bits of weaponry and sharp farm implements. A quick discussion appraised them of what I'd said and resulted in most of those with horses spreading out to make certain there were no other qorg around and to see if there was an injured wildcat likely to cause trouble. Those on foot stayed together to make certain that I got to the house for cleaning up and Jason got back to his farm. They were also talking about securing the Taggart's house after the damage the qorg caused. Dad let one of the locals take his horse so that he could walk with me back to the house.

I could tell that Dad had a lot more questions for me about the "wild cat" that chased off the qorg. His eyes asked a lot, but he waited patiently when I shook my head to indicate I didn't want to talk any more in front of the others. We arranged a couple of the local lads to watch flock for the rest of the day, and prepared to head down the hill to our house.

The boys were quick to start gathering up the herd. By the time we were ready to head down, the goats were already starting to gather around us. Jason was just beginning to get his voice back, but his eyes widened and he clammed again up as the goats arrived. A moment later, he pulled his father's ear to him and whispered something.

His father's eyes widened and his brow rose. A moment later, he looked me up and down appraisingly, then patted Jason on the shoulder and gave him a leg up onto the horse. He led the mount over to us and held his hand out to me. "Ben, I want to thank you for keeping your wits about you and helping Jason." There was moisture in his eyes.

"I did what I could, Mr. Taggart. I'm only glad it all worked out for the best."

He harrumphed a bit. "Be that as it must, but you've earned a friend today. And on that note," he turned to my father, "I should pass word around that Mrs. Simpson is up in arms about the wildcats getting into her hen house. Says they've cost a lot of good birds this month. She's going to have a crowd of men watching them overnight for the next week or two. I'm sure she'd appreciate some help if you can manage it."

Dad shook his head. "Taggart, I've told Mrs. Simpson, it's foxes, not wildcats, but I'll certainly help her. It's best that we all stick together until we find whether the qorg are going to settle down, or if there will be more trouble."

"As you will. As you will." He turned to me again. "In any event, it would be best if no wildcats turned up near her place for a while." His eyes pierced me.

Yesterday, I'd have trembled, but the world seemed a different place now. I relaxed and put on the most innocent look I could muster before answering, "Yes sir, it probably would. I've often wondered what folks see in chicken. Nan Lou won't let us eat them. She says they're dirty birds that eat their own waste if it gets in the way."

Mr. Taggart's eyes raked over me. I felt like I was being judged. He finally spoke again, softly, "Well Ben, no matter what Mrs. Simpson's opinions, Lois and I have lived here all our lives, and we like wildcats." His eyes moistened again, "And we'll always be grateful for the times when they accidentally help us out. Seems I owe at least one of them my son's life and I hope I get the chance to repay that debt someday." He winked, nodded his head, and turned to lead his horse, with Jason on it, down the hill.

A few minutes later we broke off from the group so Dad could take me home to get the cut looked after. As we walked through the yard toward the house, Dad finally got a chance to quiz me for a few minutes, giving me a chance to explain what really went on. When I told him how badly the panther was injured, he slumped a bit and got a sad look in his eyes for a moment. Then he seemed to lift himself up and congratulated me for keeping my head, both during the attack, and with the village folk after. I asked him about the strange panther, but he just got kind of vague and said it would come to me soon enough. He then left me with Mom and Nan Lou to fuss over my shoulder.

I finally clued in the next morning, when I was deemed well enough to watch the goats again. Mom was against it, said I should spend the day in bed, but Dad wouldn't give in. In the end, I headed up the hillside with bread and cheese for lunch, to take up my job. Getting the flock all going in one direction was harder than usual, and it only took me a couple of minutes to realize that Ernie wasn't helping me as he normally did. He wasn't there at all. I was miserable and panicked. I suddenly understood everything, and I couldn't bear it. I closed the gate with the herd still inside, and went yelling for dad. I wouldn't stop bugging him about going out to find Ernie. I was practically crying, as I demanded over and over that we go look for him.

Dad finally made me sit down and be quiet. "Ben, Ernie was around long before either of us was born. He knows how to take care of himself. Either he's dead, and there's nothing we can do about that, or he's holed up somewhere where the riders didn't find him. I'm sorry that you feel bad. I understand that you feel guilty. You feel like Ernie is gone because of you, but that's not what life is about. Ernie had a good life and if he's dead, then he died saving the life of one of his family and I'm nothing but proud for him. If he thought he needed our help, he'd have changed and stayed close to you so he could get it. You have to trust him now."

I was angry with that. I couldn't understand how Dad could just give up on Uncle Ernie like that. He'd been there as long as I could remember. Goat or not, he was part of the family and his absence hurt deep down inside.

—•—

Dad's talk didn't help as much as I think he hoped it would. For weeks I stared off into the woods around the meadow, frequently calling Ernie, and taking short trips into the brush to look for him. I finally had to give up when the goats got spooked by something while I was off one day. When I came out of the trees they were all over hell-and-gone and it took me a couple of hours to gather them up again. I still watched, and called, but it was less and less over the next few weeks. By mid-winter, I finally gave up and my life started returning to normal. I'd started talking to Dad again, and we spent time together.

My shoulder healed nicely. A bit stiff now and then, but it was fading every day. I was still tending goats every day after school, but after word got around about the qorg, the jokes pretty much stopped dead. Mr. Taggart encouraged me to visit with Victoria, which was fine with both of us I'm glad to say. A couple of other boys took exception to that, but I was carrying myself a bit differently now, and in the end, neither of them was willing to make an issue of it.

By spring, life was pretty much back to normal. Victoria and I were starting to make plans. It became clear that she and her father knew about our family secret, and they were fine with it. I was still herding goats after school, and starting to wonder what Victoria and I might do with our lives together.

There was still a hole inside, a place I didn't like to look, and some days it seemed like it would swallow me. But I thought about it less and less every day. It would hurt the most when someone bumped the bell and it rang. Dad never took it down. I think Gramper would have had a fit if he did. There was a curved line in the side of the door where 20 odd years of it swinging on the rope had worn a groove in the wood of the frame. Every time I noticed it, my eyes would fill up and the hole would feel big again.

—•—

Dad was waiting for me at the gate one day when I got home from school. He had a grin on his face as he spoke. "Ben, before you go up to the pasture, there's someone I'd like you to meet." He took my arm and led me into the house.

Nan Lou was on the couch next to a stranger. She laughed at something the silver-haired man said, and passed him a plate so he could take another cookie. He softly finished another sentence and she laughed again, harder than I'd heard in years.

"Ernie," Dad interrupted softly. "I'd like to introduce you to my son Ben. Ben, this is your Gramper's big brother, Ernie. He's come to stay with us for a while.

My jaw must have nearly hit the floor, as the white-haired man struggled to his feet with Dad's help. Ernie stood, leaning heavily on a cane with his left hand. My eyes travelled down to his twisted left leg as his right hand came out to take mine for a shake.

"Pleased to meet you, Ben," He said with a grin. "I expect we'll get along quite well, don't you think?"

Mouth still open, I looked over to Dad, who had his mouth open in a grin so wide it must have hurt. My vision blurred a bit and a feeling of enormous relief washed through me. "How…what…" I couldn't form my thoughts into words.

Ernie pulled me into a tight hug and whispered into my ear. "Couldn't abandon my goat-herd, could I? After all, I may be old and crippled, but I'm still feeling a little horny." He stepped back and winked at me. He leaned against the wall and reached out with his cane. A soft clang filled the room as he hit the bell with it. "What say we go for a walk up the hill, eh, Ben?"

—•—

Late that afternoon I watched Ernie in the pasture. He was mostly grey now instead of black and grey. He moved a lot slower too, with the bad leg. But the herd still paid attention to him, still followed his lead, so my job was easier again and I had time to relax and just watch. "Ernie?" The goat looked at me and cocked his head for a moment, but then continued grazing. I thought for a moment before continuing, "Is it hard for you to become a panther? Is that why you're usually a goat?"

He stood, chewing his mouthful of greens for a moment as though thinking. Then, in a flash, he shifted. From goat to silver panther, to a large, soft grey bird I'd never seen, to a huge coiling rattlesnake, then back to goat, still serenely munching on grass and buttercups.

I was confused. He clearly hadn't had any difficulty switching forms. If anything, he seemed faster and better at it than even Dad or Gramper. I thought about it for over an hour, watching him quietly grazing, wandering about among the other goats, and butting them affectionately now and then. I thought about what it was like when I was a panther. Slipping quietly through the dark with Dad there was a feeling of power, of control. But at the same time, a tension, wondering if someone would notice and send men and dogs running after us. I watched the sun disappearing behind the mountains, felt the last of its heat on my face. I spotted a particularly green patch of grass nearby, thick with sweet buttercups and wild chouflower. My mouth started to water and I felt my hands shifting into shiny black hooves.

A Sirius Situation

by
Daniel Archambault

W alter shut door of his pickup truck. He was home and the sky was clear. This excited him. February was over and the snow in the valley was almost gone. The weather was becoming ideal for stargazing.

Stargazing was just one of those things that Walter always had the energy to do. It didn't matter how tired he was; he could always take the time to lie down in his backyard and watch the constellations and planets above him. And as the sun set behind the lake and the mountains in the west, he was in his backyard, doing precisely that.

The stars of the spring sky began to emerge one by one. In the west, Walter knew Pegasus was setting along with Pisces, but it wasn't dark enough to see any of the major stars in either of them. Taurus was to the south with its bright star Aldebaran beginning to twinkle. Below it, Orion with Betelgeuse, and Canis Major with Sirius shone brightly; he could already see their outlines. In the east, Leo rose with Regulus and the planet Jupiter. In the northeast Ursa Major, known as the Big Dipper to many, climbed high into the sky. Before he knew it, day had become night and he could see all of the constellations he had imagined only moments before.

And at that very instant, he heard the growling for the first time.

It seemed to come from all directions at once. Walter stood up and looked around. He couldn't find the source. The growling became louder.

It was disorienting, and he was nervous. It was spring in the Okanagan, and the bears were just coming out of hibernation. Hungry bears.

Walter was making his way towards his patio doors when he heard a loud bark and then a crash. He was knocked clear off his feet and the next thing he knew, he was flat on his back in the garden. He stood up and dusted himself off. Looking back onto his lawn, he saw a white bear and a dog lying in a small depression. It seemed that both were unconscious, but it was dark and Walter wasn't taking any chances. He was backing away slowly when his wife Jill came running out onto the deck with a flashlight in hand.

"Walter? You all right?"

"Yeah, I'm fine."

"What happened?"

"I don't know. I was just out here observing, and the next minute, I'm lying on my back in the garden with two animals in our lawn."

"You probably got in the way of their fight. You're lucky you didn't get hurt," Jill said. She came down and took a closer look at the two animals. "We should probably take these two back to my clinic. I'll get the tranquilizers."

—•—

"They're both just a little cut up, that's all," Jill said as she stitched up a gash on the bear's face. "It seems the dog got the worst of it. Especially that cut on its shoulder. It looks like that the bear must've bit into it quite deeply."

Walter looked at the dog who was sleeping on some blankets on the other side of the room. Jill had done a good job cleaning it up. It looked like some sort of deerhound, but neither he nor his wife could place the breed. It was big for a dog, but not as large as the bear. The bear was just over a half-year old and outweighed the dog by about twenty pounds. It slept on the metal operating table over which his wife worked. He and his wife had both agreed it was a polar bear, but they wondered what it was doing this far south in the Okanagan.

Walter was getting tired. He had already nodded off in his chair a couple of times, and he didn't know how his wife could continue concentrating on her stitches; it must've been something they taught her in vet school. It was either that, or it explained the purpose of the glaring lights above the operating table that were now giving him a headache. Walter looked at his watch. It was one in the morning. They had been here for over three hours now.

Jill finally straightened herself up. "All right. That should do it. Honey, can you help me take this youngster to one of the outside enclosures?"

Walter nodded. Carefully, he helped Jill move the unconscious bear to a cart on wheels. They rolled the cart outside into one of the pens and unloaded it. In a similar fashion, they loaded the dog into another of the pens. Here, the animals would be isolated from most human contact while they healed. In a day or two, Walter would take the bear up into the mountains in his pickup and release it back into the wild.

—•—

When Walter woke up the next morning, the sun was already shining, bringing promise of a wonderful day. He was looking forward to going off to work at the park. As he was loading his truck, he noticed the state of the pens for the first time.

"Jill?" he called.

"Yeah?"

"The bear's gone."

"What?"

"The bear's gone."

It took her a few moments to run downstairs. She opened the patio doors as she was doing up her bathrobe. "That's impossible."

"See for yourself."

Jill looked inside the pen to see that it was empty. She checked the five others to make sure they hadn't placed the animals in another one by accident last night. There was no bear or dog to be seen.

She shook her head.

"Look, Jill. The worst that could happen is that they ran off back into the woods, right?"

—•—

By the time Walter returned home from work, the sun had already dipped below the mountains in the west. Another day to stargaze, but after last night and this morning, he'd stay a little closer to home. Tonight, he would be observing from his patio.

The sky was darkening to a navy blue and the stars were slowly beginning to twinkle into existence. Venus shone high in the west with unwavering brightness. In the east, Jupiter was just rising above the horizon in Leo. Walter took out his binoculars and steadied them on the railing of his deck. As he looked at Jupiter, he thought he could pick out two or three moons of the planet. He tried to remember which ones they were from the charts he'd looked at earlier in the day. Ganymede, then Io, then Callisto he thought it should be right now. He'd have to check that after dinner. Maybe later on in the night, he would come back out and see how they moved.

By the time he was done observing Jupiter, it was pretty dark already. He could see Orion was already clearing the horizon in the east. However, Sirius, the brightest star in the sky, appeared to be missing. He took out his binoculars and scanned the horizon, even though he shouldn't have needed optical aid to see it. Nothing.

Perhaps, he had just underestimated its right ascension? It must be still below the horizon. It must. With the mountains here, it was most likely the case. However, the pattern of the stars in the sky seemed wrong. He felt that Sirius should be visible now, up near the right thigh of Orion.

"Nice night, isn't it?"

The voice startled him. It was deep, but somehow it still managed to sound as if it belonged to a child. Walter looked over his left shoulder to see a translucent bear become solid before his eyes.

The bear turned its head away from him and let out one giant burp. "Oops. Excuse me," it said. It rubbed its stomach with a paw. "It seems that I've swallowed some bad gas."

Walter nearly fell over. He barely reached a deck chair, pulled it in close, and fell onto it.

"Oh. Sorry for appearing out of nowhere, but I couldn't help myself. Sunlight generally makes us invisible."

"What are you and how come you speak English?"

"Well, I'm Ursa Minor of course. My first languages are Ancient Greek and Arabic, but I figured you wouldn't understand either of those. I learned English from the constellations in the southern hemisphere. That's their first language ..."

"Jill!"

"Hey! What are you doing?"

"I'm about to confirm that I'm hallucinating. Jill!"

The bear stood up on its hind legs and put its paws against its hips. "I'm not a hallucination. How dare you insinuate that I ever was!"

"Jill!"

She poked her head out of the clinic's window. She must've been working later than usual.

"What?"

"Is there a talking bear in that cage?"

The bear waved a paw. "Hi there, Jill."

"Hi, Ursa Minor." Jill looked Walter squarely in the face. "Walter, Ursa Minor. Ursa Minor, Walter. I've been talking to Canis Major in here for the past half-hour. Do you mind cooking supper tonight, honey? I believe it's your turn."

Walter gave a slight nod.

"Thanks. I'll be inside in a few minutes." She ducked her head back into the window and was gone.

Walter made a slight whimpering noise and the bear giggled as he walked slowly back toward the house.

—•—

After dinner, Ursa Minor sat on a chair in the kitchen at the head of the table. It leafed through some of Walter's old astronomy magazines like they were old family photo albums as it sipped its tea. Occasionally, it would come across a planetary alignment, eclipse, or some other astronomical event and sigh heavily. "Ah, the good old days," it would say, or something to that effect. Once or twice, the bear was all choked up as nostalgia overcame it.

Canis Major was sitting next to Jill on the other side of the table. The dog was just finishing its serving of the chicken souvlaki Walter had made for everyone. It held its head in its right paw. Its left paw picked flecks of chicken from its teeth with a small bone. The poor dog looked like death. It was tired and quite banged up. It had a steaming mug of coffee next to it, which it sipped regularly.

Jill sat between the two constellations directly across from Walter with a cup of tea in her hands. She sipped it before Walter asked the same question he had asked for the past hour.

"So, two constellations fell out of the sky after they got in a little scuffle last night?"

She nodded.

"And one of them was injured?"

Canis Major lifted its left paw. "That's right, bud."

"And later on tonight they'll be trying to go back to the sky?"

Jill nodded.

"Oh look at them, would you?" Ursa Minor said. The bear poked Walter in the shoulder a couple of times before shoving a 1998 issue of *Skynews Magazine* in front of his face. In the magazine was a picture of the half-degree alignment between Venus and Jupiter in April of that year. The moon was no more than a degree below the pair. "Look at Zeus! And Aphrodite she … she … looks just so darling. Oh, how they squabble so beautifully together! And look, here comes Artemis, and oh, boy does she look upset!" It sighed happily, holding the magazine to its chest. "What a lovely argument that was had by all!" The bear went back to its reading.

Walter turned to Jill, confused. "Lovely argument?"

"The Gods of ancient Greece were imperfect. Quite a dysfunctional family, really."

"Oh."

"So, it's not going to bother you if they stay here for a bit?"

Walter looked at the two of them again. "Just as long as they don't ruin the furniture."

And just as Walter finished his sentence, their chesterfield flew through the wall behind him.

It stuck into the wall just about a foot above Walter's head. It and he were covered in white dust. He blinked the dust out of his eyes and spat some of it out of his mouth.

There was some screaming that came from the family room. It was a man's voice. "I'm going to kill that bear. I swear to the Gods that I'm going to kill that bear!"

Ursa Minor, who unfortunately heard this, darted under the table, hiding quite unsuccessfully beneath it. The table was a foot off the floor resting on the bear's back.

"Orion. Calm down, buddy. It was as much your dog's fault as it was Ursa Minor's," a second voice pleaded.

"Shut up, Perseus," Orion grumbled, as he appeared through the doorway.

Orion was big. He easily filled the doorway with his frame and had to slouch and turn sideways to enter the kitchen. He turned and looked down at everyone sitting at the table. His eyes caught on Canis Major.

"Canny! Oh, Canny! What has that brute done to you? Oh, Gods are you all right?"

Orion fell to his knees. His large arms were around his pup hugging it tightly. "'Rion. Yo, 'Rion! I'm fine, 'k? Just don't crush me!"

He let go of the dog's shoulders and backed away from it. Tears were running down his cheeks. His face was reddening with rage. His right shoulder gleamed brightly and began to swell.

"Oh, Gods! He's causing Betelgeuse to go nova!" Perseus pulled out a bag from his pack. "Calm down, Orion. Don't make me use this," he threatened. "I will stop you if I have to and you know that I can."

Orion shook his head. He grabbed the table with his right hand. In his grip, the wood groaned and then snapped in half. Ursa Minor, without protection, was now shaking on the floor, its paws covering its head.

"Orion. Cut it out now," Perseus said.

"'Rion, we were just playing. Don't kill him!" Canis Major pleaded.

Orion ignored them. His sword came out of its sheath, gleaming with the brightness of three stars. A red nebula obscured the point. He grabbed the bear by the scruff of the neck. As the sword came down,

Perseus jumped out in front of him with something green in his hand that seemed to squirm.

There was a flash of light, which completely blinded Walter. When the kitchen slowly faded back into view, Orion was now a stone statue. Ursa Minor looked above its paws. After suddenly realizing that there was a chance it wasn't going to be killed, it scurried to the other side of the kitchen, hiding unsuccessfully behind Walter's legs. Perseus slipped the green thing back into a bag and turned back to Walter.

"I'm so sorry about that. My friend here can have a little bit of a temper sometimes. I'll help you fix your kitchen back up."

Walter examined what was once their kitchen. "No, that's okay …"

"No. I insist. I'll fix what I can and help pay for the rest," Perseus said. He began retying the drawstring on the bag in his hands. Walter looked at it curiously.

"What's in the bag?"

"Oh, in the kibisis?"

"The what?"

"The kibisis," Perseus said. "That's what you call this bag."

"Oh. Well, what's in the kib-er whatever." He tried to peer through the open neck of the kibisis, but Perseus pulled it away from him and quickly tied it closed.

"Trust me. You don't want to peek in there."

Jill jabbed Walter in the ribs with her elbow. "Medusa's head," she whispered.

As Perseus put away the bag containing Medusa's head, Walter walked up to the newly formed Orion statue in their kitchen.

"We can't just leave him here," he said as he tapped the statue. "Just think of how many times we'll bang into it while it's invisible during the day."

"We could put him in the garden?" Jill said.

Walter thought about this for a second. He looked at the rage contorting Orion's face. "Don't you think it'll scare the neighbours?"

Jill frowned. "You're probably right."

"We could put him in the basement?"

"Yeah. We could do that."

"But, how do we get him down there? That statue looks awfully heavy."

"Leave that to me," Perseus said. He lifted the statue off the ground with ease and held it over his shoulder as if it were a sack of potatoes. Jill and Walter gawked.

"What?" He grinned. "I'm a son of Zeus, remember? Now, where do I put this thing?"

—•—

Perseus managed to successfully navigate the Orion statue down the stairs without banging up the walls too much with Jill and Walter following in tow. They moved their zodiac card table which they bought in the sixties, and placed the Orion statue between their washer and dryer. Walter began to use the statue as a clothes rack, but Jill started removing what he had hung up.

"How would you like it if I used you as a clothes rack?"

"Jill. It's not like he's going to remember anything."

"Oh he's fully aware," Perseus said. "He just can't do anything about it. Yet."

Walter swallowed and put his clothes on hangers faster than either Jill or he could ever remember.

"Can we keep this statue?" Jill said with a smile as Walter threw the last of the five shirts on a hanger. "I'm beginning to like it."

"Unfortunately, no," Perseus said. "When I get some help from the rest of the sky, I think we should be putting him back. Now, about your kitchen. Walter? Do you have any repair supplies?"

"Yeah. I have a small workshop over there," he said as he brought them around to the other side of the furnace. "There are some building supplies here and some tools over there. Are you sure you don't want me to help?"

"No, no. Orion and I caused you all this trouble, and you shouldn't have to clean up after us. I'll fix your walls and shelves tonight. Your kitchen table is going to need more work, though."

"Don't worry about that," Walter said. "Jill and I will go into

Kelowna sometime on the weekend and find a new one. Until then, we could eat in our family room."

"All right. But, I'm going to help you pay for the new table." Perseus motioned to drop a few coins in Walter's hand. He tried to refuse them, but Perseus placed them in his hand anyway. "I insist."

Walter didn't want to argue with him and put the coins into his pocket. "All right. Are you sure you won't need more than the evening to fix up the kitchen? You can have more time if you'd like."

Perseus already had all of the repair supplies together. "I wish I had time," he said, "but I have to get back to Andromeda. She was kinda tied up the last time I saw her, and I wouldn't want her to be Cetus' lunch you know."

Walter wanted to ask, but before he could, Perseus and all the building supplies were gone. There was some very quick hammering and sawing upstairs and then nothing. Walter and Jill tried to follow him up the stairs, but they were way too slow. When they looked into the kitchen, everything, except the table was repaired and cleaned. The table was still broken in half and was leaning upright against the counter.

Ursa Minor sat on one of the chairs, reading a book and Canis Major walked around the now rather empty-looking room.

"Those sandals that Hermes lent him certainly do make him travel quickly," Jill said. Walter was still amazed.

Canis Major bobbed its head in agreement. "He's already returned to the sky," the dog said, "and we should probably try to return there too."

—•—

The four of them walked outside into the moonless night. Walter could see every constellation clearly. He could see every star that would be drawn on one of the star charts in his room at home. There were, however, some exceptions that he noticed for the first time. In the north, the sky was the darkest he had ever seen. Each and every star of the constellation Ursa Minor was missing.

"That's what happens when nobody's home," Ursa Minor said. The bear grimaced after finishing its sentence.

"What's wrong?" Walter asked. "Are you all right?"

"I've had a bit of a stomach ache for most of the night," Ursa Minor said. It burped and rubbed its stomach with a paw again. "But, don't worry. I'll be fine."

"All right, but don't hurt yourself. You're welcome to stay here another night if you need it. All you need to do is ask."

"Thanks, but no thanks. I think we should try returning tonight."

Walter nodded. He looked up at the starless patch of sky. "How do you get back there anyway?"

"The opposite way I came down here. I jump."

"You jump?"

The bear nodded. It walked up a few yards ahead of Walter. "You should probably stand back. If I run into you on the way up, this could hurt."

The bear bent its four legs awkwardly and jumped. At first, it seemed that Ursa Minor hadn't jumped that high, but then Walter realized that it did not obey the laws of optics. The bear didn't diminish in size as it rose higher and higher upward. When it hit the sky, the sound it made was very much like falling down hard onto a wooden floor. Unfortunately, the bear had now changed its direction and begun falling down again.

Jill and Walter had to scramble out of the way. The bear hit the ground about five feet from them. The ground shook on impact. Soil was kicked up into the air and Walter felt a dusting of it land on his head. When the dirt settled in his backyard, there was a small impact crater with Ursa Minor in it. The bear rose to its feet and shook its head quickly.

"Let me try," Canis Major said.

Canis Major took off for the horizon, running quickly. The dog, as well, did not obey any of the laws of optics. Its image barely diminished in size as it reached the horizon. It vaulted into the sky, turning sideways. Appearing to balance on the tips of the mountains, it fell back-first toward the southern sky.

Unfortunately, when Canis Major hit the sky another loud wooden thud came. The dog's expression changed quickly. It winced and then began to yelp. Its whining seemed to come from all directions at once as it slid off the sky and back onto the ground.

Ursa Minor looked up at Jill. "It looks like we're going to be stuck here for a while."

"What's wrong? Why can't you go back?"

"I don't know."

—•—

The next day was one of those days when Walter figured he just should've stayed in bed.

He went to work. Things were going pretty good, until later that morning. He had some high school kids come for a tour of the park. It seemed that a few of the kids had been noticing that some of the stars were missing from the sky over the past couple of nights. One of them had asked him why. He said that he didn't know.

After lunch, CBC radio aired a special called "Bright Stars Missing from Sky" (guess what that was about). Supposedly, the unexplained phenomenon had a lot of Canadians worried. The announcer pleaded with the general public to remain calm. She assured the listeners that astronomers all over the world were looking for an explanation. Her plea didn't seem to register with some of the callers. Many of them were still freaked out.

All in all, Walter was glad his day was over and that he was driving home.

He stepped out of his pickup truck, and shut the door behind him. He walked around to his backyard and to the pens that held Ursa Minor and Canis Major. As the sun set behind the mountains, the bear and the dog's stars began to emerge and their outlines began to ghost into existence as they did.

But, there was something wrong. Walter knew his constellations, and if Ursa Minor was Ursa Minor, the bear had a bright star in it that didn't belong. He traced the constellation out with his fingers. The star was inside the bear's belly. When he looked back at Canis Major, who was now solidifying as well, he noticed that a prominent star was missing from its shoulder. He remembered what Ursa Minor had said last night:

"I've had a bit of a stomach ache for most of the night."

"Sirius!"

"What was that?" Ursa Minor said through a yawn. The bear was fully solid now.

"Ursa Minor. If you didn't have the right stars, you wouldn't be able to return to the sky, would you?"

Ursa Minor thought about this for a second. "I suppose that's true, but how would that happen?"

Walter looked at the gash on Canis Major's shoulder. Sirius. That was exactly where the star belonged, and there was absolutely nothing there when the dog began to solidify.

"I think that explains your stomach ache and the reason you can't get back into the sky. We've got to get Canis Major and you to Jill. You bit off Sirius and swallowed it by accident."

—•—

"That's exactly what happened," Jill said, as she put Ursa Minor's x-ray on the back light. It looked like a normal x-ray to Walter, all except the very bright, white dot in the centre of it. "Ursa Minor swallowed a star. The star Sirius actually."

"Can you get it out?" Ursa Minor said.

"I could try to remove it from you surgically," Jill said. "I have removed many things from animals before, however, I must admit that I've never removed a star." She put a hand to her chin. "It seems that your physiology is very similar to other species of bear that I've worked with in the past. Assuming the star is similar to any other foreign body a bear might ingest, it should be reasonable."

"When can you take this out of me?"

"I could take it out tonight if you'd like. It seems to be causing you some discomfort, so that is what I'd recommend. Canis Major? Is that all right with you? I'm am going to have to put this star back into your shoulder once I take it out of Ursa Minor."

The dog nodded. "Yeah. Let's do it."

—•—

Less than an hour later, Canis Major was lying next to Ursa Minor's operating table. Jill had frozen the dog's shoulder so that the star wouldn't hurt too much when she reinserted it. She was about to begin the operation with Walter assisting. He had helped his wife in the operating room before, and he knew that he could help again. He couldn't speak for Jill, but he was slightly nervous about what they would find inside Ursa Minor.

"Scalpel."

Jill made her entry cut.

Walter was always fascinated and terrified by surgery. He wondered how anyone could stay focused and calm as they worked on another living animal. He wouldn't have trouble assisting, but staying calm was another matter altogether.

Jill worked for about a half-hour before she found what was presumably the bear's stomach. When she made a small incision into it, blue light shone out. Light that was so bright that it was easily visible under the white lights of the operating room. They saw a ball of swirling blue gasses floating just below the opening.

"Forceps," Jill said.

Walter handed them to her. Just as she was about to extract the star, she hesitated.

"Oven mitts."

"What?"

"Oven mitts. This star's going to be pretty hot. I wouldn't want to burn myself."

"Okay. But, it's going to take me a few seconds to get those. Not standard O.R. equipment you know."

Walter ran from the room and into the kitchen. He grabbed the oven mitts from the stove. He ran back, washed up, and sterilized them the best he could with some bleach.

"Oven mitts," he said handing them to her.

"Okay," she said as she put them on, "I'm going to extract the star now."

She clamped the forceps down onto the star and pulled it out. It looked wispy out in the open as tiny solar flares went off during extraction process. It appeared that the star did not want to be moved. She turned to bring it over to Canis Major's shoulder.

"No! Wait!" The dog cried.

"What?" Jill asked

"I need sunblock! I don't want to get sun... er um... Sirius burn."

"Walter?"

"Already gone," he called from the other room. He got the S.P.F. 60 stuff from their bathroom, washed up, and returned to the O.R.

"Sunblock," he said, squeezing some of the stuff onto the dog's paw. Canis Major rubbed it into the shaved skin around the wound.

"Thanks."

"No problem."

"You ready?" Jill asked.

"Yeah. Go right ahead," Canis Major said.

The star burned away the stitches to the wound revealing a small cavity where it belonged. She placed it inside the cavity, which healed instantly.

"Ahhhhh!" Canis Major said. "That feels much better."

— • —

Ursa Minor rubbed the dressing that covered the small incision on its belly. It took a walk around the backyard and ended up at Jill's feet on the patio.

"I'm not that sore," it said, "But, I'm going to need help to get back to the sky. Canis Major? Would you get some help for Orion and I when you get back?"

Canis Major nodded. It seemed that the dog would agree to almost anything about now. The dog was ready to go. It broke out into a run for the horizon and quickly met it. It jumped, turning sideways above the mountains as it did. As Canis Major hit the sky, it slowly dissolved into stars and melded back into the blackness.

"I'm back! I've made it back to the sky!" It yelled, its voice coming from all directions at once.

And then, there was silence for just one moment.

With sounds that neither Walter nor Jill could identify, constellations in droves hopped out of the sky. Ursa Major jumped down from the northwest, bright stars highlighting its neck and body. The Gemini twins jumped down from almost directly above. Castor was shining on the forehead of one and Pollux on the cheek of the other. Leo jumped down from the east with Regulus shining brightly on its chest. Cancer jumped down. The large crab had the beehive cluster on its stomach. Perseus came down from the west and landed on his feet right in front of Jill and Walter.

"Canis Major said Ursa Minor needs some help back to the sky. We might as well put Orion back there too. Do you mind if I go and get him?"

"No. Not at all," Walter said.

Perseus flickered and the Orion statue was outside. "Thanks," he said as he hefted it onto his shoulders. "Hey guys," he called out to the other constellations, "I think we should put Orion back first."

The other constellations built themselves into a pyramid with Leo and Cancer at the bottom, balancing on the mountains. Gemini and Perseus hefted the Orion statue. Presumably, they were going on top. Ursa Major stood on its hind legs on the backs of the other constellations and bit into the sky just above the rabbit, Lepus. It hauled its head downwards, and the sky stretched like a sheet of rubber down to the southern horizon. Lepus wasn't too happy being scrunched up into a ball. It kicked Ursa Major in the face, causing the big bear to let go of the sky.

"You're crushing me! Stop it!"

Canis Major stuck its head out of the sky. "I'm sorry, Lepus, but we've got to get Orion back into the sky," it said.

"You're going to put the hunter back into the sky? The hunter that chases *me* every night and I'm going to let you?" The rabbit laughed.

"I won't chase you as much as I did the last millennia."

Lepus looked at the dog skeptically.

"I promise."

"And you'll give me prime viewing for the next forty solar and lunar eclipses?"

"What? That's highway robbery, pal!"

Lepus thumped its feet against Ursa Major's jaw three more times. "I can do this all night!"

"Okay. Okay. But ten."

"Thirty."

"Fifteen."

"Twenty five, and that's as low as I go."

"Grrrrr. Deal."

Lepus cackled and turned to Ursa Major. "Bite a little to the north, please."

Ursa Major obeyed and pulled the sky down to its ankles with its powerful jaws. Hercules' head was pulled just above the northern horizon, and he watched the scene with curiosity. Perseus and Gemini climbed onto Leo's and Cancer's backs, trying to wedge the Orion statue back into its spot. They hammered at him for a while before the statue was accepted again. Ursa Major opened its jowls, and let go. The sky seemed to oscillate north-south for a bit before coming to rest. Lepus got a little queasy and Hercules fell back below the northern horizon with an audible "Eeeep."

Ursa Minor was next. The bear's place in the sky was directly north, and fortunately, moderately close to the horizon. Ursa Major stood on the backs of Cancer and Leo again, and Ursa Minor climbed on top of the pyramid. The little bear looked up at its place in the sky and hopped. It turned upside down and made its way back easily.

All of the other constellations quickly jumped back to their places, leaving Walter and Jill alone in their backyard. They sat there together in the quiet darkness, looking skyward. Seemingly out of nowhere, the curtains of the northern lights began to roll in from the horizon. They covered a quarter of the sky radiating down from the zenith. As they did so, Ursa Minor flicked them with its paws and bit at their fringes. Walter and Jill could swear that the bear cub was giggling as the translucent swirls tickled its belly.

"Don't injure yourself again," Jill called out. "The cut's going to take a few weeks to heal."

The bear ignored her and began climbing the luminous curtains, running up and down them more confidently and quickly.

"Weeeee."

"Ursa Minor! Stop it!"

Canis Major stuck its head out of the southern sky. "Let me try."

"Canis Major, no! Bad dog! Canis Major? Canis Major!" Jill yelled.

But it was too late, the dog vaulted overhead toward the northern horizon. It caught the fringe of the curtains in its paws. The lights swayed upward and Canis Major began play-fighting with Ursa Minor again. When the curtains and the two constellations swayed back down, the curtains tore. A few bits of diaphanous cloth flew off and the two constellations came tumbling down, landing in the lake just offshore behind Walter and Jill's house with a large *sploosh!*

Jill turned to Walter and sighed. She rose to her feet and began walking back towards the clinic, presumably to get the tranquilizers again.

"Kids," she muttered. "They never listen."

Once Upon a Toad

by
Wen Spencer

From the high white cliffs of Spine Mountain, Norrie could see the entire kingdom. As always, the Blight covered the eastern horizon like a thunderstorm caught in glass.

"It's hard to tell, everything is so far away," Norrie told the toad, Phred, sitting on the boulder beside her. "I think the Blight has gotten closer — don't you think?"

"Yyyyyyup," Phred croaked, and she pretended that he agreed with her. He was good company, for all of being a toad. There had been a horde of toads around the wizard's tower, but Phred stood out for his size, mobility, and sheer noise. While the other toads seemed happy to lurk in dark corners of the basement laundry room, croaking only when no one was about, Phred had sat in plain sight and puffed out his throat in running commentary.

"I can remember when it was just a little black pimple that you could only see at sunrise." Even in those early days, she had to walk from town to town to find a job. She only found one as good as laundry maid to the legendary wizard, Dyndentin, because everyone else had been too scared of him. True he sometimes forgot odd things in his pockets — dried newts and bat skeletons and such — but he'd been kind and good to her.

"Hopefully it's just a trick of the light and it's no closer to the tower. They say the Blight is the stuff of nightmares."

The wizard was more grumpy than fearsome as everyone claimed, and the things that darted under the furniture — while magical and strange — were no more bothersome than mice and moths. So, maybe, the Blight appeared more frightening than it truly was.

Phred flicked out his tongue and caught a passing fly.

"Yeah, true, no sense worrying about it." Norrie took another bite out of her travel bread and tried to ignore the ominous cloud. Certainly, she had other problems to consider, like finding her way into the Dragon Caves.

For years, Master Dyndentin's health had been poor. Powerful wizard or not, he was still an old man. Last week, he'd fallen down the stairs and broken several bones. He would be bedridden for months and the Blight's shadow already darkened their mornings. Someone had to do something. Norrie had poured through the history books in the wizard's library; while they disagreed over the origin of the Blight, the cause of its periodic outbreak, and the nature of the spreading evil, they all agreed that it could only be defeated when a seeker journeyed to the Dragon Caves to call forth a hero filled with the gods' might.

Taking things she didn't think Dyndentin would miss, Norrie had set off for Spine Mountains two days ago. The map she'd borrowed, however, only showed one cave opening, yet she could see three from where they sat. Now she spread the map out in front of Phred. "What do you think this means?"

"Mmrph?" Phred croaked, a stray fly leg still sticking out of the corner of his mouth.

She pointed to the nebulous point. "Yeah, it does say 'enter here at the cave mouth' but which one of these caves is the entrance?"

He leapt forward and landed on the map, covering the words completely.

"Hey, get your wet toady butt off that!" She snatched him off the map. Where he'd landed was slightly damp and the words 'enter here' were starting to smear. "Oh, no!"

Norrie stuffed him back into her pocket where he'd spent most of their trip, and held up the map to blow dry the spot. Everything had seemed so simple, back at the wizard's tower. She only had to find the legendary hero in the Dragon Caves, and he would ride out to vanquish the Blight, as all heroes over the ages had done before him.

Hiking up to Spine Mountains had been easier than she expected. The priests of the shrines dotting the ridge maintained the pilgrimage road. What she hadn't counted on was how many caves would pock it. Who would have guessed that Spine Mountains were holey as well as holy? Thinking that all the caves might be linked together, she'd explored two yesterday, but they narrowed down to cracks only Phred could have fit through.

"Crawling around in every cave we find isn't the answer. Sooner or later we'll end up wedged into some nook or cranny and then where would we be?"

"Sssstuuuuck," Phred gave a muffled croak from her pocket.

"Exactly."

In the books, the seeker simply 'journeyed' to the caves, found the hero, and pointed him in the right direction. While the hero's life — from his first battle to the last — was recorded in great detail, the books never covered what Norrie thought was the most interesting parts. What was he doing down in the caves? Why was he waiting in the dark? Playing fetch with his dragon steed? Who made his magical armor and sword of fire? She'd have to remember to ask when him when she found him.

That led back to the problem at hand — how to find him.

She tested the damp spot on the map and found it dry, but the ink had blurred everything but the word 'mouth' into one large inkblot. The pilgrim road lead from the blotch to Taisendville, looking like a big-headed snake. Or a dragon. She squinted at the town's name; it wasn't to hard to pretend it was actually Tail's End Village.

"What do you think? Does 'mouth' mean the mouth of the dragon?"

"Yyyyyuppppp."

—•—

The problem with that theory was the pilgrimage road ended at the edge of a cliff. A little weather-beaten shrine marked the site as a holy place. The white stone peaks of Spine Mountain dropped down to this point exactly like vertebrae picked clean, so where she stood should be the dragon's head. There were no caves, nor anything that looked like a mouth.

What now? Norrie had been sure that she was right — that the road would lead to the mouth.

Phred climbed out of her pocket.

"No!" She caught him as he leapt for the ground. "It's too dangerous here!"

He squirmed in her hands and poked his head up between her fingers. "Dddoownnnn!"

"There's nothing here but cliffs," she told him as the salt wind tore at her clothes. "I'm afraid you'll hop right over the edge."

"Dddooownn."

"Besides, we're not staying. This is the wrong place. We should be standing right on top of the skull, but there's no ..." She stopped, staring at the wide flat top of Phred's head. "Oh! If this is the top, then the mouth would be down at the bottom."

"Ddddooownnn," Phred agreed.

Holding him tightly, Norrie inched to the cliff edge and peered over. It wasn't a straight drop down, more a series of steep slopes, much like the front of Phred's face. The ocean roared endlessly at the foot of cliff, foaming white over ragged rocks.

"Oh, my, none of the books said anything about this." This explained why the Blight had advanced so far without someone searching out the hero. "What is he doing way down there? I think I'm going to have a bone to pick with this hero when I find him."

She walked the edge, hoping for a safer shortcut but found nothing. Like Phred's head, the tip of land was wedge-shaped; the center point fell away in a steep slope, while the sides were sheer cliffs. If she were going down, it would have to be down the middle of the nose.

"I don't know, Phred, what if I'm wrong?"

Phred was silent, leaving her alone with her uncertainty and fear.

"I suppose, it's just like laundry, difficult and unpleasant but it has to be done." She looked down at Phred in her hands. "This is going to be dangerous. I could fall. Do you want to come with me?"

He gave her the same answer as he did at the wizard's tower. "Yyyyuuup."

"Oh good, I don't know if I'd be brave enough to go on alone." She tucked him back into her pocket. "Stay put. I won't have a hand free to catch you."

She made sure her walking stick and backpack were strapped tight across her back. The white stone of the cliff was smooth as bone, making her wonder if this was indeed the skeleton of a dragon stretched out across the land. Luckily the stone had little bumps and ridges for handholds and her arms were strong and her hands well calloused from doing laundry. The way grew steeper, and the roar of the ocean grew louder, until she clung to a sheer wet cliff face, the spray misting her like fine rain. Just as she started to worry that she have to climb the whole way down to the raging surf, she found a small opening.

"This is awfully tiny for a mouth for such a big head." Norrie eyed the cliff around her. There wasn't another, more likely cave. "Well, forward and onward."

She crawled through the tight opening into darkness. After a dozen feet, she found herself in a wide, open cave. Narrow, regularly spaced slits let light in from outside; after her eyes adjusted, she realized the sunlight shone between great teeth. She had entered the mouth where one tooth was missing.

"It is a dragon, Phred. A huge one! I wonder what it ate."

"Bbbbliiiight."

"Yes, I suppose it might have." Dragons were holy creatures, so perhaps the Blight fungus didn't affect them, and certainly there was lots of it. Also while the beasts twisted by the Blight were monstrous, nothing suggested that they weren't edible.

Norrie had come prepared for exploring caves: travel rations, fresh water, a bag of illums that magically gave off light, and large piece of chalk. "We'll mark our way as we go." She activated one of the illums. The mouth led to a narrower cave in the back, the soft glow from illum seemed pitiful compared to the darkness beyond. "It could swallow me whole."

"Wwwwwhaaat?"

She wasn't sure if she meant the dragon or the darkness. "Never mind." She made a mark to make sure the chalk left a visible white arrow, pointing back toward the entrance. "Let's go."

There were a distressing number of similar marks on the walls, some of them even seemed recent. The tunnel led down into a huge chamber, which might have been the dragon's stomach. Monstrous skeletons littered the uneven floor, huge and misshapen with too many limbs.

"Well, what do you know?" Norrie nudged a skeleton with her foot, reassuring herself that it was very dead. "It seems that Blight beasts are edible."

There was, however, no sign of the sword, the dragon, or the hero. Picking her way around the edge of the cave, she found several passages twisting away into the darkness. Numbering each one, she continued until she returned to the one she entered through.

"I don't know, Phred, a dozen tunnels and they all seem the same. I suppose I should just pick one."

Phred croaked.

"Yes, I suppose starting at number one probably would be best."

The first tunnel branched three times in twisting passages that went up and down and sideways. At one point, Norrie squirmed up through one tight hole to pop into a small cavern. "I wonder if this is how earthworms feel, wriggling blindly around in the dirt. Do they spend all their time wondering: 'Where am I? How did I get here?'"

In the end, all the branches of the first tunnel led to nothing, and she retraced her steps to the stomach to explore the second one. It, at least, came to a quick dead end. By the time she returned to dragon's stomach, she was exhausted and the illum was failing.

"I wonder how long I've been down here. It seems like hours. Do you suppose it's night now?"

"Yyyyuuup."

"I didn't know it was going to be this hard." Norrie climbed back up to the mouth, where the air was warmer. "Not that it makes much difference. It had to be done. I just wish it wasn't me doing it. Someone smarter. Someone braver. Someone who is more than just a laundry maid."

—•—

She fell the next day.

The third tunnel had been relativity wide and level. Norrie was walking slowly, but still, where there should have been solid stone, there was nothing, and she found herself falling.

—•—

"Noooooooorie."

She woke up, laying on the floor. Phred was sitting nose to nose to her. He looked as concerned as she felt. His throat puffed up as he croaked again. "Nooooorie."

The illum lay on the floor, still gleaming brightly. She could not have fallen far, or laid long unconscious long.

"Oh, that last step was a doozie." She was stiff and bruised all over, but luckily nothing broken. The hole she'd fallen through, through, was far over her head. "Hopefully there's another way out of here, Phred."

Still her heart sunk in her chest as she marked an arrow straight up. "Nothing to be done now but go on."

—•—

Norrie was lost. She was cold. She was hungry. And soon, she'd be in the dark, as she only had two more illums left.

Trying not to panic, she explored as quickly as she dared.

"Norrie! Norrie, where are you?" A voice called to her out of the dark.

Norrie turned around. No one was there. She peered inside Phred's pocket. "Phred? Was that you?"

"No, no, no, it's me." A gleaming light appeared in front of her. "Dyndentin."

"Oh, Master Dyndentin, you died?" A stab of guilt went through her — she'd thought that other tower servants — while old and frail as their master — could take proper care of the wizard.

"No!" The light brightened slightly, as if fueled by Dyndentin's annoyance. "I'm using a spell to speak with you! Where in blue blazes are you, girl?"

"I'm trying to find the hero."

"Have you gone daft?" The light flashed into brilliance.

"Well, someone had to go." Norrie blinked, suddenly blinded by the outburst. "I read all the books you have on the other heroes."

"Bah!"

"It is written …"

"Any idiot can pick up a pen and scribble complete nonsense down!"

She was getting little dots of light burned into her vision from his outbursts. "But …"

"The gods gave you a brain for a reason — why don't you use it? There's a reason why no one else has done it."

"So what's written isn't true?"

"It's like gold in river gravel, you need to sift to find the truth. Some of it is true, for all the good it does anyone. A great hero can be found on an island of white stone in the secret lake, deep in the heart of the Dragon Caves. The shining armor, the guardian dragon, the sword of fire, yadda yadda yadda, that's all true."

"So the legend is true?"

"Of course. Time to time, throughout history, they appear, in full glory, dragon and all. You can find their armor, their swords — and their very large dead bodies in the case of the dragons — here and there."

"If it's true, what's the problem?"

The light sputtered with the wizard's indignation. Dyndentin didn't like to swear around her, so he stammered out bits and pieces of words until he found something safe to say. "Dragon's flame, girl, how dense can you get? It's dangerous! The caves are a virtual maze. You could be lost forever in them. Even if you find the lake, you might not find the hero, and only a hero can call the dragon, and the only way out is via the dragon."

"Yes, I'm starting to realize that."

"Come home now. Someone else will take care that."

"I haven't seen anyone else looking." Norrie didn't want to admit that she was lost.

"Because everyone knows it's dangerous. Just come home."

"I can't."

"We'll find someone to go. We'll put out a reward — there's always fools willing to risk their lives for money."

"They say that doesn't work. They say only the true of heart can find the hero."

"Bah! It's ancient magic — who knows for sure what the laws are that govern it? The gods might have been wise and merciful but they were also obtuse. Just come home, Norrie."

"Master Dyndentin — I can't — I'm lost!"

"You're in the caves already?"

"Yes!"

The light sputtered for a minute. "Blast it girl, then there's nothing I can do!"

—•—

Norrie rounded the corner, and there it was — the lake.

Small motes of light moved above the dark water, only lighting it enough to show that the lake was enormous. She crouched to test the depth of the water with her hand. It was cold as it was dark. She used her walking stick to probe the depth of the water — all five feet of the stick and her arm up to the elbow without finding bottom.

She walked the shore, a half-arc until she reached impassable stone, and found nothing that looked like a boat, or a bridge, or hint of an island out in the darkness.

"Hello! Is there anyone there?" She shouted, and her words echoed back.

She sat down, feeling like crying.

Phred climbed out of her pocket, and croaked. "Wwwwwhat?" and it echoed back.

"Exactly — what should I do?"

Was there more than one lake? Was there really an island somewhere in the darkness? If the hero was out there, why wasn't he answering her?

With a quiet, familiar noise, Phred suddenly flicked out his long tongue, snared one of the shimmering motes, and ate it. She only caught one glimpse of the bug, something thin, long, and gleaming with pale dragonfly wings. Whatever it had been, it now gleamed dimly in Phred's stomach.

"I'm not sure you should eat those things."

"Whhhhy?"

"Well, they might be bad for you."

But Phred chose to ignore her, eating three more as they floated past. His stomach glowed brighter.

If she kept searching for a way out, there was a small chance she could find one. Swimming out into the darkness, looking blindly for the hero's island of white stone, seemed insane, especially considering how cold the water was — it would be like swimming in winter. Even if she found the island in the dark, she would stay wet and cold. It changed things from she 'might' die to 'in all likelihood.' She had been willing to risk her life — but was she ready to die?

She heard a splash and turned. "Phred?"

Phred was a bright gleam in the water, already several feet out, and swimming.

"Phred!" She crouched at the shore and reached out with the walking stick, but he was already too far out. He ignored her and continued to swim. "Phred, don't leave me alone! I need you more than ever!"

He vanished into the darkness.

She wept then, choking on the tears.

Phred's deep croaks came across the water, calling to her. "Noorrie. Nooorrie."

She didn't want to die, but the books all said this was the last step to find the hero. Nothing had really changed. The Blight was destroying the world. Only a hero filled with the gods' holy might could stop it. Daunting as swimming out into the darkness may be, it would be silly to come all this way and not carry through with it.

Steeling herself again her fear, she slipped into the water. The cold was shockingly painful. Her teeth chattering, she swam blindly forward. Phred's croaks seemed to come in that direction but if was difficult to tell, as the sound echoed all around her. After several minutes of swimming, she saw a small gleaming spot. It felt like an impossible distance, the cold sapping away her strength. She was floundering, barely able to keep her head above water, when she reached the island.

Phred greeted her at the rock's edge. "Noorrie."

It was tiny island, a ten-foot square of silvery white granite, polished until it reflected Phred's gleaming belly. She clung to the stone, gasping for breath. Except for Phred, the stone was bare — there was no hero on the island.

"Oh no," she whimpered.

Going back was impossible. She knew that if she tried, she'd drown. She wasn't even sure she could get out of the water. With cold-numbed fingers, she groped the polished stone and found a long groove cut into the stone; using it as a handhold, she scrambled awkwardly up onto the granite. Her panting rasped loudly in the still-ness of the cave as she huddled on the wet stone.

What happened to the hero? This obviously was the place — why wasn't he here? Did the idiot fall in and drown? Exhaustion dragged her down into the blackness of sleep.

— • —

Norrie woke with air blasting over her, hot and moist and smelling of the laundry room at the wizard's house. It reversed direction for a minute, turning cool as the lake, and then roared back. Sunlight shafted down from a vast hole in the cavern's ceiling, a pillar of gold centered on the island. Norrie sat up, blinking against brilliance, her clothes oddly heavy. During her sleep, her plain cotton shirt been replaced with a tunic of chain mail, so fine it flowed like silver water. Her trousers too, ending in high leather boots. The walking stick was gone, and in its place was a great sword.

The cool air rushed over her, followed by the hot again, before she wondered at the source. She turned — and squeaked in alarm at the massive dragon breathing down on her. It stood chest-deep in the lake, its pearl white scales throwing an iridescent reflection on the dark waters.

"Norrrrie." The great beast rumbled, a sound that vibrated in her bones, yet otherwise exactly the same as Phred's croak.

"Ph-Ph-Phred?"

"Yyup. Phrrred!" the dragon rumbled, and spread pearlescent wings that filled her vision. "Phredatranndth. Bbbig now."

Wow," she breathed and reached out to stroke his muzzle. His scales were hard and smooth as silver, warm to the touch. "You're the hero's dragon." Only then did she realize she was alone on the island. "But where is the hero?"

"You'rrrrre hero, Noooooooorrie."

"Me? I can't be."

"You doooooo what is nnnnneeeded. That is what makes a herooo."

Norrie stood for several moments in stunned silence, and then she picked up the hero's sword of fire. Her sword. Surprisingly light for its great length, it thrummed in her hand like a taunt clothesline on a windy day, ready for work. "I suppose someone has to clean up the Blight, and it might as well be me."

"Us." Phred lifted his foreleg out of the lake, water falling like pearls, and placed it carefully beside her.

"Us." Norrie scrambled up onto Phred's board shoulders. She felt him gathering for a leap to take them into the air. "And I think it might actually be more fun than doing the laundry."

Companions
Beyond

The Power of Eight

by

Jane Carol Petrovich

Mikhail's breath came in short, painful gasps as he dodged up the wooded hillside. Thorn bushes snatched at his school trousers. As he ripped free, his game leg almost buckled under him. The pack wasn't far behind, hooting and calling. He plunged on up the overgrown path, his bad hip joint on fire. If he could get to the top and slip away over the cliff edge without them seeing him …

He broke into the open. The bay sparkled far below in the late afternoon sunshine. He doubled over, trying to catch his breath. There, the familiar gap in the rocks that led down to the water. He started toward it.

Too late.

Jerek stepped casually out from behind the largest boulder, barring his way. He was tapping a short willow wand in the palm of one hand. Short but flexible, and painful, as Mikhail knew too well. Jerek wasn't even breathing hard. So. It was a trap.

"Thought you'd show us up, did you? Thought you knew all the answers, did you?"

There was a crunch of stone behind Mikhail. Three more of the gang had come out into the clearing. Mikhail noticed with a tiny flare of satisfaction that they were panting even harder than himself. Mikhail moved around Jerek and turned to face his tormentors. They closed in on him, crowding him closer to the edge.

"It's all in the books," Mikhail protested, knowing it was futile.

"Guardians, pah." Jerek spat, narrowly missing Mikhail's school shoes. "My da says it's all bunkum, the priests just want a soft living."

A long rumble of thunder sounded from the far side of the bay. Mikhail felt a breeze waft up behind him. He was very close to the edge now.

"They're real. You can even see them in the pictures of the old temple."

"Are you saying we can't read, that we have to look at *pictures*?" one of the other boys yelled but Mikhail kept his eyes on Jerek, the leader.

"No," Jerek answered for Mikhail, "he's saying my da is wrong."

"I didn't —" Mikhail began.

"He's disrespectful to his elders, he is, and you know what that will get him." The other boys chuckled dutifully. Then Jerek made his move, swiping at Mikhail with the wand. Mikhail dodged but it caught him a stinging blow on the shoulder. The other boys, encouraged by Jerek's action rushed in and seized his arms.

"Where are your guardians, now?" As Jerek brought his arm down in a punishing blow, Mikhail twisted to one side, springing off his good leg and overbalancing his captors. He whirled, shaking them off and saw to his horror that he stood on the very brink of the cliff.

He glanced over his shoulder at the angry boys. Too late to take back the words. Was it too late to submit to his punishment? *Yes. Never again,* he promised himself. "Guardians, help me," he whispered. Thunder rumbled louder and the wind gusted in his face as Mikhail swung his arms wide and launched himself headfirst off the cliff.

Time slowed down. Mikhail could see every bush straggling up the cliff side, the outlines of every leaf crisp against the weathered rock. He stared into the eyes of a tiny beach mouse frozen in surprise. He had dove from these cliffs before, but never from so high, and only where the cliff hung out over deep water. For a moment he felt the exhilaration of flight. Here in the air, as in the water, it didn't matter about his twisted spine.

Then he saw the gleam of the wet pebbles on the shore below. No, not pebbles, boulders. He wasn't going to make it. He arched his back, fighting for distance. If he could strike the water where it was deep enough, he might survive.

A blast of wind caught him suddenly, and he lost the perfect form of his dive. It sent him tumbling helplessly, wind roaring in his ears. He glimpsed in turn the darkening sky, tiny figures leaning out over the cliff, the stormy gray surface of the sea. With a massive effort he straightened out. He felt a tremendous impact as he sliced through the foaming waves. The world darkened and disappeared.

—•—

There were voices, murmuring in the distance. He was comfortable, so comfortable. Soft arms surrounded him. His mother? Or perhaps Appollonia? She was the loveliest girl in the whole school, the whole village, maybe the whole province of Oravka. But she didn't like folk telling her so. Mikhail had met her studying at the old priest's home. At school they never spoke but there she would talk to him quite naturally. Together they admired the finely painted illustrations of the old days and the great cataclysm. The old priest had set them to learning to decipher the ancient scripts. And taught them about the Guardians ...

Something cool brushed his brow and he woke more fully. *Appollonia holding him? How?* His eyes snapped open. Not Appollonia, not his mother. He was wrapped in great fleshy purple-white coils. More arms, crowded with huge round suckers, waved in front of him. His heart leapt in terror. The great octopus of legend, that could drag boats to their death. His mouth opened to scream.

"There you see, you've scared him. What did I tell you?" said a crabby old voice so like his great-grandmother's that he closed his mouth in surprise.

"Well, what else were we supposed to do? He called on us, didn't he? Couldn't let him break his fool neck, could we?" said a second voice as squeaky as an old gate.

His eyes were blurred and his head ached terribly. Frantically, he tried to wriggle out of the tentacles but they just tightened around him.

"Well, he's here now," said a third voice, as dry as the summer dust that blew in from the parched fields. "What do we do with him?"

What did they mean, 'do with him?' His terror peaking, Mikhail grasped the tentacles holding him and pulled but as soon as he got away from one, another curled around him. He took a great breath to scream and salty water flooded into his mouth. *I'm underwater,* he realized with shock and started to choke. A small part of his mind wondered how he had been breathing all this time.

"Arana, let the lad go," said the squeaky voice. He felt his body go free and tried to break for the surface but his arms and legs had no power. His lungs convulsed and his vision darkened again. *Of course. This is all a dream. Or the afterlife. I died when I hit the water.*

He dimly heard the crabby voice again. "Now breathe, lad, breathe."

"Water, air it's all the same. If you believe, believe, believe..." a chorus of voices chanted.

Mikhail forced himself back from the edge of unconsciousness and took a cautious breath. If he was dead, then what did it matter? To his surprise it worked. The water tasted cool and slightly fizzy.

"That's better, lad," said Squeaky-voice.

"Should have let him drown," muttered Dry-voice.

Mikhail peered through the green dimness, trying to see who was speaking. Sunlight filtered down from above. There were vague dark shapes in the near distance. It was rather beautiful, really, this afterlife. He thought sadly of his mother and father. They worked so hard, and had so little. Now they wouldn't even have him.

"Well, lad, you called us," said Crabby-voice. "Speak up now."

"And what do you ask for?" said Dry-voice, sounding even drier.

"Don't pester the child," broke in Squeaky-voice, "can't you see he has no idea where he is? Arana, bring him over here."

The great baggy mantle of the octopus floated into view and Mikhail recoiled. *I'd be petrified if I thought this was real.* One huge tentacle curled out towards him and floated, waiting. It was like a mad invitation to dance. *Why not?* he thought with a sudden prickle of curiosity and put his hand in the curve of the arm.

The tentacle felt smooth and firm against his skin and warmer than he expected. It locked around his wrist and he almost pulled back in panic but the two giant eyes regarded him calmly. They didn't look so threatening, more like a placid milk cow's eyes than a monster's. The octopus towed him towards the dark shapes, jetting out a stream of water. He blinked, looking around and realized numbly that he could see quite well. And he had heard the voices perfectly well even though he was underwater. *Maybe it is a dream. Because things like this don't happen. Except in the old stories …*

Mikhail gaped around him at the wondrous world of the seafloor. Huge coloured anemones opened up like flowers. Inquisitive fish darted towards him and then veered away into gently waving banks of sea-grass.

The blackness ahead loomed even larger and a shiver went down Mikhail's spine. It was a great curving wall, crumbled around the top and broken down completely in parts. The shape of it teased at his memory. The octopus towed him nearer and let go.

A hideous face emerged out of the blackness. Mikhail's heart almost stopped, until he realized that it was just a carved statue attached to the top of the wall. He reached out to feel the rough texture of the stone.

"There, now, I'll thank you to keep your fingers out of my ear," said the Crabby-voice in his head.

Mikhail flinched back, seeing the other statues leering down from the wall. They were even uglier than the one in front of him. He suddenly recognized where he was. The old temple. He laughed helplessly in sheer reaction. If only Jerek and the others boys could see it.

"The boy's mad, quite mad," muttered Dry-voice.

"Here, lad, get ahold of yourself now," said Squeaky-voice.

Mikhail sobered abruptly. If this was the temple then everything else was true. The cataclysm that had devastated their land. Destroyed their prosperity. Even changed the weather. And these stone statues must be … the Guardians.

"Come over here where I can see you better," said Squeaky-voice. "Blasted barnacles growing in my eye …"

Mikhail swam hesitantly over to the next statue. There was indeed a patch of barnacles growing over one of its goggling eyes.

"Can I … help?"

"You offer to help us?" said the Squeaky-voice. There was a loud murmur at this.

"Well, yes, if I can," he replied, heart racing. *What am I agreeing to?*

"Then see what you can do about these blasted barnacles, lad."

Mikhail started to pry them loose with his fingers but had to resort to his belt-knife to scrape them off. The statue didn't appear to mind.

"Ah, much better. Thank you, lad."

"You, you're, are you the Guardians?" Mikhail ventured timidly.

"Mad, *and* simple," grumbled Dry-voice.

"Of course we are the Guardians," said the Crabby-voice. "Pay no mind to Dolnici. It's been many a long year since we've been called upon, though. I'm Cravina. Go ahead, ask."

Mikhail decided to ask straight out. "Am I dead?"

The voices erupted all at once. Mikhail's head reeled.

"Doesn't even know what he's doing," the dry voice of the one named Dolnici cut through the clamour.

"You called on us," insisted Cravina.

"Did I? I don't remember." But he did remember, now. He had whispered a prayer to the Guardians, just before he went off the cliff. *What have I done?*

An entirely new voice broke into his mind. This one was lovely though, mellow and soothing. "Don't worry. They're harmless, really."

"Harmless!" came an indignant chorus.

The new voice ignored them. "You're supposed to ask them for a boon, a favor. Go ahead, don't be afraid."

The octopus jetted closer and Mikhail knew this was the source of that lovely voice.

"And ask Sevari for another favor, for clearing his eye."

Mikhail could have sworn the octopus was laughing now.

"They don't admit it, of course, but they are lonely. It's been many years since your people stopped believing in them."

The voices erupted again in denial. "Who, us, lonely?" "Perfectly happy where we are." "Just fine, we don't need them." The voices died away but Mikhail felt that they were waiting expectantly, even eagerly for him to speak.

Mikhail marshalled his thoughts and slowly began. He spoke of the gang of boys who had chased him from the school yard, jealous of his good grades and contemptuous of his limp. He spoke of his home, of his parents who wanted to protect him and couldn't. He went on to tell of the village, hunger and cold in the winter and droughts in the summer, long days of toil that brought only failed crops and meager herds as long as he could remember and as long as his parents could remember. He spoke of his studies with the old priest and of his fascination with the old days. Encouraged by the benevolent gaze of Arana, he even told them about Appollonia. He trailed off into silence at last.

The silence lengthened. Mikhail began to fear that he had done it wrong. Asked for too much.

At last Sevari spoke. "Well, lad, that's quite a bit. Didn't realize things had gotten so bad."

"Serves them right," said Dolnici promptly.

"Even so, even so —" began Cravina and stopped there as if uncertain.

Mikhail began to wonder if these stone beings had the power to help at all. The water seemed to darken and chill and he remembered that it had been late afternoon when he had gone off the cliff. How long had it been?

"Well," Sevari said at length. "Only one thing to be done. Arana, you go with him. Find out what's going on." There was a murmur of agreement.

"We'll give her the usual, " said Cravina matter-of-factly. "Earth, Air, Water, Fire. Four majors and four minors."

The Guardians began to chant. Mikhail's doubts were swept away as he felt a strange tingling in his limbs. New voices chimed in, wispy, deep, rough, scratchy, one like a cracked bell tolling far away.

Power of earth that shakes the land
Power of air that stirs the wind
Power of water that brings the tide
Power of fire where lightning strikes...

Streams of light were lancing out towards the octopus, lighting up each tentacle. The sea roiled around them and Mikhail was swept up and away from the temple. He couldn't see the ocean floor anymore, or the Guardians. The chant echoed through his head, *Power of eight, eight, eight* ...

This time when the octopus snagged him, he welcomed her grasp.

—•—

Mikhail's head broke the surface. He was in a small sheltered cove. Water streamed from his nostrils and he suddenly felt he was choking again. His knees bumped the bottom and he tried to stand up but his bare foot slipped on the rocks and he fell back in with a splash. The magic was gone, he couldn't breathe the water any more. He rose up again, lungs rebelling, and started to cough up seawater. This time he didn't try to stand on his wobbly legs but crawled up the rocks and onto the short crescent of beach. He collapsed onto his side, wheezing and retching. Finally, he got to his feet and staggered back to the edge of the water.

"Arana," he croaked, the sound of his voice strange in his ears. The octopus was just visible in the shallow water. She didn't look as big now as she had down at the temple, or even powerful enough to have towed him all this way. He felt a sudden sense of loss. How could she come with him? Maybe if he got a bucket from the stable ...

"Arana?" he said again but she didn't answer him. Maybe she could only talk to him underwater. He was just about to dunk his head back under when the tip of a tentacle poked out of the water and waved gently. Mikhail put out his hand to touch it. It felt strangely warm. A tingle ran up his arm. Or was it running down his arm towards Arana? No matter.

As Mikhail watched, the octopus seemed to shrink. Her arms stiffened and splayed out to either side of her body. Her head disappeared in a swirl of water. Unable to see her clearly and thoroughly alarmed, Mikhail reached down into the turbulent water. He felt a stinging pain in his palm and hastily pulled his hand back out. A spiky jointed leg was hooked onto his skin. He flinched back instinctively and the rest of the creature emerged, dripping. A huge black spider was clambering into his palm. He was just about to shake it off when it spoke to him.

"Take it easy, lad, you're moving a bit quick here." The voice was tiny, and raspy, but some quality in it was unmistakably Arana's.

"Arana?" he asked in amazement.

"The same." The creature peered up at him.

"You look, well, different."

A scratchy sort of sound came from it. Laughter, Mikhail realized.

"Didn't think you were going to haul a great, wet octopus around on your shoulders, did you?"

Since this was exactly what he had thought, Mikhail didn't know what to say. The scratchy sound came again.

"Well, lad, let's get on with it." Arana climbed up his arm, shrinking even further, and settled herself in the hollow of his shoulder, just inside the collar of his wet shirt.

He trudged around the headland to where the fishing boats were beached, and back to the village up the coast road. With every limping step, new aches manifested in his body until he seemed to be one flaming mass of bruises and sprains. Arana kept up a constant chatter though and it was nice, for once, to have a companion to share his thoughts with.

The village square was deserted in the last rays of the setting sun, the shadow of the old clock tower long across the cracked paving stones. Mikhail was relieved. Maybe he could sneak home without anyone noticing. Still, it was odd not to see anyone, no grandfathers sitting and enjoying the evening breezes, no mothers gathering up stray youngsters. He turned down the dusty alley that led to his home.

Mikhail heard rapid footsteps echoing somewhere just ahead. Before he could draw aside, a boy came pelting around the next corner and slammed into him. It was Saltish, one of Jerek's bunch. To Mikhail's surprise, it was the other, heavier boy who went sprawling in the dust. In spite of his aches, he felt solid, connected to the earth. Saltish was picking himself up, muttering curses. When he looked up at Mikhail, his mouth sagged open and the color drained from his face. Then his feet were slipping and sliding in the dirt as he tried to stand up and run at the same time. He vanished as quickly as he had come.

"What was that about? He looked terrified? Did he see you?" Mikhail asked, puzzled.

"Not me, you."

"Me?"

"Last he saw, you leapt off the cliff and never came up. Nice color change there, though."

"Oh." Then it hit Mikhail. "That's where everyone is. Oh no!" Mikhail started off again at a faster pace. "They must all be searching for me."

Mikhail ducked through the doorway of his family's small cottage. It was dark inside and as deserted as the village. Suddenly ravenous, he went to the tiny kitchen and rummaged amongst the meager supplies. He was just finishing a heel of bread and a couple of withered apples when his parents burst in the doorway, closely followed by half a dozen villagers.

"We thought you were dead!" his mother sobbed.

"My boy, my boy. Let me look at you," his father added.

He was enfolded in a solid and humanly warm hug. How had he ever mistaken Arana's watery coils for this?

Mikhail found himself out in the narrow street once more, where a crowd had gathered. "What happened?" "We searched everywhere!" "Where were you?" The questions came thick and fast.

"Let the boy speak," commanded Appollonia's father, the headman of the village, in the forefront of the crowd. An expectant silence fell.

Mikhail reached under his collar for Arana's furry presence. She was still there. He could see, at the back, Jerek and Saltish along with the rest of the gang. They were watching him with a special intensity. The whole school knew they had been after him. Someone must have given the alarm and set the search going. Maybe he did have a friend or two.

"Now what?" he murmured under his breath to Arana. He could condemn them with a word. The heresy alone ...

"You have the power of air, of eloquence, if you choose, but the time is not yet. Tell them... nothing happened."

"Nothing happened."

"Tell them... you're fine."

"I'm fine."

"You went up to the cliff and climbed down the face. Walked by the water for a while and came back the long way round the headland. It has the advantage of being true."

"I went up to the cliff ..."

As Mikhail spoke Jerek's aggressive stance relaxed and was replaced with an air of confusion. In his place, Mikhail knew Jerek would not hesitate to denounce him.

The headman looked at him narrowly. "Is there anything else you want to tell us, Mikhail, son of Karol and Hanna?"

"No, sir."

"Very well, then. We thank the guardians for your safe return. Go back to your homes now, everyone.

Mikhail jumped when the headman said 'guardians' but then realized that it was just a saying, he had no way of knowing where Mikhail had actually been. Appollonia had been standing behind her father and she gave him a shy smile before turning to follow the headman away. The crowd dispersed slowly.

Mikhail, feeling his exhaustion, allowed his parents to lead him back inside where the village healer prescribed a good warm soak.

"Just what I need, more water," he whispered to Arana as he carefully removed his shirt with her in it in the screened-off bathing alcove. Still, it was nice to lie back in the shallow tub and let the warm scented water sooth his aches. Arana came to perch on the edge. He felt almost happy for the first time in a long while.

"That wasn't so bad, Arana. Those boys can't touch me now."

"Guard against overconfidence, lad. They are more dangerous to you now, not less. Now they fear you as well as envy you."

"Oh." Mikhail thought about it. "But you said that I have the power of eloquence. Do I have the other powers that Cravina said?"

"You're a clever lad, no mistake about that," she answered. "Now move over." She slid into the water and began to transform.

"Arana, you can't, not here," he said, sitting up in alarm. But the spider didn't answer. Her legs had already gone all rubbery and her body had ballooned into the octopus's mantle. She was still tiny, though, when she finished her transformation. As she jetted energetically around the tub, Mikhail climbed out and dried himself off. He held out his hand for the octopus.

"Come on, Arana, they'll see you if you stay in there." She must have heard him because she jetted over to his waiting fingers and latched on as before. The tingle of power was less this time and the transformation quicker.

Mikhail carried the spider carefully to his sleeping loft. He installed her in the small box he kept for his few treasures. She immediately began spinning herself a comfortable nest. Mikhail fell asleep almost instantly and dreamed he was diving to the bottom of the sea and soaring above the mountains. All the world lay below him and he could move the rivers in their courses and command the lightning and thunder ...

—•—

It was like a new world the next day, the air sparkling fresh and clear. During the night it had rained for the first time in weeks. His parents had gone out to the fields already, letting him sleep without doing his usual chores. He felt energized and ready to face the day. He even felt taller.

"Are you coming to school with me today, Arana?"

"Of course," came the scratchy little voice. The spider leaped into his outstretched hand, a gossamer thread trailing behind her and they set off.

Arana had an inexhaustible curiosity about his life and the life of the village. She watched everything with all eight of her eyes and asked about the people, their families, their work, the land, the crops, and on and on. A few times her comments almost made him laugh aloud. Mikhail had to be careful not to look like he was talking to himself. He'd received a few odd looks already.

Later that week, Saltish tried to pick a fight but Jerek, of all people, called him off. Mikhail felt on top of the world. He even seemed to be limping less.

"So, Mikhail, tell me again why —"

"Arana, I have a question for you this time. What really caused the Cataclysm?"

"Ah yes, what you call the cataclysm… Mikhail, what's that over there, up the side of the hill?"

Mikhail smiled. She was irrepressible. They had just crossed a plank bridge over a dry gully on the way home from school. He looked over at the adjoining hill where a few stunted trees straggled up the hillside to a cleft in the rocks. There was a bit of a flat place with a tumbled down wall of stones.

"Oh that. My grandda said it used to be a shrine. There was a spring up there and a pool that overflowed down the hillside and fed the creek that used to be here. At least that's what he said."

"Talking to yourself again?" Jerek stepped out from the shade of a small grove of trees at the far side of the bridge. The usual hangers-on slouched out after him.

Not so long ago, Mikhail would have stammered and denied it. Instead he asked coolly, "And what if I am?"

Jerek looked a little disconcerted but he stepped forward to block Mikhail's path. Mikhail looked down at what Jerek was holding and his heart sank. The willow wand again. Jerek had just been biding his time. Bravado was all very well but he was outnumbered. Out here in the open he couldn't outdistance them, either.

Then a tiny voice spoke in his ear. "Ask him if that's his grandda's wand." With a flood of relief Mikhail remembered that he wasn't alone this time. Outnumbered maybe, but not alone.

"Is that your grandda's wand?" The surprise in Jerek's face was gratifying. So, it *was*. How had Arana known?

Jerek asked in turn, "And what if it is?"

"Not very original, is he?" said the scratchy little voice.

Mikhail decided to improvise a little. "You'll be the one getting switched if he finds out." Jerek's grandda's temper was near legendary. He saw Jerek's face twist as the gibe hit home. He'd felt the edge of the wand more than once, that was sure.

"Walk, now, Mikhail," advised Arana. "Walk right past him."

Mikhail did so, hoping that Arana knew what she was doing. He kept his gaze fixed on Jerek who looked back sullenly. At the last moment he put out a hand to stop Mikhail. Mikhail felt a small sting and heard a loud snap as a spark jumped from Mikhail to Jerek.

Jerek actually yelped and jumped backwards, knocking into Saltish. Mikhail risked one look back before he walked on. Jerek was nursing his hand, glaring with resentment. The other boys were sniggering until Jerek took a swipe at one of them with his good hand.

"What was that?" Mikhail asked when they were safely out of earshot.

"What he needed to be reminded of." Arana sounded pensive, if a spider could sound pensive. "His ancestors were not so petty. Once they were …"

"Yes?"

"Nothing, my friend. Do we go to the priest's house today? And meet the young female? You know, she reminds me of myself when I was first hatched."

Mikhail was still puzzling over that when they arrived at the courtyard outside the priest's home for his weekly study time. Dusty vines drooped over the walls and only the weeds seemed to flourish in the small patch of garden. Appollonia was already there, waiting in the shadow of the archway for Per Novas to let them in. Mikhail mumbled a greeting to her and felt himself blush when he remembered waking up under the ocean.

"Cool down, young man, my feet are getting too warm," protested Arana. Mikhail followed the priest and Appollonia down the flagged hallway to the library. It was pleasantly cool after the summer heat outdoors and he loved the scent of old books. As Appollonia got some help with her last translation, Mikhail ran his fingers over the cracked leather bindings of the ancient volumes. Arana skittered up his arm and onto the shelves. She disappeared into a crack between two of the books.

"Arana, what are you doing?" he whispered but there was no reply. "Come back here," he said urgently.

"Mikhail?" the priest asked. "Did you say something?"

"Per Novas," Mikhail thought fast, "I was just reading the titles. May I look at these books?"

The old man looked up briefly and nodded. "I know you will treat them with respect."

Michael took out one of the books where Arana had disappeared and peered into the space but she was nowhere to be seen. This book was one of the oldest. He laid it on the reading stand and gently turned the age-spotted pages. Some seemed to have been soaked and dried out, others looked scorched. The spidery characters of the old language ran across the pages. Small woodcut illustrations gave tantalizing glimpses of an age of glory — princes in resplendent long robes, grand palaces, tables piled with food, a proud civilization. He turned the next page and there it was. The unmistakable outline of the old temple. And there, perched upon the walls, were the stone statues.

"What are you looking at, Mikhail?"

Mikhail jumped and turned around. The old priest looked down at him kindly.

"The, the temple in this picture," he stammered, "Where was it?"

"Ah, the Temple of the Eight Guardians. Not too far from here, we believe. But it was on an island and could only be reached by boat at high tide and a causeway at low tide. An order of holy ones lived there."

"The stone statues, did they have names?"

Per Novas gave him a long considering look. "Of course. Look. Here is one of them. See if you can decipher it." He pointed to one word still highlighted with a gleam of gold paint.

"D—h—o—k, no that's an l, n—e—c—e. Dholnece." *Dolnici!* He felt a rising tide of excitement. So it wasn't all his imagination. They actually existed.

"What is it Mikhail?" Now Appollonia was looking at him, too.

He showed her the illustration. As she bent over the book, her long dark hair fell forward and brushed against his hands, cool as water. He caught his breath.

"Those are the Guardians," she said. "Why did people pray to them?"

"Not pray," replied the priest, "invoke. And there's a difference." The old man leaned back and crossed his arms. "Legend has it that they were messengers to the gods. But no one believes that anymore." He sighed. "I sometimes think no one believes in the gods anymore, either. People back then cared only for their wealth and power. When the mountains spoke and the land changed, all that wealth and power disappeared. And so did the Guardians. Although there have been tales over the years — of miraculous rescues — fishermen whose boats capsized far from land and were washed up on shore, raving and delirious." He looked searchingly at Mikhail from under bushy snow-white eyebrows.

"Do you have something you would like to tell me?"

"I, uh," Mikhail glanced aside at Appollonia, who was listening intently. Even with the undeniable presence of Arana, it still sounded too crazy.

"Well, when you are ready, then. Now, my children, our time today is short as I must be about my visits. There are still some who find comfort in the old ways." He gestured towards the door.

Arana! Where is she? Per Novas was already ushering them out.

"At least let me put the book away, Per Novas."

"No need, I can do that."

Mikhail moved his feet as slowly as he could and scanned the room. There, a flicker of motion from behind the priest. Arana came sailing down from the ceiling on a silken line. In a moment he would see her. Mikhail pretended to stumble and the old man put out a hand to steady him. His grip was surprisingly strong. For the first time Mikhail noticed the tiny spider emblem embroidered on the shoulder of the priest's shabby robes. He put his own hand instinctively to the spot where Arana usually rode. Mikhail looked up to see the priest studying him intently.

"Nothing at all, Mikhail, to tell me?"

"No Per Novas." Mikhail tried to look innocent.

Behind the priest, Arana landed safely on a dusty plant beside the door. Mikhail brushed by it clumsily on his way out. People were used to him being clumsy. He felt Arana scurry up his arm and back into his shirt. Per Novas accompanied them out to the courtyard apparently none the wiser. As he turned to go back inside Mikhail heard him say, very softly "But the legends also say the gods will return someday, if we believe …"

Out in the street again, blinking in the bright sunlight, Mikhail nodded farewell to Appollonia and turned to go.

"Do you believe in the Guardians, Mikhail?" Her question startled him. They might talk and debate with the old priest but they rarely spoke together outside of the priest's home. He knew they were too different. She was so pretty, the headman's daughter and always the centre of attention. He had noticed though, that she never asked the insightful questions or volunteered the quick answers at school as she did here. Now he wondered if her life was as constrained as his, but in a different way.

He thought about avoiding her question. He felt Arana shift around and tickle his collarbone and decided Appollonia deserved a straight answer.

"Yes, I do."

To his surprise, she broke out into a wide smile. "I thought so." She leaned closer and he smelled again the faint fragrance of the herbs in her hair. "So do I." She turned then and walked away.

Shaken by the power of her smile, Mikhail watched her go. He finally turned around to go home only to find Jerek planted in the middle of the street, not five paces away.

"Leave her alone, runt. She's mine."

"Does she know that?"

This time Jerek didn't seem surprised by Mikhail's air of defiance. He only laughed unpleasantly. "She will, runt, she will soon enough."

Mikhail was filled with a sudden fury. "She doesn't belong to anyone, Jerek."

"You tell him, lad," Arana encouraged.

Mikhail balled up his fists. "You leave her alone and leave me alone, too."

"Or what, runt?"

"Or by the Guardians, you'll —"

A shadow fell over them and both boys looked up involuntarily. The sun had gone behind the clouds, dark angry-looking masses that were piling up in the western sky.

"I'll what?"

"You'll wish you had," Mikhail finished lamely.

Arana shifted her tiny feet. "It's not a light matter, to invoke the Guardians, lad," she whispered.

"I know," Mikhail said quietly. "You'll just wish you had," he repeated with more intensity.

"You're crazy, you know that," sneered Jerek.

Arana spoke softly in his ear. "Let it go, Mikhail, you've made your point."

Mikhail just smiled and shrugged. A hot wind had sprung up, swirling the dust at their feet, catching and whirling last year's dead leaves in a mad dance. He turned and walked down a side street, half expecting Jerek to follow him or throw something. Jerek usually preferred frontal attacks, though, Mikhail could say that about him.

"Not a good enemy to have," murmured Arana. "Pity. All that energy and leadership, to be wasted …"

"I'm not afraid of him anymore, Arana," Mikhail said stoutly. "And I've got you, after all," he added more truthfully.

"That's the thing, Mikhail. I have to go back."

"Back?" Mikhail was devastated. "But I thought … they said you'd be my companion. That you'd help me."

"Seems to me that you're doing just fine by yourself, lad."

"But you're my friend!" He no longer troubled to keep his voice down and he got a few odd looks from the old folk sitting out on their front steps.

"I will always be your friend, Mikhail, but I must report back to the Guardians. They care about all of your people, you know, even if your people have forgotten them."

Mikhail felt momentarily abashed. "Well, come back soon, then, won't you?" He quickened his pace. "I just have time to take you down to the shore."

"No need, lad, just take me to the top of the clock tower."

"What are you going to do?"

"You'll see."

—•—

Mikhail negotiated the final few broken steps and emerged onto the decrepit balcony that ran around the outside. The wind was stronger here and he could see that the sky over the mountains was a forbidding black. He saw that Arana had been busy. She emerged from her hiding place dragging a small white bundle. When she reached his outstretched hand she unfurled a long gossamer banner.

"Will you be all right?"

"You're a good soul, Mikhail, son of Karol, son of Mikhail."

"When will I see you?" he called as the wind whipped her away.

"The Guardians be with you, my friend," he thought he heard her say as the tiny body went flying away over the rooftops toward the sea.

Mikhail watched the scrap of spidersilk until it disappeared. His eyes stung but he told himself that it was the dust in the air. He climbed down from the tower, now swaying alarmingly, and trudged home feeling utterly bereft. His shoulder felt achingly bare.

—•—

By the time Mikhail reached home the wind had intensified. His father put him to work securing their possessions against the storm that was surely coming. It had blown up with unseasonable suddenness. Mikhail had an uncomfortable feeling about it. *I wonder... if the Guardians are responsible...*

Mikhail and his father were tying down the worn wooden shutters when a group of people approached, heads bent against the wind. A few fat raindrops fell.

The headman was in the forefront. "Goodman Karol, a word with you," he called out.

His father paused, listening.

The headman cleared his throat. "It's about your son," he said uncomfortably.

There was a loud rumble of thunder and several people looked up nervously.

Mikhail's father reached out an arm to draw his son towards him. "Yes?"

"Perhaps you should send the boy indoors," the headman suggested.

"I think Mikhail is old enough to hear whatever you have to say." His father sounded quite calm but his hand on Mikhail's shoulder tightened slightly.

The headman cleared his throat again. "Well, there have been reports. And as you know, as the headman of Oravka, it is my duty to investigate anything of this nature. That is not to say that I am giving credence to all of these —"

"Dano," his father said patiently, "we have known each other many years now. There is a storm coming. Just tell me."

"Ah, yes, the storm. Karol, the boy has been accused of heresy. His disappearance and reappearance ... his unusual interests in the ancient ways ... he's been observed talking to himself ..."

The crowd was growing. Another group approached from the opposite direction and Mikhail noticed that Jerek and his gang were right in the center of it. He suspected that Jerek had been busy.

"Consorting with demons! He burned my boy. You can see the blisters!" shouted a man in the crowd.

Mikhail realized with a sinking feeling that the speaker was Jerek's father. The crowd was muttering now above the noise of the wind. *Arana, where are you now?*

"I am sorry, but you see the Council will have to question the boy and find out the truth of these allegations," continued the headman, with a sharp glance at Jerek's father.

Thunder rumbled again, closer. It seemed to go on and on this time.

Karol spoke up as it died away, "This doesn't appear to be the Council, Dano, it looks more like a mob. And the storm is coming." Even as he spoke rain began to splatter in the dust.

Appollonia squeezed to the front of the crowd and came to stand before her father. "You'll have to question me too then, Father, because I've been studying the old ways along with Mikhail."

The headman appeared stricken. He put his hands on her shoulders. "Appollonia, you shouldn't be here," he said quietly to her, but Mikhail overheard. Then the headman turned around and held up his hands. "Everyone go back to your homes and prepare for the storm."

The crowd jostled forward instead, led by Jerek's father, with Jerek right behind him. "We want justice now!"

"Tell him to call off the storm!" "We're being punished for harbouring a heretic!"

Lightning forked across the sky and the thunder was deafening. It seemed to shake the very ground. *No*, thought Mikhail, *the ground* was *shaking*. Several roof tiles on the adjacent homes snapped loose and cascaded into the crowd. There were screams and curses. People clung to each other and several threw themselves flat on the ground. A small group surged forward and rough hands ripped him from his father's grasp. The rain was coming down in earnest now, but it didn't seem to dampen their mood. Mikhail saw the headman pulling Appollonia away. He fought against the hands holding him. *Arana, where are your powers now? I need you!*

"Offer him back to the sea!" came a cry. This seemed to galvanize the crowd and they dragged him along out of the village toward the sea. Rain sheeted down, blinding everyone but it didn't seem to matter. Some insanity seemed to have them all in its grip.

—•—

A gigantic flash of lightning lit up the darkened skies and Mikhail found that he stood on the edge of the cliffs once more. He finally wrested free of the hands that held him.

"You're wrong," he screamed above the force of the gale. A blast of wind whirled away the rain and Mikhail looked at the soaked, angry faces of the villagers he had known and grown up with. Angry but also frightened. "The Guardians exist, I've seen them."

"He admits it!" Jerek and his father moved towards him but Mikhail continued.

Words came to him. "The Guardians would still be here, guarding and guiding us if we believed in them. We caused their downfall! We did it!"

The crowd was silent for a moment. *They are listening to me*, Mikhail thought with amazement. Then he saw, approaching from the path to the village another large group of people. His heart sank. *Have they come to condemn me too?*

Then Mikhail grinned. Per Novas was leading the group. Jerek's grandfather was right beside him, brandishing the willow wand that Jerek had borrowed. It looked like all of the ancients of the village, in fact, hobbling, limping, some half-carrying others more decrepit along. They all seemed to be clutching walking staffs, wands, rods. Behind them came the rest of the village - women, children, babies, even the dogs. It was a bedraggled little procession, but strangely impressive in the vast span of their ages.

"Listen to the boy," Per Novas began, his voice strong over the wind from the sea.

"We must give him back to the sea," yelled Jerek's father. "Otherwise the storm will destroy us all." Some of the villagers shouted their assent but others were silent now, doubtful.

"Harm him and you condemn yourselves. He has learned what we have forgotten. We have forgotten what we are. We have forgotten where we came from. But it may not be too late."

Mikhail was thrown to his knees as the ground suddenly began to shake again. He felt a lancing fire in his bad hip and his mind seized on the verse he had heard deep under the waters.

"Power of earth that shakes the land," he croaked.

"Power of air that stirs the wind," he said with more confidence into the teeth of the gale.

"Power of water that brings the tide," he said loudly. Now the ancients were joining in. He could taste salt spray on his lips, or maybe it was tears.

"Power of fire where lightning strikes." More and more people took up the chant. The ancients held up their wands and staffs and rods, some strongly, others with trembling arms. Sudden streams of fire lanced down from the heavens to the tips of each wand or staff and the villagers were suddenly encircled in a cone of light.

Power of earth that makes us strong
Power of air that makes us hear
Power of water that makes us see
Power of fire that makes us wise ...

All about them the storm raged with renewed fury. Children screamed in their parents' arms and dogs howled as lightning lanced down all around them, everywhere but within the cone of light. The ground heaved under them and great sections of the cliff fell away but the ground under their feet remained intact.

Still the chant continued. "Power of eight, we believe…" Mikhail staggered to his feet and searched through the crowd. He saw Jerek supporting his grandda's arm as he wavered under the stream of fire. Finally he located his parents, holding tight to each other and sheltering a shivering group of children. Then there was Appollonia, wet, smeared with mud and more beautiful than ever, helping her granddam hold her walking stick steady under the blazing beam of light. He added his strength to theirs. Appollonia spared him a quick glance of thanks through the driving rain.

The wind and the battering seemed to go on forever. His arms and shoulders ached with the strain and still the torment of wind and lighting continued. When he felt that he could bear no more, it ended as suddenly as it had begun. The streams of fire sizzled out and all three fell together in a sodden heap.

At length, Mikhail realized he could hear something else — the crash of waves on the beach far below. The wind had lessened. The rain had settled down to a warm drizzle. People were scattered everywhere, some flat on the ground, others kneeling and clinging to each other. Gradually they were getting up, moving around, uttering cries of joy as they found family members and friends. He got to his feet and helped Appollonia and her granddam up.

Mikhail heard an excited child's voice cut through the chatter. "Look, what's that?"

Mikhail looked around. A child was pointing out over the cliffs and people were turning to look. Huge waves covered the surface of the bay in a complicated pattern, but something was different. An island rose up where nothing but water had been. And on the island, a familiar structure. A structure he had last seen far below, as he breathed water and heard the Guardians speaking in his mind. He walked slowly to the edge of the cliffs feeling as though he was still floating underwater. All the pain in his body had vanished and his stride was sure and even. Appollonia came to stand beside him as though it were the most natural thing in the world. Soon the entire village stood on the edge looking down at a legend reborn.

Even as they watched, the waves were dying down and more of the island became visible. The rain stopped and the setting sun shone out below the clouds. The structure on the island was suddenly ablaze with light.

There was a murmur of wonder from the crowd. Mikhail could clearly see the roofless walls of the old temple with the carved stone statues high up. His eyes blurred. He saw the island was covered with trees and gardens; the dome of the temple was still intact, light shone out from the arched windows and the stone figures breathed. He seemed to hear an echo of voices in the shrieking of the gulls overhead.

"I knew he was the one."

"Nonsense, you knew no such thing."

"I suppose they'll all be bothering us now …"

Mikhail blinked and the temple was a darkened shell once more, waiting to be rebuilt.

A hand fell on his shoulder and he looked round. Per Novas stood there. The spider emblem on the priest's shoulder gleamed. "You saw it too — the temple as it was, and will be again."

Mikhail nodded in sudden understanding. He took a last look out to sea and then froze. Far below in the storm tossed bay a giant shape was just visible under the surface. Something broke the water. A piece of driftwood or a tentacle, lazily waving?

Tomorrow, he would go and see.

$\mathscr{D}$arkbeast

by

Mindy L. Klasky

I knew that I would kill my darkbeast on the morning of my sixteenth birthday.

Mother came to me that day, with all of my aunts, and my cousins, and my two older sisters. They woke me early in the morning, before the sun had risen above the hills that surround our village. They awakened me with their singing, their laughing voices that cared not for pitch or for tone, but rather, rose in joy at their shared experience, their common life.

My mother filled the bath with steaming water. My grandmother should have been the one to draw the bath. That was her honor as the oldest woman in our family, but she was too old to lift the buckets. Her stroke the year before had left her unable to move the muscles on the left side of her body, and she looked as if she was always frowning.

I knelt in the tin tub and let the women sluice water down my back. They wet my hair as well, and they washed it with soap made from lavender and lye. They scrubbed my hands and my feet, peeling away the dirt of child's play.

After I was bathed, my family took me into my mother's closet, the secret room where she kept her herbs and her draughts, the potions that made our family the strongest in the village. My sisters laughed as they brought out the gown that they had embroidered for me. The cloth was blue, which was Marguerite's favorite color, and the stitches had been done in green and white, shades preferred by Avonette. I would have wanted red, but no one asked my opinion.

They wrapped me in an underdress of clean linen, and then they settled the incredible garment over my head. My mother had me kneel at her feet, and she combed out my hair, working the snarls from my blue-black curls. Each of my cousins knelt beside us, whispering a birthday greeting and offering up a fresh flower from the fields. I remembered to thank each of them with the appropriate verse of the Family Rule, and my mother smiled as she wove the blossoms into my hair.

When my body and my hair were dressed, I was presented to my aunts. One painted my cheeks with red. One outlined my eyes with black. One shaded precious blue, the most costly of all the colors, on my eyelids. The last, the youngest, spread crimson on my lips. I thanked each of them with the Family Rule, fighting against the nervousness that clenched my belly.

It was my birthday. I should be allowed to eat some sweets. I'd settle for a heel of dry bread.

Mother squinted as she reviewed me, and I remembered to stand very tall. I looked down at her feet, blinking my painted eyelids like a demure young woman. I turned about when she commanded, stopping after one full revolution.

"Ariane," she said at last. "You make me proud." I had never heard such words from her.

They swelled inside my chest and made me want to laugh out loud, to reach out and squeeze her in my excitement. She continued: "Now it is time to kill your darkbeast."

Every girl did it. Every girl was dressed and pampered on her sixteenth birthday. Every girl was taken to Perdine's godhouse, to the round wooden building dedicated to the goddess of hearth and harmony.

I loved my darkbeast, though. I loved Caw like the brothers I never had, like the sisters I dreamed of, when my own relatives laughed at me and pulled my hair and made me feel ashamed.

Before I could protest, my family paraded me through the streets. Our neighbors looked out from their windows, laughing and calling out birthday wishes. I saw my childhood friends who had turned before me. They smiled with honest welcome, anticipating my joining them in the Women's Circle.

Kill Caw, I thought. That's the only thing that I must do. Kill Caw.

Perdine's godhouse was located in the center of town, nearly lost among the columned rectangles of the other gods. The priestess greeted me on the steps, and I bowed to her, offering up the shawl that I had woven during the winter before. She accepted my present with the expected words, smiling and welcoming me into her refuge. I paused on the threshold, looking back at my mother. Expectation shone in her eyes.

She hoped that I would become the daughter she had always dreamed of. She hoped that I would stop being Ariane the disobedient, Ariane the tardy, Ariane the sarcastic. She wanted me to be Ariane the meek, Ariane the humble, Ariane the good daughter.

As Perdine's priestess led me deep into the sanctuary, I heard small children crying in the streets, "Kill the darkbeast! Kill the darkbeast! Kill the darkbeast!" I had been one of those children dozens of times in the past. I had encouraged others to destroy their past, to embrace their future. Did I have the strength to take the step myself?

"In the name of Perdine, be welcome," the priestess said. Her dress was a simple linen shift, and her hair hung straight to her waist. Beside her, I looked like a gaudy flower. "Your darkbeast awaits you in the inner chamber. Slay your past and look to your future and your life as a woman in our village."

I knew there was some proper response, something that Mother had taught me, but I could not think of it now. I bowed my head instead, whispering thanks in ordinary parlance. If the priestess were offended, she gave no sign. Instead, she opened the door to the sanctuary, stepping back so that I could pass. "Be brave," she said.

The inner room was dark, lit only by a brazier that sat in the center of the floor. Curls of incense rose into the air, and I sneezed twice. I wiped my nose on the back of my hand, only just remembering not to rub at my painted eyes.

"*Aye,*" Caw said, laughing. "*That would leave you quite the sight.*"

"Caw!" I blinked in the dim light, and I finally made out his eyes. He was trapped in a cage, suspended from the chamber's domed ceiling. I knew that Mother had brought him to the godhouse early in the morning, even before she had awakened me.

"Were you expecting someone else?"

"Of course not."

"Then don't waste my time with your foolish words."

I heard Caw's speech inside my head. We had been bound this way since I was an infant, since he had landed on my cradle on the first day that my mother took me to the hills to harvest lavender. I had reached for his jet black wings, and I had laughed at his voice, and my mother had spoken her strongest spell to bind the raven to me.

I heard him inside me, but I spoke to him aloud. That was an old habit, one that I had never tried to break. Caw and I spent a lot of time away from the village. We ranged up into the hills, and it never seemed important to think to him silently, the way so many of my friends did.

Of course, when I was a child, I had argued that Caw was different from other darkbeasts.

He wasn't disgusting, like the rats and snakes that took the evil thoughts of other girls. He wasn't so short-lived that I needed to repeat my history to him every six months, like the girls who were bound to lizards or toads. He wasn't angry or sly or cruel or dirty. He was my darkbeast, and he was perfect for me.

I stepped toward his cage, and my jeweled sandal caught on an uneven paving stone. I fell hard, skinning my knee through the fine fabric of my dress. My bare palms scraped on the floor. I swore sharply, using words I'd heard the shepherds use, when they thought they were alone with their flocks. Tears sprang to my eyes, and I could hear Mother's sternest voice: "Take it to your darkbeast."

—•—

My first memory, or a scene retold by Caw over the years: I was a child, barely one year old. My sisters danced around me, teasing me with their mobility, while I was trapped by my short, chubby legs, by my wheeling arms. They watched me try to take a step, another, another, and they laughed when I fell hard on my bottom.

I wailed, enraged by their teasing, surprised by the sharp hurt of falling. Mother scooped me up and shook her head, saying, "We don't cry. Take it to your darkbeast."

She wrestled me into the corner of the room, swatting at my bare legs as I kicked to be free from her. She dropped me in front of Caw's cage, slipping a rag leash around my chubby wrist. I tugged and wailed some more, but my mother only repeated, "Take it to your darkbeast."

I pulled and cried and flailed until I was so tired that I could move no longer. Only when I had collapsed on the floor, one wrist secured to Caw's cage, did the raven come over and look at me. He cocked his head to one side, studying me with one shiny eye. He hopped away and spread his wings, letting the firelight catch them and turn them iridescent green.

I reached for his feathers, gulping in surprise when he let me catch him. *"You look like a fool,"* he said. *"They only tease you because they want you to try to keep up with them. They want you to fall."*

I stared at Caw, too young to form the words that were in my thoughts, to express my surprise at his voice, my indignation at my sisters' treatment.

"Practice where they cannot see you. Stand. Find your balance. Take one step. Take another. Then, when they tease you, you will be able to chase them. You will catch them. They won't tease you about walking again."

I was silent, thinking about the bird's words. After a pause, he said, *"I take your tears. Forget them. They are mine."*

That night, in my cradle, I stood. I lifted my hands from the carved wood until I could feel the balance that Caw had described. I concentrated, and I took a step. Another. I slid over the side of the cradle, stretching until I reached the floor. I practiced walking until I could cross the room without falling.

The next day, my sisters teased me, but I stood up and walked away. I looked back and found Mother nodding. I heard her say, "You took your tears to your darkbeast. No more tears."

I looked at Caw, and I forced myself to stand, to ignore the stinging of my knees and my palms. I would inspect the damage to the dress after I was outside. "It's too dark in here."

"*It's as dark as it is,*" he said, in the practical tone that drove me mad. "*Did you bring me anything to eat? I've been here for hours.*"

"I'm sorry! I didn't think!"

"*You never do,*" Caw said, but he didn't seem too concerned. All the same, I felt like a glutton, as if I had eaten all of my breakfast, and his, and my family's as well.

—•—

I was five years old, and my mother had sent me to the communal oven to get our loaves of bread. They were the fat ones, the balls, made with chestnut flour instead of wheat. They were my favorite.

I thought that I would take one bite, to sustain me on the long walk home. Then just one more, and another to conceal the ragged edge of what I'd already eaten. The new line wasn't even, and I took another bite, and then I needed to turn the ball around, and I could see that it was already half gone. I took one more swallow, and then I decided that I might as well finish all of the loaf; that was the best way to hide the evidence of my sin.

When I entered our home, my mother saw the crumbs on the front of my dress. She brushed them away from my lips and forced my mouth open, as if she could summon up the bread that was already turning in my belly. I thought that I might be sick on the floor in front of her, but she only shook her head. "Glutton!" she exclaimed. "Take it to your darkbeast."

She slipped the rag leash around my wrist, and I turned my back on the room. I did not want to see my sisters; I did not want to confront their smug smiles as they watched me transferring my sins to Caw.

"*The wheat bread is better,*" Caw said.

"It is not!" I kept my protest to a whisper.

"*It's better for the peace of the house,*" the raven said with implacable logic. "*If you had brought back a long loaf of wheat bread, you would not have been tempted to eat it all.*"

"I'll go without for the week. I'll give my portion of seedcake to mother."

He turned his head, looking at me with first one eye, then the other. *"Your mother does not care for seedcake."*

"Fine! I'll give it to my sisters, then."

He ducked his head up and down, in the quick motion that meant that he was happy. *"I take your gluttony. Forget it. It is mine."*

—•—

I said, "I didn't get breakfast, either. It's my birthday. That's not fair."

"The world's an unfair place," Caw said. *"You'd likely appreciate that more, if you watched from behind the bars of a cage."*

"I can't let you out," I said. "Not yet. You know what they expect me to do."

"And you're afraid."

"I am not!"

He hopped down to the floor of his cage, spreading his wings wide before turning to look at me with one shiny eye. *"You look afraid to me. Your cheeks are pale beneath those ridiculous paints."*

"I don't fear the things I cannot change."

—•—

I was twelve years old, and my father had died the day before. He had been harvesting grapes in the field, carrying the big vine basket on his back. My uncle said that my father had his sharp knife in one hand, that he had just cut a huge clump of fruit. He collapsed with a single wordless cry, clutching at his chest. He fell forward, and all the grapes in his basket spilled onto the ground.

"They spilled around him," my uncle said repeatedly. "All around him, the grapes spilled."

Mother wailed her grief, a sorrow far sharper than any she had given to her rat, her darkbeast when she was a girl. She reached for her apron, tore it into ragged strips. She snatched at the gold pin that kept her hair piled on top of her head, and she released the heavy braid that was more grey than black. She retreated into her closet and rummaged among her herbs and paints, coming out only after she had smudged dangerous black circles around her eyes.

And that night, she told me to go the vineyard and collect the grapes that my father had spilled.

"I can't, Mother!" I wailed, terrified of the strange woman in front of me. "There are evil spirits out there. There are ghosts!"

"You will get the grapes! We need every fruit we can harvest! Your father is gone, and things are different now!"

"Tell Marguerite to go! Tell Avonette! They can gather the grapes. They aren't afraid of the spirits! They aren't afraid of the ghosts!"

My mother's fury cut through the horrid paint on her face. She dragged me over to Caw's cage and tightened the rag leash until my fingers turned cold. "Take your fear to your darkbeast!"

I trembled with terror, imagining the creatures that waited for me under the moonlit sky.

Caw took his head out from under his wing, and he shifted from foot to foot, blinking sleepily at me. *"Perhaps we should consult with the priests about the cause of this earth tremor shaking my cage."*

I tried to still my trembling hands by taking deep breaths. "I can't go out there, Caw. She wants me to stand where my own father died. She wants me to touch the grapes that he touched just before … His ghost will catch me, Caw. I know it will."

"She wants to know that her husband did not die in vain. She wants to know that she has food to feed her family in the difficult days to come."

My teeth chattered, and my fear made me peevish. "If she wants the grapes so much, then she should go get them."

"What do you truly fear?"

"Ghosts." I whispered the word, as if I were afraid of attracting the undead's attention merely my speaking their name.

"And you believe your father's ghost would be evil? You believe that he would attack you, the last daughter of his heart?"

Hearing Caw ask the question, I felt foolish. "It's dark out there. There could be other things. Brigands. Wild animals."

"And there could be grapes, spoiling on the ground."

"Will you come with me?"

"*Aye. A night journey for a nightbird.*" He cocked his head at me as I stood straighter, as I brushed hair off my face with my free hand. "*I take your fear,*" he said. "*Forget it. It is mine.*"

— • —

"I wish things could be different," I said, wondering how long I had before Perdine's priestess came back to us. She expected me to present her with proof that I had killed my darkbeast. I was supposed to show the priestess, and then I would make Caw's remains into some totem for the house I would share with my husband.

Marguerite had tanned the skin of her darkbeast, a snake. She had scraped it clean and stretched it to dry, rubbing it with precious oils to make it soft and supple. She had given it to Thomas, the butcher's son, when he asked for her hand in marriage. The snake was a symbol of all the bitter lessons that she had learned, all the bad traits that she had left behind in her childhood.

Mother's rat had been stretched around a wooden frame and fitted with glass eyes so that it looked real. It had fallen into the fire, though.

No, I must be honest. I pushed it into the fire, in a fit of jealousy.

— • —

I was thirteen years old; one year had passed since we'd buried my father. My family was supposed to celebrate the end of our year of mourning; we had commissioned a bull to be slaughtered on Zelo's altar, and the good beef was spitted and cooked for everyone in the village. Musicians had been hired from three villages away, and the communal oven had been filled with bread three days during the week before the festivities.

And then, Mother told me that I must stay at home. Someone must be here, she said, in case Father's spirit came looking for us. We could not let him be lonely. We could not let him think that we had forgotten him.

"It's not fair!" I cried. I was thinking of the meat, all the juicy beef that had been denied to us during our entire year of mourning. "Why can't Avonette stay behind?"

"Avonette hopes to dance with Lastor." Lastor. The blacksmith's apprentice. He had shoulders as broad as the bull we had sacrificed, and hands as sinewy as Father's grapevines. I thought of Lastor, and my belly swooped. I had felt that way before, at the winter rites when our neighbor, Philippe, asked me to dance. I had refused, of course, because I was still mourning Father.

"I want to dance with Lastor, too," I said to Mother. "I've been mourning too. I deserve to dance with him."

"You're a jealous, jealous girl," Mother said, and her mouth straightened into an angry line. "Take that to your darkbeast."

The rag leash was old and loose, but I would never have dreamed of pulling my hand free. Instead, I stared after my mother and sisters as they left our home, and I listened to the strains of merriment from the green.

"*May I have the honor of this dance?*"

"Leave me alone, Caw."

"*Avonette fears that she will never find a husband. Let her dance with Lastor.*"

"But I love him!"

"*You don't know the meaning of the word love. You are jealous.*"

"I am not." I closed my eyes, and I tried to picture Lastor's face. I knew that I had dreamed of him before, nearly swooned when Mother sent me down to the forge to collect an iron poker for our hearth. Now, I lifted the poker and shifted its weight in my untethered hand.

I swept it back toward the fire, and I caught Mother's rat on the mantel. The stuffed darkbeast teetered on the wooden shelf, and I cried out, stretching to retrieve it before it hit the hearth. Leashed, though, I could not reach it, and its whiskers were singed before I could dig it out of the fire.

"*You only want Lastor because your sister wants him.*"

"That's not true!" I was brushing at Mother's rat, trying to clean her darkbeast.

"*What color are his eyes?*"

They were green, weren't they? Or were they hazel, the color that Mother called "shadows of the forest?" I muttered something, which Caw accepted as an admission of ignorance.

"You want to be the one fussed over. You want to plan your wedding. You want to be the wife of the blacksmith, but you don't care about Lastor."

I had been thinking of the fine gown I would wear on my wedding day, the cloth of gold that would cover my hair, just as my mother had covered hers, and her mother before her. I had imagined people referring to me as Goodwife Smith, bowing their heads a little in recognition of the power and prestige that I had in the village.

"Is there anything wrong with that?"

"You know that Avonette wants him more. She baked the seedcake that he likes, to give to him tonight."

"Her cakes are too dry. He'll have to drink a flask of wine to choke it down." I muttered under my breath, but Caw heard me perfectly.

"He'll know that it is dry, and he'll finish every crumb." He waited for a long moment, and then he said, *"I take your jealousy. Forget it. It is mine."*

—•—

Now, on my birthday, my mind was filled with memories. I had spent years mastering the ways of a proper young woman, learning everything I needed to know to be a wife to whatever man would have me. Only one step remained in my education.

"I can't do it," I said, my voice dry of the tears I might have shed when I was an infant. "I can't kill you."

"You must."

"I never asked for this. I never asked for you to take my evil from me."

"I came to you, though."

"I was only a baby. You landed on my cradle. You did not know what you were taking on."

"Is that pride that I hear in your voice?"

"No," I smiled. "You took that one, well enough. It's rebellion."

"Ah," my wise darkbeast said. *"We haven't quite mastered that yet, have we?"*

—•—

I was fifteen years old. I lived in my parents' house, with only my mother for company, now that Avonette had moved into the home that she shared with Lastor. Mother kept Caw's cage in the corner, but she had not used the rag leash for over a year.

Then, the Travelers came. Rumor swept before them, through the hillside villages. Lastor heard it from Philippe, who had heard it from the miller in the next village, who had heard it from the bargemen who plied the river. The Travelers were coming.

I dreamed about them. I dreamed about the stories they wove, the magical tales they told of the days when the gods still walked the earth, when Perdine came into the houses of perfect young girls, when Zelo found a dozen maidens to claim as his own.

I had heard about the Travelers' costumes, about their pure and perfect voices as they sang their plays. I had heard about their brilliant masks, the painted shapes that fanned above their brows, turning them into gods, animals, common ordinary men.

They were magic more powerful than Mother's herbs, stronger even than the spell that had bound Caw to me when I was a baby. The Travelers were the most intoxicating wine I had ever drunk, the finest feast I had ever consumed, the deepest emotion I had ever felt, all rolled into one caravan.

Mother forbade me to see them. She said that I was too young to understand their stories, that I could not comprehend the morals of their tales.

I sneaked out of the house and saw the first night of their plays, hovering at the back of the crowd until my excitement chased away my caution. I stepped forward when they finished their piece, applauding hard enough that my palms stung.

Mother leashed me to Caw's cage that night.

"It sounds as if the Travelers put on quite a performance."

"They were wonderful," I whispered. "I've never seen anything like them."

"*You were wrong to disobey your mother. She only thought to protect you.*"

"Protect me from what? I'm not a child any more. I understood every word of the play I saw."

"*Every word?*"

I thought about the story, how the mother grieved for her children lost at war. Well, of course I could not understand that. My own mother would never grieve for me. She had a heart of stone. "Nearly every one."

"*You haven't much longer to live beneath your mother's roof. Her rules will not bind you for many more days.*"

"I can't wait for the day that I'm free." But of course, the day that I was free was the day I sacrificed Caw to Perdine. It was the day I forfeited my darkbeast to the goddess of harmony. I was not ready for that. "I'm sorry," I said to Caw after a moment. "I didn't mean that."

He peered at me through the bars of his cage. "*I take your rebellion,*" he said. I thought that his voice sounded sad. "*Forget it. It is mine.*"

But the next night, I was back in the Travelers' camp. I watched their show from the shadows, and I kept from cheering at the end, but Mother caught me when I returned home late. She leashed me to Caw once again, muttering that my darkbeast was failing.

"*How was the performance tonight?*"

"It was magnificent," I said. "The Travelers move differently from anyone here in the village. It's like they're free. They don't have to follow the rules that bind the rest of us. You can't imagine what it's like."

"*No,*" Caw said, and his voice was dry inside my head. "*I can't imagine how freedom would feel.*"

I looked at the leash that bound my wrist, at the ancient rags that I could slip off anytime I chose. My fingers curled around the iron bars of Caw's cage. "I'm sorry," I said, and I truly felt contrite. "I should not have defied Mother."

"*I take your rebellion. Forget it. It is mine.*"

But I returned to the Travelers. For the four nights that they stayed in our village, I went to them. Each time, they pierced my heart with their tales. Each time, Mother caught me. Each time, Caw spoke with me. Each time, he took on my darkness. But still I longed to join the Travelers. Mother sang a happy tune the morning that they disappeared over the hills, heading off to the next village.

—•—

"No," I said. "We did not master rebellion."

"*So I failed as a darkbeast after all.*"

"No!" My insistence was so sharp it burst my lungs. "You have not failed at anything!"

Caw merely shifted in his cage, spreading his wings wide and fluttering them to catch all the dark rainbow he could command. "*It is time, Ariane. The priestess will return soon.*"

"I will refuse."

"*You must show her my death.*"

"I cannot!" How did the other children manage? How did they murder their rats and snakes, their toads and tortoises? How did they kill their teachers and their allies, their closest friends in all the world?

"*If you do not kill me, you will be outcast in the village.*"

I wanted to cry, but I knew that I must not, for Caw had taken tears from me. I wanted to take all my village's traditions, consume them and destroy them until nothing was left behind, but Caw had cured me of my gluttony. I wanted to collapse in a quaking pile, terrified of Perdine's wrath, of Mother's rage, but Caw had absorbed my fear. I wanted the other girls' peace; I envied their easy acceptance of the village rules, but Caw had peeled away my jealousy.

Caw had taken so much, but he had left me my rebellion.

I opened the door to his cage. "Be free," I said. He looked at me, first with one eye, then the other. I repeated myself, my whisper harsh as I thought I heard Perdine's priestess outside the door. "Be free!"

He flew out of the cage as the priestess's key turned in the lock. For just a moment, I thought that he would leave me without a whisper of farewell, but then I heard him say, "*I take your gift. Forget it. It is mine.*"

His wings buffeted the priestess, and she shrieked in surprise. She recovered quickly, though, dragging me out before Mother, casting me down the temple steps as if I were some sort of household filth. My relatives stared at me in disappointment; they had invested so much hope, so much planning in this day.

"I'm sorry," I said to Mother, but she only shook her head, staring at my skinned palm, my ragged knees, my torn dress. My sisters' eyes filled with tears, and my aunts began to whisper among themselves. My cousins stepped back, awe filling their eyes. No one could remember a time when a girl-becoming-woman had failed to kill her darkbeast.

I walked home alone. I removed the dress. I combed the flowers from my hair. I washed the paints from my face. I lay down to sleep, even though the sun was still high in the sky, and I turned my face to the wall when my mother, my sisters, my aunts, my cousins, even my poor, broken grandmother came in to talk to me.

At last the sun set, and the house grew quiet.

I waited until I heard the chimes in Zelo's temple strike midnight, and then I slipped out of my bed. I put on my sturdiest clothes, the rugged ones that I wore to work in the vineyards. I slipped into the kitchen and took a single loaf of chestnut bread, and one of wheat. I took a round of cheese from the spring house, and a small sack of apples.

No one was in the streets as I walked through the village. No one saw me leave the only home that I had ever known. No one was able to direct me over the hills, to the next village, or the next, or wherever the Travelers had gone. I turned my back to everything that was familiar, and I took a deep breath.

And then a shadow detached itself from the trees. "*I take your village.*" It said. "*Forget it. It is mine.*" My darkbeast settled on my shoulder and we started down the road toward my future.

Kitemaster

by

Jim C. Hines

Osa's string tickled Nial's face, jerking her awake.

Wake up, sleepyhead! For a magically animated kite no larger than Nial's hand, Osa had quite the voice. *You've got company.*

Outside the tent, one of the rebels called out, "Kitemaster, you're needed at the observation post."

Osa fluttered her panels in a rude, raspberry sound. *The Kitemaster is needed in dreamland. She's exhausted! And you need to leave her alone before I get angry.*

Thankfully, the rebel couldn't hear the tiny kite. Nobody else could. Nial stumbled out of her bedroll and fumbled with the ties holding the tent flaps shut.

The Imperials on the other side of the Rionto Valley must have launched scout kites. It was the only reason for Captain Shalen to summon her so early.

The instant the tent flap opened, Osa shot toward the rebel soldier. He leapt back, nearly dropping his lantern.

Osa floated up and began to circle, like a hawk preparing for a dive. Nial could hear her giggling.

Osa, no!

Osa returned at once, her string coiling around Nial's right arm. The miniature kite floated a foot or so above Nial's head, a hexagon of faded blue and white linen on a fragile bamboo frame. Nial grabbed her blanket and wrapped it around herself to fight the night chill.

He's only a messenger, Nial added. *Leave him alone. Do you want Shalen angry at me?* She glanced at the rebel, noting the tarnished patches on his ill-fitting armor. The reversed curve of the knife at his waist marked him as a northerner, probably one of the fishermen Shalen had recruited last month. The brass shoulder guards had been taken from an Imperial soldier's armor and hand-stitched to a battered leather breastplate. The golden lions had been scraped from the shoulder guards, replaced by crudely painted tigers, the sign of the Emperor's traitorous brother.

"Captain Shalen said there were scouts," he said, confirming Nial's guess. But why would the Imperials fly scouts at night? The moon was a mere thumbnail. In the darkness, the men harnessed to the oversized kites would see little or nothing of use.

"I don't need an escort," Nial said.

His cheeks reddened. "I'm sorry. Captain Shalen's orders."

Osa floated beside Nial's ear, muttering.

No, Nial said. *I don't think he trusts me either.*

They walked through the small camp, ducking through the low, twisted trees that covered the valley.

The observation post was built between twin pines. The concealed platform held a spyglass and several spools of thick cable. It doubled as a launch point for the rebels' own kites. The valley provided a constant wind that whipped Nial's hair into her face and threatened to tear her blanket away.

"Nial, excellent." Captain Shalen climbed down the rope ladder of the platform, jumping the last few rungs. "Our men spotted three scouts flying from the Imp outpost."

"Four, actually," Nial said. She could sense them riding the updrafts from the valley.

Shalen's shaggy brows lowered, but he gave no other sign of annoyance. "Four, then." He pointed to the ladder. "You know your duty."

"What about Lin?"

He nodded. "You'll see your brother once those kites are taken care of."

Without another word, Nial climbed the ladder and hauled herself onto the platform. She could feel the Imperial scout kites straining in the night sky. To Nial, the bulky rectangular kites were alive, fighting to break free of their bonds and ride the wind, heedless of the men strapped to their bamboo frames.

Kind of like herself, she thought. Yearning to escape, but tied here by Shalen's hold on her brother Lin.

The Imperial outpost was on the opposite side of the valley. Nial could just make out the orange glow of the torches on the stone wall surrounding the outpost. Somewhere behind that wall, linemen stood by huge wooden spools, fighting to control the scout kites.

"Hurry, *Kitemaster.*" Shalen's sneer twisted the title into an insult. They both knew she was no true Kitemaster. Nial was an untrained peasant. Her power was crude and clumsy. Shalen only kept up the façade because of the prestige he gained having a Kitemaster under his command.

Nial concentrated on the lines of the four scouts. They were taut as lute strings, and she could feel the wind strumming inaudible chords. She picked out the lead kite, and imagined a puff of wind from the side, sending the scout into a spin.

The man harnessed to the kite remained silent, even as the ground rushed to meet him.

Nial felt the line tighten again as the kite's lineman reeled in slack, trying to catch the wind before the kite crashed. The kite began to rise. Nial blew it sideways, tangling the line in the trees and swinging the scout into the branches.

The second and third scouts followed quickly, and Nial turned her attention to the last. This kite was larger than the others, hovering perfectly still in the wind.

Nial, I don't like this, Osa said.

"I know." How did it float so precisely?

Nial tried to send it into a spin, as she had done with the others. The kite drifted lazily to one side, the only sign of Nial's power.

"How goes it, girl?" Shalen shouted.

Osa's line snapped from side to side. *Give me two minutes, and I'll turn* him *into a girl!*

"Not now," Nial said, trying to shut them both out. She summoned a gust to hit the Imperial kite head-on, but the kite twisted aside. Finally, Nial reached for the cord itself, hoping to disrupt the scout's lineman.

Nothing happened. The kite's line dangled free, unanchored. "How can he fly without a lineman?"

She concentrated harder, putting all her strength into a single wind, trying to batter the kite back to earth. She pounded it again and again, beating it from above and below.

Finally, the kite began to swoop gracefully back to earth, leaving Nial gasping for breath.

"Good work," Shalen said. The sky had lightened enough for him to see the other kite's descent.

Nial's stomach hurt. She knew the effort it took to control the over-sized scout kites. The rebels often needed two or three linemen per kite, even with Nial's assistance. But that last kite had moved like a sparrow.

Nial, he flew with no lineman, Osa whispered. She sounded awed.

"I know," Nial said curtly. There was only one answer. After weeks of losing their scouts to Nial's untrained power, the Imperials had acquired their own Kitemaster. A *real* Kitemaster, strong enough to fly unassisted.

Fear followed Nial down the ladder. Shalen was bound to learn about the Imperial Kitemaster sooner or later. What would he do with her then? She found herself wishing again for the safety of a home that no longer existed.

—•—

Nial's mother had died giving birth to Lin. Their father died a little over a year ago, in the wave of sickness that washed through the village.

Nial spent a week building a spirit-kite for their father. She used his favorite cloak, the faded blue one with the white trim. She had painstakingly patched the rips and sewed the material to sticks of black-painted bamboo.

"It won't fly," Lin said. His clothes were damp and soiled. Only twelve years old, he had worked extra time in the grain fields so Nial could finish their father's kite.

"It will fly." Nial's fingers moved slowly and precisely through the knots. She had chosen a simple rectangular kite, to reflect their father's straightforward and honest manner. She looped the kite's line through the twin bridles and adjusted the knots.

"The cloak is too heavy." Lin shook his head. "It'll be like trying to fly a rock."

Heat flowed through Nial's hands as she worked. It had frightened her at first, feeling the unfamiliar power seeping through her fingers into the kite. Now the sensation was a comfort, bringing a sense of rightness. The material rustled at her touch, as if it could taste the winds outside the hut. When she stood to stretch her back, the kite glided to the dirt floor, toward the door.

"You need to rest," Lin said. "You can finish tomorrow."

"No." She picked up the kite, heading for the door. She hadn't realized how late it was. No wonder her eyes ached.

Insects chirped by the riverbank, falling abruptly silent as Nial and Lin walked down the trail.

"It's too dark," Lin said. "Unless you've suddenly gained the senses of a bat?"

"It will fly."

"Come to bed, bat-brain."

Nial kept walking. She could feel something stirring in her chest, power bubbling to life. All the grief was forcing its way upward, fighting for release. Fighting to fly.

"Nial, you'll ruin the kite. There's no wind, and …"

His voice trailed off as the spirit-kite leapt to life. Nial had wrapped the line around a maple branch as thick as her forearm. Now that branch whirled like a spinning wheel as the kite soared skyward.

She felt …joy. Freedom. A giggle slipped past her lips.

"What have you done?"

She didn't answer. For the first time since losing her father, she felt *alive*. Her heart pounded, her breathing came in gasps, and tears blurred her vision. She ran toward the river, allowing the kite to choose its own path.

She sensed other kites, far downstream. Tiny kites, woven of expensive silver and gold thread that glinted in the moonlight. She could see them, not with her eyes, but with whatever power her father's spirit-kite had awakened within her. Caught up in the excitement, she called those kites to her. She felt the lines snap as the kites raced toward her, and she sent them skyward in tribute to her father.

The spirit-kite tugged her arms. The line was completely played out. Her bare feet sank into the muddy riverbank.

Lin grabbed her arms. "Nial, get back here before the water takes you."

"Let me go!" she yelled, struggling to wade deeper. Cold water pounded past her legs. All she could think of was the spirit-kite, tugging her onward.

"Think of father," Lin said. "That's *his* spirit-kite. How can his soul travel the skies in peace if you drown to send him there?"

Even that might not have broken through Nial's haze, but as Lin spoke, the kite swooped closer, and a familiar whisper echoed within her mind.

Nial relaxed her hands, allowing the branch to fall into the water. An instant later, the kite leapt skyward.

Nial swallowed. "The kite had a message for us."

It was a measure of the night's strangeness that Lin made no quip about his sister's madness. "What message?"

"From our father. He said thank you. He asked me to look after you." She wiped her eyes. "He says he loves us."

She watched the rectangle of blue ride away, carrying their father into the afterlife. The smaller kites she had stolen followed after, gleaming like shooting stars.

—•—

Osa's line tickled Nial's ear, drawing her back to the present. *I'm okay*, Nial said.

Sure you are. And I'm a hummingbird.

That earned a small smile. Nial had created Osa from the leftover scraps of her father's cloak, hoping to hear his voice again. It hadn't worked.

I beg your pardon! I think it worked beautifully.

Nial grimaced. "Yeah. The one thing I did right."

The glittering kites she had stolen to send after her father belonged to Captain Shalen, who was using them to signal the other rebel groups. Shalen and his rebels had come to the village, seeking the one who had controlled their kites. *I led them right to us. I practically handed Lin and myself to Shalen.*

Osa drew a long double-circle in the air, trying to distract her.

I know, I know, Nial said. *Concentrate on the moment.*

Osa settled behind Nial's head as they neared her brother's tent. A single guard sat by the entrance. Lin's tent was at the center of camp. Even if he somehow got past the guard, he would have to fight through half the camp to escape. The guard nodded respectfully as Nial ducked inside.

Lin lay sleeping in the straw, an old blanket pulled over his shoulders. Osa tapped the canvas to wake him.

"Nial?" Lin rolled over, rubbing his eyes.

"The Imperials flew scouts. Shalen said I could see you again."

Lin nodded. "Hi, Osa." The little kite whirled. "What did you do to them?"

"They soft-landed." *I didn't have to kill anyone.*

Lin glanced at the open tent flap. Lowering his voice, he said, "What's Shalen doing? We've been here for weeks."

"I don't know."

"They won't wait forever," he said. He lay back, wadding the blanket into a crude pillow. "The Imperial palace is only a day's march away. Why stop here? Why this outpost?"

"Lin, they had a Kitemaster. A real one. It was all I could do to bring him down."

Lin grunted. "They've started taking you seriously."

"I don't know how long I can keep Captain Shalen from finding out. Once he does …" She left the thought unfinished. Lin's life depended on her service to the rebels. If she failed, what would happen to her brother?

So don't fail, Osa said.

Easy for you to say.

"But you did bring him down?" Lin asked.

"Easier to crash to earth than to soar among the clouds," she quoted. "I had the advantage, but he still almost beat me. I think it was a test to see what I could do, and it exhausted me. Now they know I'm not strong enough to fight their Kitemaster."

"Shalen would have killed me sooner or later anyway," Lin said bitterly. He turned away. "I'll almost be glad to get it over with."

"Lin, don't." She squeezed his arm, searching for words. She wanted to promise to protect him, to find a way for them to survive. But Lin would see right through the lie.

"At least you're useful," Lin said. "Even if you're not trained, they might keep you around."

"I won't let them hurt you," Nial said.

"Oh, good. I feel so much safer." Lin rolled, jerking the blanket over his head so it muffled his next words. "Maybe you can turn your baby kite loose on Captain Shalen."

Osa fluttered indignantly. *I'm not afraid of old turnip-brains. I could strangle that overgrown—*

Osa, no, Nial interrupted. *You can't. Lin's right.* She stared at the tent wall. *It's only a matter of time.*

—•—

Shalen's coming, Osa said. Nial swallowed the last of her mud-textured oatmeal and stood. Shalen was smiling. He looked almost cheerful. It made her nervous.

The men around Nial saluted or bowed. Nial deliberately kept her hands at her sides.

"There's my little Kitemistress," Shalen said, chuckling. "I hope you had an enjoyable chat with your brother last night."

Osa buzzed near her ear.

You're right, Nial agreed silently. *He's too happy.*

Osa projected a mental picture of a tiger pouncing from the trees. Slowly the image changed, and the tiger's face took on Shalen's wide features. Then Osa crossed Shalen's eyes and allowed the tongue to loll out one side of his mouth. It was all Nial could do to keep from laughing.

The real Captain Shalen clapped a hand around Nial's shoulders, dragging her away from the log where she had sat. "I have a special assignment for you. No more of these clumsy scouts. In a few days, you're going to fly nightwings."

"Assassins?" Several men glanced up, until Shalen's scowl made them look away.

"That's right," he said, his voice low. "Five of them. You're going to drop them right into the middle of the Imp camp."

"Captain Shalen, I —" She bit her lip. Controlling normal scouts would be all but impossible, given the presence of the other Kitemaster. Nightwing kites were little more than thin sheets of silk and string. More symbolic than practical, they relied entirely on the strength of the Kitemaster. Nial had never flown one. Even unopposed, she wasn't sure she could do it. With an Imperial Kitemaster fighting her ...

Don't worry," Shalen said. "I don't expect you to get them all across the valley. But for an untrained whelp, you've done well so far. Get even a single nightwing across, and I'll let you see your little brother again."

His smile grew, and he gestured back toward the other rebels. "My men say it's a blessing to have a Kitemaster among us. The rumors have spread throughout the country. 'The rebels have a Kitemaster,' the people whisper. 'Surely their cause is blessed by the gods.' You wouldn't want to disappoint everyone, would you?"

"No," Nial whispered.

"So what's wrong? You cower like a frightened child. Is there a problem, girl?"

"No," she said again.

It was the wrong answer. The muscles in Shalen's neck tightened like cords. "Is that so?" he asked, yanking her behind the cover of the trees. "You weren't even going to mention the new addition to the Imp camp?"

"What addition?"

He struck her on the face. It wasn't a strong blow, but it was enough to knock her to the ground.

Osa streaked toward Shalen's eyes, making him stumble back. He waved his hands, like a man trying to swat an insect. Osa's string flicked out of reach as she dove again. *Don't touch her, you walking pile of*—

Osa, no! The kite hesitated, and in that instant, Shalen caught her line.

Get your greasy hands off me! Osa struggled, but Shalen's thick fingers dragged Osa closer.

"Captain Shalen, please," Nial said. Tears of pain and fear filled her eyes. She could imagine Shalen crushing the fragile spars in his hands and tearing the old material into scraps. Her mind raced. "I need Osa. She helps me control the kites. She helps me sense the winds. *Please.*"

She held her breath, hoping he would believe her lies. She hated herself for begging, but she couldn't let him destroy Osa. With Lin trapped in his tent, the little kite was the only friend she had in the camp. Maybe in the world.

Shalen flung the kite away. Osa swooped along the ground and hid behind Nial.

"Keep the toy, if it serves you. I wouldn't want to deprive you of your resources. Especially with Edo's arrival at the Imp outpost."

"Edo. The Kitemaster?"

"The *Emperor's* Kitemaster," he said. "Only a handful of people have your gift, girl. The Emperor commands four. Three are scattered along the borders. The fourth, Edo, lives at the palace. Once the Emperor heard the rumors, it was only a matter of time before he sent his beloved Edo to handle the situation." He smiled. "And you're going to help us kill him."

—•—

For several days, Nial was kept under guard as Shalen flew scout after scout. He and his linemen flew them without her assistance, and one after another they tumbled into the trees. Sometimes she heard the men cursing and crying out as they fell, knocked down by Edo's power. Some never even made it off the launch point, dropping like the air had been sucked from beneath them.

Even within her tent, Nial could feel Edo's touch, reaching across the valley to tangle lines and drag scouts from the sky. He did it effortlessly, with a skill Nial envied. The slightest touch, and the rebel kites fell like stones.

Nial, what's Shalen doing?

I don't know. I didn't realize he had so many kites. This must be costing the rebels a fortune.

Have you heard the men? They know you're not helping, and they're not happy.

Nial nodded. She had overheard the muttering. Still, nobody dared disobey Captain Shalen.

Where is he getting the men? Nial wondered. The camp held two-hundred rebels at the most.

He's reusing them. Most crash so quickly they escape without injury, and Shalen flings them right back in the air. I hope Edo starts crashing those kites into Shalen's ugly nose.

Maybe I should talk to him again, Nial thought. *Offer to —*

Why, so he can laugh at you?

The day before, Nial had gone to Shalen, offering to help with the scouts. Not out of any desire to help, but because she wanted to earn another visit with Lin. Shalen had smiled that broken-toothed smile and ordered her back to the tent.

She thought of her last conversation with Lin. *He's waiting for something.* She wished she could figure out what it was.

—•—

Rebel soldiers woke her early that morning. Dew from the brush and scrub dampened her legs as she followed them to the observation post. Captain Shalen and several guards stood waiting.

"It's time," Shalen said. He tossed a long, leather satchel to one of the soldiers who had escorted Nial. The soldier untied the end and handed out five black-rolled bundles.

"These are the men you will fly into the Imp camp," Shalen said. "Once they're ready, launch them across the valley. Forget stealth. Forget style. Speed is your only concern."

Osa fluttered overhead, echoing Nial's surprise. "All five at once?"

"That's right." A hungry grin dominated Shalen's face. "Edo hasn't slept in three days. Even if he hasn't collapsed in exhaustion, he'll be too drained to stop five nightwings. All you need to do is get them into the outpost."

Nial swallowed her protests and turned to study the assassins. Superstitious fear made her shiver. Guild assassins were trained to kill quickly and silently, using any available means. Their bodies were weapons, as effective as any blade.

I don't think so, Osa said. *The one on the end is the same one who got drunk last week and stumbled into the privy trench. Remember?*

So? Nial asked.

The kite looped a tight, impatient circle. *You think a trained assassin would walk around with one boot covered in dung? It messes up the whole "inconspicuous" bit.*

Osa was right. Nial stared at the nearest "assassin," a young man with weary brown eyes. He had already looped ribbons of black silk around his wrists. He flexed his shoulders, testing the nightwing's fit. He looked tired and afraid. Hardly the look of a hardened killer.

The nightwing kite was a simple black diamond of dull silk. The men themselves would provide the spars. In the air, they kept their arms outstretched and their bodies rigid. A thin black line provided a symbolic connection to the earth. So long as that line remained, the nightwing was a true kite, and a true Kitemaster should be able to keep it aloft. Nial bit her lip, wondering if she'd even have the strength to get them off the ground.

Osa giggled. *A false Kitemaster, false assassins ... next you'll tell me Shalen's actually a bulldog who learned to walk upright.*

"Fly them low," Shalen said. "Close to the treetops. Try to keep the Imps from spotting the nightwings. Edo will have less time to stop you, and he'll have to push himself even harder." He sneered. "He is a loyal subject of the Emperor. He'd die before letting a single rebel nightwing into the camp. Do you know what that means?"

Nial took a step back at the sudden challenge. "I'm not sure."

"If a single nightwing makes it, Edo is unconscious, or even dead."

Suddenly things began to make sense. Shalen didn't plan to assassinate Edo. He meant to use Nial to drain Edo's strength.

But what would that accomplish, and why go to such lengths? There had to be more to Shalen's plan.

Are you sure? Osa asked. *Shalen doesn't strike me as the cunning type.*

Nial shook her head. Someone had to pay for all of those scout kites. They wouldn't have invested so much just to inconvenience the Emperor's Kitemaster.

"You know your duty," Shalen snapped.

Nial jumped. The five men had already climbed onto the observation platform and now stood ready, their arms outstretched. Long coils of line sat on the ground beside them.

"Go!"

Nial glimpsed fear and resignation on the lead rebel, and then he was leaping from the platform. Nial barely caught him, imagining a powerful updraft lifting him above the treetops.

The second man followed, and then the third. Seconds later, all five were in the air, gliding down the valley.

Nial couldn't breathe. It was like all five men were pressing down on her body, grinding her bones against the earth. She cried out, and the rightmost nightwing spun away, crashing roughly into a treetop.

"Concentrate," Shalen said. He slapped the back of her head.

Like that's going to help me concentrate. From the corner of her eye, she saw Shalen cut the line of the fallen kite.

Tension made the remaining four lines quiver. Other rebels held the lines, feeding out more and more as the wind carried the nightwings deeper into the valley.

They were almost to the bottom when Edo responded. Before she could react, one of the nightwings fluttered downward. No matter what Nial did, she couldn't control it. It was like Edo had created a bubble of stillness around the kite.

"Let it go," Shalen said. "You still have three kites. Fly them. Keep Edo on the defensive."

Nial blinked. He was right. She was doing it. *Three nightwings at once!* Excitement bubbled through her chest, but passed quickly as the kites reached the bottom of the valley and began to climb.

Regaining lost height was harder, and the effort sobered her. Nial dropped to her knees, gritting her teeth as she fought to fly the kites uphill, skimming the trees.

She pitied the soldiers strapped to the nightwings, helpless and unable to see what was happening. All flew facing backward, the strings tugging their chests as her winds carried them higher.

They've got it easy, Osa said. *You're the one doing the work.*

She sensed Edo reaching for another kite. Instinctively, she stilled the air, allowing all three kites to dive before scooping them up and pushing them onward.

It worked. At least, it was several seconds before Edo recovered, and she managed to gain a bit more ground. But now Edo was ready, and when she repeated the trick, he warped the line itself, tangling it into the tip of a pine tree. The nightwing dropped gently into the branches and hung there, leaving the soldier flailing helplessly.

Nial was over halfway up the far side.

"Our Kitemaster is strong!" Shalen pronounced. "She *will* succeed."

She heard others muttering in agreement, and wondered if any of them heard the unspoken *"or else"* in Shalen's words. Osa's line gave Nial's arm a comforting squeeze.

Edo sent his winds to buffet both kites, choosing brute force over the subtlety of his earlier attacks.

"You can destroy him," Shalen said.

The lust in his voice sickened her, but she pushed those feelings aside. Even after three days, Edo was still stronger. She crouched, knees bent as she braced herself against the winds.

If he's stronger, stop fighting him head-on! Osa fluttered sideways, cutting through the air like a blade.

Thank you! Nial turned the kites sideways, mimicking Osa's movements. Before the nightwings could fall, she flipped them in the opposite direction, zig-zagging closer to the Imperial outpost. The rebel on the nearer nightwing doubled over as the chaotic ride cost him his lunch. His motion bent the kite itself, wrenching it free of Nial's control. Edo pounced before Nial could recover, dragging the nightwing softly to the ground.

But the final nightwing had reached the ridge atop the far side of the valley. Edo made one last effort, but his winds were weaker than before. Edo was nearly spent.

"They're shooting at our scout," Shalen commented. He could have been remarking on last night's dinner.

Nial couldn't see the arrows, but she heard the occasional *thud* as they buried themselves in the earth. Nightwings were meant for stealth, but thanks to Edo's presence, the entire outpost knew what was coming. Orange streaks colored the sky as the Imperials began shooting flaming arrows, hoping to burn the kite out of the sky.

Edo couldn't stop her, but the rebel strapped to that kite was still doomed.

Nial...Edo could *have stopped you,* Osa said. She sounded uncharacteristically serious. It took a moment for Nial to understand why.

You're right. All four downed soldiers still lived. Edo had wasted his own strength to save them. Nial hesitated, floating the nightwing a bit higher. "Captain, the archers ..."

"You know your duty. Force Edo to respond, if he still can."

Nial wanted to weep. If Edo hadn't weakened himself, the rebel on the nightwing might have survived. Instead, he would die, and the nightwing would become his spirit-kite.

Don't blame yourself, Osa said. *It's not your fault.*

I can't just let him die.

Fists clenched, Nial allowed the nightwing to glide lower. It touched down amidst the scrub, well short of the Imperial outpost.

She turned to face Captain Shalen, bracing herself. "I'm sorry. Edo ... he was too strong."

Shalen didn't appear angry. "So, the old man still has some life left in him." He glowered as one of the false-assassins limped past, carrying the ruined remains of a nightwing.

Shalen shook his head. His satisfied look made her think of a cat after a good meal. "Your mistake was saving the ones who fell. Let them die, and concentrate your strength on the survivors."

Nial said nothing. *He thinks I saved the soldiers.*

"Thinks" is a bit generous, wouldn't you say? Osa asked innocently.

With a laugh, Shalen continued. "Still, you did well enough. I had my men launch a scout from the far side of the camp several minutes ago, and he flies without interference. Edo is unconscious. Possibly dead."

"No ..." The word slipped out before Nial could stop it. Osa's string tightened around Nial's arm, a not-so-subtle warning.

"What's that?"

Nial blinked. The fear had hit so suddenly, stronger than anything she had felt since her father's death. "I ... I don't think he's dead. I think I would have known." She searched her feelings, recognizing it as the truth. Edo had chosen to let go at the end, when Nial saved the scout.

Shalen studied her closely, then shrugged. "It doesn't matter. He's no longer a threat. Even if he lives, he'll need several days to recover. That's all that matters."

"What do you mean?" Nial said. "The assassins failed. *I* failed."

"Of course you did," Shalen snapped. "Stupid girl. Edo's death would have been a gift, but what do we care about one old man?" He grabbed her by the neck of the robe, no longer bothering to hide his contempt. She heard the other rebels whispering. "Who is the tyrant keeping us in chains?"

You are, Nial thought bitterly. But she gave the answer he wanted. "The Emperor."

"That's right. And you're going to help us put his brother on the golden throne."

She thought of the Emperor's palace, a day's ride through the mountains. "We're going to the capital?"

Shalen began to walk, leading her past the observation post to a pile of broken rock and boulders. The dusty smell of seed and droppings told Nial what was hidden here. Cages of wood and wire sat stacked behind the rocks. Pigeons fluttered their wings as Shalen approached. Their beaks opened, but no sound emerged.

Looking closer, Nial saw tiny pink scars on their necks, and realized their vocal cords had been cut to keep them silent.

A spindle-armed woman stood beside the cages. At Shalen's curt nod, she opened a pot of blue dye and set it on the ground. Reaching into one of the cages, she snagged a pigeon and dipped its tailfeathers into the pot. She held it close, cooing softly and blowing on the birds feathers while the watery dye dried.

Nial, what's going on? Osa asked.

"I don't understand," Nial said.

"It's a signal for the rebels hidden in the hills to the east. It tells of our success, and orders the men to prepare for the arrival of our Kitemaster."

"So we *are* going to the capital," Nial said.

Shalen shook with laughter. "I said a Kitemaster, girl. A real one. Not some useless commoner from the villages."

He began to pace, glancing at the birds to check whether the blue-dyed pigeon was ready for flight. The old woman shook her head.

"When the Emperor's brother heard about you, he devised the plan himself," Shalen said. "We already had a Kitemaster, but he wanted to wait for the right time to use him. Already the rumors were spreading. The Emperor knew about our Kitemaster, and he feared us. So we used you, dangling you like a worm before the Emperor's nose. The fool sent Edo running here to deal with you, leaving the palace unprotected.

"If we were to march on the capital in force, the Emperor's army would overwhelm us. But he thinks he has our Kitemaster trapped here. He won't expect nightwings to approach from the east. Thanks to you, this war will be over within days."

Shalen watched as the old woman released the pigeon and grabbed a second. Shalen waved his hand, and two soldiers grabbed Nial's arms.

"Don't worry, girl. I'm sure our new Emperor will be happy to repay your services once he takes his place on the throne."

—•—

Osa buzzed around Nial's head like an angry wasp, drawing nervous glances from the two men escorting her back to her tent.

"I want to see my brother first," she said.

One guard shook his head. "Captain Shalen's orders. I'm sorry."

Nial looked back. In the pink-orange light of the rising sun, she could just make out the gray speck that was the second pigeon.

It's my fault, Nial said. *I let him use me. I wasn't strong enough to —*

Do you think the self-pity could wait? Osa interrupted. *If we're going to do something, it has to be soon. Those birds are fast. They'll reach the other camp by sundown.*

Yes, they're fast. Fast for birds, at least. An idea began to form. But what about Lin?

Her father had asked her to watch over her brother. If she fought back, she would put them both at risk.

You heard your brother, Osa said. *This is destroying him.*

I can't leave him here.

So don't.

Slowly, Nial nodded. *I can't do this alone. You know what I need?*

Child's play.

"Go," Nial whispered.

Osa's string slid free of Nial's arm so fast it burned, and then the little kite was darting through the air like an arrow.

One of the rebels tugged Nial around. "What's it doing?"

Nial ignored him and concentrated. An instant later, several battered kites exploded from the observation post. The first one crashed into the rebel's back, wood splintering from the impact. He dropped, barely conscious.

Her second guard ducked a silver signal kite. Nial caused the line to loop round his legs, yanking him to the ground. And then she was sprinting toward Lin's tent, praying she got there before the rebels figured out what was happening.

—•—

Several rebels rose as she neared Lin's tent. She summoned more kites, sending them ahead to clear the way. These men hadn't heard Shalen's words. They hesitated to fight back against Shalen's "precious Kitemaster."

Nial didn't hesitate. Her kites smashed themselves apart as they bludgeoned rebels out of her way. By the time she reached the tent, the rebels had all fallen or fled.

"Lin!" She ducked into the tent and hauled her brother to his feet. "We have to go."

"What happened?" Barefoot, he followed her outside, where he stopped in shock. Torn kites lay scattered about. Nial could hear Captain Shalen's angry shouts, and she saw rebels regrouping by the observation post. "Nial, did you do this?"

"Come on," Nial shouted. She called more kites, slowing their pursuers. She smiled grimly. If not for Shalen, she wouldn't have known she could command this many kites at once.

Confusion reigned as they raced for the edge of camp, dodging more rebels.

Behind, Shalen's men were beginning to gain on them. A few others had stayed at the observation post, shredding the few remaining kites to stop her from using them as weapons.

Nial seized one of the scout kites, lifting it free before they could damage it.

She studied the kite as it neared. One edge was torn, and the bridles were tangled, but it was otherwise intact. "Get in," she said.

"What?"

The kite's line had snapped. She had maybe two hundred feet, but that was enough to drop Lin down the valley. It would give him a head start on his pursuers, who would have to climb down the treacherous slope.

Lin didn't move. "I know what you're thinking, and I won't do it. Both of us or neither one. We're small. The kite can support us both."

"But I can't fly it!" She called the kite around so it bumped Lin from behind. "Shalen was right. I'm no Kitemaster. I need an anchor for the line. If I try to fly us both, we'll probably crash."

So you crash. Better than sticking around here!

"Osa!"

The little kite clutched several blue-tipped feathers in her line. *Those poor birds will have nightmares for years,* she said, giggling. *They won't be flying anytime soon, though. Hard to steer without tailfeathers.*

Osa, I can't do it, Nial protested. *Maybe Edo can fly without an anchorman, but I'm no Kitemaster.*

Excuse me? Osa asked indignantly. *You're my master, and last I checked, I was a kite. Besides, what do you have to lose?*

Nial whispered a quick prayer to her father and mother, then slipped one arm through the leather ties of the scout kite. They seemed to tighten on their own, pressing her elbow against the bamboo spar.

Already the wind threatened to pull her off balance. She called a broken kite from the branches and sent it hold off the approaching rebels. "Lin, tie my ankles, then wrap the waist strap around us both. You'll need to hold on to me."

Lin obeyed, pulling the ties so tight it hurt. He stepped onto her feet as he knotted the last tie around his waist. He stretched out, grabbing the horizontal spar with both hands.

"Um … how do we do this?" he asked.

Nial pushed onto her toes and imagined a gentle wind raising them from the ground. The kite lifted a few inches, then veered to one side, toward a low, twisted pine.

Osa, grab the other end!

Osa's string twined with the line of the scout kite, and she tugged back with all of her strength, providing enough of an anchor for Nial to control her flight. The kite rose higher.

"Stop!" Captain Shalen held a cocked crossbow in his hands. He was breathing hard, but his mouth twisted into a triumphant smile. "It was a nice try, girl. But I can't have you running off to warn the Imps."

He still thinks his birds got through, Osa said, a nasty edge to her voice. *Won't he be surprised?*

"I don't mind shooting children," Shalen warned. "It's your choice. Surrender and live, or find out what it feels like to take a crossbow bolt in the belly."

Osa vibrated her line, producing a rude noise.

Nial found herself thinking of Edo, who had risked his own life to save rebel soldiers.

"Come down," Shalen said. "I wager we can still find a use for you."

"No," she said softly. She twisted her head to see the agreement in Lin's eyes. "We're through being used."

"Suit yourself." Shalen fired.

Osa's string sliced through the air, knocking the bolt aside. *Weren't expecting* that, *were you?* Osa crowed. She flew in tight circles, her own triumphant dance. *So much for the rebel Captain and his big, bad crossbow!*

Nial's kite began to fall. *Osa!*

Whoops! Osa caught the line and tugged, helping them fly once again. *Sorry about that.*

They flew higher, moving as fast as Nial could push them. Another bolt shot past her legs. Lin buried his face in her shoulder, but Nial felt nothing but joy. After launching so many scouts for Shalen, finally she got to experience it herself. She was flying!

Concentrate, Osa snapped.

Nial nodded, fighting to create another updraft. She was upside down now, her arms spread like wings as she stared down at the valley. The leather ties cut harshly into her ankles and wrists.

The kite shuddered and dipped to the side. Nial saw a small hole in the material. Shalen was still shooting, and it was hard to control the damaged kite.

"I can't keep us up here much longer." Already she could see Shalen's men hiking downhill, hoping to intercept them when they crashed. She closed her eyes. *Osa, I need your help.*

What do you think I've been doing?

Not that. She explained as quickly as she could.

You're crazy!

Do you have a better idea?

Grumbling, Osa released her hold on the kite and shot away. Without the tension Osa provided, the scout kite was like a boat adrift in a typhoon. Lin groaned as they twisted and jerked from side to side. It took all of Nial's strength to keep from dropping.

"What are you doing?" Lin yelled.

"Just hold on," she snapped. "We're *not* going back."

Nial struggled to control the kite. They kept listing to one side, and it was hard to balance the winds. They were probably out of crossbow range, but what good did that do if they crashed to their death?

The kite's wooden frame creaked with the strain. They slipped a good ten feet before Nial managed to create a new wind. That sent them twisting head over heels toward the other side of the valley.

Lin's hands slipped free. He flailed about until he managed to regain his grip on the main spar. The tie around his waist kept him from falling, but he still gasped like a child after a nightmare.

"Hold on," Nial said. "A little longer." She tried not to think about what would happen if Osa failed.

They dropped again. She glimpsed Shalen standing with his hands on his hips as he watched them fall. Anger gave her a brief burst of strength, and she managed to lift them a bit higher. Then the hole in the kite ripped, becoming a gash. A triangle of material flapped like a flag.

Nial fought to control the fall, pushing them farther from the rebels. If she was going to crash, she was going to do it as far from Shalen as she could.

Did you miss me? Osa snagged the line, doing her best to steady the dying scout kite. The choppiness diminished slightly. Then a second wind began, like a cushion rising beneath their feet.

"What's happening?" Lin said. Sweat covered his pale face.

"Edo. Osa was able to rouse him." Nial grinned. "She can be more than a little obnoxious. It's impossible to sleep through."

Is that any way to talk about the kite who just saved your life?

She could sense Edo's weariness. The extra breeze was weak and unsteady, but she could feel him fighting to save her, the same as he had done with the rebel scouts. It wasn't much, but it was enough.

The kite began to rise, pulling them toward the Imperial outpost. Toward safety. Her stomach tightened at the thought.

"How did you know Edo would even be able to hear her?" Lin asked.

"He's a Kitemaster," Nial said. Bound to the kite, she couldn't see where she was going. She had to trust Edo to lead them into the camp. Nial watched as Captain Shalen and the rebels began to shrink from the distance. "Like me."

〜●〜

Singing Down the Sun

by

Devon Monk

It wasn't the music that changed, bell-sweet and delicate as a moth's wing. Jai always heard the music no matter where she had hidden it. But the silence within the melody was different, the pauses between each note too long, then too short. Jai tightened her grip on the handle of her hoe and glanced up at Black Ridge where a forest of yellow pine stood dark in shadow. She knew what the changes in the song meant. It meant Wind and Shadow had found a new child to do their bidding.

"What will you do?" a soft voice asked.

Jai startled at the sound of the ancient corn snake, Sath, who sunned on the flat stone at the corner of her garden. He was her forever-companion, the one creature who had promised to never leave her. But he had been gone for nearly a year and returned this morning as if he had never left. As if she had not spent long days and nights worrying that Wind or Shadow had found him, killed him.

His sinuous body looked like a rope of sunlight, his scales like jewels of orange and yellow with deep black outlining the patterns down the length of him. She had forgotten how beautiful he was, but had not forgotten how afraid and betrayed she had felt when he left.

"There's nothing I can do," Jai answered.

Sath lifted his head, black tongue flicking out to taste the air, the wind, the song. "The song has changed."

Jai didn't answer.

"Wind and Shadow will take the child," he whispered.

Jai blinked sweat from her eyes. "You have been gone for a year. Did you come back to tell me what I should do? I won't teach another child. The gods can fight without me this time." Jai went back to hoeing the dirt between the summer-green shoots at her feet.

"I am home now," Sath said.

"That is not enough."

Sath rocked his head from side to side, his black eyes never moving from her. "I am sorry you were alone. But the child is —"

"— the child is not my problem."

"Even if he dies?"

The wind carried the song to her, melody and pauses chilling the sweat on her back and neck, tugging her faded cotton dress and the handkerchief covering her thick black hair.

Jai did not answer the snake. She pulled the hoe through weeds knowing that Sath was right. When Moon discovered Wind and Shadow had caught a child, there would be a battle for the music, and the child would die.

It'd happened before. She found the first child who played the music many years ago. He was a fine strong boy named Julian. Julian had been a quick student. He'd learned how music had come into the world. He learned that Wind and Shadow wanted it, and that Moon wanted it more. He had fought to keep the music hidden in the world, like she had, like it was meant to be. Maybe he'd been too strong. Like an oak cracking down under a storm.

He had been only six years old.

And that slip of a girl, pretty and bright as the sunrise, Margaret Ann. Jai had taught her too. Tried to teach her to ignore Wind and Shadow. But Margaret Ann had gone walking in the night and was swallowed up by moonlight. Poor little bird, Jai thought, poor sweet child.

"I've buried enough children," Jai said. "Teaching them didn't help." She struck the dirt, broke clumps, uprooted weeds, but the memory of the children would not go away.

Sath drew into a tighter coil, resting his fiery head upon circles of scales. "Not teaching helps less," he said. He gave a slow, gentle hiss, "please, forever-companion?"

"Forever-companions don't leave each other." Jai finished weeding the row and the next, following the curve of the land. All the day Sath watched her with dark unblinking eyes. And all the day the music drifted down to her, sweeter than she'd ever heard it before.

There was power in that song and there was power in the player. But she had made up her mind.

At the last of the last row, Jai straightened her back. The shawl of night would soon come down. Time to fix a meal, boil water for tea, soak her feet.

"Are you coming?" she asked Sath.

The snake uncoiled and slipped off the edge of the stone like a ribbon of orange and umber and gold. He crossed the rich tilled soil and stopped at her foot.

"Will you teach the child?" he whispered.

"No." Jai said.

"Ahh," Sath said sadly.

The sound of his disappointment made Jai wish she could take the words back, but she did not want to teach another child, could not bear to see the gods tear a soul apart again. Jai ignored the snake and made her way to her house: a sturdy square cabin with two windows and a pitched shake roof shaded by a gnarled hickory that combed the wind in leafy exhale.

Just as she reached the edge of her yard, just as she looked up at her doorstep and saw the small silent figure standing there — that very moment — she realized the music had stopped, leaving nothing but the warble of the night bird and the whisper of the old hickory tree.

The child was small, dusky-skinned and red-haired. A boy. Long in the leg, and serious of eye. He looked to be ten, still dream-slight, as if not yet anchored to this living world.

Oh, please no, Jai thought. "What are you doing out this late, child? Won't your mother be looking for you?"

The child blinked, shook his head. He pressed his back against her front door. He held a wooden bowl-shaped instrument tightly against his chest — string and wood and magic itself. There. On her doorstep. In his arms.

No one had ever pulled it down from the mountains. No one, not one adult who had no chance of it really, nor one child who could still hold magic bare and true in their hands, had ever gone up to the mountains and brought the music down to her.

"Please," Sath said from the grass at her feet.

Jai put one hand on her hip and tried hard not to show her fear. She did not want to fight the gods again.

"There's no place for you, child," she said. "No place for that music. You should go home to your mama now."

"I don't have a mama," the boy said, and his voice was honey and starlight, the sound of a barefoot angel begging on her doorstep. "I don't have a daddy either."

Jai shook her head. None of the children who were taken by Wind and Shadow had kin.

"There's no room for you here, child," she said again.

"Jai," Sath whispered, "please don't turn him away."

The boy looked down at the snake.

"He told me," the boy said. "Told me I should find you. Said you would help me. Please. I don't have another place to stay."

Jai was surprised the boy could understand the snake — Sath had never spoken to anyone but her. She was even more surprised that Sath would tell the child to come to her, that he would expect her to help again.

"You should have stayed gone," she said to Sath.

Sath lifted up, high enough the blunt tip of his mouth could touch her fingertips. His whisper was so soft, she could feel it on her fingers more than she could hear it. "We are — we were forever-companions. You trusted me for many years. Trust me now. Then I will go."

Jai opened her mouth to tell the boy to leave but a gust of wind whipped by. The wood and string bowl in the boy's hands hummed a sweet, low, soul-tugging tone. Even at half the yard away, Jai could see the child sway beneath the music's power.

"Please don't be mad at the snake," the boy said. "It's not his fault. I will try to pay you back any way you want if you'll help me."

Holy, holy, always the sweetest children. How could she turn her back on him now? Jai glared again at the snake. Sath arched back down to the ground, and slipped through the grass toward the house, toward the boy.

Jai stepped forward with a heavy sigh.

"I'll do what I can, child. Don't expect miracles. You are tied to this thing," she pointed at the instrument, "until the end of time." *Your time,* she thought. "But that doesn't mean you have to fear. You are the one who plays the music. It doesn't play you."

As if to prove her wrong, the wind snatched at the strings again, and the boy's fingers found their place on the strings. His eyes glazed and two strong notes rang out.

Jai put her hand on the boy's shoulder, breaking the spell. "First rule is you keep your hands off the strings if you want into my house."

The boy's eyes cleared. He swallowed. "Yes, Ma'am."

"Second rule is to listen to me, child. This is not an easy thing." *For either of us,* she thought.

The boy nodded. "I'll try to do right."

Jai stepped past him, avoiding even a casual brush with the instrument. She did not want to feel its power in her hands again.

"Come inside, and I'll get us some food. We have some time yet before night thickens and Moon wakes."

The boy followed her into the house and stood in the middle of the small living room, a shadow in the uncertain light. Jai moved around the room and lit the kerosene lamps. The light revealed a wood rocking chair and padded couch, a braided rug and a rough stone fireplace with a mantel made of a lightning rod. Sath was no where to be seen, though she was sure he had slipped into the house ahead of them.

Once all the lanterns were lit, the boy gasped.

The stronger light showed walls covered by hundreds of musical instruments. Hung by cords, hung by nails, hung by strings, every conceivable musical instrument rested against the walls, repeating the sounds of Jai's footsteps in gentle harmony.

"Do you play them?" the boy asked.

Jai raised an eyebrow. "Didn't think I spent all my days hoeing the field, did you? I've been a few places in my long life, boy — what is your name, child?"

"Julian Jones," he said.

"Julian?" Jai's heart caught. Her first. Her oak-strong boy. Buried so many years ago beneath the moss and loam of a continent far and an ocean away. But this boy was different than her first Julian. This boy was built like a supple willow and had a voice as sweet as an afternoon dream.

"I haven't heard that name in a long, long time." Jai walked into the small clean kitchen and lit the lamps. There were no windows here to let in sun or moon light. Sath might be here, but she did not see him.

"That name has strength, child," she said.

"Will it help?" his voice was almost lost to the wind blowing outside.

"Every little bit helps when Wind and Shadow want you to serve them. Do you know the old stories, Julian? About how music first came to the land?"

Julian shook his head and took a step toward the kitchen, then stopped.

"Come on, child. Sit at the table."

Julian came into the room and a long streak of orange followed at his side. The boy settled into the chair, keeping the instrument cradled in his lap. Once he was settled, Sath slipped up the wooden rungs of the chair until his wide diamond head rested just above the boy's shoulder.

Jai wondered why Sath was so protective of the child, wondered if he had promised the boy to be his forever-companion. That thought made her heart ache. She turned to the sink and pumped water into the kettle, putting the hurt aside. They had only an hour before Moon woke.

Jai had told the story of music to every child. She had tried every way she could think of to defeat Moon and Shadow and Wind. But no matter what she taught the children, no matter what they tried, the gods always won, always drank the music down, and with it the child's life.

Wind scraped across her rooftop, clawing to get in.

She rekindled the wood stove and pulled the morning's bread out of the warmer. Her thoughts raced. What way to destroy the instrument? What way to stop the gods?

"In long ago days," Jai said, "Sun would walk over the edge of the horizon to the dreaming world each night. Sun's dreams were beautiful and terrible, frightening and foolish. They were so filled with wonder, the sound of them caused the stars to blink in awe and all the world to tremble."

She put the kettle on the stove and turned to place a plate of bread in front of the boy. Outside, Wind rattled in the hickory tree.

"Every night sister Moon listened to Sun's dreams and grew jealous of the beauty she would never see in her dark world. She wanted those dreams, wanted what her brother, the Sun, had.

"So Moon sent Wind to catch Sun's dreams and bring them into the night. But Wind had no hands, and the dreams slipped away before he could reach Moon. Then Moon sent Shadow into the dreaming land. But even in dream, Sun shone too brightly for Shadow to touch."

Julian was perched on the edge of his chair, looking as if at any moment he would fly away. Jai hurried.

"Moon was crazy with want. A greedy, selfish want. She shone that hard cold eye of hers down across all the lands, across the seas, and into the hearts of every soul until she found herself a strong child. A girl with more curiosity than good sense."

"A brave girl," Sath whispered.

Jai shook her head.

"A foolish girl who listened to Moon's call and let her feet follow. She found her way over the edge of the world and into the dreaming land.

"There, the girl scooped up armfuls of dreams that glittered like jewels. She put the dreams into the wooden bowl she carried and ran back to the waking world.

"But Moon was waiting for her at the edge of the horizon. Waiting with Wind and Shadow. All three of them so greedy, they tussled for the bowl of dreams.

"The girl tripped and the bowl flew. Moon tried to save the dreams by sealing the bowl with silver light, but Shadow and Wind wanted it too and tore at the bowl, shredding Moon's light into strings.

"The bowl up-ended and dreams poured out between the moon-light strings, crying a sweet music as never a soul on earth had heard.

"The music of Sun's dreams soaked into the land and was caught in every river, every stone, every tree, bird, beast, and all the souls between."

Wind buffeted the roof. Shadow crept down the walls, leaching light from nooks and corners. But Julian watched only Jai.

"What about the girl?" he asked.

He didn't ask about the bowl. Didn't wonder where the magical instrument had gotten off to. Of course, he shouldn't wonder. He held it against his heart.

"A snake who had been resting on the edge of the world whispered for her to get up just as the Sun came into the waking world and discovered the spilled dreams. Sun was angry, but the snake told Sun it was not the girl's fault. Instead of killing the girl, Sun bound her to guard the moon-strung bowl, to keep it hidden from Wind and Shadow, and most of all, from Moon.

"The girl did this for a long, long time. She hid the bowl in all parts of the world, but always, always, Wind and Shadow found it. Always, always, they lured a child to play the music for them and jealous Moon."

"They still want the Sun's dreams," Julian breathed. His hands clutched the bowl so tightly, his knuckles were white.

Jai did not want to tell him the rest — the worst. "No mortal can endure playing the instrument for long. Maybe a day, maybe a week. But Sun's dreams are so pure, so strong, they burn flesh and bone to dust."

"I won't play for them," he said.

Jai's skin chilled.

"I'll break the bowl, cut the strings, or, or throw it back over the horizon."

"No mortal power can break that bowl, boy. No answer as simple as that." Poor, sweet bird, she thought, what more could she give him? What words to guide him?

"Teach him," Sath whispered.

Jai knelt at the boy's feet and placed one hand on his knee. He was trembling. "I can teach you how to survive this night," she said.

"What should I do?"

"Don't say no to the wind, child. Don't refuse the shadow. Play the music for them, let them have their song through you. Bend like a blade of grass, and they'll let you free for at least a little while."

Dark eyes searched hers. "That's never worked before, has it?"

Wind tore at the shakes. Shadows spread like spilled ink across the ceiling.

"We'll make it work," Jai said. "You are strong enough to bend."

Julian closed his eyes, his mouth tugged down. When he opened his eyes, Jai could see his fear, fresh and sharp. A fear she shared.

Shadows licked out. A lamp dimmed.

"Did you try to break it?" he asked.

"A hundred, hundred times." Beyond the living room, the front door bucked beneath pounding gusts. Instruments within the room rang out in answer.

Julian stood and walked into the living room, facing the door, his back to Jai.

"Did you play the music for them?"

"For a thousand, thousand years." She stepped up behind him and placed her hand on his thin shoulder. Sath had wrapped around Julian's waist and rested his head on the boy's other shoulder.

Hinges groaned, darkness swallowed lamp light.

"Did you try to play it wrong?" Julian asked.

"There is no wrong way to play a dream, child. There is only your way."

The door burst open. Wind stood beyond the doorway, larger than the room could hold. His arms and legs were ragged tornados of dust and dead grasses, his face the flat cold mask of storm. Only his eyes seemed solid, and those were bottomless swirling vortices that drank thought and emptied minds.

Behind him skulked his brother, Shadow. Against the dark of the night, Jai could only see Shadow if he moved, a nightmare shaped like a great cat or monstrous dog, with only the razored glint of fangs and claw to show his passing.

Wind and Shadow strode toward the house.

"Bend child," Jai said, wanting to close her eyes and run from here, but unable to do either beneath the hold of Wind and Shadow. "Play for them."

"Your way," Sath whispered beside the boy's ear.

"My way," Julian said.

He placed his fingers against the strings. But instead of plucking, his fingers lay flat, muting the music, denying the gods.

Wind howled. Shadow swelled and grew, filling the air, until it felt the house would crush beneath the weight of the night.

Jai squeezed Julian's shoulder, hoping to hold him steady against the gods while Sath whispered to him.

"Play," she said again.

Music, soft as a sigh, rose to fill the room. It was not the burning power of Sun's dreams pouring through moonlight strings. It was a softer song, a child's melody. A lullaby.

Julian was singing, his voice sweet and clear, like river against stone, like time against the world.

Please, no, Jai thought, *don't fight the gods*. But Julian did not stop singing. This was his way, his denial of the music, his choice to stand strong and not bend. Just like her other oak-strong boy.

And Sath was singing with him.

Jai could not let them fight alone. She added her warm, low voice to their song. The instruments on the walls echoed the lullaby. Note by note, they stood against the gods. Wind tore at the room trying to stop them. Shadow crushed down.

Still, they sang.

In a moment of song, in a beat of three hearts, Wind and Shadow pulled away from the house.

Julian swayed. "Are they gone?" he asked.

But Jai knew that in only a moment, a beat of three hearts ...

Wind struck the house. The door exploded. Splinters of wood knifed through the room. Julian cried out, turned toward Jai.

Shadow leapt through the doorway, so hard and cold, it was as if the air was made of claw and ice.

Blinded, deafened, Jai pulled Julian behind her and reached for the bowl in his hands. Her palm touched the strings and moonlight left blistering burns. Wind snatched the bowl from her fingertips and hurled it against the wall. Wind struck her and Jai fell to her knees, holding Julian close against her, trying to protect him from Wind and Shadow.

Julian struggled free of her grip.

No! she tried to say, but shadow clogged her mouth and the wind stole her words.

One step, two, and Julian was gone. She could not see him, lost to Wind and Shadow, but she could hear him, his halting voice, his soft song.

Wind and Shadow saw him too. They tore out of the house so quickly, the natural darkness brought tears of pain to Jai's eyes. In that light, she saw Julian. He stood in front of the open door, his clothes tattered, his thin body straight, bloody, Sath wrapped around him like braided armor.

In his hands was the moon-strung bowl. He lifted the bowl up above his head and called out.

"I have them! I have all of Sun's dreams and all of the songs."

From the black sky, Moon woke. Moonlight poured over him like platinum fire, the cold cruel eye of a jealous god.

"Julian!" Jai called. "Come back."

He glanced over his shoulder, his dark eyes filled with fear, his mouth set in a thin line. Sath lifted his head and whispered, "Good-bye, forever-companion. I am sorry."

Then the boy turned back to the door and held the bowl out in his hands.

"I won't play for you," he said. "They aren't your dreams to hear." Julian softly sang the lullaby.

Moon's anger was like sharp fingers pressing into Jai's ears. A snap, a flash of pain, and her ears popped and bled. Beyond the door, Wind roared like a great ocean, and the air filled with Shadow, choking out all light except that single beam of ice surrounding Julian and Sath.

Jai pushed up to her feet. She had to pull Julian and Sath away from the moonlight. She couldn't let them die.

Wind and Shadow and Moon pulled back to strike.

"Now!" Sath hissed.

Julian yelled and held the bowl before him like a shield. Moonstrings snapped. The bowl shattered. A thousand, thousand glittering dreams fell from between the splinters of wood. All at once, beautiful notes cried out, the pure, the last song of Sun's dreams.

Wood and moonlight sliced through the room, whipped by the wind. Jai stumbled toward Julian, but could not reach him through the flying debris.

The walls groaned. Instruments fell and shattered against the floor.

Wind and Shadow clawed into the room, snatching at the remaining bits of the bowl — wood and broken strings that would never sing again — then screamed away to the distant face of Moon. As if released from a spell, clouds crowded the night sky and smothered the moonlight.

When Jai could hear again, when she could see, she found a lamp and match and brought both back to find Julian lying dazed in the middle of the destroyed room.

He was covered in dust and splinters of wood and reed, Sath still wrapped around his thin chest and waist. A trickle of blood ran tracks down his arm and hand, too dark to be his own.

"Sath?" Jai said. Her hands shook as she ran fingers against Sath's cool glossy scales trying to find the source of the bleeding. Not a fast flow, she realized. Just scratches, no deep wounds.

Sath shifted, his head appearing from near the boy's neck. "The child?"

Jai brushed dirt and wood from Julian's hair and felt for his pulse.

"Fine," she said, her voice trembling with relief. "He's fine."

Julian looked up at her, his eyes wide with shock. "Should I go now?"

Jai brushed the dust from his cheek. "No. I think you should stay right here."

"You said there was no place for me here, and your house, the instruments, Sun's dreams. I broke them. I ruined them all," he whispered.

"Hush, child," Jai said, "you didn't ruin anything. You made it right again. Something I'd never been strong enough to do."

"But the music, your music ..."

"The music wasn't mine. It was Sun's."

She drew him into her arms.

"So I can stay?" Julian asked softly.

"Yes," Jai said.

"And so can the snake?"

Jai brushed her fingers across the top of Sath's head, remembering the hurtful things she had said to him. "If he wants to stay with such a foolish girl."

Sath tipped his head to one side, his dark eyes warm and deep. "I promised a brave girl I would be her forever-companion. My home is here with her."

"Thank you," Jai whispered. And she held the boy and the snake in her arms until Sun walked to the edge of the waking world and brought with him the warmth of day.

About the Contributors

DANIEL ARCHAMBAULT

Daniel Archambault lives in Vancouver where he continues an active lifestyle, having competed in short track speedskating from 1987-97. When not writing or reading weird stories, he is pursuing a Ph.D. in Computer Science at the University of British Columbia. A member of the Royal Astronomical Society of Canada (RASC Kingston Centre) since the late 1990's, Dan had his astrophotography published in the March/April 1998 issue of *SkyNews Magazine*. As a writer and reader of fiction, he chaired Green College's read/write café at UBC, and has recently become a member of the West End Writers' Club. "A Sirius Situation" is his first fiction sale.

KRISTEN BRITAIN

Kristen Britain is the author of the bestselling fantasy novels, *Green Rider* and *First Rider's Call* from DAW Books. She grew up and attended college in the Finger Lakes region of New York. After earning a bachelor's degree in film production, with a writing minor, she served for several years as a national park ranger, working in a variety of natural and historical settings, from high on the Continental Divide, to 300' below the surface of the Earth. Currently she lives on an island in Maine with two cats, a dog, and her kayak (none of which, thankfully, talk), where she continues to work on the next book in the *Green Rider* series.

HEATHER BRUTON

Born in Halifax, Nova Scotia, and currently residing in Kitchener, Ontario, Heather Bruton has spent her whole life drawing. Having little formal training, she has nonetheless made her living as a professional artist since 1991. Since then she has illustrated book covers, role playing games, collectible card games, tattoos, T-shirts, cloisonne, book marks, and magazine illustrations. At the same time, she has produced hundreds of her own paintings for sale at Science Fiction conventions and for private commissions. A long time SF/F reader, the fantastic realm is her favourite genre, although she has dabbled in wildlife, pet portraits, landscapes, and anything else that catches her fancy.

Along with her artwork, Heather pursues other interests including bird watching, travelling, horses, reading, zoology, ancient history, and cultures, archeology, paleontology, folk music, art history, Egyptology, reading, needle-point, and collecting way too much stuff to fit into her house.

JOHN C. BUNNELL

John C. Bunnell — no relation to the police-video host — has been writing and reviewing speculative fiction for two decades. His book reviews presently appear in *Amazing Stories* (marking the third incarnation of the magazine to which he's contributed), and were previously featured in a long-running column for *Dragon*. He has published fiction in *Swashbuckling Editor Stories* and *Deals with the Devil*, as well as in several middle-grade anthologies edited by Bruce Coville. "Dances With Coyotes" draws on his family's long interest in Pacific Northwest history and Indian mythology, and is dedicated to the memories of his grandfather, C.O. "Bun" Bunnell, who collected the stories in *Legends of the Klickitats*, and of Martha Alick ("Indian Martha") from whom some of those stories came. John lives and writes in Oregon, where he fights a never-ending battle against spending too much time on the Internet.

JANET ELIZABETH CHASE

Janet Chase was born and raised in Northern California. That might explain some things right off. She has a degree in Visual Arts from UC San Diego. After discovering that she was better at editing than at filming she began her own post production house. She 'retired' from television shortly after taking on her full-time position of mom. Her part-time hobby of writing soon followed. After much cajoling (and just a wee bit of shoving) she finally wrote something worth publishing. Janet lives with her husband, two children, and an assortment of interesting pets in Reno, Nevada. She blames the children for the pets though her husband knows differently.

DORANNA DURGIN

Doranna Durgin spent her childhood filling notebooks first with stories and art, and then with novels. After obtaining a degree in wildlife illustration and environmental education, she spent a number of years deep in the Appalachian Mountains. When she emerged, it was as a writer who found herself irrevo-cably tied to the natural world and its creatures — and with a new touchstone to the rugged spirit that helped settle the area and which she instills in her characters.

Dun Lady's Jess, Doranna's first published fantasy novel, received the 1995 Compton Crook/Stephen Tall award for the best first book in the fantasy, science fiction, and horror genres; she now has fifteen novels of eclectic genres on the shelves and more imminently on the way; most recently she's leaped gleefully into the world of action-romance. When she's not writing, Doranna builds web pages, wanders around outside with a camera, and works with horses and dogs — she's currently teaching agility classes. There's a Lipizzan in her backyard, a mountain looming outside her office window, a pack of agility dogs romping in the house, and a laptop sitting on her desk — and that's just the way she likes it. You can find a complete list of her fantasy books (*Dun Lady's Jess, Wolverine's Daughter, A Feral Darkness* ...), franchise tie-ins (ANGEL, MAGE KNIGHT), and action-romance (*Femme Fatale, Exception to the Rule, Checkmate*) at Doranna's website, along with scoops about new projects, lots of silly photos, and a link to her SFF Net newsgroup. And for kicks, Connery Beagle has a LiveJournal (connery-beagle) presenting his unique view of life in the high desert — drop by and say hello!

SARAH JANE ELLIOTT

Sarah Jane Elliott is a Canadian author of Speculative Fiction. She currently holds an Honours Bachelor of Science Degree from the University of Toronto as a specialist in Zoology and Behaviour, which she earned by taking as many English courses as possible.

Sarah was one of the 2001 winners of the Isaac Asimov Award for Undergraduate Excellence in Science Fiction and Fantasy Writing, earning an Honourable Mention for her short story, "To Soothe the Savage Beast." Her first published fiction, "Tides of Change", appears in Odyssey, fourth in the Tales from the Wonder Zone anthology series designed for use in the classroom, edited by Julie E. Czerneda.

When not writing, Sarah works in a variety of places, including North America's oldest Science Fiction bookstore, and the Royal Ontario Museum. She continues to work on her first novel, and finds herself constantly plagued by a vast menagerie of characters demanding to be let out to play, including a certain griffin.

JIM C. HINES

Jim C. Hines has been a busy little writer these past few years, appearing in such markets as *Turn the Other Chick, Sword & Sorceress XXI, Realms of Fantasy,* and many more. He recently took a break from short stories to focus on longer works. His humorous fantasy novel *GoblinQuest* is now available from Five Star Books. Jim lives in Holt, Michigan, where he fixes computers to support his writing habits. His own fantastic companions include 2.75 cats, his wife Amy, daughter Skylar, and the as-yet-unnamed child who should be showing up around the time this anthology goes to print.

CATHERINE DYBIEC HOLM

Catherine Holm lives in the northern Minnesota woods with her husband and a menagerie of cats, dogs, and chickens. She enjoys being outside as much as possible. Her short fiction has appeared in *Strange Horizons, Electric Velocipede,* and the Polish magazine *Tawacin.* Catherine attended the Clarion Writers' Workshop in 2002 and won a Minnesota arts grant in 2003 for her writing. She's completed a cat fantasy novel, and is at work on a sequel, as well as another surreal novel featuring humans. Catherine is a freelance writer/editor and a co-active coach. When she's not writing, working, or daydreaming, she enjoys camping, playing with her cats, gardening, bellydancing, and yoga.

MINDY L. KLASKY

Mindy L. Klasky is the author of the award-winning, best-selling Glasswright Series. When Mindy was learning to read, her parents encouraged her, saying that she could travel anywhere with a book in her hands, and Mindy has never forgotten that advice. While growing up, Mindy's travels took her from Los Angeles to Dallas to Atlanta to Minneapolis. (She now lives in a suburb of Washington, DC.) Mindy's academic travels ranged from computer science to English to law to library science. Professionally, she has moved from practicing trademark and copyright law to managing a large law firm library. When Mindy is not reading, writing, or working as a librarian, she enjoys cooking and quilting. She is an active member of the Science Fiction Writers of America, many legal bar organizations, and a number of library societies. Her husband (Mark) and their four cats, (Christina, Dante, Ted, and Yaz) fill the rest of her spare time!

JAY LAKE

Jay Lake is the winner of the 2004 John W. Campbell Award for Best New Writer, as well as a nominee for the 2004 Hugo and World Fantasy Awards. His stories appear in half a dozen languages in markets around the world, as well as his collections: *Greetings From Lake Wu, Dogs in the Moonlight* and *American Sorrows*. Jay is editor or co-editor of the *Polyphony* anthology series, *All-Star Zeppelin Adventure Stories, 44 Clowns, TEL : Stories,* and other projects. He lives in Portland, Oregon.

FRAN LAPLACA

Fran LaPlaca lives in the northwest hills of Connecticut with her husband and children, and a rabbit named Midnight. She is currently at work on her third novel. "Wings To Fly" is her first published piece.

JOHN MIERAU

John Mierau was born in the same year as the Intel microprocessor, so perhaps it was inevitable he would grow up to work in Information Technology. He continues to insist the whole computer thing is just a fad, and took a degree in Adult Education to fall back on 'just in case.' He hopes the degree will help him train his yellow Lab to stop hogging the bed, and all his footspace when he writes (it's a work in progress). Comic books and mysteries led to his true passion and lifelong addiction: the literature of the fantastic. John lives with his long-suffering partner in southern Ontario.

DEVON MONK

Devon Monk lives in Salem, Oregon with her husband, two sons, several fish, and a dog. The third oldest of seven siblings, she is surrounded by an odd and wonderful extended family who all live nearby and often gather in her home to catch up on news and celebrate holidays. She has a love for music and magic that goes back to her youngest years, and the story in this volume is inspired by those two loves.

Her short stories have appeared in anthologies such as *Year's Best Fantasy #2, Rotten Relations,* Marion Zimmer Bradley's *Sword and Sorceress,* and *Maiden, Matron, Crone.* Her stories also have been seen in *Cicada, Realms of Fantasy, Amazing Stories, Black Gate,* and *Talebones* magazines. In addition to writing short stories, she is currently working on several fantasy novels.

RUTH NESTVOLD

Once an assistant professor in English, Ruth Nestvold now works as a technical translator to feed her writing addiction. She has sold short stories to a variety of markets including *Asimov's, Realms of Fantasy, Strange Horizons, Andromeda Spaceways, NFG,* and *Futurismic.* Her novella "Looking Through Lace" made the short list for the Tiptree Award in 2003, was nominated for the Sturgeon Award and been reprinted in the first Tiptree Award anthology, *Sex, the Future, and Chocolate Chip Cookies.*

JANE CAROL PETROVICH

Jane Petrovich was born in Thunder Bay, Ontario and has always felt at home in a rocky land where evergreens march down to the water. That was probably why, after obtaining a degree in Biochemistry she studied Chemical Oceanography in Vancouver (where she had an underwater encounter with one of the characters in her story). She has been an oceanographer, chemist, community college professor, and technical writer. Currently, she is becoming certified as an elementary school teacher after years of amusing and edifying children of all ages with imagination, invention, and storytelling. "The Power of Eight" is her first professional fiction sale. She lives with her son and cat in the gently rolling country north of Toronto in view of the (rocky) Niagara Escarpment.

KENT POLLARD

Kent Pollard is a full time bookseller who devotes much of his spare energy to promoting Canadian science fiction and fantasy. He has lived all his life on the Canadian Prairies, currently making his home in Saskatoon, Saskatchewan with his wife, Victoria, and the assorted cats and dog who permit them to share space. His favorite ways of avoiding writing are Gardening, Computers and RPGs. Despite a preference for writing science fiction, his favorite piece of writing to date is the fantasy short: "Uncle Ernie was a Goat," which is also his first published work.

WEN SPENCER

When Wen was young, she accidentally licked a toad instead of the lollipop that was in her *other* hand. The experience left an impression. She is the author of the Ukiah Oregon series by Roc Books, and *Tinker* by Baen Books. She won the 2003 John Campell Award for Best New SF Writer. Wen currently lives in the Boston area with her husband, son, two cats, and a small swamp filled with toads.

MATT WALKER

Matt Walker lives at the edge of a vast forest, where daily he debates matters of philosophy with the bears and the moose and the crows. With his dog, though, he usually only talks about food and why the garbage is spread across the kitchen floor. Word is, Matt writes under another name as well, but a secret isn't any good if everybody knows what it is.

K.D. WENTWORTH

K.D. Wentworth has sold more than sixty pieces of short fiction to such markets as *Fantasy & Science Fiction, Hitchcock's, Realms of Fantasy, Dying For It, Return to the Twilight Zone, Marion Zimmer Bradley's Fantasy Magazine,* and *The Chick Is in the Mail.* She is a two-time Nebula nominee for short fiction and currently has seven novels in print, the three most recent being *This Fair Land,* an alternate history Cherokee fantasy, from Hawk, *The Course of Empire,* written with Eric Flint, and *Stars/Over/Stars,* both from Baen. A third book in the House of Moons series, *Moonchild,* will be published in the coming year by Hawk. She serves as Coordinating Judge for the L. Ron Hubbard Writers of the Future Contest.

JANNY WURTS

Janny Wurts is the author of twelve novels, a collection of short stories, and the internationally best-selling Empire trilogy written in collaboration with Raymond E. Feist. Her current fantasy release *To Ride Hell's Chasm,* and the lastest volume in her Wars of Light and Shadow series, *Traitor's Knot,* are the culmination of more than twenty years of carefully evolved ideas. The cover images on the books, both in the US and abroad, are her own paintings, depicting her vision of characters and setting.

Through her combined talents as a writer/illustrator, Janny has immersed herself in a lifelong ambition: to create a seamless interface between words and pictures that will lead reader and viewer beyond the world we know. A self-taught painter, she draws directly from the imagination, creating scenes in a representational style that blurs the edges between dream and reality.

Says Janny of her work, "I chose to frame my stories against a backdrop of fantasy because I can handle even the most sensitive issues with the gloves off — explore the myriad angles of our times with the least risk of offending anyone's personal sensibilities. The result, I can hope, is a moving journey of the spirit that rises to the challenge of exploring compassionate understanding."

Beyond writing, Janny's award-winning paintings have been showcased in exhibitions of imaginative artwork, among them a commemorative exhibition for NASA's 25th Anniversary; the Art of the Cosmos at Hayden Planetarium in New York; and two exhibits of fantasy art, at both the Delaware Art Museum, and Canton Art Museum.